House of Rejoicing

THE BOOK OF COMING FORTH BY DAY
Part One

LIBBIE HAWKER

The Book of Coming Forth by Day:
Part 1: House of Rejoicing

Copyright 2015, 2016
Libbie Hawker

Running Rabbit Press
San Juan County, WA

Second Print Edition

Cover design and formatting by Running Rabbit Press.
Original cover illustration copyright Lane Brown.

290 ½

MORE BOOKS BY LIBBIE HAWKER

For Paul.

The names of the sacred cattle are:
House of *Kas*, Mistress of All;
Silent One who dwells in her place;
She of Chemmis, whom the god ennobled;
The Much Beloved, red of hair;
She who protects in life, the particolored;
She whose name has power in her craft;
Storm in the Sky, who holds the god aloft;
The Bull, the husband of the cows.

-*The Book of the Dead*, Spell 148.

Ankhesenamun

Year 1 of Horemheb,
Holy Are the Manifestations,
Chosen of Re

THERE ARE MANY WHO SAY that I have no voice. Still more would claim that I do not have a thoughtful heart. They think a woman who keeps quiet must be simple. They think that my eyes have forever been on the floor—shy, like a gazelle among the thorns. They do not suspect that I know when to look up—that when their eyes are turned away, that is when I *see*.

It is true that the gods—and there are many gods, I know—never blessed me with boldness. It is true that I haven't my mother's beauty. I cannot stand before a crowd and know that they will love me, as she could do. I haven't the pluck of my eldest sister, nor my father's fatal focus, nor the silent, watchful certainty of my grandmother. I haven't the buoyant, trusting charm of my brother—my dear brother, whom I loved so well.

They are all with you now, Waser, oh merciful god of the dead. I know that you live, that you have ever been, that you and all the gods of Egypt will take your rightful places once more.

I know, too, that I will not live to see that glorious day. I am what the gods have made me: the watcher in the shadows, the eye that sees the whole world. I have looked on as, one after another, my family has fallen. I am the last of my line—and perhaps that is for the best. But soon I must fall, too.

There is no fear in my heart—only quiet determination. As the last small drop in a bloodline of reckless divinity, I cannot help but feel as if I bear all their sins upon my back—that I must carry the blame for all the darkness my family has cast upon the world. It is I who will be called to account, who will stand in the underworld caverns of the Duat, and answer to the gods for all my family's crimes.

Goddess Iset, you who know all names—you know my *ren*, the name of my heart. You know that when I was shaped on the divine potter's wheel, I was given but little voice. My voice is not in my throat, but in my writing-brush—and what trouble my writing-brush has wrought for me! I have sealed my fate with a letter, so now, if you are willing, Iset, let me salvage my afterlife with the words I write.

I will tell you—whoever you are, whoever comes to find these papyri when I am gone—everything I know of my family. I will tell it full, and tell it true, and hope that it is enough to rinse their sins from my soul. For on the day when I stand before Anupu, when he places my heart on the Scales of Judgment to weigh it against the Feather of Truth, I must be cleansed of my family's stain. I must speak these words with a clear conscience:

I have not done crimes against the people. I have not sinned in the Place of Truth. I have not known what should never be known; I have not harmed any man. I have not blasphemed a god, nor done what the god abhors. I have not caused pain, I have not caused tears, I have not killed, nor ordered any killing. I have not made anyone to suffer. I have not stopped a god in his procession—I am pure, I am pure, as pure as the heron of Henes.

You might ask, "How can she know these things? How can she tell of deeds that happened when she was a child—even before her birth—and claim that she speaks the truth?"

I can answer you in one way only: it is often the silent

ones who see the most, who think the deepest, who *observe*. If a woman speaks but little, then she has more time to listen. And in my short life I have heard many tales from those who know the truth .

So now hear the truth. Hear all who came before me, speaking with the tongue of this scroll. Let me be cleansed before death comes to claim me. Let me read my name in the Book of Coming Forth by Day. Let all be known—let me add not to the weight of the balance, nor falsify the plummet of the scales.

Let me walk in the Field of Reeds forever.

Kiya

Year 36 of Amunhotep,
Ruler of Waset,
Lord of Truth in the Sun,
Strong Bull Arising

HER GOODS PRECEDED HER INTO the city—
the flat, sun-baked, clamoring city. Although the
princess of Mitanni remained aboard her ship, watching
from a strange, detached distance as the wealth of her
dowry flowed down the ramp and onto the shore, the air
was not perfumed with the river's gentle clarity. It smelled
of city life—it *stank*. Egypt reeked of sweat, of anger, of the
desperation that comes when men live atop one another
like beasts in a narrow pen. She had smelled it for days
as the ship made its way down the long silver stretch of
the river, the bright, pure scent of open water gradually
giving way to the reek of this far-off land. The city stank
of beer and the cheap perfume of whores, of fish rotting
in the unforgiving sun, of the waste of animals and men.
She struggled to keep her hands still, hidden in her heavy,
tasseled sleeves, so she would not pinch her nostrils shut
and betray her true feelings for all to see.

She watched the procession of her dowry wind from the
docks, up toward a broad, stone-paved lane, which was
flanked by tall, narrow, mud-brick houses the color of
sun-bleached hides. The houses seemed to lean inward, to
press upon one another's shoulders just as the Egyptians
did in the alleys below, struggling to gain a better view of
the princess's goods.

From the foot of the ship's ramp all along the great processional way, the road was lined with ranks of the Pharaoh's soldiers, dressed in the striped blue-and-white kilts of their trade. Their belts were heavy with blades; each man was armed with a long spear and adorned by a single, small, round shield. The soldiers held their bucklers across their naked, well-browned chests. The shields were set with bronze studs, polished and slicked by the blows of swords. They glimmered in the sunlight so that they looked like suns themselves—like twin river banks made of little suns fallen to the earth. River banks—between which all the princess's possessions were drifting steadily away.

First went the fine textiles, so that they would not be soiled by the dust of the procession—her light silk gowns and woolen robes with heavy, layered skirts of many-colored tassels. Next went her jewels, displayed in open cedar cases so that all the king's subjects might gape and admire. Ebony furniture for her house—furniture she would never be allowed to use, she felt certain—and mirrors of silver and copper; a golden spindle and distaff that were more beautiful than utilitarian; drinking vessels set with agates and platters inlaid with turquoise. A camel carried a fine litter balanced on its hump—the Egyptians pointed and cheered at this oddity—and a golden war chariot, drawn by two equally golden stallions, burnished and prancing, with floating manes as pale and airy as undyed, fine-woven linen.

Last, the procession was joined by dozens of slaves—and nearly as many free servants, who were nevertheless not so free that they might refuse to accompany their mistress to Egypt, never to see the hills and fragrant coastal forests of Mitanni again. Each was dressed in a silk robe, and the slaves carried themselves straight-backed and sure, for they, at least, knew their work and their purpose. Even the slaves looked infinitely more confident than the princess felt.

She watched, silent and trembling, as the last of her servants steadied themselves on the ship's ramp and prepared to descend into the midst of this new land—into the stink and the clamor, the press of bodies half-undressed, with their strange kilts of linen swinging loose around their knees and their backs bared to the heat. This was Waset, the grandest city in all the world. It was her home now. By her father's decree, this was to be her place in the world for all the days to come—until the end of her life.

A team of litter-bearers readied the double-chaired platform that would carry her to her husband. The last servant on the ramp, a girl the princess's own age, hesitated and turned back. The sun was bright on her braid, hair the color of newly founded bronze, like the princess's own—and for a fleeting moment, before the servant controlled her face with a professional will beyond her years, the princess noted hesitation and fear in the girl's green eyes and on her tight-pressed mouth.

The princess stepped toward her litter, for there was nothing else to be done, no direction to go but forward. But the servant girl cried, "Wait!" and rushed to her side. The princess of Mitanni watched as her servant pummeled and fluffed the chair's cushions.

"You should be comfortable on your wedding day, Lady Tadukhepa," the servant said. She bowed, and when she bobbed up again she was smiling. One of her front teeth was gone—knocked out, Tadukhepa imagined, by an angry father or a jealous lover. Was that how the girl had found herself in this predicament—part of Tadukhepa's entourage, serving in a foreign land—a virtual exile?

The missing tooth marred the girl's beauty, but not her warmth. Tadukhepa smiled back at her. "What is your name, please?" she asked quietly as she settled onto the cushions.

The servant dropped her eyes. "My mother called me Inanna, after the goddess. It's a silly name for one such as I—I am not worthy of it." The words lisped slightly through the gap in her teeth.

"I like your name." Tadukhepa took her hand, a brief expression of thanks. Inanna's hand was warm, and Tadukhepa's fingers burned suddenly in the girl's grip. Despite the heat of Egypt and the weight of her Hurrian robes, fear had chilled the princess to her bones.

"Won't you please call me Nann, then," the servant said, squeezing Tadukhepa's hand.

"Stay beside my litter," Tadukhepa whispered to Nann. "I would have someone... someone close." *Someone who does not make me feel afraid in this strange, new place.* She did not dare speak her fears aloud.

The priest of Ishtar came forward, muttering his prayers as he cradled the golden statue of the goddess close to his chest. The eight-pointed star tied to his forehead sent a flash of blinding light into Tadukhepa's eyes. She blinked rapidly as the priest set the goddess on the chair to her right. Then, when her dazzled tears were gone, she risked a sidelong glance at the goddess. Standing tall upon her sharp-taloned eagle's feet, her wings falling down her back like a cloak, Ishtar looked unafraid. But then, statues always looked unafraid. Tadukhepa swallowed hard and nodded to her litter bearers.

They lifted the platform onto their shoulders. The litter, decorated with strings of bells and tassels of beads, made a cheerful music as it descended the ramp. But when it reached the flat stone of the processional way, one bearer stumbled. Only for a moment, and he caught himself at once—but it was enough to make Tadukhepa's heart leap, and to rock Ishtar perilously in her seat. Tadukhepa reached for the goddess in a panic, fumbling to right her—

and then she flushed. Was it ill luck to touch the goddess in this way, or good luck? She could not decide, and not knowing made her sick with worry. She kissed both her hands to take in the goddess's blessing—if indeed a blessing had been conferred—and to apologize if she had caused offense.

From the height of her bearers' shoulders, Tadukhepa looked down on the citizens of Waset. Men and women alike glanced up at her with minimal interest, their curiosity waning now that the last of her treasures had passed. Their glances were cynical. Some eyes even looked pitying in their stark rings of black kohl. Some turned away before her litter had reached them, finding the dull, daily work that waited in the bread-and-beer shops or at the stinking dockside far more interesting than the king's latest bride.

Tadukhepa was glad she had commanded Nann to stay close. The girl's presence was the one familiar thing to which she could hold in a world that saw her as nothing remarkable—just another woman for the king; one of a great many.

Tadukhepa had known what these Egyptian rulers were like from her earliest days. She'd heard tales of King Amunhotep at her nurse's knee. The Pharaoh had several palaces full of women, she knew—so many women that he could never visit them all, never sire even one child on each of them, and the poor creatures were fated to live and age and die untouched and unloved, locked away in the gilded cages of the royal harem.

As a child, these lurid tales of Egyptian proclivities had amused her, filling her with a pleasant kind of disbelief, a bubbling, mischievous shock. When she had reached her seventeenth year and her father had called her to his throne room to announce that she would go to Egypt as a bride—as a pawn to maintain the fragile peace between Egypt and Mitanni—all the pleasure of the stories had shattered, and she had fallen to her knees, weeping shamefully before the eyes of the Hurrian court, pleading for mercy. But her father had refused to hear her cries, and for weeks afterward as she prepared for the journey, no matter where she looked, her vision was obscured by the floating, faint suggestion of the bars of a fine golden cage.

By the time the procession reached the temple complex on the northern edge of the city, Tadukhepa had allowed a haze to fall across her senses, a misty half-awareness through which reality filtered slowly—the throbbing heat, the sweat trickling down the back of her neck, Ishtar's cool composure, and the crowds turning away—as if she saw it all through the weave of a thick veil.

A small gasp of shock from Nann, who walked close beside the litter, brought Tadukhepa out of her miserable reverie. She looked up, eyes focusing for the first time since leaving the lower city. The gateway to the temple district rose above her, two soaring, solid pylons of golden-hued limestone. They were stern and imposing, in true Egyptian style—blocky and slanted faintly inward like the sides of the great pyramids far to the north, which Tadukhepa had observed several days ago from the deck of her ship as she had sailed past. The pylons stretched into the hot, blue-white sky. They were the height of six or seven men at least, and every surface, every enormous block was carved and inscribed with the images of kings from generations gone. They surrounded her, frozen in postures of striding might, lifting clubs against enemies, holding doomed transgressors tight by the hair, driving their chariots into the sun. And all around the kings' bodies, the strange, illustrative characters of the Egyptian sacred script wreathed them like Ishtar's protective power.

Tadukhepa could not read the sacred script—its precise, carefully incised rows of birds and snakes, human figures and flowers were a mystery to her. She had only just gained the smallest understanding of low Egyptian writing, the characters used for everyday communication. But she did not need to read the words to know that this towering gateway admitted her into a place of great and fearsome power. She could sense its import, could feel it bearing down upon her as if, like a thinking creature of malignant will, it sought to sweep her from her litter and cast her small, unworthy body into the dust.

She glanced down at Nann, tempted to reach for the girl's hand again. But she would only look graceless and cowardly, leaning from her litter to cling to a servant's paw. And so she folded her hands firmly in her lap and sat up straight on her cushions, gazing straight ahead as the litter bore her into the city of temples.

Once beyond the imposing gate, temples seemed to crowd all around her: small red-granite shrines, their lintels carved with winged scarabs; larger houses dedicated to this god or that, with porticoes framed by bright-painted pillars. Strange stone beasts crouched on limestone plinths along the processional way, their human faces watching her with icy judgment above lithe, leonine bodies. In the distance, a low, broad stair led to the massive pillars and yawning black entrance of a huge stone temple, larger by far than the rest. Tadukhepa could see her dowry procession making its way up that stair, into that blackness—and she knew that she must follow. She swallowed the lump in her throat and clasped her hands together to still their trembling.

The litter proceeded up the broad staircase. Nann puffed slightly as she climbed and wiped the sweat from her brow with a thin, pale wrist. The blackness at the temple's mouth at least provided relief from the heat, cool and sudden as a springtime rain in the mountains. It nearly made Tadukhepa gasp aloud. She breathed deeply as the litter sank to the ground, allowing the shade's caress to soothe her, and smelled the thick, sweet odor of incense and the raspy char of burnt meat.

Nann shuffled close as Tadukhepa stood. The servant girl offered her hand and guided Tadukhepa from the litter's platform.

"It's so dark here," Tadukhepa said. Nann whispered back, "What is this place?"

Two of Tadukhepa's other servants emerged from among the umber pillars. They lifted the goddess with reverence from her seat, then disappeared again into the shadows.

As the litter was carried away, the darkness slowly receded. It was evident now that some flickering, shifting light source—torches, perhaps—burned deep in the temple's heart. A long, wavering tunnel of faint orange light seemed to reach for Tadukhepa, extending toward her out of a blackness that was as deep and bottomless as the Underworld. She gasped and clung to Nann's arm, heedless now of showing weakness or fear. She *was* afraid—afraid and alone, save for her servant, who was trembling as much as Tadukhepa.

A quiet ripple of voices drifted down the tunnel of light—a man's voice, deep, but with an animation that spoke clearly of his youth—and the high, light, musical laughter of a woman. A moment later she heard footsteps, the soft scrape of sandals against stone: a confident, unhurried tread.

Their linen garb was so brightly bleached that it emerged first from the darkness. Tadukhepa blinked at the bobbing shapes, swaths of fabric lightening from gray to a white tinted strongly by the orange light that trembled behind them. Then she saw their forms—the perfect, smooth curves of the woman, her graceful, almost dancing movements, and the silhouette of the man's body, broad through the shoulders, tall for an Egyptian, his legs as strong and straight as pillars. His head darted as he looked from Tadukhepa to Nann and back again. The locks of his short wig seemed to separate and settle again, like the feathers of a black bird ruffling. Tadukhepa stepped away from Nann, forcing herself to stand alone under the man's scrutiny. Was this the king, then—the Pharaoh whom she was to marry?

The two figures drew close enough that she could at last make out their faces. They were beautiful—both so beautiful that their perfection struck her with a deep, icy dismay, and she had the peculiar sense that she had traveled not to a land inhabited by mortals, but into the realm of spirits and gods.

The man's face was strong, his chin and jaw well-angled. His nose was long and prominent, but it did not overwhelm his face, and his lips were full and curving, indicating Kushite heritage. He had deep-set, very dark eyes—the kind of eyes that could look stern, even naturally angry—but they took in Tadukhepa's face with a soft glow of pleasure, and as he looked at her, she felt some of her fear abate.

No, this was not her husband. She knew that much as she offered him a feeble smile. This man was certainly too young to be the Pharaoh. He could not have been more than nineteen or twenty—barely older than Tadukhepa herself—and the current Pharaoh had sat his throne for longer than that. The prince—Tadukhepa felt instinctively that he was a prince, if not a king; what else could such a fine, supremely self-assured man be?—smiled broadly and dipped his head in welcome. No lines marred the skin around his eyes. He was youthful indeed.

The woman said something in her native tongue, and Tadukhepa blinked, tearing her gaze from the prince, struggling to comprehend the words. Although she had been tutored thoroughly in the Egyptian language, all understanding fled from her when she met the woman's eyes.

She was lovelier than any woman Tadukhepa had seen, with a face that seemed carved by the finest sculptor, every stroke of bone and flesh made with fastidious care. She was a being of perfect balance—her breasts neither small nor large, but as round and appealing as sweet fruits; her waist slim and her hips neatly curved; supple shoulders giving rise to a long, graceful neck. And her face—not even the goddess Ishtar could claim such flawless, frightening beauty. Wide cheekbones framed a small, Greek nose and lips nearly as full as the prince's. The long, careful curls of her wig fell like dark water to her waist, and eyes the color of tilled earth gazed at Tadukhepa with patient, faintly amused expectation.

"I... I'm sorry..." Tadukhepa stammered in Hurrian, the language of her homeland. Faced with such impossible beauty, every word of the Egyptian tongue escaped her mind.

The prince gave a low, gentle laugh. "She asked," he said in heavily accented Hurrian, "what is your name?"

Tadukhepa gaped at him. She had not expected anyone in this country to speak Hurrian. Nann gave her a subtle nudge with her elbow, and Tadukhepa finally spilled out her name.

The lovely woman made a show of tilting her head, as if she could not hear the response. Then her perfect mouth moved, trying out the Hurrian syllables.

"Tadoo... Tadoo..." the woman said, and her eyes sparked with a quick, fierce light—mockery, Tadukhepa realized, withering inside.

The woman tried one more time. "Tadoo...*kiya*." She laughed musically and shrugged her smooth shoulders.

The prince gave his companion a tight, uncomfortable smile. "Tadukhepa," he corrected without difficulty.

The beautiful woman tossed her head and turned away,

back toward the temple's faintly glowing heart. Then she called over her shoulder in perfect Hurrian, "Come along, Tadoo-Kiya," and swept into the darkness.

Tadukhepa shared an uneasy glance with Nann. The servant's face was as pale as bread dough, even in the temple's dim interior.

Then the prince stepped forward, offering his arm. "That was the Lady Nefertiti," he said. "I'm afraid she has a cutting wit to balance out her lovely looks. You mustn't mind her. She is only jealous."

"Jealous?" Tadukhepa said, taking the prince's arm with a trembling, hesitant hand. "Why?"

"Because you are a King's Wife now, of course—or you will be, as soon as you marry my father. Nefertiti is only a lady of the courts. And also, she envies you because you are very beautiful."

Tadukhepa flushed; her thick wool robes were entirely too close, and prickled against her heated skin. "Thank you," she said meekly. "What is your name, please, Prince?"

The prince chuckled. "That's a strange word—*prince*. What does it mean? I should know it, I'm sure, but my tutors always had to scold to make me practice my Hurrian."

She blinked up at him in surprise, so startled that she did not notice the temple growing cooler as they moved into its depths; nor did she notice the rows of bronze bowls that lined its thick, smoke-darkened walls, nor the flames dancing among the fragrant oils they held.

"Don't you have a word for *prince* in Egypt?" she asked him. "A prince is a king's son."

"Well, I am that, certainly," he said with a sudden bravado that made Tadukhepa smile. Then he ducked his head again, as if bashful of his own flare of pride. He gazed down at her while they walked. "I am the first son of the Great King Amunhotep, and heir to his throne. You may call me Thutmose."

"Prince Thutmose," she said, careful to keep her voice soft and low. She knew that this was a sacred place, even if it was as dark as the Underworld.

"King's Son Thutmose," he corrected gently, forming the Hurrian words with care. "In Egypt, all status, all power derives from the king. It is your relation to the Pharaoh that determines your standing. A *prince* is not a man of power in his own right. He is only great because he is the King's Son. And so you see, even a minor King's Wife, as you are, stands high above the most beautiful ladies of the court. That is the soil from which Nefertiti's mockery springs. You'll forgive her, won't you?"

"Of course."

They walked on in silence for a few paces more. Tadukhepa watched the flames dance in the braziers and saw how the light picked out the crevices and curves of old carvings—darkened by generations of incense, the long, powerful legs of gods, the dipping, dancing arms of goddesses, and the prostrate forms of worshipers seemed to descend down the temple's walls, slinking into rings of lamplight which stretched and flickered upward to meet them.

"Nefertiti has double cause to envy you," Thutmose continued. "You come to us a King's Wife, and you are even a King's Daughter, though the king of Mitanni holds little power in our court. Yet for all her beauty—yes, I saw how you stared at her—Nefertiti has no real standing." He gave a little chuckle, then added, "Not yet, at any rate. She and I will be married soon, and one day, when my father's well-earned rest is at hand, I'll be the Pharaoh. Nefertiti will be satisfied then, I dare say."

"She is lucky," Tadukhepa said, flushing at her own audacity, "to have such a kind and courteous husband."

Thutmose patted her hand where it rested in the crook of his elbow, a familiar gesture, as if they had known one another since childhood. "You mustn't let her teasing disturb you. Nefertiti *is* kind and good, I swear it—when you get to know her."

At last they reached the inner sanctum of the temple. Here the burning bowls of oil were plentiful, and illuminated a rough half-circle of men and women dressed in the long, flowing linens and jeweled ornaments of nobility. They conversed quietly in small groups, and servants moved about the crowd, offering cups of chilled wine and bowls of dates and spiced nuts, refreshments against the heat outside. The air was one of subdued festivity, balanced by reverence for the temple. As Thutmose and Tadukhepa approached the crowd, several of the nobles turned toward them and fell silent. Nefertiti, standing out in their midst like a lily among plain, brown grasses, offered Tadukhepa a soft smile that held none of her earlier mockery.

Beyond the waiting crowd, two great sets of double doors stood waiting, recessed into the temple's wall. Both were carved with images of Amun, the Egyptian sun-god. The doors were leafed from top to bottom in bright yellow gold and set with several rows of polished stones. Even in the fitful lamplight the doors sparkled, and Tadukhepa inhaled sharply at the sight. There was more wealth displayed on those doors than an entire farming district of Mitanni could produce in three months. She had come to a land of gods and spirits, indeed.

"Come," Thutmose said. He led her through the crowd; she could feel the eyes of the nobles following her, assessing her, taking in her long, heavy robes and the sweat that still beaded along her brow, noting the fear on her pale, wide-eyed face. Thutmose halted beside one set of doors—the smaller of the two—and tapped lightly on its frame.

A moment later it swung open, creaking on its hinges.

The chamber within was darker still, a dense black, which not even the closest lamps could penetrate.

"You may go in," Thutmose said.

Tadukhepa balked.

"It's quite all right," he assured her. "Your audience will be short, and then we'll proceed with the marriage." He added in a whisper that only she could hear, "There is nothing to fear."

Tadukhepa felt a surge of gratitude for his discretion, but still she hesitated, staring into the core of black.

Nann stepped quickly to Tadukhepa's side. "I'll go first, Lady," she said, and although Tadukhepa could see how she trembled, the servant walked into the blackness without hesitation. Before she could lose what little courage still remained to her, Tadukhepa followed. She reached out, groping for Nann's hand as Thutmose shut the door behind them.

"Why is everything so dark here?" Tadukhepa whispered. "It's unnatural!"

She heard the soft rustle of unseen servants in the darkness—silent, accustomed to the black, waiting at their ease like birds in a night-time roost. Then the squeal of another door sounded somewhere ahead. A pool of coppery light spilled from a doorway into the chamber where Tadukhepa stood.

The lamp was carried by a man—perhaps thirty years in age, with a simple white kilt and an unadorned, chin-length wig—a style Tadukhepa had seen at the Mitanni court on stewards from Egypt. These were, she knew, the men who did the bidding of the Pharaoh and his most favored nobles.

A figure moved behind the steward, small and delicate of proportion, but not a child—this one had the unmistakable poise, the confident, easy grace of a royal woman. As she and her steward came forward, the woman shifted in and out of the lamp's reach, now revealed, now cloaked again in shadow. Tadukhepa caught glimpses of her face and form—fragmented impressions like fish darting in the shallows of a lake. The small woman had a dark complexion, and her face was lined by late middle age—especially around the mouth, which seemed to frown more naturally than it smiled. The skin of her cheeks and neck had just begun to sag, but in the brief flashes Tadukhepa could see, and in spite of her cool, unamused expression, the woman still held a stark sort of beauty, reminiscent of a mountain's stony peak. The pleats of a blue gown stirred in the breeze of her brisk pace, and resting atop her intricate wig she carried with practiced ease the weight of a tall, ornate crown—two high, golden plumes rising from a gilded sun-disk.

The steward stepped aside, holding his lamp before him. The small, aging woman halted in the ring of light. The folds of her gown swung and settled about her feet; she stared at Tadukhepa silently, expressionless save for the scowl that was evidently hers by nature.

Nann shifted uncomfortably. Tadukhepa gripped her hand harder, desperate for reassurance.

"What should I do?" she breathed.

Nann began, "Perhaps..." but the stately woman said in a clear, powerful voice—in her own language— "Do you have our tongue?"

The Egyptian she had worked so hard to learn flooded back into Tadukhepa's mind. Relief washed over her; she sent up a tiny prayer to Ishtar in thanks for this one small mercy. "Yes, Mistress," she answered.

"Good."

The woman came forward a few steps. Though slight of frame, she nevertheless bore a palpable force of personality—it preceded her like a perfume or an aura, sweeping across the room in advance of her stride, so that she seemed to grow in size as she closed on Tadukhepa, until the fact of her presence towered over the princess of Mitanni like the cold, blocky gates of the temple precinct.

Instinctively, Tadukhepa lowered her eyes, then dropped her chin. She would have sunk into a trembling bow, but the woman's hand flashed out—small and frail-looking, yet so precise in its movement—and a single finger caught Tadukhepa beneath her chin. The finger was as hard as iron. It pressed irresistibly upward until Tadukhepa's head was tilted back, held at an arrogant, uncomfortable angle. In the silence she could hear the wick of the steward's lamp crackle, and she swallowed once, her throat as tight as a stretched thread.

"You are a King's Wife now," the woman said. Her voice filled the room, though she did not shout. She had no need of shouting. "*Queen*," she said in Hurrian, so there could be no mistaking her meaning. Then she resumed in Egyptian. "You are not a concubine, nor the wife of a mere noble. You hold your head up proudly. You do not lower your eyes. Do you understand?"

"Yes, Mistress," Tadukhepa managed. With her head stretched back, her voice was nothing but a dry breath.

The finger flashed away, and Tadukhepa inhaled in relief, lowering her chin a fraction, resisting the urge to rub at her neck.

"You must call me King's Great Wife, or Great Wife," the woman said—not unkindly, but not warmly, either—simply informing. Then she added, "Tiy."

"I am Tadukhepa, daughter of King Tushratta of Mitanni—" Tadukhepa began.

But Tiy said shortly, "I know," cutting short the speech Tadukhepa had rehearsed for her arrival in this new land. "Do you know *why* you have come, Tadukhepa?"

"I... I come..."

Because my father has sent me, she thought miserably. *Sent me into exile to suit purposes of his own, and I must now find some place in this strange, foreign court, in a land so hot the very sun seems to hate me.* She felt the first sting of tears and blinked hard to clear them from her eyes before Great Wife Tiy could notice their shine. *I come at my father's bidding. He has sacrificed my happiness, and I will never see my home, or my mother and sisters, again.*

She drew a deep breath to steady her heart. "I come to maintain the critical bond between Egypt and Mitanni." She was pleased that she managed to say it without a quaver, that she sounded almost as confident as Tiy herself.

"Yes," Tiy replied. "And here you are. Do you know what your father Tushratta has demanded as your price? Statues of his goddess, cast in solid gold."

Tadukhepa flinched. She had not known that Tushratta demanded a payment—that in spite of her elegant dowry, she had, in the end, been purchased like a sack of grain. Her head drooped again.

"Ah," Tiy said shortly, a warning. With effort, Tadukhepa lifted her chin.

"It doesn't matter," Tiy told her. Something like warmth creased the corners of her eyes.

"I would have come willingly," Tadukhepa said. In spite of the misgivings she still felt, her anger flared. "I love my country—my home. I would have come willingly to Egypt, to seal the peace—to keep Mitanni safe—if only I'd been *asked*." This was not true, Tadukhepa admitted to herself. But it was a noble ideal. She liked to think that in time she could become that sort of woman—the sort who would sacrifice for the land and the people she loved. *I will be brave enough one day*, she said silently, *and then it will be true of me.*

"Instead..." Tiy prompted.

"Instead I was sold. Like a slave—like a whore."

Tiy's dark eyes sharpened. "Are you a whore?"

She asked it very directly, with no hint of coyness, without any of Nefertiti's coltish play. The matter-of-fact question raised Tadukhepa's ire; now there was no need for Tiy to remind her to lift her chin.

"With respect, Great Wife Tiy," Tadukhepa said coldly, "how dare you ask such a question? I am a virgin, as befits a new bride."

One side of Tiy's mouth curled, transforming from its natural frown into a wry, approving smile. "Virgin brides, indeed," she said, nearly laughing. "This is Egypt, King's Wife—you are a long way from Mitanni. But it makes no matter. So long as you are devoted to the Pharaoh from this day forward, it is all one to me, whether you were as pure as an uncracked egg, or whether you used to spread your legs for every Hurrian shepherd that came your way."

Tadukhepa could think of no response to such an outrageous statement. She flushed with anger, and was glad that the light was dim.

"How old are you?" Great Wife Tiy asked.

"Seventeen."

"Young," Tiy said. "My husband will like that."

Tadukhepa bit her lip. It had not occurred to her until now that she must share the king with this woman—this sharp, bold, fearsome woman. Surely the Pharaoh had other wives, and their status was above that of his vast, unloved collection of lower concubines. Tadukhepa now held that same elevated position. Tiy must be used to the Pharaoh's broad interests—used to sharing the king. Tadukhepa devoutly hoped it was true. The petty envy of Nefertiti was a challenge she could learn to handle, given time—but if Tiy took it into her head to hate Tadukhepa, she felt sure there was nothing she could do to preserve herself from this tiny woman's implacable wrath.

"Don't look alarmed, child," Tiy said. "I am sure your duties will be light. The Pharaoh is a man of habit, and he is not inclined to alter his routines, even for a pretty face. It was a different story some years back. If you'd come to us then, you would have had a harder time of it. But of late... well, you shall see."

Abruptly, Tiy sighed, rubbing her forehead with the tips of two fingers. "My head aches. Waset always makes my head ache. The smell, you know—and the crowds. I feel sure the presence of so many people does something foul to the air, poisons it in some way, though the magicians have always told me it isn't so." She turned to her steward. "Huya, tell one of my maids to prepare my special wine."

The man bobbed a small bow, bending over his lamp. "Great Wife, I believe all the wine and herbs we brought with us from the West Bank have been used up."

"What?" Tiy rounded on him. "Did those entitled heifers who call themselves my maids drink it all themselves? I shall beat them with my own hand!"

"No, Great Wife," Huya said smoothly. "*You* drank it all. Last hour, you recall—while we waited for King's Wife Tadukhepa to arrive."

Tiy sighed again, like a woman enduring a veritable plague of offenses. "There is nothing for it, then, but to soldier through." She dusted her hands together, brushing away the prospect of unpleasant work ahead. She said to Tadukhepa, "Once this business is concluded and Amun has approved of your marriage to the Pharaoh, we will leave this stinking city, thank the gods."

"Leave the city, Great Wife?" Tadukhepa said. "But where will we go?"

"To the West Bank, of course. Back to the Pharaoh's

palace—the House of Rejoicing. It's beautiful there—serene and quiet, and it smells sweet; it's so far from the stink of Waset. The air is wholesome." Tiy reached out and took Tadukhepa's hand. Her fingers were hard and cold, her nails as sharp as the gripping toes of a falcon, but Tadukhepa sensed that the Great Wife meant the gesture kindly. "You will like the House of Rejoicing—you'll see. But until we are back there, in our sanctuary, you and I must both soldier through."

"What do you mean, Great Wife? Soldier through what?"

Tiy leveled a dark stare at Tadukhepa. The copper lamplight played over her face, forming unsettling, flickering shapes beneath the older woman's eyes. "When you see the Pharaoh—your husband—you must not show any distaste."

Misgiving filled Tadukhepa, curdling her stomach. "Distaste?" she stammered.

A gentle tap sounded on the door. "The Pharaoh has arrived," Thutmose's deep voice said, muffled by the door's thickness. "He is in Amun's sanctuary. All is ready."

"Show *no* distaste," Tiy said again, and led Tadukhepa by the hand, out of their chamber and into the circle of waiting nobility.

The courtiers bowed low as Tiy swept past. They held their hands up, palms facing the Great Royal Wife. Tadukhepa was obliged to stride quickly to keep up. Tiy was small-framed, but moved with a directness and purpose that could have left a large man panting in her wake. Tadukhepa held her thick, heavy skirts well clear of her ankles and thanked the goddess that she did not break into a fresh sweat. The crowd of nobles remained bent in their postures of obeisance until Tiy barked, "Rise."

The second set of doors—the larger of the two—swung wide. Lamplight flashed off the tall, strong, gilded carvings of the god Amun, rippling like the streams of a fountain over bands of lapis lazuli and malachite. Nann whispered a few Hurrian words to the Mitanni servants who bore Ishtar carefully between them; the crowd seemed to draw itself in like a single body taking one expectant breath, and then Tiy led the way into the god's sanctuary.

A cloud of perfumed smoke spilled from the doorway, rising at once into the black heights of the temple. It was lulling and sweet, rich with myrrh, Amun's favorite scent. The low, rhythmic voices of women followed the incense, twisting and flowing like the smoke-clouds themselves. As she stepped into the sanctuary, Tadukhepa could see that each chanting woman—there were perhaps a dozen of them arrayed in a half-circle—was dressed in a simple, white linen robe, tied at the waist with an unadorned sash of blue. Each held a tiny oil lamp in her hands. The flames illuminated the undersides of their faces, so that proportion and perspective were thrown out of balance and the women appeared to hover like spirits in the darkness. Their mouths seemed to open and close without regard to the rhythm of their song.

The little oil lamps spilled just enough light that Tadukhepa could make out the faint outlines of Amun himself—Egypt's lord of the sun, who, she had learned, paradoxically preferred to remain cloaked in darkness. He was slightly larger than a mortal man, and sat steady and straight upon his throne, his face turned toward the double doors—though in the dimness, Tadukhepa could discern nothing of his features. The sparse light was just enough to limn his square shoulders, his confident posture, and the two enormous plumes rising from his crown, not unlike the plumes Great Wife Tiy wore.

There was a rustle in the darkness behind Tadukhepa— the crowd of Egyptians bowing once more, offering their palms to the statue of Amun. She did the same, and heard Tiy give a little hum of approval.

As she straightened, Tadukhepa heard a grunt, followed

by a thick sigh. It came from somewhere near the foot of the statue, but in the darkness she could not determine its source. Once more, Tiy took Tadukhepa's hand and pulled the princess closer still to the sun god.

It was only then that she saw the Pharaoh. Amunhotep sat hunched in a chair, shrouded in the shadows that gathered around the statue's feet. His trembling hands were braced on the chair's arms. He grunted and puffed again, struggling to rise from his seat. In the dim light, Tadukhepa took in the great belly that pushed over the top of his white kilt, the sickly pallor of his skin, the mottled face with its sagging jowls swaying between the locks of his wig. He wore the Double Crown, towering, red and white, but as he struggled the crown tipped precariously, and with a muttered curse he steadied it with one age-spotted hand.

"You should remain seated," Tiy said smoothly, going to him, easing him back gently with one hand on his shoulder. "You are the Lord of Waset; there is no need to rise if you do not wish it."

"Nonsense," Amunhotep said thickly.

He made another effort, levering himself carefully against the throne's arms, and at last he rose ponderously to his feet. Now Tadukhepa understood what Tiy had meant— *show no distaste*. The Pharaoh Amunhotep was draped with folds of fat, his flesh softened and overfed from too many years of royal excess and too few years on the battlefield. He was a man of advanced age, but not yet so old that he ought to find such great difficulty in rising. It could only be his bulk that hindered him so—and his indolence, which was evident in the heavy-lidded laze of his eyes. Below the scent of Amun's copious myrrh, Tadukhepa detected the faintest trace of sourness rising from the Pharaoh's body. The odor held a suggestion of danger—of disease. She understood at once that quite apart from his astounding heaviness, the king of Egypt was ill. Perhaps seriously so.

She bowed low once more, holding out her palms in supplication, grateful that in this position the Pharaoh could not see the look of shock and disgust on her face. But in only a moment his dry, warm hand closed on hers, and Tadukhepa straightened and made herself look calmly into his eyes.

"I welcome you to Egypt, Wife," the Pharaoh said. "You are as beautiful as your father, King Tushratta, promised."

And even as a queen I shall be locked away in the harem, to wither and die of loneliness, she thought with a stab of desolate pain. It was certain that a man in such a state would have no real interest in a new wife.

Tadukhepa resisted the urge to glance toward Prince Thutmose. She did not desire the Pharaoh—he was nothing at all like his beautiful, courtly son. But she might have hoped at least for a child to ease the years of loneliness and confinement that lay ahead of her. There was no question, though, that Amunhotep could not sire a child on her, even if he possessed the inclination to try. A man in his condition was surely devoid of fertile seed—and probably devoid of the energy to go planting in any wife's field. She hadn't even motherhood to hope for. Despair drew around her like the folds of a thick, woolen cloak.

But she felt Great Wife Tiy's gaze upon her face, so Tadukhepa made herself smile. "I thank you for your graciousness, Mighty Horus," she told him softly. "I am pleased that you have chosen me, and hope to make both Mitanni and Egypt proud."

The Pharaoh nodded.

"I have brought Ishtar," she added, gesturing to the servants beside her, who held the statue of the goddess up so that the Holy Lady might examine and commune with her fellow deity, Amun. "My father sends her with his blessings for you, and his hope that she might extend her healing powers over you."

"Very thoughtful," Amunhotep said, and Tadukhepa could read neither dryness nor gratitude in his voice.

The chanting women concluded their song. Silence enveloped the dark shrine. A bald-headed priest emerged from the shadows behind Amun's throne, the skin of a leopard slung over his shoulder. He carried a small bowl in one hand, a tiny vial in the other. Both objects were carved from pure, thin alabaster, and seemed to glow in the light of the lamps. The priest offered both vessels to Amunhotep.

The Pharaoh took a pinch of salt from the bowl, and Tadukhepa, well-schooled in Egyptian marriage customs, turned her face toward him and opened her mouth. She closed her eyes so that she could not see the king's plump, sallow fingers approaching. When the bitter grains of salt dropped upon her tongue, she swallowed hard to keep from gagging.

"With salt I feed thee," Amunhotep said.

Next he accepted the white stone vial and raised it over Tadukhepa's head. Warm, fragrant oil pattered against her hair, trickling down to mingle with the sweat on her scalp.

"With oil I anoint thee."

Tadukhepa stood with her chin raised, as Tiy had bidden, while the High Priest of Amun recited a long, poetic litany of praise to the sun god. Then he called down Amun's blessing upon the union and asked the god to favor Tadukhepa's womb that it might bring forth many healthy children.

At this, she stifled the laugh that clawed at the back of her throat. It felt hysterical, wild—desperate. She blinked hard, forgetting the foreign tongue she had studied, allowing the priest's words to blur into a mess of meaningless sound. Tadukhepa had come to Egypt a virgin, and a virgin she was likely to remain.

Finally the gathering paused, waiting in the darkness to hear whether the god's golden statue would speak, whether he would offer any condemnation on the union or lay a curse that would shatter this marriage before it had even begun. Tadukhepa allowed a foolish hope to spark in her breast... but all too soon the High Priest raised his hands in benediction and pronounced the marriage acceptable to the god.

"Go now and celebrate," he said, and as one the gathering bowed before Amun. No one saw the two small tears that slipped down Tadukhepa's cheeks, falling silently on the cold tiles of the sanctuary floor.

It took an hour for the procession of noblemen and their gaily dressed wives to make its way back to the heart of the city, through its finer districts, and on down to the quay where a fleet of glorious pleasure-barques waited. The barques' bright pennants flapped in the breeze, and the gold-leafed eyes adorning their bows seeming to blink as the boats bobbed on the river's gentle current. Wine and strong beer appeared like mushrooms after a Mitanni rain, and skins and jugs were passed from hand to hand among the celebrating crowd.

Throughout the revelries, Tadukhepa remained silent and placid-faced on her litter, sitting as still as Ishtar beside her. She watched the rear of Amunhotep's huge, electrum-plated carrying-chair as it progressed slowly before her, borne on the backs of sixteen broad-shouldered men. Not once did the Pharaoh deign to look around, to catch sight of his new bride in the sunlight. He only slumped in his seat, his body stirring faintly with the thick rhythm of his breath, while Tiy on her own litter moved smoothly beside the king like a boat drifting on a current, observing the revelries with a detached, unreadable stare.

When at last the singing, laughing crowds filtered

onto the pleasure-barques and Tadukhepa herself was conducted aboard a small, private boat with a few of her Mitanni servants, she crept into the shelter of a curtained cabin, taking only Nann with her. Nann drew the heavy drapes tight and turned to Tadukhepa with her mouth hanging open, a look of sorrowful disbelief painted on her pale features. Tadukhepa's chin quivered. She felt as knocked out of place, as wholly *gone* as Nann's missing tooth.

"Oh," Nann said slowly, "Mistress..."

"He's horrible," Tadukhepa whispered. She covered her face with trembling hands, wishing Nann couldn't see her weeping, but grateful the serving-girl was there.

"He was polite," Nann offered.

It was a lame attempt at comfort, and Tadukhepa nearly lashed out at her before she recalled that Nann, too, was condemned to exile, trapped in this terrible place against her will or whim.

"We only have one another," Tadukhepa said.

With a strangled sob, Nann rushed toward her. They clung together, burying their faces in each other's hair. Tadukhepa breathed deep, tasting the last faint traces of Mitanni in Nann's scent—the green fragrance of the coasts, the softness of spring flowers, the sacred smoke of sandalwood. Soon, she knew, those memories would fade.

"You must be brave," Nann said, her voice muffled by Tadukhepa's shoulder. "You must bear up and be a true queen. It's all you *can* do now."

"I know," Tadukhepa said.

The sailors on deck shouted and cast off their boats' lines. The gilded barque pushed out into the great, gray-brown river, shuddering lightly in the grip of the current. But Tadukhepa did not peek from her curtained enclave, did not join her servants on deck to watch as Waset shrank to a grimy dot on the eastern bank, and the bright, glowing walls of the House of Rejoicing grew larger to the west.

Instead the two girls threw themselves down on the scattered silk cushions, locked in one another's arms, weeping for the world they would never see again.

Nefertiti

Year 36 of Amunhotep,
Ruler of Waset,
Lord of Truth in the Sun,
Strong Bull Arising

IT WAS DAWN BEFORE NEFERTITI returned to her father's estate. She crossed the lanes of the West Bank in blissful silence as the sun rose to fill the sky with a rose-petal blush. Her train of servants followed behind, yawning and shuffling. The light of a fresh, new day crept up the street, a slow but inevitable flow like honey pouring from a jar. Everything it touched was tinted with warmth. Nefertiti held up one smooth, elegant hand as she walked and examined it in the glow of dawn. Even her skin was touched by a golden hue, just like the skin of a goddess. *Apt*, she thought. *How perfectly perfect.*

The wedding feast celebrating Amunhotep's union with the Hurrian foreigner had stretched into the late hours. The ailing Pharaoh had begun to look pale and afflicted well before the second course, and had taken his leave midway through the third. Great Wife Tiy and her perpetual frown exited with him. The Pharaoh had turned over the seat of honor to Thutmose, his heir—and Nefertiti, as Thutmose's betrothed, had settled herself to the left of the throne.

She had enjoyed the view from the dais, raised above the heads of the West Bank nobles—those considered important enough, grand enough, of high enough birth to live near the king and his House of Rejoicing, buffered from the stink and lowly clamor of Waset by the wide, gray-green expanse of the River Iteru. Few experiences had pleased Nefertiti as much the simple act of sitting so high above the best and wealthiest families in the Two Lands.

The dais—the throne—was where she belonged. She had felt the certainty of it coiled tight inside her like a bud on the verge of bursting open. That gloried elevation was what she had been preparing for, nearly her whole life. Or rather, it was what her *father* had been preparing her for. Throughout her eighteen years there had been many times—uncountable times—when Nefertiti had felt convinced she would never attain the status she wanted, the greatness for which she had been groomed. When her fingers went awry on her harp strings and her tutor scolded, when her voice broke as she sang, when her sister Mutbenret cried out from the sting of the cane because yet again Nefertiti had been caught walking gracelessly through the halls, or because their father Ay had seen a defiant flash in Nefertiti's eyes...

But at last she had found herself there, seated on the golden chair, and raised above them all—even her father— as a King's Great Wife ought to be. She was untouchable on the dais, and all the eyes of Egypt were upon her.

Of course, Nefertiti was not Great Wife yet. She would not be raised to that exalted status until she and Thutmose were married, and old, fat Amunhotep finally went down into his tomb. *It won't be long now*, Nefertiti mused comfortably as she strolled from the House of Rejoicing to her father's estate. The current Pharaoh weakened by the day, plagued by pains in his teeth that spread and throbbed through the bones of his face—or so the servants' gossip said. He looked so powerless now, a wilted petal from some waxen, yellow bloom, that it felt obscene to even think of him as 'king.'

Time to make way for my betrothed—my beloved—for a strong, young king who can be the demi-god a Pharaoh must be.

38

She imagined Thutmose back in the House of Rejoicing, reclining on his cedar-and-ivory bed where she had left him. By now the light of dawn would be slanting through his window, falling on his bare skin, turning him to gold, too, like the god he was inside.

We are all gods here, she thought. *We hold ourselves apart from the rabble—the east-bank* rekhet *with their low blood, who mill like cattle and bleat like the senseless goats of the fields.*

Long before Nefertiti was born, the Pharaoh left the dull, mortal-fleshed city of Waset behind and established his court across the river. Better—far better this way. What commoner would dare to approach this shining new city of the Pharaoh? Only the chosen dwelt here, the well-bred, the valuable, the pure. West was the direction of death—the direction in which the sun died at the close of each day, the direction in which the tombs lay, those cold, dark, stale-aired chambers bored into the rocky bones of the earth. The House of Rejoicing and the estates that surrounded it—homes of those families chosen by the king himself—existed like a veil between worlds, an ethereal place hanging between the living and the glorious, immortal dead. Egypt's most noble families drifted here like mist above the water, set apart—untouchable, and more beautiful than any mortal heart could comprehend.

She was one of the lucky ones, Nefertiti knew. The gods could have caused her to be born into any other family. They could have made her the child of *rekhet* farmers, scrabbling in the black Iteru mud for her livelihood, whelping litters of young in the fields just like any common beast bred for the harness. But the gods were good. They had made her *this*: daughter of a famed charioteer who had risen to the king's closest favor; niece of the King's Great Wife; betrothed to the heir to the Horus Throne... and beautiful. As beautiful as the sun rising, and golden as the goddess she would soon become.

The lanes of the West Bank stirred slowly to wakefulness

as the servants of the noble houses rose to their morning tasks. She heard the quiet conversation of women drawing water from a canal, the metallic *chip-chip-chip* of two fire-flints struck together in the seclusion of an estate's walled courtyard. Soon the outdoor ovens would be lit, and the gardens would fill with the sweet, tempting odor of baking bread. For now, the morning still clung to the crisp perfume of dew and well-watered greenery, and Nefertiti could still smell Thutmose, his compelling scent of musk and myrrh clinging to her skin.

How pleasant it was to drift down the lanes of the West Bank, alone but for her sleepy servants. How good of the gods, to make Nefertiti what she was, to fit her into this time and this place, smooth and easy and just so, like a carpenter fitting a peg into a piece of fine, ebony-wood furniture. In the days before Amunhotep had taken his court west to dwell in this veil between the worlds, she would have been obliged to go everywhere with an escort of guards, or carried on a litter as she was for yesterday's wedding procession to and from the Temple of Amun. In Waset, and elsewhere—everywhere in the Two Lands—the world was not a gentle place. But here, where the homes of the blessed and precious clustered around the House of Rejoicing like chicks around a she-goose, there was nothing to fear. She was safe. She was always safe.

Nefertiti turned onto the path that led to her father's gate. Her servants sighed with relief. It had been a long night for them—for her, too, though she would not have it any other way. She was eighteen years old. At that age, life itself is one great, extended celebration, full of song and dance and endless displays of beauty. When a woman is young and beautiful, she can taste every dish life sets before her, drink from every cup, and never stop to sleep, never pause for rest. What good is sleep when it only interrupts the pleasures of the waking world?

The porter opened the gate when Nefertiti's maid rang

the bell, bowing low when he saw the young mistress standing there in her rumpled red-linen gown, the long, curled locks of her wig matted and disarrayed from the fragrant beeswax sticking to its black strands. The wax had been a festive white cone at the beginning of the feast, tied carefully to her wig like a little crown of alabaster. As the night wore on and the feast hall grew hotter with the presence of so many bodies—and with Thutmose's enticing proximity—it had softened, then melted drip by drip to fill the air around Nefertiti with the intoxicating scent of night-blooming jasmine.

The porter bowed and stood back for her to enter. Nefertiti breezed into the courtyard, brushing past the household servants who busied themselves with the ovens and pans of risen bread dough.

"Go to your chambers and rest," she called over her shoulder to her own train of attendants, and gratefully, her servants scattered.

The courtyard gave way to a portico, the space between its pillars retaining the river-damp coolness of the night. Her gold-threaded sandals tapped lightly on the paving stones; the vines thriving in the shade brushed her cheek with leaves like long, soft fingers. Beyond the portico was the entrance hall of Ay's fine, two-story house, its doors flung open so the servants might bustle back and forth between courtyard and hall unimpeded. Nefertiti slipped in easily—it seemed her father and her stepmother Lady Teya were still asleep—and climbed the stairs to her chamber.

But before she could reach her chamber, Mutbenret's face, still round with the last traces of childhood, peered from the alcove that hid the entrance to her own room.

"You're back," Mutbenret called softly.

Nefertiti smiled. "Of course I'm back, silly duck. Would I stay all night and all day, too? Eventually even the House of Rejoicing becomes a bore."

Mutbenret took a hesitant step down the hall, hands clasped at her waist.

"Well, come on," Nefertiti said, pushing open her chamber door. "I know you're dying to hear all about it."

All about the party—the late-night revelries, the entertainments, both planned and unplanned, that were offered when the hours grew late and the wedding feast stretched on into the deep of the night. Mutbenret had been obliged to leave with Ay and Lady Teya when they'd had their fill of the feast. It was just as well, Nefertiti thought. The late-night celebrations were nothing for a girl of eleven to see, and any girl as compliant as Mutbenret, as used to doing what she was told without question or complaint, might get into trouble at such a wild carousal. Parties became *truly* good when the older nobles trickled off to their beds, and the young and adventurous were left to steer the boat where it most wanted to go.

Nefertiti sank onto her bed, sighing. The night had been exhausting, after all; she could still feel its heat and frantic rhythms pulsing along her limbs. A nap before breakfast would be welcome. But first she must tell her little sister everything. The day would soon come when Mutbenret would be allowed to remain at a feast after Ay departed, and the girl must know what to expect. She held out one arm and Mutbenret came to her eagerly, tucking herself against Nefertiti's body, resting her shaven head with its youthful, braided side-lock on Nefertiti's shoulder.

"The music became loud and wild just after you and Father and your mother left," Nefertiti said. "It was like the baying of hounds! It made all the handsome young men eager for a hunt."

"A hunt?" said Mutbenret, smiling lightly.

"*You* know. I've told you all about that."

Nefertiti pulled the wax-covered wig from her head and tossed it across the room. It missed her cedarwood wig stand by several feet and landed on the floor with a comical smack. Both girls giggled.

"But it's always best to let any hunter dream of his prey before he goes prowling," Nefertiti went on. "It makes him sharper and keener, and the sport is so much better that way."

Mutbenret nodded sagely, as if she were wise in the ways of men.

"When the seventh course came out from the kitchens it was followed by a troop of naked acrobats, male and female. Their displays left little room for imagination." Nefertiti gave a short, sharp laugh, which made her sister sit up and peer enquiringly at her face. "The Hurrian—the new King's Wife—was mortified by the acrobats. I could see it on her face. She had asked leave of the Pharaoh to remain at the feast when he and Great Wife Tiy departed. Poor dear, I think she was trying to avoid consummating her marriage, though the gods know Amunhotep is in no state to lie with a woman. I don't blame her. If I were married to a man of his size, and in such poor health, I'd avoid my marriage bed, too. He would crush his wife before he could beget a child!"

"You shouldn't say such things about the Pharaoh," Mutbenret said, tensing as if she expected punishment from some unseen watcher.

"Oh, but it's only the truth. The gods were merciful to me—they promised me to Thutmose." Nefertiti slitted her eyes, smiling dreamily. "It's hard to believe a man as handsome and... and *vigorous* as Thutmose was sired by Amunhotep. Ah, well—the poor Hurrian girl. When she saw the acrobats bending and twisting around one another, naked as they were, I believe she regretted her choice to stay in the hall! You know how prudish foreigners can be.

But what a choice: stay and be embarrassed, or go and be stripped naked before Amunhotep! I wouldn't trade places with King's Wife Kiya for all the riches in the treasury."

"Kiya? Is that her name?"

"It's what *I* call her. A good name, don't you think?"

Mutbenret frowned. The name meant *monkey* in the Egyptian tongue. "I hope you were kind to her, Nefertiti. She's so far from her home."

"Of course I was kind, my sweet, soft-hearted little sister. She remained up on the dais with Thutmose and me, and we were both very solicitous and thoughtful. We gave her first choice of all the dishes that were presented, though I think by the time you left the feast hall she was stuffed like a goose ready for roasting, and she didn't eat much more. Her Egyptian is quite good, I must admit. She has a funny accent, but she speaks the language well enough. She even told a few amusing stories, and made Thutmose laugh." She paused. "Did you see me up there, sitting on the dais, right beside the Pharaoh's throne?"

"How could I not see you? The whole banquet hall saw! You looked finer than any King's Great Wife who has ever lived."

"Finer than Tiy?"

Mutbenret gave a shy laugh. "Auntie Sour-Face." Then her eyes darted around Nefertiti's chamber, as if she were afraid the walls might be listening.

"Auntie Sour-Face was a spectacular beauty in her younger days," Nefertiti said. "Father always says so. 'She won the Pharaoh's heart with her beauty,' he says, 'but kept her place with her wits.'" Nefertiti tossed her head. Her natural hair, dark and curly and tightly bound in a roll against her nape, lay flattened on her scalp from long hours spent beneath the heavy, wax-laden wig. "I'm meant to take a lesson from that, I suppose. But I'm glad I didn't have to win any Pharaoh's heart—not that I couldn't rise to the task. It's better this way, promised to Thutmose, with everything planned out in advance. And now we need only wait for the gods to call Amunhotep to the west. When he dies, I'll be King's Great Wife, out of all the women in Egypt. Just think of it, Mutbenret! Your own sister, wife of the Pharaoh!"

The younger girl smiled faintly. "You looked a natural up there, sitting beside the throne. It's where the gods intend you to be."

Nefertiti wrapped her half-sister in a tight embrace. "It will all be worth it, then. Everything we've suffered..." though Nefertiti knew well that Mutbenret had suffered far more than she. "We'll be free from all these expectations, all these rules, the training, the watching... the punishments. Oh yes, *we*. I'll take you with me to the House of Rejoicing and Father will remain here, simmering behind his walls like a soggy old dumpling."

Mutbenret pulled away, eyeing Nefertiti with doubt.

"I'll be King's Great Wife," Nefertiti said, perhaps a bit too forcefully. "*I'll* be the one in charge. Of everyone—of all the Two Lands. That includes Father. He'll have to do what I say, and I'll put a stop to everything. You'll be safe, Mutbenret—I swear it. We have only to wait a little while longer. Soon Thutmose will be Pharaoh, and I'll be his wife—and then you'll see."

"Tell me more about the feast," Mutbenret said.

Her smile was hazy, distant—and Nefertiti could tell that she didn't believe anything would really change when Nefertiti took her place in the king's palace. Perhaps the poor girl couldn't allow herself to believe. The gods could be whimsical and cruel in their caprices—even a child as young as Mutbenret knew that much. *Maybe*, Nefertiti thought, *the girl is wise to temper her hope.*

Nefertiti spoke on, telling all she could remember of the

night's lush details: the dancers with their gauzy costumes, their wrists and throats glinting in the lamplight with bangles of turquoise and gold; the decadent sweet courses of sugared figs and lemon juice and rose petals crisped in honey; the jests the young men made down among the lower tables, their mock battles for the hearts of ladies— fought with ducks' bones and the long, pale spears of radish roots instead of swords and daggers. She told of fleeting romances that lived and died in the shadows of pillars, all in the space of a few moments—the courtship of whispers, the victorious kiss, the slap across the face, the furious woman striding away with her rumpled dress hanging askew. The music had changed as the night wore on, altering itself subtly, one song at a time, until the harpists no longer plucked ballads from their strings, but darker, more compelling rhythms, throbbing and low. The wind had changed several hours before sunrise, carrying the wet, fertile scent of the garden indoors where it twined quietly with the savory, spicy odors of the feast and the perfume of women's half-melted, waxen crowns. The garden beckoned to young lovers, and two by two they slipped outside to allow themselves to fall under the spell of moonlight and stars.

Nefertiti trailed off here, remembering. She no longer felt Mutbenret's slight frame tucked against her. She felt only Thutmose, his arm around her shoulder, guiding her toward the garden—the hard slab of his muscular side, his body as well-trained as any general's—and the slight twist, the shifting of his ribs as he turned to glance back into the hall at the empty Pharaoh's throne and the little Hurrian bride who sat beside it, huddled in her dark woolen robes, staring dull-eyed into the rising, pulsing chaos of the feast.

He led Nefertiti out into the fresh night air. It worked its way beneath her wig's curls, teasing the back of her neck with a breath of coolness that raised a delicious shiver along her skin. He kissed her there on the garden path, his tongue forceful in her mouth, his hands ardent on her hips and the soft swell of her behind. Anyone could have seen—several people likely did, though Nefertiti kept her eyes tight-shut. She blushed with mingled pleasure and shame at the thought of the revelers catching sight of the heir and his betrothed, displaying their passion in such an undignified way. She broke from Thutmose's kiss with an effort, panting out her protests—*not here, not where everyone can see*—although she made no move to disentangle herself from his arms.

In short order he pulled her into one of the flower beds, where a wall of shrubbery, just high enough to hide them both from immediate view, provided a rather flimsy screen. He backed her up against the thick trunk of a sycamore and pulled her gown up around her hips, lifting her easily to lock her legs around his waist. Nefertiti could still feel the tree's rough bark biting into her shoulders.

Rutting in the garden, just like a rekhet slut. What would her father say if he knew? The memory made Nefertiti shiver with bliss.

But her shiver quickly changed to a shudder of disgust. As Thutmose worked steadily, driving Nefertiti back against the tree while the moonlight and indigo shadow of the leaves dappled across his shoulder, a crackle in the nearby shrubbery made Nefertiti glance around sharply. A man had pushed through the screen of foliage and stood watching them, a small, coolly amused smile on his fleshy lips. Nefertiti nearly screamed, until she recognized Thutmose's brother.

"Stop," she panted in Thutmose's ear. "Stop!"

Reluctantly, Thutmose slowed his efforts, then eased Nefertiti down until she could get her feet beneath her and stand. She couldn't straighten her gown quickly enough. She felt the dark gaze of Young Amunhotep, Thutmose's strange, eerily watchful brother, slide over her bare skin.

Thutmose turned to find Amunhotep standing there. "Gods," he shouted, lunging at his brother. "Get out, you rat—you dog!"

Unperturbed, Amunhotep took an easy step back, out of the range of Thutmose's swinging fist. The black leaves of the night-time garden framed his face like a lion's mane.

"Dog," Amunhotep had said. His voice was slow, lazy, with a musical smoothness that would have been pleasant in another man. A laugh rippled his words like a sluggish, muddy current. "Dogs always come sniffing when they hear a bitch in heat." Then he raised his voice—*Yi! Yi! Yi!*—yipping in rhythmic imitation of Nefertiti's passionate cries. His teeth flashed pale in the starlight.

Thutmose lunged at him again, and laughing, Young Amunhotep melted into the shadows of the garden.

Thutmose turned back to Nefertiti then, shaking his head and growling. "That foul creature. That blight! I wish Father would send him to the army for training—and that a spear would miss its mark and land in his guts instead."

Nefertiti said nothing. Amunhotep departed without raising any further trouble, and the relief that he was gone now flooded her limbs, making her tremble with a violence that surprised her.

Thutmose returned to her then, kissing her neck, moving the locks of her wig aside to tease her earlobe with his tongue—but she pushed him away. "No, not here," she insisted. "What if your brother comes back?"

Thutmose clicked his tongue in annoyance. "Where, then?"

"Your chambers. We can bar the door there, and be certain Amunhotep won't come spying."

They remained in Thutmose's chambers, tangled in the cool sheets of his wide, leopard-legged bed, until it was finally time for Nefertiti to locate her servants and leave the House of Rejoicing. Those hours with her betrothed had been sweet, but now, in the privacy of her own bedroom, she could recall almost nothing of the time she had spent there. All she could remember with any clarity was Young Amunhotep in the garden, his long, leering face melting into the shadows, his eyes sweeping her naked flesh, his teeth gleaming and predatory when he laughed.

Mutbenret sensed Nefertiti's discomfiture. "What's the matter?" she asked, sitting up and once more staring in earnest concern.

Nefertiti made herself smile lightly. "I was only thinking of the time I spent with Thutmose when we took leave of the feast."

"And what did you do together?"

"Tried to fill my belly, of course," Nefertiti said archly. "Don't you think it would be splendid for Thutmose to begin his reign as Pharaoh with a son and heir already in the cradle?"

"I suppose..."

"When the old Pharaoh dies, Thutmose will inherit more than just the Horus Throne, you know. He'll gain all his father's harems, too. Imagine, all those palaces and estates just brimming over with women. Any of them might bear a son to Thutmose—I'm not fool enough to believe he'll only ever desire *my* bed. You know how fickle men can be. I need to get the jump on the harem girls, don't I? The faster I can produce a son, the more secure I'll be on the throne of the King's Great Wife."

But gods grant I never have a son like Young Amunhotep, Nefertiti thought. With his alienating silence and intensely watchful eyes, the Pharaoh's second-eldest son was enough to turn even a mother's heart away. Nefertiti wondered whether her aunt Tiy loved her second son, or whether she saw him clearly for what he was. The gods would have been merciful if they'd sent a fever to claim Young Amunhotep in the cradle, or made a nurse roll upon him in her sleep, smothering the breath from the child before he'd grown to manhood.

As Nefertiti sat in brooding silence, the high, light notes of Lady Teya's voice drifted up the stairs and floated down the hall. She was singing in the portico below, as she did at the start of each new day, greeting the god in the form of Khepri, the climbing sun of early morning. It was the form of the god which Lady Teya revered the most, for she was ever the optimist, ever the believer in fresh beginnings.

"Your mother is awake," Nefertiti said. "Tra-la-la, just like a lark outside your window who insists on singing when you'd rather sleep in."

Mutbenret smiled.

"I'd hoped to catch a nap." Nefertiti yawned and pressed her fingers against her stinging eyes, careful not to rub lest she smear her eye-paint. "But the praises to Khepri have begun, so there's no hope of that now. Will you help me dress and freshen my paint, Little Sister? Father probably assumes I've been out all night, but he won't be pleased if I look it."

Dressed in a fresh, neatly pleated gown, and with her face powdered and her eyelids newly colored, Nefertiti looked as light and airy as the morning itself. She combed out her hair, then re-rolled and pinned it while Mutbenret chose a new wig from the collection stored inside Nefertiti's large, free-standing closet of costly cedarwood. Soon the maids would come to tidy the room; they would tend to the old hairpiece that still lay on the floor, heating bone combs in a flame and pulling them through the wig's strands until all traces of the sticky perfumed wax were melted away. Nefertiti settled the clean wig in place and pulled Mutbenret close as she studied herself in the mirror.

NEFERTITI

"Perfect. Don't we look a lovely pair?" She tweaked Mutbenret's braided lock. "Not long now before you are a woman grown, and then off comes your lock, and on with a stylish wig!"

"Will I have your old wigs—the ones you don't like anymore?"

Nefertiti took her by the shoulders and laughed. "Goodness—never! You'll have new wigs, new gowns all your own—the best and finest of everything. You'll be sister to the King's Great Wife. There will be no cast-offs for you."

In the portico, the final notes of Lady Teya's praises died away. There was a momentary silence, as if the creatures of the garden were waiting politely in case Teya wished to continue. Then a chorus of birds and insects whirred and chittered as the world greeted the sun in its own fashion.

"Come," Nefertiti said, moving toward her door, already walking with the stately grace her father expected, even though there were no watchful eyes as yet on the young beauty and her little sister.

They found Ay, Overseer of All the Horses, on the portico with Lady Teya. Nefertiti bobbed a tiny bow to her step-mother, who did not return the greeting. Lady Teya's face still beamed vacantly with the bliss of her morning ritual. Nefertiti produced a deeper bow for her father, bending her neck to a precise angle, holding the pose for the exact length of time to indicate the honor Ay expected from his daughters.

The household servants had just produced a table and four stools; Ay had seated himself to enjoy his wife's ritual song, and looked up with a nod of approval for Nefertiti. Ay was past the prime of his life, though he was not yet old; he had settled comfortably into that age when men give up all their youthful passions and turn their hearts and hands to industry, to useful works. Ay worked tirelessly toward his goals—no one could ever accuse him of indulgence in leisure—and he expected the same ambition, the same unflagging drive from Nefertiti.

Ay gestured curtly at the empty stools; the girls took their seats while breakfast was laid before them.

"A fine wedding," Ay said at last, biting into a boiled duck egg.

"The Hurrian is so lovely," said Lady Teya. "What a fine King's Wife she will make."

The Hurrian was terrified, and as meek as the sheep her father rules over in Mitanni. But Nefertiti did not speak. Lady Teya would never have noticed the new bride's meekness— or would have chosen to ignore it if she had. Lady Teya saw nothing but what she wished to see, and what she wished to see was beauty, harmony, peace—good things only, never any flaw, never any darkness that might cast a shadow over her bright and hopeful world. Nefertiti tore bits from the still-warm round of bread that lay steaming in her bowl and dipped the pieces delicately in the little wells of colorful sauces, which sparkled like jewels in the center of the table.

"You looked very fine atop the dais," Ay said to Nefertiti. His voice was heavy with significance.

She glanced at him and noted the satisfaction, the self-congratulatory gleam in his eye. *Soon enough,* his fractional smile said. Nefertiti lowered her eyes demurely. She wished she had the knack of making herself blush. Other girls could do it, but Nefertiti had never been able to master the trick. It would have pleased Ay, if she had managed to color just then—a flush of gratitude for all the work he'd done on Nefertiti's behalf. That was what Ay would see in the pinking of her cheeks.

"Your betrothed looked quite stately there, too," Ay went on. "King's Son Thutmose—what a fine young man. He'll make a great Pharaoh one day."

"Oh, you must tell her the news," said Lady Teya suddenly, coming out of her fog of blissful unawareness, focusing on her husband with a radiant smile. "Don't withhold it any longer; Nefertiti's heart is so full, and she longs to hear—"

Ay held up a hand to hush Lady Teya; she lapsed into complacent silence, turning her face to beam unseeing out at the flowers of the garden, at the cloud of glowing flies that swirled above the fragrant blooms, their delicate wings backlit by the rising sun.

Nefertiti cleared her throat. "Tell me what, Father?"

It was an audacity, to speak when Ay had already indicated that he wished for silence. Nefertiti saw Mutbenret go tense, and felt a quick stab of guilt for making her sister worry. But she could tell from Ay's gratified air that she had not overstepped—*could* not overstep today.

Ay glanced around the table, his smile growing by the moment. He looked as pleased as a cat on a sunlit cushion. "Some weeks ago, I wrote to the astrologers at the Holy City of Annu."

Nefertiti leaned from the edge of her stool. Astrologers? And from the Holy City, no less. Ay wanted to be very certain of his plans—whatever was in that letter.

He said, "They have returned my letter at last. It was a long wait, but I am sure they only wished to be thorough in their consideration."

"What did you ask of them?" Nefertiti prompted.

"They have declared the most auspicious date for your marriage to Thutmose. The wedding shall take place ten days from this morning, as the sun rises, at the Temple of Amun."

Nefertiti kept her wide grin in check. With exquisite control, she managed to smile only very softly, almost coolly. She did not clap her hands or reach to hug Mutbenret as her racing heart commanded, but dipped her head gracefully toward her father. "I thank you for the news. I am very pleased."

Ay watched Nefertiti for a long moment. As she returned to her food, slicing her duck egg into cubes so she might nibble delicately from the point of her knife, she could feel Ay's level stare as surely as she felt the weight of the wig on her head. His eyes assessed her every movement, judging her grace and aplomb. She went on eating as if this was an average morning, a normal day—and soon Ay turned the conversation to other topics, though Nefertiti followed his words with only half her heart.

But this was no average morning. The sun had finally risen on a world that would soon belong to Nefertiti alone—a world in which she was free to do as she pleased, to live as she pleased, to love Thutmose with all the passion in her heart and to fashion the world to her own pleasure, rather than conforming herself to Ay's narrow expectations.

When Ay's gaze finally left her face, Nefertiti reached beneath the table and found Mutbenret's hand. She squeezed it without looking up from her plate. Her sister's warm fingers squeezed back.

At last, after a lifetime under her father's thumb, dwelling in his shadow, the sun had risen for Nefertiti. In ten days she would be free.

Kiya

Year 36 of Amunhotep,
Ruler of Waset,
Lord of Truth in the Sun,
Strong Bull Arising

TADUKHEPA WAS ALONE. The garden's afternoon shade had crept from the bank of tall, fragrant, glossy-leaved bushes behind her to cast an ever-shifting pattern of blue and gold onto the bench where she waited. The shade kept the worst of the day's heat away, yet the stone of the bench was still warm from the lingering height of noon. The feel of it—the warmth, the faint graininess of the stone—passed easily through her light linen shift, and the sensation was intrusive, as if the whole of Egypt pressed itself against her skin.

At the request of Great Wife Tiy, she had given up her Hurrian clothing and donned the correct, courtly garb of an Egyptian queen—long, pleated linen gowns with a loose, airy weave. Tadukhepa conceded that the linen was much better than her Mitanni wool when it came to coping with the brutal heat, but some of her new dresses were made of such fine fabric that they were nearly transparent. She felt naked, bared to the scrutiny of all who looked upon her, as vulnerable as a fish in a net.

She had drawn the line at wigs, mustering the courage to put her foot down no matter how it deepened Great Wife Tiy's frown. In the five days since her marriage to the Pharaoh, Tadukhepa had had opportunity enough to handle the wigs these Egyptian women wore. She had attempted to make friends with the women who shared her fate—the concubines and other minor queens of the king's harem—and had shyly joined in their leisure, helping them sort through their old gowns and the contents of their massive cedar chests and carved, freestanding closets. The wigs prized by the Egyptian women were ornate and lovely, but too heavy for the arms to hold, let alone one's head and neck. Far more hair was rooted into the wigs' silk caps than any woman's head could naturally grow, and the braided and curled locks were laden with beads and ornaments of gold. Just the idea of trying to balance one on her head while she reeled in the heat was enough to make Tadukhepa feel faint.

She heard the shuffle of feet on the garden path and looked around, plucking at the distressingly low neckline of her gown as if she might be able to tug it up and cover herself to the chin. Past the gentle curves of the pale limestone path and the mounds of cool-green flower beds, whose shapes overlapped one another like the peaks and valleys of Mitanni mountains, the rear wall of the harem palace stood blazing in the sun, its surface washed by a brilliant white paste of lime. Most of the women were inside the palace where the air was slightly cooler, spinning and weaving in their private rooms or gathered in the game hall over their *senet* boards. The day was still too hot for outdoor leisure. Tadukhepa preferred the solitude of the garden when the sun was still high, even if the heat was fierce; she cherished the silence, the music of birdsong, and the simple comfort of thinking in her own Hurrian tongue rather than struggling to converse with the other women in Egyptian. As Tadukhepa watched, her servant Nann came around one of the path's many bends, carrying a stone jar whose sides were already beaded with moisture.

Nann set the jar down in the shade, then eased the straps of a linen bag from her thin shoulder. She hissed in quiet pain as the straps scraped against her skin, for her pale shoulders, like her nose and cheeks, were reddened and tender from the sun.

"Did you use the ointment?" Tadukhepa asked. "The one Great Wife Tiy gave me? It takes away the sting of the sunburn and keeps your skin supple as it heals."

Tadukhepa had been dismayed on her first morning in Egypt when, waking and looking into her hand-mirror, she had found her face as red as a carnelian and burning with pain. Tiy had come to check on her, to see that Tadukhepa had settled into her new apartments, but the moment she set eyes on Tadukhepa's face, Tiy had sent her attendants scurrying for a translucent, sharp-smelling salve in a bright faience pot. The ointment had eased the pain immediately. Tadukhepa was grateful to the sour-faced little woman for the thoughtful gesture.

"I haven't tried the ointment yet," Nann confessed. "I don't quite trust Egyptian medicine. I heard they make concoctions out of ghastly things—human blood and the dung of crocodiles! But I will try it if you insist, Mistress."

"What have you brought me?"

Nann pulled two silver cups from her bag, set them carefully on the end of the bench, and then poured a stream of red-gold liquid from her jar.

Tadukhepa took one cup eagerly and tasted it. "Sweet! Oh, I'm so relieved. All these people ever seem to drink is bitter beer. It's enough to make me choke."

"I convinced the kitchen girls to juice some melons, just for you. They chilled it overnight in a cellar. Isn't it divine? I must admit that I tasted some on the way here."

The juice was a miracle in Tadukhepa's mouth, cool and refreshing, with a mellow flavor that reminded her of mountain summers, of picking berries with her sisters on a high hillside while the sea broke and whispered against the base of the gray cliffs far below. She set the cup down, sighing.

"What is the matter, Mistress?"

"I'm lonely—that's all. I miss my sisters and my friends at Father's court. I've tried to make new friends here, but most of these Egyptian women treat me so strangely, as if I'm some creature to be gawked at, like the gazelles and jackals they keep in their menageries—as if I'm not a person at all. And all the servants who came with me from Mitanni have already been absorbed into the Pharaoh's household—all except for you."

"Sometimes I feel as if we're sitting on an island," Nann said. "A very small island, just you and me, with all the rest of the world flowing by around us, all these people going about their business, never taking note of us at all. How is it possible to feel so isolated in such a busy place?"

"If only we had more companionship," Tadukhepa agreed.

Nann made the sign against evil, an ironic smile on her face. "Be careful what you wish for! You might be called to the Pharaoh's bed after all. There is one companion you wouldn't want."

Tadukhepa seized her cup again and drained it in one long draft. It had been five days since her wedding, and in that time she had been spared her marital duties—thank the goddess—for the Pharaoh was even more unwell than usual. *Perhaps it is wicked of me*, she thought contritely, but in truth she prayed often that the king's illness would continue. She had no wish to remain a virgin forever, but even that fate might be preferable to lying beneath the heaving, grunting Pharaoh while the sweat of his exertion dripped down onto Tadukhepa's face. The thought made her shudder.

Nann raised her own cup of melon juice to her lips, but then lowered it again quickly. The servant girl stared into the depths of the garden, suddenly as tense and focused as a hound on the hunt.

"What is it?" Tadukhepa whispered, glancing around. A prickle of foreboding crept up her spine.

"I thought I saw a... a *man*. There, in the bushes."

In Mitanni, Tadukhepa had heard tales that the Egyptian kings kept their women shut away forever in palaces, never leaving those walls, and protected by gelded men. Since her arrival she had learned that these stories was not strictly true. The harem women often went across the river to the marketplace in Waset, to trade the fine cloth they produced for expensive goods—or they enjoyed pleasure excursions, boating up and down the glittering Iteru, their barques crowded with musicians, cooks, dancers, and acrobats. Sometimes they accompanied the men of the western court on hunts in the sere, golden-brown hills. The hunts often lasted for days, and Tadukhepa had heard tell that the women took just as much part as the men did, firing bows into flocks of geese or pursuing antelope in chariots with spears clutched in their fists. And although there were guards at the door of the harem palace—and patroling along its walls—the women who had so far deigned to speak to Tadukhepa had giggled at her naïve questions, assuring her that the guards who watched over the Pharaoh's women were certainly *not* geldings.

Sometimes a visiting foreign prince, or a noble most favored by the Pharaoh, would be allowed to choose a woman from the harem and amuse himself with her body—an indignity Tadukhepa would never be made to suffer, praise the goddess, for she was a King's Wife and not a mere concubine. She had been mortified—and, she was forced to privately admit, somewhat intrigued—to realize that the concubines looked forward to being debased, passed about in such a cheap and tawdry fashion. *I should not judge them*, she'd told herself. *Doubtless they are just as lonely as I, and derive no joy from the sickly Pharaoh's rutting.*

Perhaps it was a relief to be treated as a whore when the alternative was to remain an isolated, untouched virgin for the rest of one's days.

Still, regardless of the Pharaoh's policy of generosity toward his favored men, it was known by all, even the newest King's Wife, that no men were allowed to freely enter the harem palace. Approved visitors were always accompanied by guards dressed in the red kilts that identified them as keepers of the harem.

"A man?" Tadukhepa clutched Nann's hand. "Should we call for the guards? Should we scream?"

"No," Nann said sensibly. She raised her voice and said in Egyptian, "Let him show himself, if he is not a coward."

The shrubbery rustled. A young man stepped from a nearby flower bed. He drifted to the middle of the path, walking with his face turned casually down toward the ground, his hands clasped behind his back. He never looked at Tadukhepa and her servant until, a good twenty paces away, he peered up at them with a quick flicker of his dark eyes. That one brief glance seemed a palpable, striking force, an intrusion on Tadukhepa's senses, like the perpetual heat or the rough granite of the bench. She felt the man's eyes upon her face, her body, and the sensation made her shiver. His full lips curved in a languidly amused smile as he turned away and strolled down the path.

Blinking in astonishment, Tadukhepa watched him go. His shoulder-length wig bobbed with his stride and the counterbalance chain of a large golden pectoral swung across his back, glinting in the bright afternoon sun. The man kept walking until he was a few flower beds away, then stopped, turned, and folded his arms across his chest. He stood staring frankly at them, distant but shameless in his audacity.

Tadukhepa watched him for a long moment, then turned to Nann with wide eyes.

"Who *is* that?" Nann asked, glaring at the man as if the force of her stare might shove him bodily from the path.

"I remember him from the wedding feast. He's one of the King's Sons. His name is Amunhotep, like the Pharaoh, if I recall correctly."

"Well, King's Son or no, his staring is impolite. Surely even Egyptians know that it's offensive to stare at women so openly. And you, a King's Wife—the wife of his own father!"

Tadukhepa shrugged. "As much as a wife as I can be, unbedded as I am."

"You certainly don't want to be bedded by the old stallion if *that* is the kind of colt he gets." Nann snorted, rather like a horse herself.

Tadukhepa did not answer; she only gazed wonderingly at the prince, rolling her silver cup between her palms. Young Amunhotep had stared at her the same way during the wedding feast. Tadukhepa was sure of it, though much of that long night's details were a miserable blur in her memory. She remembered this, though: the second-eldest prince standing, stalk-still, arms folded in a gesture of unshakable confidence. He had simply *watched* her, while the festivities had roiled about the foot of the dais, the feast growing more wild and animalistic by the moment. Young Amunhotep's stillness and self-possession had seemed compelling then, as if he had set himself deliberately apart from the needs and entertainments of mere mortals. He had only solidified Tadukhepa's earlier impression that she had traveled to a realm of demigods. That notion made him somehow attractive to her, as one cannot help staring at a statue of a god—even as his bold, unapologetic stare unnerved her.

Now, with a clearer head, and lit by the sun instead of the lamps of the feasting hall, Tadukhepa examined Young Amunhotep more closely. He was near her own age, and at least as tall as his elder brother. His broad shoulders spoke of natural strength, yet his body lacked the finely toned, masculine definition of Thutmose's arms and abdomen. His stare still made her feel wary, but his face was handsome and finely carved, if a bit long and narrow—and his lazy, curling smile made her curious. What exactly did the prince find so amusing?

"I think," Tadukhepa said to Nann, "I would like to get to know that man better."

"What?" Nann rounded on her, incredulous. "Mistress, you can't be serious! Look at him! He's arrogant and strange—anybody can see that, just from the way he holds himself. And what in the name of Ishtar is he doing here in the harem palace?"

"He seems rather interesting."

"Lady Tadukhepa, I beg you, as your devoted servant: don't be so naïve. There stands a dangerous man. You can see it in his eyes—in his stance. Look at him: he's like a lion watching its prey! Any woman is better off keeping him at a distance, and the greater the distance, the better."

"His brother Thutmose knows some Hurrian. Do you suppose this Young Amunhotep knows our language, too?"

"Let us not find out," said Nann drily.

But Tadukhepa raised her voice, calling out in her own tongue, "King's Son!" Undoubtedly it was her isolation and boredom that compelled her to do it. She felt mischievous, like a child stirring up trouble, dropping a spider into the wine jug just for the fun of watching nurses and aunties shriek and dance about with all their careful dignity forgotten.

Young Amunhotep dropped his arms and tilted his head, considering the two women on the bench. He took one step toward them, and there was something powerful and leonine in his movements—for a moment Tadukhepa felt a chill of regret, a sudden flutter of fear, and she wished she could call her words back into her mouth. But then the prince tensed, turning to stare down an adjoining path that snaked between two high walls of shrubbery. From her place on the granite bench, Tadukhepa could not tell what had stalled him.

Then, with a burst of laughter aimed at Young Amunhotep, Prince Thutmose appeared, swinging his arms easily, his long white kilt rippling and the thin braids of his wig tossing about his strong, chiseled chin. With a mocking grin, Thutmose shook his head at Amunhotep, and with one last, long stare at Tadukhepa, the silent, catlike prince turned on his heel and vanished into the garden.

Thutmose approached, ducking his shoulders in a courtly bow. "King's Wife," he said in Egyptian, smiling broadly. "I heard you call out for the King's Son, and here I am, at your service."

"I had thought to speak to your brother," Tadukhepa said. "But then I thought..."

Thutmose raised one brow. She could see that it had been darkened and defined with a sharp line of kohl, like the paint that lined his eyes. "Better not to speak to Amunhotep," he said. "My brother has always been strange. My father thinks his second son was touched by the gods, blessed with some kind of divine discernment— but I think the only vision Young Amunhotep cares about is how much of a woman's body he can glimpse through the tangle of a flower bed."

Nann was picking up more Egyptian every day—she was remarkably fast with languages, Tadukhepa had discovered—and at Thutmose's words, she levelled a justified glower at her mistress.

Tadukhepa ignored her servant. "But why are you both here in the harem palace?" she asked Thutmose. "On some business for your father?"

"Yes, indeed," he said. "May I sit? The shade is so inviting."

Nann rose to make room for the King's Son. He settled with an appreciative sigh close beside Tadukhepa. She could feel the warmth radiating from his bare arm, the memory of the sun's heat pouring from his flesh like a fountain in the hills, like perfume from a bank of wild flowers. He was ever so much finer-looking than his father. Tadukhepa gazed off into the depths of the garden, counseling herself to dignified stillness, as befitted a King's Wife of Egypt. But her heart pounded inside her chest, beating so insistently that she feared it might make the soft linen draped across her breasts tremble with its speeding rhythm, and betray her excitement to the prince.

"Today marks the six-year anniversary of the wedding of Lady Henuttawy to the Pharaoh. You may have met her—the rather plump woman with the sweet, lovely voice."

"I have heard her in the garden," Tadukhepa said. "She sings just like a sparrow, all high trills like a shepherd's flute."

Thutmose smiled. "That is King's Wife Henuttawy, for certain. And you have a very charming way with words."

Tadukhepa blushed.

"Father couldn't rise from his bed this morning," Thutmose went on. "The pain in his mouth was too great. The pains take him this way, you know, waxing and waning just like the cycles of the moon. There is not a magician or doctor in the Two Lands who's been able to cure him—not yet, though he keeps searching for an end to his torment. In any case, he wanted to present a gift to Henuttawy to mark the day, so he sent me in his place. Young Amunhotep never misses an opportunity to prowl about the harem, so of course he came along, too."

"I am sorry to hear that my husband is unwell,"

Tadukhepa said. "But it was kind of him, to remember Henuttawy's anniversary."

Thutmose laughed. The low, rich tones of his voice, rumbling in his chest, only deepened Tadukhepa's blush. "In truth, it's my mother, Great Wife Tiy, who keeps track of all the dates—the anniversaries of each marriage, the birth dates of all the king's children. She runs the Pharaoh's personal life as smoothly as she runs his political affairs."

"Tiy?" Tadukhepa turned to the King's Son with earnest surprise.

"Of course. Someone must see that Egypt sails smoothly along in its course, even when the Pharaoh is ill. Mother has a fine heart for it, too. She's been handling Egypt's reins for years now, and she's as deft as any king. But soon—" Thutmose paused, and his eyes lingered on Tadukhepa's face, taking in her soft, pale skin, the rosy flush along her cheeks— "Soon I shall be king, and Mother may finally take a well-earned rest. Egypt will be in my hands. All of it."

"Even the harem?" Tadukhepa blurted. Her own eagerness surprised her, and she looked away from the prince, pressing her hands to her stomach to fight back a sudden rush of queasiness. How shameful, to be so outspoken about her unladylike desires!

Thutmose blew out a soft, gentle laugh. She felt his breath puff along the sensitive skin of her bare shoulder, and felt the fine hairs on her arms rise in response. Then his hand lifted; his warm fingers found her chin, and turned her face toward him.

"You haven't been to my father's bed yet, have you, Lady Tadukhepa?"

She swallowed hard, staring into Thutmose's eyes. They were like two deep pools, as dark as tilled earth, and they held all his regal, self-assured amusement. But his gaze was not mocking. It was kind and confident—so confident that Tadukhepa's heart leaped again; her belly heated with desire. She knew Thutmose longed to speak frankly to her, and she desperately wished to hear all that he had to say.

"Leave us, Nann," she said, without breaking the prince's gaze.

"But Mistress—"

"I told you to leave. Don't worry—I'll be all right. I shall see you in my apartments when the King's Son and I are done talking."

Nann hesitated a moment longer, looking helplessly from Tadukhepa to Thutmose and back again. Then she gathered up the silver cups, spilled their dregs onto the path, and threw them into her linen bag with an indignant clatter. Nann scooped up the jar of melon juice and stalked away down the length of the garden, fuming as she went.

Thutmose spoke to Tadukhepa as if Nann's interruption had never occurred. "I know the Pharaoh is not well enough to tend to his wives' needs just now. He has been in this state for several years. We all pray for his health and vigor to return, of course, but I do not think the gods mean to grant our prayers."

Caught by Thutmose's steady, intense eyes, Tadukhepa nearly looked shyly down at her lap, but she recalled Great Wife Tiy's admonishment and kept her chin resolutely high. To stare into the eyes of the King's Son this way seemed an intimacy greater than any she could imagine, and the heat inside her grew to a warm throb.

"Look at you," Thutmose said. His voice was soft and low, like the purring of a cat. "Not from our land, and yet you are as proud and possessed as any native-born King's Wife."

Was this, Tadukhepa thought with dizzy delight, an end to her isolation? For Thutmose showed no inclination to look away from her. He *saw* her, as the women of the harem did not. And oh, he was beautiful—strong and capable, as manly and virile as the Pharaoh was not.

The Pharaoh. Tadukhepa's timidity was eclipsed all at once by condescending anger. She could have spat, but Thutmose still held her chin in his hand. The Pharaoh of Egypt and Tushratta, her royal father, who had sold her into captivity for a few golden statues. Well, now here she was, behind the bars of the harem, surrounded by Egyptian women with their revealing clothing and their low, sly laughter, with their smoky eyes and their liberal behavior. And she was a queen among them—not only one of their kind now, but set above them, set apart. She thought of the concubines and their unfeigned pleasure at being handed like a parcel from man to man. *I was sold into Egypt*, she told herself as Thutmose's thumb moved slowly along her cheek, stroking her gently. *I might as well become an Egyptian. I might as well comport myself just as they do.*

"It is true," she said calmly, "that my marriage has not yet been consummated."

"What a shame. A woman as beautiful as you shouldn't go untouched."

"If what you say is true—if the Pharaoh will not recover from his illness, and you will inherit all, even the harem..."

Thutmose smiled. "You will be mine one day. Perhaps soon—who can tell?"

Then, to her surprise, his hand left her cheek and reached into her hair. He pulled the combs and pins loose from her long, bronze-golden locks and her hair tumbled down around her shoulders. Thutmose ran his hand through it, slowly, and his deliberate movements wracked her body with a tantalizing chill. She gasped when his fist tightened in her hair, close to the nape of her neck—a possessive gesture that should have frightened her, should have set her crying out for Nann to return. But instead she leaned toward him a little, half pleased with this rebellion against her fate, half appalled at how very *Egyptian* the whole affair was.

"Do you want your marriage consummated, King's Wife?" Thutmose's voice was barely more than a hoarse whisper. Tadukhepa licked her lips. "My father is unable, but I am his heir—I may act in his place. I can give you what you want, and do it better than the Pharaoh ever could."

She almost said, *Yes. Yes, do it now—here—who cares whether anyone sees?* But the memory of Nefertiti intruded suddenly on her bliss—a vivid image of that perfect, serene face, with laughter sparking in the dark, mocking eyes.

Tadukhepa stammered, "Your betrothed—what of her?"

"Nefertiti?" Thutmose gave a dismissive shake of his head. "What of her, indeed? I'll marry you, too. You won't be demoted to the level of a concubine after my father goes to his tomb. I'll make you *my* King's Wife. You are too beautiful for any other fate."

"But won't Nefertiti be angry if we... if we do this now, before you are Pharaoh yourself—before you own the harem?"

"Nefertiti doesn't need to know." Then he pulled her sharply toward him, and his mouth pressed hard against her own. She opened her lips to gasp in surprise, and his tongue slipped inside, flicking and teasing until she felt like molten pitch, dark and flowing and ready to burst into flame.

Thutmose pulled away. Tadukhepa's eyelids fluttered. No man had ever kissed her before. Moments ago, before she had decided to behave like a true Egyptian woman, she would have been indignant at the prince's audacity. Now she just wanted him to kiss her again. But he loosed his grip on her hair and gently lifted one bronze lock, rubbing it between his fingers, studying it as the patchy shadows and light flickered over its shining strands.

"Such lovely hair," he said quietly, as if to himself. He raised the lock to his nose and inhaled deeply. When his lungs were full of her scent, he held his breath, savoring her. After what seemed an eternity, Thutmose exhaled. "I am in love with you, Tadukhepa," he declared.

She laughed. She couldn't help it—the idea of this King's Son loving her when he had a woman as beautiful as Nefertiti to adore, to look forward to lying with... it was an absurdity of the highest order.

"It's true," Thutmose insisted. "You will be mine—my King's Wife. And I will cherish you and see to all your desires, for as long as the gods permit me to live. You will want for nothing, and you will be always at my side, where my eyes can feast upon you, where I can always smell the perfume of your burnished-gold hair."

"And Nefertiti?" she said, still bubbling with laughter. "She will be very pleased by my presence, I am sure."

"She will cope. She knows what it means to be a King's Great Wife. She knows she must share me. Besides, it's the title Nefertiti wants—the throne—not *me*. She is as ambitious as she is beautiful, but you—you are soft and giving. And lonesome, and fragile—I can see it in your eyes. Let me be good to you, Tadukhepa, all the days my life."

Now she did lower her gaze. She couldn't help it. He had cut to the heart of her feelings with one sure stroke, as boldly as he had kissed her.

"You don't deserve to be alone and unloved," Thutmose whispered. Her hair slipped from his fingers. "Let me show you how it will be when I am king, when you are my wife. You need fear nothing—not Nefertiti, not my father. I am the heir; my power is almost as great as his. Meet me tonight, and I will show you the love you've been denied."

This was wrong—a grievous sin. She was *not* Egyptian. She knew that with a sudden, painful rush. She was a good girl of Mitanni, and Ishtar was her goddess and guide. It was wrong to lie with a man who was not her husband. Wrong—and she would be punished for it.

Tadukhepa opened her mouth to rebuff him, to tell him she could not—that they must wait until Thutmose was truly the Pharaoh, no matter how long it took for the throne to pass into his hands, no matter how her heart ached in her terrible isolation.

But the words that came from her lips surprised her— and pleased her. She answered, "Where shall I meet you, and when?"

TADUKHEPA WAITED BESIDE HER CHAMBER window, perched in the bowl seat of a carved cedar stool. She watched through the tall, narrow opening as the garden transformed, the indigo blue of late evening deepening to the dense black of night. The last of the roosting birds had hushed, the night-dwelling insects had raised their choruses of rough, rattling song, and beyond the formless silhouettes of the treetops, stars bloomed, one after another, like pale flowers on a shadowy hill.

She watched until the red star rose, climbing slowly up from behind the black line of the garden wall. Then Tadukhepa, trembling and pale, still astounded by her own audacity, stood quietly and lifted her embroidered cloak from its peg beside the door. It was made of thick-woven linen and dyed a rich indigo shade. Its deep color would blend her form into the shadows of the night-time garden.

As Tadukhepa slung the cloak around her shoulders, Nann looked up from where she sat, spinning flax beside a flickering oil lamp. "Mistress? Where are you going?"

"Only out into the garden, Nann. It feels close and stuffy in here. I want some fresh air."

Nann eyed her soberly for a moment, then let her spindle fall into her lap. "It is *not* close in this room. In fact, it's quite breezy. I'm nearly cold, which should count as a miracle in Egypt." Nann frowned, and her green eyes clouded with suspicion. "What did he say to you?"

"Who?"

"Who, indeed! That prince who sat with you in the garden this afternoon. What did he tell you?"

"Nothing important," Tadukhepa said, waiving one hand in dismissal.

"You're going to meet him, aren't you?" Nann scrambled to her feet. Her flax and spindle dropped to the tiled floor and lay there in a tangle. "Oh, Mistress, you *can't!* I beg you, don't do this!"

"Stop, Nann—be quiet! One of the other women will hear you."

"Let them! You know this is wrong."

"It is not. You saw the Pharaoh at our marriage ceremony. He is very ill—near death, and getting worse by the day. Thutmose told me the court has all but given up hope. It won't be long now before the King's Son inherits the throne."

"What of it?"

"When he does, he'll make me his wife."

Nann threw up her hands, rolling her eyes up to heaven as if entreating Ishtar for patience. "Mistress, men say these things to sweeten women and lure them into outrages. You should not believe the prince's stories, no matter how pretty they may seem."

Nann's words struck at Tadukhepa's heart. As she'd waited, watching the garden transform from twilight to deepest night, she had wondered whether Thutmose could be trusted. This tryst he proposed was a sin—she had no doubt about that. But she wanted so desperately for his affection to be genuine, for her isolation to end at last, and above all else, she wanted a future at Thutmose's side—adored by him, favored by him, living her life near him, as he had promised.

"He will be the king someday—someday soon," Tadukhepa said. "And it is time I became a King's Wife in more than just name. Whatever you may think of me, I *am* going. It is not your place to scold me, Nann. You must remember that you are my servant, not my mother or my nurse."

The exasperation fled from Nann's face, replaced by wide-eyed panic. "Mistress, please. Forgive me—I am only afraid for your safety. We are in a strange land. We don't know who we can trust. How do I know you'll be safe? How do I know you'll return to me, and what will I do if you're harmed? You are the only thing I have—the only piece of home the gods have permitted me to keep."

Tadukhepa swept to Nann's side, trailing her dark cloak behind her. She took her servant in her arms, kissing her sun-burned cheeks. "Dear Nann. I will be safe—I promise. Remember that I am a King's Wife, and we are safe here on the West Bank, so far from the dangers of the city. There is nothing to fear in the House of Rejoicing. Great Wife Tiy told me so, and I believe her."

Nann stepped away, dabbing her eyes with one linen sleeve. "Very well, Mistress. I know I cannot stop you, and I can't force you to listen to sense. But I shall wait for you at your window. If you don't return in two hours, I will call the harem guards."

TADUKHEPA MOVED SWIFTLY through the garden. The damp chill of night, heavily scented by the dense vegetation that clung to the banks of the Iteru, worked its way past the opening of her cloak and wreathed her body, making her skin feel cold even as she burned with anticipation and desire. She shivered.

The main path twisted through the harem gardens. Tadukhepa moved along it like a wraith, keeping well to one side, nearly treading through the flower beds, fearful that any woman's stray glance from a window of the palace might expose her iniquity to every god and goddess, every man and woman on the western bank.

Soon the main path terminated in a wide, grassy sward. Tadukhepa hesitated on the edge of the lawn, drawing her cloak tighter about her body. Under the starlight, the grass was the color of tarnished silver, dark and dully reflective with the first traces of dew gathering among its short-trimmed stems. Night distorted the world, melding distance and depth into a flat blackness of shadow, so that the lawn seemed an interminable plain, a vast space across which she might walk forever without ever reaching her goal. And there was her goal, where Thutmose had promised it would be: the raised, rough-stone wall that served as the shoreline of an artificial lake, and moored along that wall, rocking gently on the lake's dream-like ripples, a miniature pleasure-barque, just large enough for two. The curtains of its private cabin were lowered, hiding the boat's interior from her view.

Tadukhepa drew a long, deep breath. The air was rich with comforting scents, compelling scents—the spice of night flowers blooming and the wetness of black Iteru mud. There was nothing to fear. This was a time for joy. Thutmose loved her—he had said so—and her isolation and sadness would end tonight. She would be a queen in truth, the bodily consort of a king, beloved of a great ruler. No matter that Thutmose was not king *yet*. He would be, and then all sins would be forgiven.

She stepped out onto the grass. The gathering dew soaked

through her slippers and chilled her toes. She walked slowly, so that she would not lose her footing on the damp lawn. The nearer she came to the barge, the slower her body seemed to move. She was not reluctant—not anymore—but the sheer boldness of this thing she did, this act of taking her fate into her own hands, seemed to solidify the air around her until she felt as if she pushed through layers and veils of awe, of amazement at her own bravery. Who would have thought that Tushratta's good, obedient daughter could turn the tables on her father so thoroughly—could choose which king she would go to as a wife, rather than meekly accepting her own sale, the trade of her body and her heart for gold, as if she were nothing but a goat or a slave?

Tadukhepa paused and turned to look back at what lay behind her. Her footprints left a faint trail through the dew, and beyond, the main garden path curved like the body of a pale, lazy snake. The walls of the harem palace looked as gray-blue as storm clouds in the dim of night. Hardly a light flickered in the black slits of its windows.

She pressed on, her stomach tight and sick with excitement. She reached the lake's wall and dropped her hold on her cloak. A breeze, lifting off the cool water, stirred the heavy linen, pushing it away from her body. The sudden force of cold wracked Tadukhepa with a shudder.

"Thutmose," she called softly. "Are you there?"

She waited. There was no answer, save for the hollow slap of water against the boat's dark, curving hull.

Tadukhepa stepped closer, until her knees brushed the limestone of the retaining wall. The breeze rose again, lifting a strange smell from the lake—a salty, metallic odor that gripped her with the chill of a sudden, unnamed fear.

"King's Son? It is I, Tadukhepa."

Stretching, she reached for one length of the drapery

that shielded the cabin from view and drew it carefully aside. The interior of the boat was darker than the starlit lawn, but some fluttering instinct told Tadukhepa that someone was there—that a shape was lying in the hull of the boat—a human form, stretched along the small barge's length, silent and unnaturally still.

"Thutmose?" she whispered.

A heartbeat later, her eyes adjusted to the darkness, and she saw what lay before her. Thutmose's strong, lean body lay on a heap of cushions, one shoulder and arm twisted back in a posture of agony. His face, darkened like bruised flesh, was frozen in a grimace of pain and desperation. And his eyes—wide and sightless, they stared unblinking past Tadukhepa into the depths of the night.

Tadukhepa screamed, high and sharp. Wild with terror, she reeled back from the wall, tearing at her hair, staggering as her legs tangled in her cloak. She fell to her knees and caught herself with her hands in the wet grass, then crouched there, gagging and heaving, struggling not to vomit. When the spell of retching passed she screamed again, and kept on screaming, her eyes blinded with tears, her hands ripping frantically at the earth.

It was only when she heard the guards' feet pounding down the garden path—and Nann's voice shouting her name, Nann pleading with the guards to let her mistress be, begging them to allow Tadukhepa to return to her apartments—that she realized she had been a fool to scream. With one half of her mind, with perfect clarity and eerie calm, she realized that she was now a suspect in the prince's death—and saw, too, that a foreign woman from Mitanni would find no justice in Egypt. But the other half of her mind was like a poor, small animal caught in a snare, leaping, thrashing—and she could see nothing through her tears but the rictus of Thutmose's face, and the blank stare of his dead, empty eyes.

ANSWER THE QUESTION," the priest said. His face drew near Tadukhepa's. The pungency of onions on his breath made her wince away.

"I... I did not hear the question," she stammered.

The priest, not particularly large of stature but imposing in the intensity of his stare, struck each word with emphasis, like a stone carver pounding with his mallet. "Why were you at the lakeside in the middle of the night?"

Tadukhepa looked around the room helplessly. It was small—a tiny cell in the west wing of the harem palace, its mudbrick walls narrow and unadorned, the floor dusty and bare. She had been in this room for hours, enduring the harsh interrogation, yet only now was she beginning to really see her surroundings. Only now was the chilling vision of Thutmose's glassy stare receding mercifully from her mind. She was in a servant's room, Tadukhepa thought dimly, and one that had been long unoccupied. She sat on a low stool in the center of the room while two guards and her interrogator paced around her—a priest from the Temple of Amun, summoned hurriedly from the eastern shore to investigate the killing. The men were like lions circling a wounded gazelle. The room was close with the smell of their breath, their suspicion and anger. A small lamp sat on the floor in one corner, for Tadukhepa's stool was the only furniture. Its guttering flame added the stench of cheap oil and greasy smoke to the miserable atmosphere.

As Tadukhepa looked around in dull confusion, struggling to make sense of the priest's words, she noted that the sky was lightening through the tiny window, casting a bar of pale pink light, no wider than her hand, into the room. The light mingled with the sickly glow of the oil lamp, picking out the rough texture of the walls and the grime accumulated on the floor. Morning had come. She had spent the better part of a night here in this cell, facing the questions of this priest and his guardsmen.

"I..." Tadukhepa faltered.

The priest dove toward her like a falcon, once more thrusting his thin-skinned, skull-like face into her own. "You were the only person nearby when the King's Son was murdered. Now tell us, *what* were you doing there?"

"I've told you already," she flared, anger eclipsing her fear. "You've asked me the same question a hundred times, and my answer has not changed: I found myself unable to sleep, and I went walking in the garden, taking the air. I had nothing to do with the murder of the King's Son. I only looked inside the boat because I thought it was curious, that it should be moored there at night."

The priest straightened, turned abruptly toward the window, and stared outside in brooding silence. The leopard skin draped over his shoulder shifted with the slow rhythm of his breath.

There was a brief commotion on the other side of the door. The guards shifted, eyeing one another, turning toward the priest of Amun as if waiting for his instructions. Tadukhepa heard the sobbing voice of Nann outside, pleading with the guards who stood sentry in the hall. It was not the first time Nann had tried to talk her way into the room, or talk Tadukhepa out of it. But all the efforts of her loyal servant had been in vain. Tadukhepa's body was cramped from hours spent huddled on the stool, her mind was fogged from exhaustion and terror, and for the past hour she had felt a desperate need to relieve herself.

She listened as the outer guards turned Nann gruffly away, as they had done before. The weeping of her servant faded as the girl trudged back toward Tadukhepa's apartments. There was nothing Tadukhepa wanted more in that moment than to return to her apartments, too—to lie across the thick, comfortable, woven matting of her bed and allow sleep to carry her far away from the terrible memories of this night.

I must end this, she told herself. *I am a King's Wife, after all, and they have no cause to detain me.*

She summoned the memory of Great Wife Tiy, picturing the woman's stern frown and hard eyes. Tadukhepa looked at the priest, opening her mouth to speak, to demand her release in the queenliest voice she could summon—a voice that would make Tiy proud. But before she could form a single word, the priest spoke quietly, without turning from the small window's view.

"Your story simply does not add up, King's Wife. You are withholding something crucial fom me—from the god Amun himself—and my patience has run its course." He nodded to the nearest guard. "Take her to the quay. She will be transported to the Temple of Amun and put to the question." To Tadukhepa he said, his bony face sharpening with a grin of anticipation, "I know a few ways to make a woman talk. I'll get the confession out of you, King's Wife, no matter how you think to deceive me."

All Tiy-like pretensions fled. Tadukhepa's mouth fell open; her heart seemed to shrink inside her chest, constricting painfully between frantic beats. She tried to speak, to plead for mercy, but her throat had gone dry as old bone. A guard seized her by the arm and jerked her to her feet; she cried out in pain as her cramped legs were forced suddenly straight.

Outside the door, over the rasping of her own panicked breath, Tadukhepa heard the snap and stamp of the hallway guards coming to neat attention. A male voice—low, smooth, languid with regal confidence—gave a few brief commands, though Tadukhepa could not discern the words through the closed chamber door.

Finally a deferential tap sounded on the door frame. "My priest?" one of the outer guards called. "The King's

Son wishes to enter."

The priest of Amun tensed. His angular face pulsed as he clenched and ground his jaw; his eyes were wide, bloodshot, angry. But at last he controlled himself and said, "Very well. Open the door."

With a loud creak of dirty hinges, the door swung wide. Tadukhepa recognized at once the man who filled the doorway. His long face held the same faintly amused expression he'd worn the afternoon before, when he had stepped out of the garden shrubbery and shown himself at Nann's insistence. His full lips curved with dry satisfaction when he met Tadukhepa's eye. It was Thutmose's brother, Young Amunhotep. He looked at ease, unruffled despite the fact of his brother's death. The pleats in his kilt were neatly pressed and a short, white linen cape draped about his shoulders with fashionable care.

"What is the meaning of this?" Amunhotep asked the priest—calmly, with a detached note that was very near indifference.

"My lord," the priest said, bowing low, "your brother—"

"I know about my brother." Amunhotep came to Tadukhepa's side. He moved with a curious, casual grace, a waterlike flow that was almost feminine. The King's Son laid his hand gently atop the guard's, who still held Tadukhepa in a hard, hawk's-talon grip. After a moment the guard loosed his hold, glancing between Amunhotep and the priest with unconcealed confusion.

Amunhotep said, "How dare you treat a King's Wife in such an undignified manner, Priest?" But the prince's words were not harsh, not accusatory. He sounded as if he were acting out a role in a play, and had long since grown bored with this pageant.

"My lord," the priest of Amun said, "this woman was found beside the boat where Thutmose was killed. She—"

"Yes, poor Thutmose. What a terrible thing for us all, to lose such a strong and noble King's Son. We must find his killer, and bring that man to justice. But I can tell you with certainty that this woman did not kill my brother."

"I..." Now it was the priest's turn to falter. He narrowed his red-rimmed eyes at Young Amunhotep. "With respect, King's Son... how do you know she is innocent?"

"Because I was with her in the garden all night long."

Tadukhepa could not restrain herself from turning sharply toward him, blinking in surprise. Amunhotep laid a hand on her shoulder, a comforting caress. "It's all right, Tadukhepa. There is nothing to fear by telling the truth. You must never fear the truth, for it is *maat* itself—divine truth—that orders the whole of the world. We have nothing to fear, you and I."

He said to the priest, "I was at this good lady's side when she spied the boat on the lake. I was trailing her when she approached it to peer inside. I was there when she found my poor brother—dead, may the gods protect his *ka*. My eyes beheld the same sad vision as her own. I would have been at the lakeside, too, when the guards arrived to apprehend her, but I had run into the garden to search for any trace of the killer, and so I was not there to vouch for her innocence. But I vouch for it now. Lady Tadukhepa could not have killed King's Son Thutmose, for she was in my company, and never left me all the night long."

Tadukhepa swallowed hard. Her throat burned; a great, twisting, pressing force seemed to swell moment by moment within her chest. She feared it might burst out as hysterical laughter.

The priest pursed his lips, considering Young Amunhotep. The leopard skin bunched on his chest as he folded his arms tightly, a gesture that spoke of deliberate and very difficult self-restraint.

"I know what you are thinking," Amunhotep said. His

voice, warm and slow as honey, filled the chamber with its strange, rich music. "You are thinking that I might have killed Thutmose. But why would I do such a thing? My brother and I always got along well. And anyhow, Lady Tadukhepa can vouch for my whereabouts."

The priest turned his searching eyes on Tadukhepa. Her lips trembled when she met his gaze, but she knew that the gods had granted her an exceptional mercy. Amunhotep's tale, however false, would spare her from torture. So she firmed her resolve, forced a mask of calm onto her face, and said steadily, "It's true. I was with King's Son Amunhotep all night, and we were not near Thutmose, nor any boat—not until we found him dead."

"Of course," Amunhotep said, "we might be lying. Perhaps we conspired together to kill Thutmose, and to vouch for one another's innocence." He smiled, and gave a gentle laugh. It startled Tadukhepa, to hear such light amusement in that chamber after her hours of fearful torment. "But I cannot imagine why we might do such a thing. I always got on well with my brother, and Lady Tadukhepa is new to our land. What ill could she wish on the King's Son?"

"Still," the priest said, "suspicion cannot be so easily laid to rest."

Amunhotep tilted his head slightly, a regal acknowledgment. "I entirely agree. You may take me to the Temple of Amun and put me to the question, if you like. I will go willingly. My *ka* and *ba* are both unstained by guilt. I have no reason to fear your knives and your hot irons. Shall we go now? I can send a message to my father the Pharaoh, to inform him of where I'll be—"

The priest held up a hand. Tadukhepa was startled to see that it trembled. "That won't be necessary, my lord."

"No? But after all, a King's Son—the heir himself—has been killed. This is a very important matter, Priest. Let us leave no stone unturned. Let us not fear to seek the truth, wherever we may find it. You and I both revere *maat*, I know."

A bead of sweat gleamed on the priest's forehead, a drop of rosy light in the window's glare. Tadukhepa watched as it slid down the man's temple, disappearing into the braids of his wig.

"It will be sufficient," the priest finally said, "that is to say, the god will be satisfied by your story if you merely swear to its veracity."

"That I will gladly do," Amunhotep affirmed.

The priest's voice gathered force, and he twitched up a hand to wipe the sweat away. "It must be a holy oath, a solemn vow that binds your *ka* and *ba* to your words. You must agree to surrender all hope of the afterlife if you speak falsely."

"I so agree."

The priest reached beneath the edge of his leopard skin and withdrew a faience amulet. It hung from his neck by a thin leather cord; the bright pendant glittered in his palm for a moment as he considered it, his lips thinned in thought—or in hesitation; Tadukhepa could not be sure. But at last he pulled the amulet over his head and presented it to Young Amunhotep.

The King's Son took the sacred pendant, holding it with reverent care in both hands. He gazed down at it, smiling, eyes alight with sudden fervor. Tadukhepa peered at the faience form of the god Amun, his blue body strong and erect, the plumes of his crown rising high and proud.

Amunhotep enclosed the amulet in his hands. Lifting his face to the tiny, narrow window, closing his eyes as the morning sun fell upon him, the King's Son made his vow. "I swear these words on this sacred amulet, on the body of the god himself: I did not kill my brother, the King's

Son Thutmose. I know that the King's Wife Tadukhepa is innocent of my brother's murder. For Tadukhepa and I love one another, and spent all night in each other's company. If I lie, may I be forever barred from the afterlife. May Anupu find my heart wanting. May my heart be cast into the maw of Ammit; may Ammit the Devourer consume me, and may I never again find Amun's grace."

He turned to the priest, smiling serenely, and handed the amulet over. "Will my oath suffice?"

The priest held Young Amunhotep's gaze for a long moment, then said quietly, "It will."

"Good. Then you will allow me to escort the King's Wife back to her apartments, where she may rest. It has been a difficult night for her."

Amunhotep offered his arm, and Tadukhepa seized it with both hands, gripping his warm, soft flesh desperately, afraid the priest and his guards might tear her away again and confine her once more to the tiny, stinking chamber. But the King's Son led her from the room without another word. She stumbled along beside him on nerveless feet, leaning against his arm for support.

The hall of the palace's west wing was dark and deserted. Amunhotep moved easily through the pillars of the colonnade, gliding in and out of umber shadow while Tadukhepa struggled to keep up with his unshaken gait.

They reached the garden. The sun had climbed nearly over the wall, and the tops of the trees and hedges glowed with golden light—but deep shadows still huddled near the ground, slinking along the paths and beds like demons on the hunt. Watching the movement of those cold, indigo veils, Tadukhepa recalled the dimness of the night, the terrible vision of Thutmose's slain body. She remembered how his still form, his staring eyes had revealed themselves from cloaking darkness with sudden force, and she shivered.

Amunhotep paused. Gently, he disentangled her hands from his arm, then removed his linen cape and draped it around her shoulders—for she had left her cloak behind in the interrogation room.

"Thank you," Tadukhepa said meekly.

They walked on through the garden in silence, side by side. Now that the threat of torture was behind her, Tadukhepa felt questions rising and falling inside her, each one piercing and sharp, but all of them clamoring together in one great, undifferentiated mass like the calls of a flock of sea birds. She grasped at her questions, seeking just one she might isolate—for even one answer, one certain thing, would be a comfort to her now.

She managed to seize one, and braced herself to ask it. "When you... when you said that we'd spent all night together, that we were in love..."

Amunhotep glanced at her with an amused, lazy smile.

"The priest never questioned it," she said. "It didn't faze him at all, that a King's Wife would be in love with a King's Son—that a son would be in love with his father's wife."

Amunhotep chuckled. "Why should it disturb the priest of Amun? We are not citizens of Waset, here on the western bank. We live so close to the veil between the living and the dead."

Tadukhepa looked at him, shaking her head in confusion.

He said, "We do things differently here. The world is different for those of us who are set apart. We make our own world, our own rules, our own morality. The priests of Amun know that. They know better than to question it."

Tadukhepa lapsed into miserable silence. That was hardly an answer at all, and certainly no comfort to her.

After a moment, as they drew closer to the palace

wing that contained her own small apartments, she tried another question. "Why were you so quick to swear, when you knew your words were untruthful? Ishtar preserve me—you consigned your soul to damnation, and did it with a smile on your face!"

He smiled hazily, watching the sun rise with dreamy, heavy-lidded eyes. "I'd swear anything on Amun, and have no fear for my soul. Amun has no power over me, nor over you, my lady."

Tadukhepa frowned. "But all gods have more power than men—even than King's Sons. How could you make such oaths, and have no fear of damnation?"

They reached the outer door that led from the garden into her bed chamber. Amunhotep watched her in silence for a moment, smiling placidly. The slant of morning light lit the side of his face, warming the tones of his skin so that his long, lazy-eyed countenance stood out sharply against a cool background of shadow.

"Do you fear for my soul now, King's Wife? Do you believe I'm in danger of Amun's wrath?"

"I..." Tadukhepa bit her lip, then said firmly, "Yes. I do fear for you. You know that you swore to a lie."

He stepped close to her. His bare chest smelled of myrrh, of temple smoke and crushed grasses. "Then let us erase the lie," said Young Amunhotep. "If you kiss me—if you love me as I love you—then my oath will become a true one, and you may rest easily, knowing that my immortal *ba* is safe."

And before she could step back or turn her face away, he pressed his lips to hers. His mouth was sweet and warm. It made her think of summer sunshine, of berries in the hills above the sea—of the sun, full and bright, shining on her skin.

Tiy

Year 36 of Amunhotep,
Ruler of Waset,
Lord of Truth in the Sun,
Strong Bull Arising

The journey across the night-dark Iteru was long and silent. Tiy sat as unmoving as a stone on the narrow, wooden thwart of the boat—the same plain, inconspicuous *rekhet* fishing vessel that had crossed to the west bank from Waset, bearing a messenger sent by Huya, her steward. Opposite her, huddled close together and swathed in dark, hooded cloaks, the children made neither movement nor sound.

Huya's message had been simple, but for Tiy, who had waited all day and long past sunset for his word, it was compelling—and a relief. *It is done*, the scrap of papyrus had read. Written in Huya's unmistakable hand, sealed with his distinctive mark—the secret ring he wore not on a finger or on a lace around his neck, but in a hidden pocket sewn on the inner side of his belt-sash, the seal-ring he used for communication with Tiy alone. The King's Great Wife was certain of the note's origin. She was certain of little else, now. *Come at once. The boatmen know where to go.*

She had been ready for hours, but the gods were kind, to arrange fate just so: the fishing boat slipping quietly to the pier long after dark, on a night with only a pale sliver of a moon, the stars half-obscured by a rare vaporous haze. If anyone had chanced to look out from the wall of the House of Rejoicing, or had peered down from the cool rooftop terrace of the king's palace, they would have seen nothing. The night was far too dark, the boat too low in the water. And the children had come when she'd summoned them, emerging from the shelter of a small waterside shrine with perfect, obedient silence.

Aside from Huya's messenger, the children in their dark hoods, and one palace guard whom Tiy trusted—as much as she dared trust any man in her husband's employ—there were only a pair of rowers in the fishing boat. Their backs were turned away from the two small, cloaked figures as they bent and pulled at their oars with rhythmic monotony.

A diffuse wash of starlight shimmered on the surface of the river like a spilled slick of lamp oil. Over the patient slap and swish of the oars, Tiy could hear the distant cries of night birds—the piping of an owl somewhere near the outskirts of the city, and the loud, barking, repetitive voice of a crake, its drumlike calls repeating from the high cliffs of the western bank with a faint, delayed echo. From somewhere ahead of the boat's dark prow, the Iteru gave a loud splash and gurgle, and a moment later the boat glided through the spreading rings of a great ripple that fractured the slick of starlight, alternating its sheen with curves of black shadow.

Crocodile, Tiy thought, watching the ripples spread. She pictured the long, grinning, coolly expectant face of Sobek, the crocodile god, who had the power to ward away evil. *Dispel this evil from my path, Sobek*, she prayed, gazing into the dark of the river, to the place where she thought the crocodile's splash had come from. *Tear this cloak of deception away from my family, I ask thee, and cast it off, that we may be freed from all manner of wrongs.*

But was she not a deceiver herself? This errand in the dark of night—it was the greatest deception of all. *But necessary*, she told herself—told Sobek.

Some distance away, the crocodile resurfaced, and the weak silver of the moon's light redoubled itself in the creature's small, curiously reflective eye. As she watched that orb of steady light burning, gazing back at her while the boat slid quietly past, she recalled with a jolt of fear the old spell from the tombs of kings long dead: *The king has appeared as Sobek, green of skin, with alert face and raised fore. The king will eat with Sobek's mouth, and copulate with Sobek's phallus. The king is the lord of semen, who takes women away to the place he likes, according to his heart's desire.*

How apt, Tiy thought, her mouth twisting bitterly. So then, did her husband the Pharaoh see her even now, peering across the expanse of dark river through Sobek's glittering eye—watching her grand deception unfold? Was this scheme doomed to fail before it had even begun? *It must not fail. It will mean my death if it does.* Her death and worse. For if the king knew how Tiy plotted, there would be no preservation of her body, no tomb with its magical texts to guide her soul through the trials of the Underworld, no eternal life, no forgiveness. When she died, she would die forever and exist no more.

She drew her cape tighter, shutting out the night's chill, and turned her face resolutely away from the crocodile's watchful eye.

At last, the fishing boat slid into its mooring, cleaving between the dark, blocky shapes of Waset's piers. Tiy allowed her guard to hand her up from the boat to the stone platform of the fishing docks. Nearby, along the quay that reeked of fish and refuse, men staggered in the short, rough, soiled kilts of the low-born, booming out their drinking songs with all the appeal of a chorus of courting frogs. From some unseen quarter came the slap of a hand against flesh, a woman's shriek, and then a burst of female giggling.

While the guardsman helped the children climb from the boat, Tiy watched Huya emerge from a nearby alley, little more than a thin black mouth between the sallow cheeks of a beer shop to the left, and a low brothel to the right. Her steward was dressed like a *rekhet* man, his unbleached kilt falling to his knees, his wig simple and plain. The cloak draping his shoulders was drab in color and unadorned by embroidery. But he moved with his usual, unmistakable confidence, shouldering easily through the jostling crowds, stepping lightly around the foul puddles that dotted the packed-earth lane.

When he reached Tiy's side, Huya's bow was quick and surreptitious. "Follow me, my lady."

Tiy glanced toward the children. They stood close together on the pier, holding hands. Between the shroud of darkness and the long folds of their cloaks, those two small hands were the only parts of them visible.

"I advise you to leave the children here," Huya said. "What I must show you is... not a sight for young eyes. Let your guard watch over them. The oarsmen, too, will protect them. I can vouch that they are trustworthy."

Tiy nodded and followed her steward, moving briskly across the lane toward the narrow alley. She kept close to Huya's back, dodging and weaving through the crowd as swiftly as she could manage. She felt an unaccustomed thrill of fear at the thought of being separated from him. The crowd pressed all about her, shouting and belching and singing as they staggered between the beer shops. She felt this stinking tide of humanity rise up on every side, as if Waset itself would soon swell into a flood of *rekhet* and drown her out, obliterate her, scour her away.Once Huya and Tiy reached the alley, the pressure of the crowd broke off suddenly, and Tiy staggered forward into her steward's back, gasping with relief. He swept one arm around her, ushering her into the narrow darkness, guiding her steps with his voice. Deep between the mudbrick buildings, the clamor of the streets abated somewhat. Tiy caught sight of a faint yellow flicker along the wall ahead; the light skittered over the surface of the mudbrick, pushing back the shadows and causing the details of the alley's walls to leap in sharp, if fleeting, relief. The cracks between bricks flared and faded with the light's guttering. Obscene carvings, depictions of crass sex acts scratched into the friable brick, bloomed and faded before her eyes in the span of a heartbeat, as did words scrawled by coarse, uneducated hands. The words were never illuminated long enough for Tiy to decipher complete phrases, but what she could make out displeased her.

West Bank gods...

Hounds and men...

The Pharaoh fucks...

Tiy narrowed her eyes and swept past the dim engravings. At last she reached the source of the dancing light. She could now see that it came from a shallow alcove recessed into the mudbrick wall. A tall, broad man stood inside the alcove, holding a tiny clay lamp. His kilt was tied with a sash striped in Huya's colors. The man's lamp was so small that the flame seemed to flicker directly in the palm of his hand. When the guard recognized Tiy's face, he bowed low, and the lamp spilled its light over the alley's damp, unappealing floor, revealing filth Tiy would rather not have seen. The guard's body blocked her view of the alcove behind him.

"Stand aside," Huya said to the guardsman.

The man stepped into the alley with alacrity. When he turned to face the alcove, its close sides caught and held the fitful light from his clay lamp, so that its depths glowed with a sudden intensity of amber. Lying on the floor, stretched at his length among the muck and foul puddles as if he slept at ease in the finest bed, was the body of a young boy.

Tiy covered her mouth. Her breath came short and fast, and the stench of Waset flooded her senses. She hadn't thought this far ahead, to the moment when she would look on the body of the child. But here he was, lying at her feet, small and very still. She made herself study the body with detachment, with a calm that befitted the King's Great Wife. The slack, peaceful face was too round, too young. This boy was perhaps eight or nine—not quite the correct age. But he was big for his years, and his body was the right size.

"How did you do it?" she asked the guardsman. She had no doubt that it was he who'd dispatched the boy. Huya had many skills, but dealing out death, even to young children, was not one of them.

"Broke his neck, Great Wife. It was fast and clean. The boy did not suffer. He didn't even know that death had come for him. He had no time to feel fear. It was done in an instant."

She nodded. "That is good." Tiy stared down at the boy once more, and she felt her *ba* and *ka* recede until they were as numb as her body, as if she watched this strange and shameful scene from a great, hazy distance. "That is good," she said again, absently.

Huya indicated the guard with a curt gesture. "My man will take the boy's body to the embalmer straight away, so no one will see his face."

Tiy would rather have carried out their plan without a body—without taking a young life, even if it was a *rekhet* life. Had it been entirely her decision, she would have claimed a crocodile had attacked, that there was no body to mummify and place inside her youngest son's tomb. But Huya had been quick to point out that concrete evidence of death—a child's wrapped corpse prepared for eternity, and all the accompanying ceremony of a royal funeral—would leave no doubt in anyone's mind, no room for suspicion, no reason to search for a missing King's Son. Tiy had seen the necessity readily enough, and had agreed to Huya's plan. What choice did she truly have?

The guard blew out his lamp and lifted the boy's limp body with a tenderness that surprised Tiy even as it sickened her. She watched in silence as the man carried the child further down the alley until he vanished into the blackness.

"Did your guardsman learn the child's name?" Tiy asked quietly.

"No," Huya said.

She sighed, and with her heart's inner vision she saw again the cold, glowing orb of the crocodile's eye, unblinking, all-seeing, floating in the dark heart of the river. *It is necessary*, she told herself. *The boy will be laid to rest in the tomb of a King's Son. It will be a finer start to his afterlife than he could have received if he'd been buried here in Waset, in some* rekhet *graveyard*.

Yet the spells on the tomb's walls carried the name of Tiy's youngest son, not of this anonymous *rekhet* child. How would the boy ever find his way out of the tomb, without the magical charm of his name to infuse his spirit-body with strength? Would the boy's soul be trapped forever within those dark stone walls, an eternal prisoner of Tiy's necessity?

She would have tucked some secret spell into the boy's coffin if she could—some token with his true name to give him the faintest chance of a decent afterlife. But no one knew the child's name, and there was nothing Tiy could do to change his fate.

I do this thing because I must, she said silently. But she did not know whether the thought was meant to reassure herself, or to excuse her actions to the dead *rekhet* boy—or to placate the cold, watching presence of Sobek.

"All we have done," Huya said quietly, "is in service to the gods."

Again Tiy nodded, blinking away the sting of tears before they could gather in her eyes. "I know."

She had no doubt that Young Amunhotep killed Thutmose, and no doubt that the Pharaoh would do nothing to bring about justice. The king had always been convinced that his second son was specially blessed—too pure of heart to do any evil. But Tiy knew Young Amunhotep had always been a watcher, a schemer. *Like me*, she thought bitterly. *And he is far more ambitious than anyone but I would suspect. How like his mother he is!*

"This plan is a good one," Huya assured her. He placed one hand on her shoulder; Huya was allowed such familiarity, after so many long years of loyal, unfailing service to Tiy's causes—to hers and no other's, not even the king's. "You must trust in its strength, my lady. Trust in the righteousness of your cause."

"Righteousness—yes." She gave a short, hard laugh. There could be nothing less righteous, less conducive to *maat* than for Young Amunhotep to take the throne. For a man to slay his own brother—that was one of the darkest evils the world could ever know.

How did this vileness come forth from my womb? Tiy wondered, her thoughts distant and stunned. *We have set ourselves apart, to live like gods on the West Bank—and now it seems I have borne two gods in truth.* Like Set, who envied his brother-god Waser and struck him down so cruelly, Young Amunhotep had done this foul deed out of jealousy, for personal gain— to claim the greatest prize any man could ever hope to possess: the Horus Throne of the Two Lands.

Tiy had heard the report of the priest of Amun that very morning. The man had told her how sincerely Young Amunhotep had sworn—on a sacred image of Amun's own body, no less—that he had not murdered Thutmose. The priest had assured her that the oaths had been most terrible, that only a madman would make such a vow falsely, and damn his eternal soul. Tiy had sent the priest away, then sat in the empty throne room, staring down its pillared length, seeing nothing. *Only a madman, indeed.* Tiy had seen then what she must do—what steps she must take to preserve the safety of the Horus Throne, of Egypt itself, and to maintain her own firm but shadowy grip on Pharaonic power.

"Come, my lady," Huya said, breaking into her dark thoughts. "The night will soon be over, and by the time the sun rises I must be well downriver from Waset."

He led her back through the crowds of the quay, back to the pier where the fishing boat was tied. When Tiy looked once more upon the two small, cloaked figures, her chest swelled with the pain of guilt and relief. She went to them slowly, and despite the memory of the dead boy lying on the alley floor, when the children's shadowed faces turned up to look at her, Tiy smiled. She sent the waiting guard and the oarsmen away, down to the end of the pier. She sent them all away, save for Huya—the one man in all the world whom Tiy knew she could trust.

Tiy eased the hood back from her youngest son's face. The gods only knew whether she would see him again in this life. He looked up at her, his eyes round and trusting in his soft face, the brave little banner of his side-lock stirring in the river breeze. A hard hand of loss closed around her throat as she filled her eyes with the sight of him.

She knelt on the dock before him and took his soft cheeks between her hands. "Smenkhkare, my son. You must go with Huya, downriver."

"North?" The boy's voice was high and sweet. He was still many years shy of manhood. "But why, Mother?"

"In service to the throne. You want to serve the throne, don't you? Like a good King's Son?"

Smenkhkare drew himself up, squaring his narrow

shoulders within the heavy folds of his cloak. "Of course. But where am I going, Mother?"

"Huya will take you to a man I know—my cousin, who is a priest of Ptah. That man will raise you just like his own son, and you must honor him and show him every respect, and always do whatever he tells you without question, even though you are a King's Son."

Smenkhkare nodded gamely. He was always such a good, biddable boy, and Tiy could have cursed the gods for sending him to her womb last of all her children. She glanced at the other child, Sitamun—the girl who clung to Smenkhkare's hand with her hood still hiding her features. What sorrows could have been prevented, Tiy wondered, if Young Amunhotep had been born last—or never born at all?

"When will I come back, Mother?"

Tiy brushed her fingers over his forehead, caressed the soft braid of his side-lock, held his shoulders in her shaking hands. "A long time from now, my brave boy. You are going off to learn many things, and to grow into a strong man of the royal family."

"To learn from a priest—like my sisters?"

Tiy had managed to send her eldest daughters, Henuttaneb and Iset, off to far-flung temples several years ago, where they could learn the stations of a priestess and the duties of a King's Daughter in peace. She had not thought to send Sitamun with them. The girl was still so young, and Tiy had assumed her youth would keep her safe—for a few more years at least.

"Yes," she said to Smenkhkare. "Just like your sisters. All the priests of Ptah will have so much to teach you—and the priests of other gods, too. You'll be quite a learned man when I see you again." *And may the gods grant that I do see you again, one day.* She kissed the boy's forehead. "You must do everything Huya tells you, too. He will see you safely to my cousin's house, but until then, you will obey him just as if he were your own father, yes?"

Somberly, the boy nodded.

Tiy stared into the black void of Sitamun's hood. Even now, the Great Wife still argued with her own thoughts. She wished to send the girl away, too—to ship her off to some temple, far from the House of Rejoicing. In fact, Tiy had brought the girl along because she had still been so uncertain when she'd left the western bank. Ought she to send Sitamun away? Or was the girl better kept close at hand, where she might be useful to Tiy's designs, even if she could not be kept safe?

But no one would accept such an unlikely coincidence: the loss of *two* young royal children, the day after the heir to the throne was killed. Smenkhkare's feigned death would already stretch the bounds of credulity, and Tiy would have to put on a performance worthy of the finest court entertainers if her story was to have any hope of being believed. No, as much as it galled Tiy's *ka*, Sitamun must remain in the royal court.

Finally, her decision made, Tiy said, "Kiss your brother, Sitamun."

The girl pulled her hood back, revealing a face of exquisite, if nascent, beauty. At barely thirteen years, Sitamun was already lovely enough to come close to rivaling Nefertiti, Tiy's splendid, haughty niece, whose divine face and unequaled charm were even discussed by *rekhet* women at their looms and wells. Sitamun's cheeks were flushed with a gentle, rosy hue from the river's damp chill, and her delicate, bud-shaped mouth drew downward in a sorrowful frown. She stared back at Tiy for a long moment, her dark eyes sensitive and searching. Then she turned to Smenkhkare and bent to place a sisterly kiss on the young boy's brow.

When Sitamun straightened, the front of her cloak fell

open, exposing the girl's seven-month belly. The round, linen-white frankness of Sitamun's condition stood out against the black of night, an accusation, a rebuke from which Tiy could not look away.

Huya took Smenkhkare's hand. "We'll go quickly, my lady," the steward said. "I've a boat ready at the other end of the quay."

"Good," Tiy said absently.

"I shall be back in seven days, if the winds favor me on the return passage."

My steward will return, but not my son. Tiy dismissed Huya with a wave of her hand and turned away. She could not watch as the steward led Smenkhkare down the pier. It would be more than she could bear, she knew, if she were to watch the small, frail shape of her one remaining worthy son disappear into that unclean crowd of *rekhet.* Instead, she beckoned to her guard and stood waiting as the man helped Sitamun with her swollen belly down into the fishing boat. Then she took the guard's hand and clambered into the craft, too, settling herself with her back to Waset.

Sitamun regarded Tiy calmly as the boat was unmoored, as the oars slipped softly into the water.

After a time, when the boat had found the swifter current far from the quay and the sounds of drunken song had faded on the shore behind her, Tiy turned to her daughter. "Do you know why we did this thing?"

Sitamun answered at once. "To keep Smenkhkare safe."

"Yes. It was necessary. I fear your brother Amunhotep is a dangerous man." Tiy turned her face to the river, watching for the crocodile's steady-burning eye, so she would not be tempted to glance at her daughter's belly.

"Is he?" Sitamun asked. Her voice was so gentle, so light, that Tiy could almost imagine she was still a naïve child.

"Whatever you may feel for Amunhotep, he killed your brother Thutmose," Tiy said, "and he will kill Smenkhkare, too, if the boy threatens his throne."

Sitamun's eyes lowered, disguised behind her dark lashes. "Young Amunhotep will have the throne now."

"He will," said Tiy, and her hand tightened on the wale of the boat, for far out on the river, one golden, glowing eye was shining in the pale starlight—watching her, seeing all. "Unless I can stop him. Unless I can change fate."

She and Sitamun both fell silent. As the boat glided smoothly toward the western bank, the crocodile's eye flickered, blinked, and extinguished its yellow light as it slid beneath the surface of the river.

Nefertiti

Year 36 of Amunhotep
Ruler of Waset,
Lord of Truth in the Sun,
Strong Bull Arising

NEFERTITI SET HER KOHL BRUSH carefully on the towel that lay folded on the gleaming surface of her cosmetics table. The tremor in her hand nearly sent the brush tumbling to the floor. She stared at the sharp black point of its bristles, watching as the oil in the dark mineral ore dried, the sheen dulling away as it hardened on the brush. Her maids would fuss over the extra work, for now they must soak the brush and recondition its bristles. Nefertiti didn't care. She felt like ruining a hundred brushes, angering a thousand maids, just to make some satisfying display against the cruelty of the gods and the unfairness of creation.

She raised her eyes to her mirror as the notes of Lady Teya's morning song died away. Nefertiti had eaten almost nothing in the six days since Thutmose's death. Now her cheeks were hollow, her face as sallow as that of a woman in a sickbed, and the kohl did little to distract from the dark rings beneath her eyes. But at least today she had applied it in a steady line. The effort left her exhausted. It had been all she could do, to will her hands—her grief-riddled body—not to shake while she touched the wet brush to her lids.

For a long moment, she simply stared, noting dully that even in the depths of her grief she was still lovely. What a terrible joke the gods had made, to cast her in such beauty, to promise her to Thutmose, who had been as pleasing to the eye as Nefertiti was herself—and then to tear them apart in this vicious, abrupt manner.

When she had first heard the news, Nefertiti had been wild with grief. She had run to the gate of Ay's estate, screaming and crying—and had only caught herself on the threshold, clinging to the rough, white-washed mudbrick of the garden wall, when she recalled Mutbenret. For her sister's sake, she had forced herself to stay inside, rather than running to the House of Rejoicing as she longed to do, tearing her hair and her garments, to throw herself across Thutmose's lifeless body.

If she'd put on such a public display, word would have gotten back to Ay, and he would not have been pleased. It was only the fact that Ay had gone into the western cliffs to inspect a possible site for his tomb that had spared Mutbenret so far—for even Nefertiti's show of shock and grief in the confines of Ay's own estate would have displeased him. For her sister's sake, Nefertiti had taken herself back to her chamber, stumbling on numb feet, and there she'd remained for six days, keeping her sorrow as private an affair as she could manage. When the pain welled up in her heart, she buried her face in silk cushions so thick that even she could barely hear her own cries, though they tore her throat raw and filled her mouth with the taste of blood.

But Ay had returned late last night. Nefertiti knew he would wish to speak with her soon, and so she had done her best to make herself presentable—beautiful and calm, the way her father liked to see her.

She heard a timid tap on the frame of her door, and knew at once that it was her sister.

"Mutbenret," Nefertiti called softly. "Come in."

Mutbenret sidled around the door, closing it carefully

behind her. She leaned her back against it, watching Nefertiti in silence as if she were afraid to approach—as if Nefertiti's grief were a great, reaching force that stretched beyond the confines of her body and made her as unapproachable as a fortress on a cliff-top or a temple built on an island. But when Nefertiti held out her arms, longing for her sister's embrace, Mutbenret rushed into them, holding her close, rocking her slightly, as if Mutbenret were the elder of the two, and not Nefertiti.

"Sister," Mutbenret whispered, and it was all she needed to say.

Nefertiti fought back fresh tears. They would only ruin her carefully applied paints, and anyway, she was tired of weeping. Her eyes burned constantly, and her nose had not ceased to run since she had learned of Thutmose's death.

"I wish my real mother were still alive," Nefertiti said. She had never known her true mother—the poor woman had died shortly after Nefertiti's birth—but when the trials of life seemed more than she could bear, she often longed for a true mother's presence, for another ally in this bitter world. The only friend she had, now that Thutmose was gone, was Mutbenret—and though her little sister was kind and sweet and loyal, she was too frail to protect Nefertiti's heart.

"What will become of us now?" Mutbenret asked tremulously.

Nefertiti pulled away from her embrace, staring in shock at her sister's face. In all her sorrow over Thutmose, she had not considered what the death of the King's Son would mean for their future—Nefertiti's and Mutbenret's. Surely Ay would now find some other match for Nefertiti—a nobleman who was positioned well in the courts, to be sure. But would her new husband have enough stature that she could take Mutbenret with her when she went to her new home? As a King's Wife, or even as the wife of an heir who was not yet king, Nefertiti could have demanded anyone she pleased as part of her household. But now...

"I'll find a way," she promised Mutbenret. "I won't leave you here. Whatever happens, wherever I go, you're coming out of here with me. I swear it."

Mutbenret nodded, but her face was blanched and sickly. Reluctantly, she said, "Father sent me up to fetch you. He's waiting in his reading room."

A sudden twist of nausea rose in Nefertiti's gut. She drew a deep breath to ward it away, and rose steadily to her feet. "Do I look well enough?"

Mutbenret adjusted the sash of Nefertiti's pleated, mourning-green robe, then stepped back, nodding.

"Then I shall go and face our fate," Nefertiti said, and left her chamber with Mutbenret trailing hesitantly behind.

She found her father lounging in a high-armed chair, in an angled beam of morning light that spilled through the window of his reading room. One ankle was crossed over his knee—a posture so uncharacteristically casual that Nefertiti checked at the sight. Ay was engrossed in a scroll. It lay open on the fabric of his kilt, which was tight-stretched between his knees, the way scribes sometimes stretched their kilts to serve as makeshift writing-desks. Although his lined face was turned down and only his eyes moved, running over the lines of the scroll, there was a certain tight, buoyant energy about him that redoubled Nefertiti's anxiety.

Ay glanced up from his scroll. "Ah. Nefertiti."

She ducked her head in a proper bow.

"I was sorry to hear of the death of King's Son Thutmose."

At the sound of her beloved's name, Nefertiti's throat tightened. But by the grace of the gods, she kept her stance poised and steady, her face clear of the sorrow that welled inside her. "A most terrible occurrence," she said.

Ay laid his scroll aside and stood, clasping his hands behind his back as he regarded his eldest daughter with a satisfied smile. "Fortunately it need not be so terrible for you. I've spoken to my sister, who has consulted the Pharaoh, and all are in agreement: you will still become King's Wife—and with time, King's *Great* Wife."

Nefertiti shook her head. The last six days hung heavy on her heart, and through that thick, cloudy veil she could not discern the meaning of Ay's words. "I..." she faltered.

"You are to marry the Pharaoh's other son—Young Amunhotep, who is to be the heir now. I see no reason to delay the wedding we had already planned. In four days' time you will stand with him in the Temple of Amun and make your sacred vows."

The air left Nefertiti's lungs. She did not gasp; she did not exhale. The sustaining breath of live simply vanished from her chest, leaving a panicked black void around her heart, and a loud rushing in her ears. She struggled with her mouth open, staring at her father wide-eyed as his pleased grin slowly collapsed into a disapproving glower. Then, before she could stop herself—before she could consider her sister—she choked out a single word: "*No!*"

Ay's voice was dangerous, low. "What did you say to me?"

"I said *no*." Nefertiti drew herself up. Her jaw clenched and she stepped toward Ay boldly, staring hard into his stunned, angry face, though the gods alone knew where she found the courage to do it. "Young Amunhotep is a foul, disgusting, gods-blighted *beast* of a man. It's very likely that he killed Thutmose, too. Would you do that to me—send me to wed a murderer, to lie with a brother-killer? You know there is no man more accursed than one who destroys his own brother!"

Ay stared at her steadily, his brows lowered, his face as cold and hard, as unfeeling as granite. "You will do as I say, Nefertiti."

"I will *not*. Not this time—not anymore!"

"I have worked too hard on behalf of this family—too hard and too long—for you to throw away *years* of my efforts. You will marry whom I send you to marry, and you will be gracious about it, as befits the King's Wife I have raised you to be."

Nefertiti laughed bitterly. Her heart raced, and with each frantic beat she struggled to rein in her words, to bring herself under control. But after so many years of doing Ay's bidding, her *ka* and *ba* had finally rebelled. She could not stop herself—and she realized as she advanced on her father, her words rising to a frantic shriek, that she didn't want to. "Efforts on behalf of our family? Our family? The only one you work for is *yourself!* You care for no one else—no one!"

"Watch yourself, Nefertiti. You've already stepped well beyond your bounds."

"What of it? What will you do, old man?"

As fast as a scorpion's sting, Ay reached out one hard, bony hand and seized Nefertiti by her upper arm. She tried to jerk away from him, but his fingers bit into her flesh.

"You ungrateful bitch," Ay hissed. "Who do you think put your aunt Tiy in her place as King's Great Wife? It was me—" he shook her, and Nefertiti stifled a whimper of pain. "Me! Now Tiy is growing old. She cannot hold the Pharaoh's heart for much longer. But you can."

"The Pharaoh?" Nefertiti said, her voice breaking. "But if I'm to marry Young Amunhotep—"

"With you in the palace—with your exquisite beauty— you will be well placed to work your charms on the king. And when he dies, you will do the same with his heir, whether Young Amunhotep succeeds him, or some other man. It matters nothing to me. You will go into the House of Rejoicing and do the things I bid. I will make of you the same thing I made of my sister Tiy—the power behind the throne."

Nefertiti wrenched her arm from Ay's grasp. "Your tool—your puppet—so that *you* can control the Horus Throne? Never! It flies in the face of *maat*."

Ay was a courtier of great power, but he was not of the royal line—not born of the divine blood. Nefertiti tried to picture it—Ay's hand, forever sullied by his common blood, taking the holy staffs of the Pharaoh's crook and flail in a clandestine grip. The image wracked her with a superstitious shudder of fear. There was no telling how the gods might curse Egypt, if Ay's plans were to become a reality. Nefertiti would not allow herself to be used in this way, the shameful instrument of his secret and dangerous sacrilege.

"I will not do it," she said again. "Marry me off to anyone else—to any noble you please. Marry me off to a *rekhet*, for all I care. But do not think to use me in your twisted schemes."

Ay stared at her a moment longer, the anger on his face giving way to a calmness that chilled Nefertiti even deeper than her dread of the gods did. He brushed past her and opened the reading chamber's door.

"Go find Lady Teya," he said to a passing servant. "Tell her to bring Mutbenret to the courtyard."

"No!" Nefertiti threw herself at Ay, clinging to his arm, pulling at her father desperately. But he shook himself free without sparing another glance for his eldest daughter, and swept out onto the portico.

Nefertiti staggered after him, choking on her tears, heedless of her ruined kohl and her shattered dignity. She pleaded with every step, begging Ay to relent, but her father ignored her, as if her desperate sobs were the soughing of a winter wind, her wails the unheard cries of a lost and wandering *ka*.

Lady Teya came to Ay's summons. She propelled Mutbenret before her with one hand on the back of the girl's neck, and Mutbenret's face was still and pale with terror. Teya hummed to herself, her eyes soft and vacant. She saw nothing of Nefertiti's distress, heard nothing of Mutbenret's soft, sobbing whimpers. She deposited her daughter in the bright sunlight of the courtyard, then drifted back inside the house, and her lovely, well-trained voice rose in the refrain of a cheerful song.

Ay had selected a switch from one of his sober-faced servants—a thick, heavy one—the kind that could bruise flesh and break bones. He turned to Mutbenret, eyeing her coldly for a moment, then commanded her to lie on the ground.

Weeping, Mutbenret complied.

Nefertiti lunged between Ay and her sister. "No! Leave her alone. I won't see her beaten for my wrongdoings anymore." Shivering, already anticipating the strike of the switch—although she had never been beaten in all her seventeen years—Nefertiti lay face-down on the sun-warmed pavers of the courtyard, beside Mutbenret's small, quaking form. "Beat me instead," she said to her father. "It's I who've defied you, not Mutbenret. I will take the punishment."

Ay clicked his tongue in annoyance. He stooped and took Nefertiti once more by her arm, raising her to her knees. She was dimly aware that the stones of the courtyard had soiled her robe with dust and bits of dried leaves. She would receive a blow for that, too. But she would bear it—she would bear anything Ay wished to give her, if she could spare Mutbenret the pain.

Ay took Nefertiti's chin in his hand, with a touch so gentle it frightened her. She stared up at him, choking and sniffling.

"You know I cannot beat you," he said softly. "What would you be worth to me if your beauty was marred—if you were scarred or bruised? No, Nefertiti. Your perfection is my currency, and when have I ever squandered what is mine?"

He stepped around her. Nefertiti shut her eyes tight as Ay lifted his arm. She heard the switch whistle through the air, then a hard, flat thud as it connected with Mutbenret's back. An instant later, Mutbenret let out a thin, high-pitched scream, a more painful sound than Nefertiti had ever heard her sister make before.

She staggered to her feet and caught Ay's hand as he raised the switch for another blow.

"Stop," she sobbed. "I'll do it. I'll wed Young Amunhotep. I'll do as you say, Father—whatever you say."

Ay cast the switch into the courtyard's dust. It clattered as it fell, and the sound made Mutbenret wince and sob.

"Good," Ay said brightly, patting Nefertiti's cheek. "Was that so difficult, my girl?" And he sauntered back under the shade of the portico, leaving Nefertiti alone with her racing heart and the sound of Mutbenret's weeping.

Tiy

*Year 36 of Amunhotep
Ruler of Waset,
Lord of Truth in the Sun,
Strong Bull Arising*

TIY STOOD ON THE THRESHOLD of her chamber's outer door, watching, listening. Her private garden was a haven of serenity in the gathering glow of evening. Orderly rows of flower beds and paths footed with gleaming white gravel began to take on the rosy tint of sunset, and beyond, Tiy's lake was as dark and vibrant as a pot of indigo dye. A flight of ruddy geese appeared over the garden wall. Their pale wings beat a warm-hued blur and whistled gently as the geese descended toward the surface of the water. The lake broke beneath the birds' plump bodies in a great rush and clamor, sending up a joyful, soothing sound like *sesheshet* rattles, like the sacred rites of the temples that roused the gods to their duties and made all of Atum's creation move to its appointed rhythm. Thus disturbed, the water gave up its rich perfume, the thick, lulling, dizzying odor that clung to the undersides of leaves in damp shade.

The perfect peace of the garden stood in sharp contrast to the mourning cries that rose and wavered beyond. The western bank of the Iteru rang unceasingly with the terrible music of sorrow. Thutmose's death had been bad enough—momentous, terrifying—for murder had not been done in all the long years since the Pharaoh had moved his court away from the dangers of the low masses in Waset. Violence had no place here, where the chosen few lived between the realm of waking and dreams, between life and the afterlife, between gods and men. For an unknown assailant to strike out at all was shocking enough, but for the killer to take the life of the King's Son, the heir to the Horus Throne, in whose body the divine blood had flowed, was simply unthinkable.

But to lose Smenkhkare, youngest of the King's Sons, so tragically and so close upon the heels of his brother's death... it seemed more than a misfortune to the inhabitants of the House of Rejoicing, and to their favored courtiers who cried out from the rooftops of their nearby villas. It seemed like a blow from the gods themselves, deliberate and final.

Tiy watched the geese paddle smoothly across the water, bending their necks toward one another with movements as graceful as a dancer's wrist. That peace, amid such a tumult of mourning, filled her with a poignant sense of righteousness—*maat*. She allowed the mourners' cries to pierce her, to assault her heart with sharp points and cutting blades, and for the first time since learning of Thutmose's death, the King's Great Wife dropped her face into her hands and wept.

In the first frantic hours after Thutmose's body was found, Tiy had had no time to mourn her eldest son. Huya had awakened her with the news, bending over her bed to whisper urgently while her maids, half-dressed and sleep-tousled, clustered behind him, their faces pale and their eyes wet with tears. When Huya's words had finally penetrated Tiy's haze of sleep, her only coherent thought had been, *It has come at last. The evil I've always feared has finally made itself known.* She knew, with a chilling, bone-deep certainty, that Young Amunhotep was responsible. In the darkness of her chamber, the linens of her bed had been tangled about her legs, as if she had roused from the clutch of a terrible dream—as if she had spent the last nineteen years of her life, ever since Young Amunhotep's birth, in a nightmare's grasp, and was only now waking.

After scrambling from her bed, allowing her maids to dress her in a fog of fear and distraction, Tiy had declined the offers of the palace guards to lead her to Thutmose's body. She had no desire to see what one of her sons had done to the other. She closeted herself at once with Huya, even before going to the Pharaoh, to discuss the dreadful occurrence with her steward—to make her plans. For she had seen immediately that grief must wait until the affairs of Egypt were set in order. Now her most urgent need— the need of all of Egypt—was to save her youngest son.

Smenkhkare was only ten years old. But he was a King's Son, and as such, Young Amunhotep might see the boy as a threat. Tiy had realized that Smenkhkare's only hope for life lay in death—for if Young Amunhotep could bring himself to kill one brother, he would not hesitate to slay another. Only in his tomb would Smenkhkare be out of his brother's reach. And only in his tomb would Smenkhkare be preserved for Egypt's sake—safe, whole, living—capable of taking the Horus Throne when he grew into manhood.

Now, at last, with Smenkhkare safely out of the way, Tiy could allow herself to grieve. She leaned on the threshold of her garden door as the sun sank into its western tomb, dying gently, its last warmth blanketing her body. She hugged herself, and beneath her own hands her body felt thin, diminished—almost frail.

One hand brushed against a stiff, crackling object tucked in the sash of her robe. Tiy hesitated, feeling the folded papyrus beneath her fingers. She had forgotten it was there. Sighing, willing her tears to leave her, she pulled the scrap from her sash and examined the grim information it contained.

Huya had provided it to her during their initial meeting, sliding the folded papyrus across the table with one finger, his eyes dark and sober. He had gone to see Thutmose's body even before he'd come to Tiy's chamber, and he had sketched and notated his observations.

"Don't look at it until you feel yourself ready," he'd told her. Tiy, focused on the fate of the throne, her grief shut firmly away in the farthest corner of her heart, had taken the papyrus in impatient hands and nearly opened it then and there. But Huya's hand fell upon her own, staying her.

"I am King's Great Wife," she had snapped. "I am ready now. I am always ready—always."

"You are King's Great Wife," Huya agreed with gentle deference. "But you are also a mother."

And so Tiy had tucked the papyrus away—and forgotten about it, until now. She unfolded it with trembling fingers and stared in blank shock at its contents.

Huya had carefully drawn out the shoulders, neck, and chin of the King's Son, including every detail—even the chain of the pectoral Thutmose had worn, and its unnatural angle as it lay draped across his felled body. Around her son's neck—his throat—Huya had noted small, regular indentations, and the flush of initial bruising around the marks. Careful measurements were noted, indicating regular spacing between the bruises. In the margin, Huya had written with a neat hand: *Strangulation by knotted garrote.*

The *pat* of Tiy's tear startled her. It landed on the papyrus, blurring a bit of the ink. She sniffed loudly and folded the papyrus again, shoving it back into her sash.

Strangulation. A terrible way to die. Did Thutmose see his attacker, she wondered dully? Did he look upon his brother's face as Young Amunhotep wrapped his knotted cord around his neck and choked the breath of life from his throat?

Tiy watched the geese move quietly in the water. The birds were oblivious to the cries that rose and fell around them. And she wept, not only for Thutmose, though the gods knew that his death gave her reason enough to grieve. She wept for Smenkhkare, whom she would not see grown to manhood. She wept for his soft presence at her side, for the comfort of a son who still needed his mother's touch. She wept for his smile, his laughter, his biddable ways. Most of all, she wept because she knew the House of Rejoicing would rip all his innocence and goodness away, sooner or later, when he returned to his rightful place to claim the throne that was now his. The power and privilege of a Pharaoh would change Smenkhkare forever, erasing the boy, building in his place a man to whom no law applied—a man who would take what he pleased, who would live in any manner that suited him—a man who had no need to conform to any custom, or fear any taboo.

The Horus Throne had already done its grim work on Tiy's husband, changing him from the just, attentive, loving man he had been to the creature he was now—remaking him year by year, deed by deed. She had preserved her best and sweetest son for the sake of the Horus Throne, but when his time came to claim his birthright, the glittering snare of power would trap Smenkhkare, too.

There was no way to escape that fate. Tiy knew it as well as anyone. The potent lure of the Pharaoh's throne remade everything and everyone it touched, and once its appealing poison was in the wound, there was no way to cast off its influence. No one was strong enough to sever the golden bonds. The demands of power had done their worst to Tiy, making her what she was now: a steady hand that would pick up and use any instrument the gods pleased—even her own children, if it would serve divine ends. Or even more temporal ends. She saw herself clearly, and did not deny what she was.

Tiy wept for Young Amunhotep, too—for what the gods had made of him. He had once been a babe in her arms, a delicate egg just on the verge of hatching into a rare and brilliant bird. Long ago, when he was only a helpless, mewling bundle, Tiy had loved her second son. But he had grown quickly, as healthy children do—and soon it was obvious to all who knew him that Young Amunhotep was a boy unlike any other. In place of a child's guileless purity, the boy had possessed a piercing, unwavering stare, which had always filled Tiy with a chill of foreboding, as if the power of the Horus Throne—its slow, seductive poison—had already seeped into Young Amunhotep's *ka*. It was as if the gods had made him in reverse, fashioning him in Tiy's womb first in his vast ambition, then in his habit of patient, crafty observation—and only then, when they could be sure that the clay of his *ka* and *ba* were hard-fired and forever set, did they deign to craft for him a body.

The Pharaoh was pleased with his second son, enchanted by his quiet, thoughtful ways. "He will be a great priest—the greatest priest of all," the king had often said. "He is the favorite of the gods, touched by their hands and blessed beyond all mortal men."

Tiy did not believe it. Even the instincts of a mother could not make her see Young Amunhotep for anything other than what he was: a predator, a lion hiding low in the grass, waiting for its moment to leap upon its prey.

And yet, what could Tiy do about her son? Send him away? A King's Son could not simply be packed off to some distant outpost—not without military training, without rank in the army and the pursuit of battlefield glory as a suitable excuse. But the Pharaoh fondly indulged Young Amunhotep's disinterest in military life, and so he was spared from service at a distant fortress.

As Young Amunhotep had grown into manhood, Tiy had been forced to turn her face away from his outrages, for how could she rebuke her son's indulgences when she could not stop his father from committing the same offenses? How could she tell him, *What you do affronts the gods*, when Young Amunhotep would only answer as his father did—his father, bloated with power, who would roll on his broad bed amidst his perfumed linens, and laugh, and say, *I am a god now, Tiy. It is mine to determine what is an affront and what is sacred. It is mine to take what I will, to craft the world to my liking.*

Tiy could ignore her dangerous son no longer. She had hoped he would reform—would develop interest in some temple, perhaps, and channel his fervid intensity toward religion—or take up hunting, or even find distraction in the beds of Waset's whores, and there, on the eastern shore, safely away from the seat of Egypt's power, become as indolent and bed-bound as his father. She had hoped he would tear his unwavering gaze away from the Horus Throne. The last dim, fragile spark of that hope had died with Thutmose, draining away with each faltering beat of the heir's heart.

Yes, Tiy had awakened in truth. Her eyes were open, and now she saw how her life was tangled about her in the darkness, and she could never go back to sleep again.

For that, she wept most bitterly of all.

Behind her, in the brown shadows of her apartment's interior, a door opened and closed. Tiy straightened, wiping the tears from her face, casting one long, final look at the geese on the lake. She drew their serenity into her *ka*, breathing steadily, her eyes dry now. She turned as the sound of soft footsteps approached, and looked at her bowing maid with expectation, brows raised.

"The Pharaoh summons you to his chambers, King's Great Wife," the woman said.

Tiy nodded. She had known Amunhotep would call for her again once the news of Smenkhkare's death reached him. But it had taken him all day to send the summons. What had occupied him in the meantime? Perhaps he had only just awakened from a long slumber—a sleep induced by the poppy juice the physicians recommended for his painful mouth? Or induced by his own idleness? Tiy gave either possibility equal odds. Or perhaps, she thought, frowning, the king had found some other means of whiling the hours away—something close and familiar, to distract him from the fierce double blow of losing two sons in a handful of days.

Whatever caused the king's delay, it did not matter to Tiy. Her hour was now at hand. She must be convincing—she must play her part well, if Smenkhkare was to be safe in his distant seclusion. For the maid's benefit, she drew a deep, shuddering breath and covered her face briefly with her hands.

"I find I cannot do it," she told the woman. "The Pharaoh will expect me to tell everything I know. How can I speak of it? Will it only draw down more of the gods' anger, if I speak aloud of... of losing my youngest son?"

The maid gaped and shook her head. Great Wife Tiy was not given to such displays of brittle emotion—and certainly was not prone to doubt her own way forward. Even in the midst of crisis, the King's Great Wife moved with surety and wore cool dignity like a crown. Tiy had no doubt that word of the Great Wife's overwhelming grief would soon spread throughout the palace. *Good.* Let the rumors flood through the halls like water spilling from a dropped pitcher. When word of Tiy's crumbling composure reached the Pharaoh, it would only bolster the veracity of the tale she must now weave.

The maid seemed about to speak, to offer some awkward words of encouragement—*The poor frightened child,* Tiy thought, *what simple servant expects to be called upon to comfort the King's Great Wife?*—but Tiy gave a convincing display of pulling herself together, and the maid's mouth snapped shut, her face blanching with relief.

"I'll go," Tiy said, a slight tremor coloring her voice. "I'll go to my lord, and if the gods will it, I shall be able to speak."

She swept from her apartment, moving briskly to distract herself from the anxieties that trailed her through the pillared halls. Her fears reached for her with demon hands—unseen, but the whisk of their grasping claws was plain enough to feel—and they seemed to clatter and bump as they dragged along in her wake.

Tiy's route to the Pharaoh's chambers carried her past a wide portico that opened onto a common garden—one of the many pockets of blooming green that beautified the House of Rejoicing, waiting around corners or between stewards' offices to delight the senses and soothe the *ka*.

A flash of linen-white moved in the shade of a slender young sycamore. Tiy paused, watching from the portico's shadows. Young Amunhotep was there, speaking earnestly with his head half-bowed, for the one who listened to him was much shorter than he—Tiy could make out the barest suggestion of a female figure in a white dress, obscured behind the dense screen of a climbing vine. As she watched, lips thinning with displeasure, her son smiled, then issued a short, happy laugh. It raised a sour swell in Tiy's gut, to see him laughing when he had wrought such havoc on the world. Tiy continued to stare as Young Amunhotep lifted a hand, caressing the face of the woman behind the vine, looking into her eyes with his typical, piercing intensity.

Then, in the act of turning the woman's face toward him, he caused her to shift her weight slightly. The swell of her pregnant belly peeked out from her hiding place, just enough that Tiy could be sure of her identity.

Tiy turned before she could see more, and pressed on toward the Pharaoh's chamber.

The king's own steward met her at his outer door,

standing as still as a monument before the two huge cedarwood doors. The doors were carved with the likeness of Bes, the dwarf god Pharaoh Amunhotep favored, and brightly painted to enhance the god's features—his squat but muscular body, his frightening grimace, the beard that spilled like a lion's mane down his chest, the phallus erect and ready for the wild carousing and sexual indulgence that Bes so greedily enjoyed.

Tiy allowed the steward to see her hands tremble. Then she clasped them firmly at her waist. "I am here at the king's summons. Is he within?"

Of course he was within. Years' worth of pain in the Pharaoh's teeth and jaw had made him reluctant to leave the comforts of his own apartments for any reason. The spells and potions he used liberally in a mostly fruitless attempt to keep that pain well-controlled ensured that he often stayed bedridden, even on days when the pain was not severe. The physicians had warned the king—and Tiy—that too much poppy juice would cloud his thoughts, would make him lazy and weak. Even a king, they had said—even one who was half-god, as Amunhotep was--would succumb to the dulling effects of the poppy, sooner or later.

Tiy had not discouraged the king's use of the potion. She had ordered his attendants to make it fresh for him whenever he called for it, and had told them to never attempt to distract him from his desire. She had personally seen that the palace had an ample supply of the stuff, and that it was kept at the ready whenever Amunhotep felt need of its transporting delights.

Now Amunhotep only ventured out from his seclusion when state occasion called for his public appearance—as on the day when he wed the Hurrian girl in Amun's temple. For several years, content with the hazy oblivion of the poppy and the carnal delights that soothed him in the privacy of his chambers, the king had left the shepherding of Egypt in Tiy's capable hands. It was a privilege she had won for herself through many years of long and delicate labor, first weaving gossamer threads of trust and reliance, then affixing them carefully to the king, and finally, with motions so subtle Tiy could scarcely detect them herself, tugging on the Pharaoh's threads to move him in the directions she pleased.

But Tiy had learned that her light, fragile threads broke on the threshold of the Pharaoh's chamber. Outside his private realm, where the eyes of men were upon him, Tiy could influence him—direct him. Whatever happened behind his closed doors, though, with their grinning double visage of the god that knew no self-denial, was beyond Tiy's control.

The steward turned to swing the chamber doors wide, and Tiy wished for one sinking moment that she could have met her husband in the throne room—or in one of the little gardens, as Sitamun and Young Amunhotep had met—anywhere but here, where she knew she had no grip on the Pharaoh's invisible rein. She braced herself, picturing her spine as hard and unbending as bronze, then stepped inside and listened with stony composure as the heavy cedar doors thudded shut behind her.

In spite of the faint, clinging odor of sweat and old vomit, through its oppressive air of heavy-lidded sleep, the Pharaoh's chambers far exceeded even the West Bank ideals of opulence. Here the ceilings were twice as high as in Tiy's own apartments, soaring to such lofty heights that their surfaces were obscured by the thick smoke of the incense and charred meat which Amunhotep burnt daily in offering to his household gods. An enormous couch stretched across the open forechamber, its lion-paw legs tense, ready to spring up and give chase to the delicate, leaping gazelles of the mosaic-tile floor. A table stood beside the couch, and two servants moved quietly around it, gathering up the remains of a large meal. When they saw

Tiy they bowed low, offering their palms in supplication, then turned back to their work, stacking bowls still brimming with untouched food in their carrying baskets.

Beyond the two servants, an alcove full of musical instruments stood, the strings of the harps silent. The bright silk cushions scattered about the floor were empty of the pliant, naked bodies of harem girls and dancers who, years ago when the Pharaoh was well, would have rested there day and night, so that whenever the king's appetites were roused, he would have a selection of playthings close at hand.

The walls were a riot of intense colors, for the House of Rejoicing was new enough that the scenes painted in all its chambers and halls—vines and blooming flowers, flocks of birds lifting to clamoring flight, fish leaping from the brilliant blue of the Iteru—had not yet begun to fade. Along the far wall, niches broke a mural of a marsh at regular intervals, each one occupied by a different god, the statues formed of the finest materials—translucent quartz, polished lapis lazuli, precious turquoise and carnelian the color of flame. The gods stood in their niches amid the flags and banners of papyrus plants, the marsh foliage painted in such a realistic fashion that it all seemed planted here in the king's chambers and halted in its breezy swaying by some miraculous command of the gods themselves.

In the largest niche of all, a statue of Amunhotep stared out at Tiy. It had the face and form she remembered from their youthful years—hers and Amunhotep's. The statue's rounded cheeks were almost boyish, his chin lifted in confidence, his body strong and trim, his stride straight and true. From its brow rose the rounded Khepresh crown, the war helmet of a potent young king, symbol of his ferocity and vigor.

Tiy stepped toward the niches, eyeing the contents of the little faience-glazed offering bowls resting at the gods' feet. None of the bowls held the ash of recent offerings, save for Bes's and Amunhotep's own. *So he has been worshiping himself*, she thought, her eyes narrowing. It was as if the Pharaoh thought he might regain his health and his long-fled youth if only he burnt enough myrrh at the feet of his own image, if only he tempted his divine *ka* with ample slices of raw, bloody flesh.

"Tiy," the Pharaoh called thickly from his bed chamber.

Quickly, Tiy stepped away from the gods' niches. She was annoyed to feel her face heat, like a child caught out at some mischief, though she knew that Amunhotep could not see her from where he lay on his bed. She steadied herself, and when her cheeks were cool again, she passed through his bed-chamber door.

The Pharaoh lay on his large, round stomach, his chest and swollen face supported by cushions. The thick beams of his bed frame creaked as he raised a hand, beckoning Tiy to come closer. As he did so, the linen sheet that covered his pale body slipped to the floor. Tiy bent to retrieve it, and shook it out before replacing it across Amunhotep's broad back. She noted the sheen of oil on his skin before the linen settled. So the king had been at his leisure, after all, enjoying the attentions of his female slaves—a massage, a feeding, perhaps something more—not asleep, not lost in some understandable oblivion. The deep slumber of grief would be all too human a reaction for Amunhotep.

How is it that even through years of pain, even as his body distends and weakens and deteriorates... how can he truly have convinced himself that he is in fact a god? That he is immortal—that death can never touch him?

A Pharaoh was a holy conduit to the gods, the necessary physical manifestation of divinity whose ceremonies and decrees directed the gods' will among men—whose soul, carefully bred for uncountable generations by the gods' inscrutable husbandry, ensured that the universe moved in its correct and righteous order—whose presence made the Iteru's waters rise and fall in their season. But the Pharaoh had never been *truly* a god—not until he died and was resurrected in spirit by his son, on whom the divine Pharaonic responsibility would then fall. Yet somehow, so insidiously that Tiy could not recall the precise day, or even the season, or the year—Amunhotep had altered that truth, and reshaped *maat* itself to suit his own whims.

Farther south, in the frontiers of Upper Egypt, and here and there in Lower Egypt, too, Amunhotep enjoyed the benefits of his own temples. Not the proper mortuary temples that provided sustenance and worship to a deceased king, who was now converted by death to a divine being in truth. No, Amunhotep's worshipers made offerings and obeisance to the image and *ka* of a living Pharaoh. And for reasons Tiy could not understand, Amunhotep's cult was growing.

He had even given Tiy the gift of immortality-on-earth, and built for her a temple in Kush, in the lands of gold and electrum. There Egypt's conquered subjects worshiped her at the Pharaoh's command, revering Tiy as the living image of Hathor, the goddess of love and joy. There was nothing that made Tiy feel less joyous than the thought of Kushites bowing before her statues. But oh, how her brother Ay had laughed with pleasure when he'd heard the tale of it.

"I have learned the sad news," Amunhotep said.

His voice had the soporific drawl of the poppy juice, and he said the words with such an utter lack of emotion that Tiy felt a rush of indignation, followed at once by a cold wave of sorrow so overwhelming that tears leapt into her eyes.

"Yes," Tiy said.

"To lose Smenkhkare so soon after Thutmose's death... it is an evil thing."

"Evil, indeed." What word could better describe Young Amunhotep's violence?

"Tell me how it happened."

Tiy sighed and sank onto a nearby stool. Its surface was still faintly warm—no doubt some ornament of the harem had sat here, her firm young body within reach of the Pharaoh's hand while his slaves worked the scented oils into his skin.

She had rehearsed the story so many times that it came out easily, more naturally than she had dared to hope for. "I was distraught when I learned of Thutmose's death. I crossed the river to attend the shrine of Mut. I thought to seek the comfort and counsel of the Great Mother."

Amunhotep tutted. "You—a goddess yourself?"

Tiy almost rejoined that she was not a goddess—had never believed herself to be, and would not accept Amunhotep as a god until he was dead and silent in his tomb. But losing her temper would not aid her cause. Instead she said simply, "Who better to comfort one goddess in her grief than another? And Mut is a goddess far older and wiser than I."

This seemed to please the Pharaoh. He smiled and nodded awkwardly against his cushion.

"I took my steward with me, of course, but also Smenkhkare." Her voice broke, for the memory of the boy's face, so brave and serious in the side-cast, amber light of Waset's quay, crowded with sudden force into her heart, and she was reminded that she would likely never see her son again in this world. "He was distraught, too, and wanted to pray at Amun's temple, and make offerings to Waser to guide and protect Thutmose's *ka*."

Tiy fell silent, staring at her hands in her lap. She waited until Amunhotep prompted her: "Go on."

"Pardon my hesitation, Lord Horus. These are difficult

words to speak." Tiy waited a moment longer, and then, on a ragged breath, she said, "As we were climbing from the boat to the quay, Smenkhkare... he slipped. He fell into the river." She stopped and pressed the knuckles of her fist against her lips, as if fighting for control. "He has ever been a strong swimmer, but something prevented him from reaching safety—perhaps a cramp, or perhaps he was tangled in an unseen fishing net; I don't know. Huya and I both tried to reach him, but all our efforts were in vain. He... he drowned very quickly, my lord." Tiy gave a convincing sob and wiped her eyes. "At least the gods granted him that one small mercy, and did not leave him to suffer long."

Tiy felt the king's eyes on her own, their black depths sharpening through the poppy haze. She would not look at him, for fear that here in his chambers, the one place where the force of his *ka* still held its original and potent sway, he would discern the lie in her face.

At last Amunhotep said, "Where is the boy's body?"

"On the east bank, with Waset's best embalmer." *The* rekhet *boy is already lying under the salts by now. Even if you send men to verify my story, they will see nothing but a mound of white natron in the House of Death, the same size as Smenkhkare's body.* Tiy made her voice flat and low, as if her grief had run dry and all that was left to her was emptiness. "Huya is there with him, to pay the officials at the House of the Dead, and ensure that the preparation of Smenkhkare's body goes as it ought, with all the care due to a King's Son."

"That is good," Amunhotep said. Sleep crept around the edge of his voice. "The poor boy. Such a good child, so full of promise."

Tiy risked a glance at the Pharaoh. His eyelids, curiously thin and delicate-looking with their shimmer of sweat and their suggestion of blue veins, slid closed in his plump face, then opened again. He fixed Tiy with a dull stare.

Perhaps, she thought, ill as he was today, she might influence him after all—even here, in the last territory that was truly his. She knew she must try, at least. Young Amunhotep would have no regard for the dead—for the seventy days of mourning due to both of his brothers. He would push the Pharaoh hard to declare him the new heir, and sooner rather than later. Young Amunhotep's aspirations had been left to simmer for nineteen patient years. But now that he had pulled the lid from the pot, his dark ambition would boil over. Tiy knew she had little time, and must act whether the setting was ideal or not.

"Smenkhkare was full of promise," she said. "He would have been a fine choice to take Thutmose's place as your heir. But now that he is gone, you must choose someone else—someone who is worthy."

Amunhotep's laugh rumbled, sleepy and slow, against his cushions. "I have another son."

"Someone *worthy*, I said," Tiy replied. "Amunhotep is not fit to be called a King's Son, much less to be called your heir."

"He is of my blood," the Pharaoh said. "The blood of a living god. That gives him more worth than any man could dream of having. And besides the purity of his blood, you know that he is blessed—cherished by all the gods."

"He squanders the gift of your blood by mocking you. He spits into your eye by taking what is not his—what you, in your divinity, have already claimed for yourself."

The Pharaoh's eyes narrowed. "What are you talking about? Speak plainly, Tiy."

"Sitamun."

The name crashed like a temple drum in the silence of the Pharaoh's bed chamber. Amunhotep stared, wide-eyed with disbelief. Then he pushed himself up with a loud grunt, rising to his hands and knees, his belly hanging like the great, drooping udder of Hathor's cow. "What?" Spittle flew from his lips as he spoke.

Tiy wiped the droplets from her cheek with a calm that belied the thrill of victory racing along her limbs. "It is true. Your would-be heir has gone planting in your favorite field. I've heard rumors that he has summoned Sitamun to his chambers, and she has gone, as often as she's come to visit you." Her voice sank, weighted by her bitterness. "I've seen the way he looks at her. And I've lived in the House of Rejoicing long enough to know what those looks mean. I do not know who got to Sitamun first—you or he. But I would not stake my life that the child she carries is yours."

The Pharaoh sank back onto his cushions, his face distorted by pain and by something else—an emotion so foreign to Amunhotep that Tiy lost all composure and stared at him in frank astonishment, her eyebrows raised. It was the sadness of betrayal. The thought that his own son might scoop up the Pharaoh's favorite plaything was nearly enough to reduce Amunhotep to tears.

Tiy frowned at him in disgust.

She had come from a non-royal family, ascending through the court under the guidance of her clever brother Ay, until she had achieved access to its highest ranks—and there she had made Amunhotep, the young heir to his own father's throne, fall in love with her, and set her apart as his Great Wife when he came, in time, to rule from the Horus Throne. Tiy had known, even in the early days of their courtship, that Amunhotep would one day take his own sisters as wives, too. The rite had not troubled her, for although such close marriages were forbidden— by laws and by nature—in families of her own class, the divine family of the king lived and loved by different rules. Among the half-divine, in the bloodlines that bred kings, for brother to marry sister was a holy order—a decree of *maat.* The gods themselves had married sister to brother, since the dawning of divinity, since the siblings Shu and Tefnut created the earth from their blessed union. Why should kings, who were the earthly conduits to the gods, do any differently? Since she was a girl newly arrived in Waset, climbing the ranks of the court, she had understood this, and had felt no disturbance at the tradition.

But this thing the Pharaoh did—taking Sitamun for his own—was no part of sacred tradition. There was no holy precedent for a king to lie with his daughter. It was a base gratification, his greed made manifest. It was proof of his dangerous conviction that he was beyond reproach—of law, of death, even of the gods themselves.

And his selfish indulgence had spread through the House of Rejoicing, like a foul air that brings disease riding on its fetid gusts. Why else had Young Amunhotep thought to take Sitamun to his bed, if not because his father had twisted *maat* to suit his own pleasures? Young Amunhotep could not be free to copulate with his sister until—*unless*—he attained the Horus Throne.

If the gods were good to Tiy, she would see that it never happened. She would sooner end this great and long-standing dynasty altogether than sit passively by, watching as the Horus Throne was handed to a brother-killer, to the embodiment of Set himself. No—Tiy had never been the passive sort, and she would not conjure up timidity now.

"And so you see," she told the Pharaoh, who panted and twitched on his bed, "Young Amunhotep is not a trustworthy man, even with your divine blood in his veins. It is better if you renounce him. Name some other heir, some loyal and pious man whose cooperation you can be sure of. If your second son could think to steal Sitamun out of your bed, how can you be sure—"

The Pharaoh raised a shaking fist. "The child *must* be mine!"

Tiy blinked at him. Amunhotep heaved, trying to raise himself again, but he fell once more onto his cushions and lay there, struggling feebly. "The child?" Tiy said.

"Bred of my seed," Amunhotep panted. "Seed planted... in a daughter of my own breeding. He will be... a strong son... a righteous Horus... to receive my soul."

Tiy sat back on her stool, aghast. So the Pharaoh's primary concern was not Sitamun at all, but merely her womb—and the monster that grew inside it, the product of an unholy union, whether its father was the Pharaoh or the King's Son. "I don't understand," she said, loathing the weak, tremulous sound of her own voice.

The poppy overtook Amunhotep, and he sank once more toward sleep. "To receive my soul..." he muttered, "after I die."

"After you die?"

"I shall go on living," Amunhotep said quietly. "A magic child... bred of trebled divinity. Its *ka*... will be my *ka*... and I shall go on living. Forever."

The Pharaoh's breathing deepened, slowed. Tiy sat in the silence of his bed chamber, staring at the line of windows that looked across the garden—westward, the direction of death. The newly set sun had painted the sky with a wash of brilliant red, but it was rapidly giving way to the pale violet of evening, and here and there, hanging above the tops of the sycamores, stars opened like the silver eyes of distant gods. A breeze moved in the west. It whispered over the windows' sills, carrying the fresh odors of flowers and sand into the Pharaoh's chamber, relieving the place of the stink of illness even as it bore the wails of mourners over the garden wall, amplifying their cries and setting the sounds to echoing in Tiy's heart.

So the king has realized that he will die, after all, Tiy thought. *He is not the god he thought he was.*

The knowledge should have filled her with grim satisfaction, but all she could think of was the child growing in Sitamun's belly—the Pharaoh's last hope for true divinity on earth, a living spell he had conjured up with the hopes that it would make him immortal.

Madness. It is the poppy that has rotted his heart, and stolen all his clear thoughts away.

But Tiy knew it wasn't true. The kernel of this madness had begun to sprout and grow years past, long before the pains had begun to afflict the Pharaoh's mouth. It had begun when Amunhotep had turned them both into gods on earth—set up temples so that their living selves might be worshiped like Amun and Mut.

Why didn't I try harder to stop him then? Tiy asked herself. Tears welled in her eyes, sliding down her cheeks to fall lightly on the bright tiles of the floor. She knew well why she hadn't tried to stop the king. Because the thought that she could truly be a goddess had intoxicated her, seduced her—because even while half of her heart was repulsed by the idea, the other half clung to it, and whispered in her dreams, *Yes, this is right—this is* maat.

In a sudden fury at how she had been seduced, Tiy hated the Pharaoh, loathed him with a force that struck her breathless and left her trembling there on her stool, in the gathering dimness of his bed chamber. She raised herself on shaking legs and bent over Amunhotep. She hissed in his ear, "You shan't go on living forever. There will be no magical, young body into which your *ka* and *ba* may flee. For Sitamun's child was sired by your son, not by you, old man. I know it in my *ba*—I swear it is true. The gods mock your efforts, and your bloated pride. You will die soon, and when you do, it will be forever."

She straightened, smiling coldly. But when she saw the Pharaoh's face, her satisfaction slid from her lips. The Pharaoh's eye was open, staring up at her with a defiant hate that matched the rage twisting in her own heart. Tiy held his gaze a moment longer. His glare sharpened and softened by turns as his consciousness slid in and out of the poppy's obscuring veil. Tiy waited until his stare was sharp, until she could feel its full ferocity—until she was certain that he truly saw her. Then she deliberately turned her back and left him, sweeping through his apartments with her head held high.

TIY HARDLY SLEPT THAT NIGHT. Even after the last mourning cries for her sons had died away, the King's Great Wife lay fretting in her bed, her heart so pummeled by terrible visions—Sitamun pulling back the hood of her cloak; the bruises ringing Thutmose's neck; the Pharaoh's single black eye catching Tiy in its hateful glare—that she could hardly form a coherent thought. In the darkness of her chamber, she tossed and kicked at her bed linens. A fever of dreadful certainty burned her skin—certainty that Egypt would soon fall away—*her* Egypt, the power she held in her small, clandestine hand.

Sometimes she dozed, drifting into dark, unsettling dreams, only to wake with a violent jerk of her body, staring into the blackness that filled her chamber, her thoughts suddenly sharp and clear. Young Amunhotep was a force beyond her control. She could never hope to guide him from the concealment of shadows, as she had done with his father. She had no doubt of that, for she hadn't the necessary leverage over his *ka*—and in truth, she could see no way to determine what sort of leverage might work against her son. His heart was a cold and distant thing, inscrutable even to Tiy, who had spent so much of her life watching others, learning their desires, understanding how to *control*.

Tiy stared hard into the dense, cool darkness, searching for something familiar, straining to pick out the shapes of her chamber's pillars or the gray shadows of the mural on her wall. But everything she looked upon was shrouded, occluded—hidden.

Had she planted a strong enough seed of doubt within the Pharaoh's mind? Would it take root, and produce the fruits she hoped for? If the Pharaoh was hurt enough, angry enough to send Young Amunhotep away, to strip him of his birthright, then all would be well. The Horus Throne would remain in Tiy's control. The Pharaoh would choose some other man as his heir—but it would be a simple thing for Tiy to undo that proclamation when Amunhotep finally died. Then she would be free to recall Smenkhkare from his hiding place, to put him forth as a child of the king's divine blood, the true and undisputed claimant to the throne. Tiy would reign on as her son's regent, and if the gods were good, she would make of Smenkhkare a better king—a better man—than his father had been.

She must hope that the gods would nurture her carefully planted seed, and clear the way for Smenkhkare's return. If they did not, her only other course would be to do as Young Amunhotep had done, and soil her hands and her *ka* with murder. If the King's Son was struck down before he could take the throne, then the Two Lands might still be saved. But if he ascended to the rank of Pharaoh, then the gods would have made their divine will plain—and then Young Amunhotep would be far beyond Tiy's reach. The only soul more accursed than a brother-killer was one who took a Pharaoh's life—for to strike down the Pharaoh was to strike down the power of the gods made flesh. Tiy knew that such a blasphemy was beyond even her calculating heart.

But before the King's Son became the Pharaoh...?

Is a mother who slays her child more accursed than a man who slays his brother? Tiy sent the question out like a prayer, searching and desperate. She waited for an answer, but felt no stir of whispers in her chamber—or in her heart.

Be good, gods, Tiy pleaded in the darkness. She pulled her coverlet up past her eyes, like a little girl hiding from the demons of the night. *Grant me mercy. Do not require me to face such a terrible task. Leave the Horus Throne in my hands. Thou knowest I am capable of ruling well. Clear the way for Smenkhkare to return. Remove Young Amunhotep from the House of Rejoicing—from the world itself—but do not require me to damn my own ka. Do not ask me to do the task myself.*

TIY WOKE, GROGGY AN RED-EYED, to the sound of her maids' whispers. She lay still in her bed, listening as they eased open the door of her great cedarwood closet, trying to keep the hinges from squeaking. The fine linens of Tiy's gowns rustled gently as the maids sorted through them. Something bumped, and one of the servants cursed another in a quiet hiss. There was a sense of urgency in their bustle. Warily, Tiy sat up and squinted at her maids suspiciously.

All three of the women bowed low, raising hasty palms toward her. "Please, Great Wife," said Akhbet, who had served Tiy since the earliest days of her marriage to the Pharaoh, "forgive our intrusion. But the king has called for you, and we thought to lay out your best gown and wig, and allow you to sleep a little longer."

Tiy frowned. She climbed from her bed, clad only in a sleeping shift that trailed behind her petite body like a boat's dropped sail fluttering on a river breeze. She made her way to her cosmetics table and seated herself, staring into the mirror. *They thought to let me sleep? Do I look so haggard, then—as if I need sleep?*

The reflection that scowled back at her was so gaunt and sad-eyed that at first Tiy did not recognize her own face. Grief and the strain of her long, nearly sleepless night had pinched Tiy's brow and shadowed her eyes with pain. She looked exhausted, as dried-up and useless as a stooped, ancient crone, as brittle as a dead leaf.

Tiy folded her arms beneath her breasts and gave her own reflection a solid, chilling glare.

"As you are up," Akhbet said, coming up behind Tiy, "allow us to dress you, Great Wife. The king wished to see you most urgently."

"Most urgently—is that the way of it?" Tiy fastened a scarf around her brow, pulling her hair back from her face. She selected a pot of cleansing oil from her cosmetics table and began massaging it into her lined face, as if she had not a care in the world. "Well, the king can wait on my pleasure, for once. I'll have my breakfast first, and then you women will do up my paint and perfume me. Then perhaps I'll stroll in the garden for an hour or two." Tiy returned the lid to the oil pot and set it back on her table with a heavy clatter. She picked up a neatly pressed towel and began rubbing the excess oil from her face, muttering as she did so, "Most urgently, indeed. I'll teach that wallowing old lout to send my maids in to fill my chamber with noise while I'm trying to sleep." She turned on her stool to stare pointedly at her maids. Then, with a shout and a scattering motion of her hands, she sent them running to fetch her breakfast.

But by the time they returned with a tray full of stewed fruits and soft bread, Tiy found she had no appetite. Fear had settled, cold and hard, in her stomach. All the misgivings of her restless night had returned to haunt her, and she found herself staring dully into the mirror, repeating the same desperate prayer she'd offered to the gods as she'd lain shivering in her bed.

Tiy rejected the food and stood, silently holding her arms out so that her women might dress her. The maids seemed relieved by her change of heart, and worked with quiet efficiency, forgoing their usual happy chatter and amusing gossip. Their grim focus only deepened Tiy's anxiety, so that by the time her face was painted and a long, heavy wig was set on her head, its neat, thick braids falling past her breasts, she was relieved to depart the eerie quiet of her apartments and make her way toward the Pharaoh's audience hall. Whatever new twist of fate the gods had planned for Tiy, at least she would face it quickly, and move beyond it all the sooner.

She hesitated outside the high, red-painted double doors of the audience chamber. As she paused, a palpable force of fear seemed to rise up and strike her from behind, as if she had been outpacing it with her brisk stride, racing it down the halls of the palace from her apartments to this very place, where her new fate awaited her. Now it overtook her, flowing up her body and over her head in one fierce, cold wave. She had the sickening, panicked sensation that she had been plunged into the river, held below the surface by some grasping force she could not see.

Then the sensation passed, leaving only a slight shiver in its wake, and she was mistress of her own emotions again. She nodded to the guards on the doors and stood firm and straight as the doors swung open.

Nothing could have prepared Tiy for the sight that greeted her—not a direct word of caution from the goddess Mut herself, and certainly not the warning shadows of the previous night's half-glimpsed, dimly remembered dreams. At the end of the hall, flanked by two massive, lotus-painted pillars, the Pharaoh sat in his raised throne, the folds of his loose stomach piled upon his lap, his head tipped back with a look of satisfaction. Beside him, on the ebony throne of the King's Great Wife, Sitamun sat stiffly, her small hands gripping the arms of the chair, her eyes so wide that Tiy could see their whites from where she stood. From Sitamun's brow rose the double-plumed crown of the sun disc—the crown that had always been

Tiy's. Dozens of lamps lit the hall with an intense, forceful glare, and the two golden plumes sparkled with light as Sitamun shivered.

"Come, Tiy," the Pharaoh called, as if she were a dog in a hunter's pack.

Struggling to marshal complete serenity, Tiy paced slowly, regally toward the thrones. *You hold power over him here*, she told herself, *outside his private realm, beyond his doors guarded by Bes. He is yours here; you are in control.* But she found it more difficult to believe in her own power with every step she took. Even the soft soles of her slippers seemed to ring against the polished stone floor, as loud as the bronze gongs of the temples. With a tremor of apprehension, she imagined Amunhotep could hear the rapid beat of her heart just as clearly as he heard her footfalls.

Tiy reached the foot of the dais and bowed, gazing up at Amunhotep with a mask of perfect calm.

"I have been thinking" the Pharaoh said, "about what you told me. Yes, I recall our conversation, Tiy—all of it, every last word."

Tiy tilted her head. The braids of her wig swung gently. "Do you? Can you be sure of my words, Mighty Horus? The pain in your mouth was great, and you had taken much of the poppy juice. You know how it clouds your thoughts."

Tiy's cool demeanor—even if it was feigned—seemed to serve her well. The briefest flicker of doubt crossed Amunhotep's face, swollen on one side from the demon that did its work inside his teeth and jaw. His confidence broke for only a moment, but it was enough to reassure Tiy. Perhaps her gossamer strings were not yet snapped— not all of them, not entirely.

The Pharaoh said, "I have considered what you've said about Sitamun's baby."

The girl shifted one hand quickly from the throne's carved arm to her belly, as if the Pharaoh had threatened the child by merely speaking of it.

"Yes," Tiy said, "Sitamun. And is there a reason why my daughter is sitting in my place, Lord Horus, and wearing my crown?"

Amunhotep's sudden laughter filled the hall, bouncing from the pillars, beating at Tiy like the stinging sands of a wind storm. She breathed deeply to stop herself from flinching.

"Your place no longer," the Pharaoh said. "Your crown no longer. I married Sitamun this morning, at dawn. I have named her my Great Wife."

Tiy cast a glance at her daughter. A single tear slid from Sitamun's eye, tracking a wet line of kohl beside the girl's nose.

"What purpose can it possibly serve, to marry the girl?" Tiy asked.

Amunhotep sat forward on his throne. "The child. Now that I've married her, the gods will make Sitamun's child my own issue, no matter whose seed it sprouted from. My own son, born of my blood."

Tiy shook her head, resisting the urge to back away from the dais, as one backs from a dog with a foaming mouth. "That is utter madness. You've lost your senses entirely."

"It is true," the king insisted. "A great magic—an incantation never known before in the hearts of men. But I know it—I alone was granted the knowledge. I saw it in a dream last night, after you left my bed chamber."

"A poppy dream. A hallucination."

"A vision from the gods."

Tiy gave a harsh, mocking laugh, threw it at the Pharaoh like a stone. "What god would grant you a vision? I've seen the offering bowls in your private quarters. You've abandoned all gods, save for Bes and your own image. Who was it, then, that sent you this great revelation? Your dwarf god of drunkenness and greed? Or was it your own twisted *ka*?"

Amunhotep levered his great weight up, staggering to his feet. His legs were water-swollen and flushed, but they held his body as straight and firm as they had done in his youth. "Watch your step, Tiy. You mock divinity. Do not insult a god."

Take care, Tiy told herself, for she felt her precious few remaining threads strain as the Pharaoh towered over her, staring down at her from the height of the dais. She bowed low, raising her palms in supplication. "Forgive me, Lord Horus."

"I will," the Pharaoh said, easing himself back into his throne. "I know that you are mourning the deaths of Thutmose and Smenkhkare. It is you who've gone out of your senses, Tiy, with grief. But I am a merciful lord. I will not rebuke you for your insults. In fact, I will do you a great favor."

Tiy straightened, eyeing Amunhotep warily. "A favor?"

"I had thought to send you away to one of your northern estates, where you may grieve in peace, and where you'll be untroubled by the rigors or court life."

Tiy's heart seized; her eyes widened before she could master her face.

"But my new Great Wife has a gentle heart," Amunhotep said, gazing at Sitamun with a soft-eyed fondness that twisted Tiy's gut. "She pleaded with me, to allow you to remain on the West Bank."

Tiy raised her brows. "I am grateful to my daughter for her thoughtfulness and mercy. However, you cannot put me off as Great Wife, my king. It has never been done before, in all the long history of Egypt."

Amunhotep grunted. "It has now. You will move into the harem palace, to take up your new station as a minor wife. Sitamun will have your apartments here in the House of Rejoicing. Count yourself lucky, Tiy. I remember the words you spoke last night. I am doing you a far greater kindness than you deserve. Be content with it, or I may change my mind, no matter how Sitamun pleads to spare you."

Abruptly, Tiy bowed and spun on her heel. As she swept back down the hall, her eyes intent on the huge red doors at its far end, she heard Sitamun's loud sniff behind her. But Tiy would not allow herself to glance back at her daughter. She would not take the risk of appearing so weak and emotional before the king, for as long as she maintained her composure, her unflappable confidence, she still held some gossamer threads in her hand.

The Pharaoh had told Tiy to count herself lucky, and she did. Demotion to the harem was a blow, but one Tiy knew she could bear. For as long as she was near the House of Rejoicing, and not banished to some far-off estate—or worse, to her tomb—she might still hope to retain her unseen grasp on the king. For now, and until the time was ripe to call Smenkhkare back to her side, that was all that mattered.

Sitamun

Year 36 of Amunhotep
Ruler of Waset,
Lord of Truth in the Sun,
Strong Bull Arising

SITAMUN WAITED, QUIETLY SPINNING FLAX beside her garden window, until her chattering maids left the vast, vibrantly painted apartments of the King's Great Wife. The girls were headed for her old, much smaller quarters, to fetch the final load of Sitamun's belongings and move them here, to her imposing new home.

Only a few baskets of linens and some small, decorative objects—cups and a wall hanging or two—remained in her former room. The rest of her goods were here now, scattered so widely across the three large rooms that they reminded her of the islands her brother Thutmose had once shown her on his war maps—insignificant dots separated by a vastness of blue-painted sea. Across her new bedroom, far from the narrow but elegantly gilded frame of her bed, stood the tiny cosmetics table her sisters had given her, years ago, as a New Year's present. Through the archway that led into the receiving room, she could see the little couch wrapped in cool silk where she took her meals. Its orange cushions and ebony feet felt so far away that Sitamun was sure it would take her half a day to walk to it. The cedar closet that had looked so grand and imposing in her former chambers seemed a poor and sad thing now, cringing in a corner as if it feared the great, myrrh-scented heights of the ceiling that reached as tall as sycamore trees.

In her previous room—the quiet, cozy chamber that had been her refuge for so many years—Sitamun's things had looked welcoming and fine. Here, their smallness and the distance between them only made the apartments of the King's Great Wife feel all the more cold and impersonal, and Sitamun was sure that she would never feel at home here, never feel comfortable with this new part she must play.

When she was certain the maids had gone, Sitamun laid her spinning aside and went to her bed. Though the girls had already dressed it with fresh, crisp linens and even perfumed the sheets with soothing herbs to help Sitamun sleep soundly in her strange new surroundings, she moved the padded crescent-moon of her carved headrest aside and pulled the sheets up, shaking them briskly until they popped in the silence of the chamber like a boat's sails in a strong wind. Her body felt strange and awkward as her arms reached up, up, as if she might toss the sheets to the tops of the pillars. Her belly was so large now that she could do nothing gracefully anymore, not even this simple task. But she did not allow her ungainly body to rob the fun from the moment. She held the sheets high as they fluttered slowly back onto the bed, landing perfectly straight, as they always did.

Sitamun smiled. She found it soothing, to dress a bed with her own hands. It was a simple pleasure; the straightforward work brought her joy, and the task was unchallenging—she could always be sure that she would do it well. She ran her hands over the soft linen, though there were no wrinkles to chase away. There never were. She was an expert at shaking out sheets—a fact that would no doubt scandalize her maids, if they knew.

Sitamun glanced up at the gods, who watched her from their new niches in the far bedroom wall. The little painted statues smiled down at her with distant, knowing expressions.

"Sometimes," she said aloud to any god who might be listening, "I wish you had made me a *rekhet* girl." She would do very well as the servant of a King's Wife. Every bed she dressed would be perfect, smooth and cool and inviting, ready to bring her high-born mistress sweet, untroubled dreams.

She turned the upper edge of the sheet back smartly, but as she moved the headrest back into place at the top of the gently sloping bed frame, Sitamun heard the far-off squeal of door hinges. Her maids had returned from her old chambers, it seemed. Much sooner than she'd expected. Sitamun left the bed reluctantly, calling out as she went—she was obliged to shout, for her voice was unused to giving commands in such airy quarters—"You may leave the baskets unpacked. I am going to find a new closet to buy, anyway, for my old one is much too small for this room."

But it was not her gossiping maids she found in the receiving room. Sitamun checked on the bed chamber's threshold. The baby inside her twisted, sensing her sudden anxiety, and her hands reached of their own accord to comfort it with gentle caresses.

"Hello, Mother," Sitamun said.

Tiy scowled, but the scowl did not look any different from the frown she usually wore. Across the empty length of the room, they stared at one another, Tiy's habitual glower unreadable, Sitamun faintly trembling.

"You look pale," Tiy said. "You should sit."

"I am well."

"Nonsense." Tiy came briskly toward her, holding out one hand like the wing of a gliding bird. Sitamun watched that hand fly across the space between them as Tiy advanced, afraid her mother might strike her—and Sitamun would not blame her for it if she did. But as the former Great Wife drew close, the hand went around Sitamun's shoulders, turning her gently but firmly, guiding her back through the bed chamber door at her mother's usual lively pace.

Tiy led Sitamun to her bed and eased her down with unfamiliar care, until Sitamun sat with her legs swinging. The baby was heavy and warm where it rested in her lap.

"How fares the child?" Tiy asked, business-like, glancing out the garden window that had once been hers with her arms folded tight beneath her breasts.

"Well, I think," Sitamun said. "The king made me stand in the throne room yesterday while a whole line of priests cast spells of protection over me, and read the signs and made every kind of divination you can imagine. It took hours, and I was so tired and weak by the end of it, all I wanted was to sit down."

Tiy's mouth tightened, and Sitamun felt her cheeks flame with embarrassment. Yesterday, Tiy's possessions had been moved from these very rooms and taken to her quarters in the harem palace. No doubt her new accommodations were not nearly as fine as these.

But Tiy did not comment on how she had spent the previous day. She only asked, "And what did the priests say about your child?"

Sitamun lowered her eyes. "They all swore it is a boy—a healthy King's Son, who will live and thrive."

Tiy's frown deepened. Her shoulders jumped with a silent, ironic laugh. "I am sure the Pharaoh was pleased to hear it."

"Oh, Mother." Sitamun's hands itched to reach out, to seek her mother's embrace. But Tiy had never been demonstrative. Sitamun could not recall a time when her mother had ever offered her comfort, preferring to leave such soft gestures to her children's nurses and tutors.

And anyway, Sitamun thought miserably, *I don't deserve her kindness. My sins have been too great.*

With a terrible effort, Sitamun calmed herself, steadying her voice, forcing herself to adopt the cool composure which Tiy always wore so easily. "Is it true, what the Pharaoh says?" Sitamun asked.

"Is what true?"

"That my baby..." her composure cracked, but Sitamun mended it quickly, grasping at the ragged ends of her wits and pulling them together with force. "That my baby will be a magical one—a vehicle for his *ka* and *ba*, to make him live forever?"

Tiy eyed Sitamun for a long moment. Her arms were still folded, and despite her small stature and advancing age, the former Great Wife looked as strong and imposing as an obelisk in the sun. Sitamun trembled under that steady stare.

Finally Tiy said, "Do you want your father to live forever?"

Sitamun swallowed hard. She felt the baby move again, shifting and turning inside her, as if it, too, rebelled against the idea. She whispered, "No."

The deep lines of Tiy's eternal frown softened. She came to the bed, and Sitamun was surprised at how heavily she sat—how her mother's weight pulled at the springy, tight-woven platform, as if Tiy were infinitely larger, infinitely *more*, than her small, feminine frame suggested.

"It was only a matter of time before Amunhotep shuffled me off to the harem," Tiy said. "A part of me knew it was bound to happen, I think, so I was not as shocked as I might have been."

"But it has never been done before, as you said in the throne room."

Tiy cast a glance at her daughter's belly. "The reign

of Amunhotep has seen many wonders," she said drily. "Many things have been done under your father's rule that have not been done before. Let us hope they will never be done again."

Blushing, Sitamun looked away.

Tiy said, "The Pharaoh knows his time is running short. He knows his death is near. He can feel Anupu's breath on the back of his neck. I am sure of it, no matter what airs he might put on for his slave girls and his harem ornaments— or for you. He truly thought himself immortal—eternal in his physical form, as no Pharaoh has been before. But the pains in his mouth have eaten away at his mad convictions, day by day, year by year. And now he can no longer deny the truth."

"But my child..."

"The baby will not be a vessel for Amunhotep's *ka*, Sitamun. It simply is not possible, so have no fear on that count. Your child will have his own *ka* and *ba*—his own identity. You will know it's true when you bring the baby forth, and look into his eyes."

Tiy smiled, her face filling with unaccustomed tenderness even while her own eyes grew distant with a poignant sorrow. Sitamun wondered whether her mother was thinking of her—Sitamun—when she was a babe in Tiy's arms.

Tiy went on, "And anyway, have you ever heard of such a thing before—any magic of the sort? A man cannot breed himself. How can such a thing be done?"

"A god can breed himself," Sitamun said. "Atum the Creator fashioned himself out of his own seed."

The tenderness fled from Tiy's face, replaced by her usual stony, narrow-eyed chill. "Has the Pharaoh been professing that he's the Creator now? We shall see, after I've sealed him in his tomb, whether he comes forth like

143

Atum from the darkness. But I tell you, I shan't hold my breath waiting for him to reappear."

Sitamun smiled, then laughed lightly. She couldn't help it. The idea *was* absurd—old, fat, drooling Amunhotep as the vigorous, virile god Atum.

"Your father's time is coming soon," Tiy said again. "He will not trouble us for much longer. It's someone else we must worry about now. And that's why I've come to see you today."

Sitamun looked at her mother gravely. "Young Amunhotep."

"Yes. I told you, on the night when we... when we crossed the river, that he is dangerous, and must be prevented from taking the throne."

"But why? He is the heir, now that poor Thutmose is gone."

"He is not the heir yet—not until the proclamation is made. And he is not a good man, Sitamun. He slew his own brother. Who knows what evils may befall our family—to say nothing of Egypt in its entirety—if a brother-killer takes the throne? The gods will not suffer such an offense to *maat*. There is no man more unclean than one who takes the life of his brother."

Sitamun remembered Thutmose, unrolling his war maps on the floor of her chamber, pointing out all the lands, their routes and boundaries, as she curled in his lap, listening to his deep voice rumble through his chest. She had been just a little girl then, trusting and innocent— and she had always liked Thutmose's smile, his laugh. Her eyes welled with tears.

"I have been cast aside," Tiy said, "traded in for a consort who is younger and more enticing."

Again, Sitamun's cheeks heated. She did not enjoy the thought of having displaced her mother. But she was the

Pharaoh's subject as well as his daughter. What could she do, when the very voice of the gods commanded her?

"You must take up my work, Sitamun. You must do what I can no longer do."

She gasped. "I? But what do you mean? What work?"

"It is you, now, who is dearest to the king—closest to his heart. It is you who must influence him toward good."

Sitamun shook her head, a frantic, frightened denial. "I cannot influence him. He'll know if I try. He'll—"

"You have done it already," Tiy reminded her, "by begging his mercy on my account. Am I not here before you, on the West Bank, instead of withering away in an estate clear up in Ankh-Tawy? I am the very proof of your new power, my girl. And you must go on using it, for the good of the Two Lands."

"But I have no power. I only… I only cried when I learned what he meant to do, sending you away from the court forever."

"Cried?" Tiy's kohl-darkened brow arched. "Tears were never my style, but I can imagine that weeping might work very well on him. However you do it, Sitamun, you must be careful and subtle—clever, like me. You must convince your father to abandon Young Amunhotep. He must choose another man as his heir instead. Or, failing that, you must make him delay the business—put off the choice for two years more, until Smenkhkare is educated and grown enough that we can bring him back to the House of Rejoicing." Tiy tossed her head. "I could even make one year suffice. Some way might be found to divert Young Amunhotep in a year's time—to break his claim on the Horus Throne."

Convince Father to abandon Young Amunhotep… Sitamun's *ka* quavered at the very thought. Such a thing was beyond her power, beyond her desires, and certainly far beyond her skill. She felt caught, trapped like an insect beneath the heel of a sandal, on the verge of being crushed by the great weight of her mother's expectations.

Sitamun covered her face with her hands. The child inside her kicked as her chest heaved with welling, choking sobs.

"Why are you weeping, girl?" Tiy's voice was confounded.

"I want no part of this," Sitamun wailed. "I don't want to be King's Great Wife, or live in your apartments, or convince the Pharaoh of anything. I only want to have my child in peace—*my* child, not the king's—and live a simple life."

The bed lurched, the web of its woven surface creaking as Tiy abruptly stood. "A simple life?" the former Great Wife said. "There is no such thing, child. There never was for you—not for anyone in the king's household. We are where we find ourselves—I, demoted to a harem wife, and you, positioned to whisper in the king's ear. That is your task now, to use what power the gods have given you. So save your tears, and use them on the Pharaoh, where they'll do us all some good."

Sitamun clutched her rounded belly as her mother swept from the bed chamber. She listened to Tiy's hard, staccato footsteps fading down the great length of the receiving room, and then the outer door opened and shut with a boom like thunder over the far western hills.

Tiy's words hung in the air, repeating as a whisper inside Sitamun's heart. *Use what power the gods have given you.* But for whom should Sitamun use this sudden, unlooked-for power? There was no doubt that Tiy intended to marshal Sitamun's influence for her own ends. Sitamun had no wish to be her mother's puppet.

A few tears dropped from her downcast eyes, falling on the pure white linen of her robe. The moisture soaked into the cloth and spread, isolated drops like islands in a sea. Sitamun remembered the feel of Thutmose's arms around her, the curled edges of his map, the brilliance of its yellow and blue paints. She remembered his smile, his laugh—and that he had always been kind to her, always a good and gentle brother. The tears fell harder then, until there were no more islands, only a swath of damp linen clinging to the swell of her belly, cloaking the child inside.

Tiy

Year 36 of Amunhotep
Ruler of Waset,
Lord of Truth in the Sun,
Strong Bull Arising

S HE WAS UNUSED TO WALKING such long distances, and her body was not as strong and youthful as it once had been. Long before the wedding procession had passed the dusty, stinking lanes of lower Waset, Tiy's hips and knees had begun to ache. There was still another league and a half to go until they reached the temple complex of Ipet-Isut and the steps of the great Amun Temple within.

On the outskirts of Waset, the finer estates of well-bred civic workers and successful merchants stood in relative peace and seclusion, their high walls enclosing gardens which helped to sweeten the stale east-bank air. Women and servants gathered on the rooftops, raising bowls of beer in salute, lifting children up to peer down on the bright river of nobility that flowed along the Processional Way: the West Bank men in their long, meticulously pleated kilts, some of them sporting fine jeweled pectorals that sent up flashes of sunlight to dazzle the eyes of the observers; the wives of nobles and women of the Pharaoh, clad in gowns of every conceivable color—pale blues and deep indigos; scarlets and oranges like dancing flames; hues of violet-pink, soft as a lotus petal; yellows and greens as bold as the skins of newly ripened fruits. Each woman wore her finest wig, long and thick after the current fashion, and each wig was enhanced with bright beads and ivory charms, lappets of electrum and circlets of filigreed gold. The sounds of these ornaments, clattering together with every step, rose above the sound of many walking feet, many murmuring voices, so that the wedding procession formed a constant, light, percussive movement, like water pouring over stones.

Servants of the surrounding estates scattered baskets of petals from rooftops and garden walls. The procession of West Bank nobility trod the petals underfoot, filling the lane with a bruised, sickly-sweet perfume that was nearly as bad as Waset's natural stench. Tiy reached toward Huya, and he handed her a skin of herbal wine. The sharp, bittersweet taste in her mouth was a relief, a distraction from the assault on her nostrils. But it would take some long time, Tiy knew, before the concoction did its work on the dull ache in her lower back or relieved the pain in her legs.

The head of the procession, several lengths away from where Tiy walked, cleared the last estate of Waset and began the trek across the open farmland that lay between the city and its temples to the north. Tiy gazed ahead at the litters that led the parade. They were raised on the shoulders of tireless bearers, swaying gently with the stately pace. Tiy clenched her jaw, noting the bright gilding of the Great Wife's litter, its thick platform decorated with vultures' wings, the tall back of its chair made in the image of Mut, the mother-goddess. She could just make out the tips of the double-plume crown peeking above the edge of the chair's back. Sitamun sat in that chair, riding at ease on that litter—in a place that was Tiy's by right.

The Pharaoh lounged on his litter to Sitamun's left, and directly behind the royal pair, two more platforms bore the bride and groom—Young Amunhotep, grinning like a cat in the sun, and Nefertiti, whose pale-faced silence and hollow stare told Tiy all she needed to know about the girl's opinion of her new husband. Tiy did not blame her niece for her reluctance. She took another long swallow from her wine skin, thinking wryly, *For Nefertiti*, hoping the herbs would do their work all the sooner, and numb away her pain and disbelief.

Huya took the skin when Tiy held it out to him, hanging the strap over his shoulder so it would be close at hand. He gestured to a nearby slave who bore an ostrich-plume fan on a long, red pole. The slave came at once, fanning Tiy as she walked.

Tiy glanced at Huya with a grateful smile. Her steward had returned from his mission in the north just two days before, angry, but not at all surprised to find Tiy displaced from her lofty position, relegated to the harem like some forgotten toy. He had declined the Pharaoh's offer to continue serving the King's Great Wife, and had opted instead to remain in Tiy's employ—even though, Huya had affirmed drily, she was now nothing more than a minor wife. This display of loyalty had raised Tiy's spirits. If the gods allowed her to keep her steward, perhaps they did not mean take everything from her, after all. Perhaps she even still held power over the Horus Throne—or could gain some of it back, at any rate. With her clever steward still firmly by her side, her prospects seemed fair enough.

Huya drifted closer to Tiy's side. He said quietly, "Tell me how affairs went with Sitamun."

Tiy glanced around the procession, eyeing the other King's Wives who moved about her. But with their constant talk, the shuffling of so many feet, and the din of their swaying ornaments, there was little chance that Tiy and Huya would be overheard, providing they kept their voices low. In fact, she thought, a conversation in the midst of a wedding procession, with the celebrants distracted and on the move, was likely to be more private than a discussion in Tiy's new chambers in the harem palace. She nodded and gestured for Huya to move closer still.

"It's hard to say," Tiy said. "I explained to her the need for some influence over the king, and the advantage her new position affords her. But she is so young, and frightened, and I don't believe she ever had the heart for these political games. Sitamun is as gentle and meek as a kitten."

In the rippling shade of the ostrich fan, Huya's face grew long and thoughtful. "It's somewhat discouraging, to know that such a frail, easily manipulated girl now stands behind the throne."

"It's not the worst curse that could have befallen us, you know. Amunhotep was beginning to suspect me anyway— beginning to chafe under my influence. I'd long believed that he was noticing more and more of my subtleties, and was growing ever more conscious of my secret shepherdings. Now he believes me safely out of the way, with all my power stripped. He thinks himself far beyond my reach. But I can shepherd and mold Sitamun as much as I ever did the Pharaoh."

"Hopefully she will even be easier for you to manage than the king."

Tiy pursed her lips, giving her steward an annoyed look. "I hope you are not suggesting that I am not as competent as I was in my youth—that I require less onerous tasks."

"Of course not, Great Wife." Huya laughed. "You are as sharp and capable as ever."

"You cannot call me Great Wife any longer," she reminded him. "It would never do for word to get back to Amunhotep that I still fancy myself his chief consort. If we are to turn Sitamun to our use, the Pharaoh must think me utterly defeated."

"Very well. You seem sure enough that Sitamun will prove useful."

"With time."

"What, then, do we do about the heir—Young

Amunhotep?"

Tiy frowned up at the head of the procession, where the litters moved like pleasure-barques on the river, languid, drifting and smooth. From where she walked, many paces behind, she could not see her son's face. The high back of his chair blocked most of his body from her view. All she could discern of Young Amunhotep was one arm hanging casually from his chair, the hand limp, relaxed, his skin shining with the gold bracelets that covered his wrist. The unconcerned angle of that dangling arm set Tiy's teeth on edge. It spoke eloquently of Young Amunhotep's self-contentment.

"Yes," Tiy said. "That is the puzzle. I have hope of convincing Sitamun that she must change her father's mind and convince him to renounce Young Amunhotep as heir. But we must prepare for the worst. If Young Amunhotep *is* proclaimed the heir, we must be sure of holding onto him—of steering him somehow."

"Nefertiti?" Huya suggested.

But Tiy shook her head. Nefertiti was her niece, it was true—but Tiy had never been especially close with the girl, and had heard from her brother Ay all about the scene Nefertiti had made when she was informed that she must wed Young Amunhotep. Tiy knew the marriage would not be a fond one. She could already predict the way this union would play out—she had seen it all before in the small, ever-present dramas of the Pharaoh's court. The passionate arguments of two ill-matched partners would soon dwindle to cold silences, bitter resentments, and as many lengthy separations as the couple could engineer. With no hope for affection, or even respect, between bride and groom, Nefertiti would make an ineffectual tool in Tiy's hand.

"Then what of the foreign girl?" Huya asked quietly. "The Hurrian—the new King's Wife."

Tiy frowned. "Tadukhepa?"

"Yes, that's the one."

Tiy recalled the pale, bronze-haired girl on her wedding day, sweltering and trembling inside her dark wool and Mitanni tassels. The shrinking, wide-eyed Hurrian seemed a more unlikely tool than Nefertiti, until Tiy recalled the flash of Tadukhepa's temper when she had asked the girl uncomfortable questions, and confronted her with the reality of her sale into Egypt.

Perhaps the girl has just enough pluck, enough of a sense of self-preservation...

Tiy reached for the wine skin again. "Why Tadukhepa? What makes you think Young Amunhotep will take to her?"

"It seems," Huya said, speaking so quietly that Tiy could scarcely hear him, "he already has. When I returned from... my errand in the north... I stopped at the Temple of Amun to pay my respects to my god, and to invoke his protection on... the cargo I transported for you."

Tiy was touched. "How thoughtful."

"I spoke with one of the priests—the man who interrogated Tadukhepa, on the night Thutmose died."

Tiy pulled the stopper from the wine skin and took another long, bitter draft. "What a waste of time and effort that interrogation was. A farce! Anyone with half his senses could see that Tadukhepa couldn't have killed Thutmose. A woman that small, disabling and strangling a man of Thutmose's strength and size?"

Huya shrugged. "You saw my notes, my lady. Even a small woman might kill a very strong young man, if she used a knotted garrote—like the one I suspect took your son's life."

Tiy hissed through her teeth and looked away from her steward.

"Regardless, though," Huya said, "Tadukhepa is innocent. I'd stake my life on that."

"Of course she is. We know who killed Thutmose—the only man who had a reason to wish him dead. To think that fool of a priest spent hours questioning Tadukhepa when he could have been interrogating Thutmose's real killer..." Tiy could have spat into the dust of the Processional Way, and would have, were there not so many people around her to witness such base behavior. "We gained nothing from that priest's antics. I ought to—"

"Ah," Huya interjected. "That is where you're wrong, my lady, if you'll pardon my saying so."

Tiy eyed him curiously.

"It seems Young Amunhotep made quite an oath, swearing on the body of the god himself."

"I know all about that," Tiy said. "What of it? It was a lie, clearly, and when I go down into my tomb, perhaps the only comfort I'll take with me into the Field of Reeds is the knowledge that Young Amunhotep damned his own *ka* by falsifying a sacred oath."

"He not only swore to his innocence, but also that he and the lady Tadukhepa were in love."

Tiy folded her arms tightly, examining this new piece of information from all angles as the procession bore her onward, toward the golden-yellow pylons of Ipet-Isut, which grew larger and more imposing with every step she took.

Clearly, Tiy reasoned, if Young Amunhotep would readily stake his soul on his innocence, then he was capable of lying about anything. This was no shock to Tiy. But why involve Tadukhepa in his oath? What good did it do him—which of Young Amunhotep's strange, inscrutable purposes was served by weaving the Hurrian girl into his careless vow? Tiy could think of no purpose—no connection, no conceivable rationale—except that Young Amunhotep's oath had freed the girl from captivity and absolved her of the crime. Spared her the ordeal of being questioned at the temple, even. *Why would he do such a thing?* Tiy wondered. *What did it matter to him, whether the girl was cut or branded with hot irons, or even held for another hour of interrogation?*

Her eyes widened, and Tiy turned to Huya with sudden comprehension. "He *does* love the Hurrian girl."

"So it seems."

Tiy shook her head. "I truly thought him incapable of loving anyone, save for himself."

"Whether he honestly loves her, or merely covets her for some reason only he knows, it seems the gods have provided the very thing we need."

"Yes."

Together, Tiy and her steward turned their heads to glance across the breadth of the wedding procession. Across the jostling, laughing crowd, beyond the brilliant blurs of the women's gowns, Lady Tadukhepa walked sedately, clad in a simple, old-fashioned gown of dark indigo blue. She wore no wig; the bronze waves of her hair were piled atop her head and kept in place with ornate ivory combs. Her pale face flickered in and out of the shade of ostrich-plume fans, while her maidservant, a Hurrian with a missing front tooth, chided the fan-slaves, ordering them to keep her mistress well shaded from the sun's brutal rays. Tadukhepa was an island of modesty and self-containment amid a sea of riotous color. But Tiy noted with satisfaction that the Hurrian showed no trace of her former shyness. Her hands were clasped primly at her waist as she walked, but she did not cast her gaze down to the dust of the road. She held her chin high, as Tiy had instructed her to do. She looked like a true King's Wife— intelligent, canny, and young and pretty enough to catch any ambitious man's heart.

Tiy nodded to her steward.

"I think she will do," Huya said.

"I hope she will," said Tiy. "She had better."

THE PROCESSION PAUSED in the forecourt of the Temple of Amun. As the litters were lowered and the king helped ponderously to his feet, the west-bank women milled, chattering gaily, their rich perfumes of myrrh, lotus, and galbanum mingling in a cloud so thick, Tiy felt she could practically see it. She peered through the crowd, past the dark fringes of wigs and women's narrow shoulders, which were protected from the sun's browning effects by thin, nearly transparent capes of loosely woven threads. Now and then a woman would toss her sun-cape lightly as she laughed with her friends, or one would go drifting up as a lady spun to call out to the slaves who bore food and drink—and the filmy veils obscured Tiy's view as they floated in the hot, mid-morning air. She watched her husband and daughter as if through the shrouds of a dream, each moment fragmented, separated from its place in time by the careless fluttering of the women's capes. Amunhotep staggered as he rose, and Sitamun, hampered by the weight of the double-plume crown on her head and the weight of the child in her body, took the Pharaoh's hand. The brief flash of Nefertiti's face was hard-angled and pale, and she stepped briskly from her litter to set one sandaled foot on the temple steps. Young Amunhotep grinned, lifting a lazy hand in a gesture of victory. Nefertiti's hips swung in slow motion as she climbed. Her gait was reluctant but steady, like a mourner climbing up to the cliff-top tombs. At the pinnacle of the broad stairway, as the Pharaoh continued on without her, Sitamun paused, turning back to look out at the procession. Save for her great, round middle, her body was small and thin, and the white of her gown stood out with poignant clarity against the black of the temple's mouth.

Tiy turned away. She took one last swallow of her herbal wine, then made her way through the press of the celebrants to Lady Tadukhepa's side.

The girl from Mitanni looked at Tiy with round-eyed surprise. "King's Great Wife," she said, and then flushed, recalling herself. "Oh," Tadukhepa stammered. "I meant to say—"

"It's quite all right," Tiy said, smiling and taking Tadukhepa's arm. "It is time I enjoyed my retirement—a well-earned rest, don't you think?"

Her voice was happy and light. This optimistic demeanor was clearly not what Tadukhepa expected; the girl pressed her lips together, her green eyes squinting down at Tiy in confusion.

"Tell me," Tiy said, tugging the girl toward the temple, "does it feel strange to you, to be here at the Temple of Amun so soon after your own wedding?"

"It is rather strange," Tadukhepa admitted. "It has not even been half a month since I arrived in Egypt, and yet it feels as if a lifetime has gone by. So much has happened since I came..." She trailed off, glancing at Tiy from the tail of her eye as they climbed the temple steps, arm in arm. "Lady Tiy," the girl said, "I am very sorry for your losses."

Now it was Tiy's turn to look at her companion in open startlement. Since finding Sitamun on the throne of the King's Great Wife, Tiy had spared little conscious thought for Thutmose—and less for Smenkhkare, whom she at least knew was still alive. When the Pharaoh stripped her of power, Tiy's reaction had been to survive—to salvage— to build something she could use out of the heap of rubble she was standing in. As quick as a blink, she had found herself without the luxury to mourn—and so she had not mourned. There were far more pressing matters at hand,

and Tiy knew it. Yet the sudden reminder of her losses—all of them, not only Thutmose and Smenkhkare—reared up before her like a cobra from the shadows. Despite her years of rigid self-control, Tiy dropped her eyes.

Tadukhepa gave a gentle, bell-like laugh. "No, no," she chided softly. "Hold your head high, like a true King's Wife. For you *are* still a King's Wife, after all."

"Yes," Tiy agreed, and squeezed the girl's elbow. "After all."

The wedding procession flowed into the dark of the temple, working its way past the storerooms and the small, curtained alcoves where priests received supplicants to the god. The air inside was dense with the odors of charred meat and the yeasty, earthy scent of beer left in shallow offering bowls. The celebrants grew quiet as they approached Amun's sanctuary, and clustered in reverent groups outside the two huge, gilded doors.

Nefertiti, her perfect face smooth and serene in spite of her troubled eyes, stood with her hands clasped below her waist, speaking to no one and declining to look at Young Amunhotep, as unmoved by his presence as if he were a circling gnat. She wore a splendid blue gown, a wisp of pleated, flowing linen that drifted from the tight, beaded band below her exposed breasts to trail like a river mist over her hips and down to the floor. Wide straps embroidered with gold accentuated her slender shoulders and framed the twin indentations of her collar bone. Her long, graceful neck was unadorned by any jewelry, as if she believed her own skin was splendid enough to dazzle the eye on its own—and indeed, the golden threads of her gown's embroidery did bring out the rich, copper-brown tone of her flawless complexion.

Or perhaps, Tiy thought, looking more critically at the drape of Nefertiti's skirt, *she refused to wear gems because she is in mourning.* The gown's shade was nearer green than blue—green, to honor the dead. The realization startled Tiy. She had always believed Nefertiti more concerned with status and politics than love, or even mere affection. She had assumed the girl was pleased to marry Thutmose because the match would one day win her a throne—not because she had felt any real warmth for Tiy's dead son. Thutmose himself had thought the same, Tiy knew.

But now, as she watched Nefertiti pluck absently at the pleats of her green-blue skirt, her stricken eyes turning away from her new bridegroom whenever he moved across her vision, Tiy realized that she had read her niece quite incorrectly. Perhaps, after all, it was not Nefertiti's ambition to claim the throne of the King's Great Wife. It was certainly her father's ambition—Ay's. Tiy wondered— if the matter had the matter been left to Nefertiti, would she forsake all the power and glory a royal marriage would bring her, and settle gladly into a quieter life? Surely no offspring of Ay's—no creature of his household—could be as innocent as that. But even if she was Ay's puppet, still she did not deserve to be bound in marriage to Young Amunhotep.

The poor girl, Tiy thought, her hand tightening on Tadukhepa's elbow. *I fear much sorrow lies ahead of her.*

But there was nothing Tiy could do to ease Nefertiti's burden. In fact, if she was to make good use of Tadukhepa, Tiy would be obliged to pile more bricks on Nefertiti's already-heavy load.

She tilted her head, whispering close to Tadukhepa's ear. "I fear this will be a loveless marriage, though it is ill done of me to say so, near to the god's sanctuary as we are."

"Loveless?" Tadukhepa asked. "But Nefertiti is so beautiful. Surely any man would love her."

"Nefertiti is very beautiful, that is true--but beauty alone doesn't make a man's heart beat faster. My son Amunhotep loves another woman." Tiy turned the full force of her intense, dark stare on Tadukhepa, raising her brows in a silent indication of significance.

Tadukhepa blinked rapidly; the light of the temple's many lamps flickered like a night-fire's sparks in her eyes. "Do you mean..."

"I do," Tiy whispered.

Tadukhepa said nothing more, but Tiy could feel how tense she was, the tight, nervous stiffness of her body.

"Do you love him, as well?" Tiy asked quietly. "I know my son cares very much for you."

Tadukhepa glanced around as if looking for a place to flee. She said under her breath, "Young Amunhotep told the priest of Amun... he swore on the god..."

"Pardon?" Tiy tilted her head again, as if she had not heard.

"Yes," Tadukhepa said, too loudly. Several heads turned to stare at her impropriety; Tadukhepa blushed and lowered her eyes. Then she whispered close to Tiy's ear, "Yes, of course. Of course I love the King's Son."

Tiy felt a moment of pity for Tadukhepa, too, as strong as the pang she'd felt for Nefertiti. The poor girl's discomfiture was obvious. Only days before, Tiy had cautioned her to be loyal to the king, yet how could any woman of reasonable wit tell a fond mother that she did not love her son? Tiy had trapped her, and unsettled the poor, delicate thing's heart. But she had no leeway for regrets.

"I am glad to hear it. No mother likes to imagine her son in a loveless marriage. When Young Amunhotep takes the throne—" *may the gods grant me the strength to stop that from ever occurring*— "he must take you as his wife, too. To cheer his heart, and be his true companion."

"I would like that," Tadukhepa said. "To be his companion—to be with him."

160

Tiy examined the girl's face, and saw, in the trembling of her lips and the downward cast of her green eyes, that this much was true. Tadukhepa was lonely. Very likely, she still had not found her feet in the harem palace and craved some other setting, where she might be an individual—valued and respected, not merely another face in an anonymous crowd.

"I am certain that he take you as a wife," she assured Tadukhepa. "But understand this, my dear: when he does, and even before that day, you will be in competition with Nefertiti."

The girl's smooth, pale brow furrowed in a frown. "You said that he loves me—and does not love Nefertiti."

So our little gift from Mitanni is sharp, beneath that fragile, fluttering exterior. Tiy was glad to note it. It was perhaps easier to work with a flighty or dull-witted girl, but Tiy appreciated clever companions—clever partners in her schemes—ever so much more. She watched as Tadukhepa's face turned toward Young Amunhotep, and saw a flash of wonder and longing sharpen the girl's soft gaze. Tadukhepa quickly suppressed the emotion, and turned her eyes coolly away. *Yes,* Tiy thought. *I can work well with this one. There is more to her than one might think.*

"Oh, the King's Son does love you best," Tiy said. "But Nefertiti—look at her. She is like the goddess Iset walking among us. It takes more than beauty to capture a man's heart, but nothing distracts a man from his true desires quite like a beautiful woman."

Tadukhepa glanced at Tiy with another pretty little frown. Tiy bit back an ironic laugh. Her words sounded foolish even to herself, but she knew if she maintained an air of easy wisdom, Tadukhepa would believe her. Even the cleverest young women were insecure at heart, and would believe what a wise mother-figure told them.

"You must be formidable," Tiy said. "You must show

the King's Son that you are more than merely pretty. You must be every inch a King's Wife—a Great Wife—in your stance, in your words, even in your stare."

Subtly, Tiy pulled on Tadukhepa's arm, tugging the girl up to her full height. In that moment, Nefertiti chanced to look their way, and something—perhaps the way Tiy clung to Tadukhepa's arm—made Nefertiti's dull, trapped-animal gaze linger on the Hurrian's face.

Tiy felt Tadukhepa begin to quail under Nefertiti's rather desolate look. "Don't look away," she breathed. "Stare her down."

Tadukhepa swallowed hard—Tiy could hear it in the quiet of the temple—but she held Nefertiti's eyes, and did not shift or tremble.

After a moment, Nefertiti faltered, and she frowned, dismissing Tadukhepa with a toss of her head. Tadukhepa exhaled in relief.

The sanctuary doors opened, groaning hollow and sad on their hinges. The Pharaoh was waiting inside, somewhere in the ring of chanting priestesses, to witness and approve of the royal marriage. Sitamun was in the darkness beside him—Tiy pictured her, hesitant and small, her hand on her belly, the double plumes of her crown tipping slightly to the side as she lingered in the darkness, unaware.

Nefertiti paused, staring into the dark of the sanctuary. For a moment she drew herself up and stood straight-backed at the threshold. Her fine, lovely face was hard and resolute, her black eyes sparking with sudden defiance.

Tiy's heart gave a leap—she felt sure that Nefertiti would refuse this marriage, here in front of everyone, before the court, the king, the god.

Do it, Tiy willed her niece. *Walk away. Go and be happy.*

But in the next heartbeat the bride stepped forward, the momentary resolution falling away. A veil of sorrow dropped across her eyes as she stepped inside the sanctuary, and the shadows reached out to consume her.

I will be one of those shadows, Tiy thought. *I will do what I must—break my niece's heart, ruin any hope she had for happiness, because I must. Because it is necessary.*

She watched the last whisper of Nefertiti's blue-green dress vanish into the dark.

Nefertiti

Year 36 of Amunhotep
Ruler of Waset,
Lord of Truth in the Sun,
Strong Bull Arising

NEFERTITI SAT IMMOBILE at the table of honor, just below the Pharaoh's great dais, looking out into the feast hall with regal calm. The hall was alive with merriment and laughter, though perhaps not as loud and reckless as it might have been, days before. After all, the Two Lands were still in mourning for Thutmose and little Smenkhkare. Too joyous a celebration would have been unseemly. As she watched the servants drift from table to table, offering platters of roasted meats, honey-glazed onions, and cubes of melon with mint, she was pleased to note that many of the guests wore green—some had even forgone most of their jewels, as she had—in honor of the dead King's Sons.

Thutmose. His name repeated in Nefertiti's heart, echoing with each hollow, painful beat. It should be Thutmose beside her tonight, his handsome face grinning at the dancers who twisted and gleamed in the spaces between tables as their oiled, gold-dusted bodies trailed veils of bright colors. It should have been Thutmose's hand reaching for the jar of wine, his laughter close to her ear, the warmth from his body raising a flush on her skin— rather than Young Amunhotep, whose voice, whose presence—whose very *existence* curdled her stomach and turned her blood to cold, sluggish water.

The dancers finished their performance, and a girl dressed in a flowing white gown appeared. She was accompanied by a harpist, an old, bent man whose gnarled fingers spoke of many years practicing his craft. The young singer bowed first to the dais where the Pharaoh sat with Sitamun on a small throne beside him, then to Nefertiti and Young Amunhotep at their table below. Nefertiti's new husband ignored the singer's graces and made some coarse jest to one of the passing courtiers. Their laughter struck a sharp pang in Nefertiti's heart. It seemed impossible, that anyone in the world could be so joyous when her *ka* had turned to ashes. And for the gods to allow Young Amunhotep to feel such happiness when he was the very cause of all the world's sorrows... it was a monstrous cruelty.

The harp began to play, its delicate, soft notes rising over the buzz of conversation, and a moment later, the girl in the white gown lifted her voice in song. It was a happy song, lilting and full of joy. At the sound of its simple gladness, Nefertiti wanted nothing more than to turn her face down toward her untouched bowl of antelope stew and weep. But she felt Ay's gaze from amid the crowd, his look sharp and assaying, and so she kept her posture erect, her face smooth, her eyes as unconcerned as she could manage.

Ah, my heart, the girl sang,

Hathor has filled it with joy

For my lover is beside me,

And ever shall be,

And I have hope of eternal love,

Of a hand to hold all my days.

Even in the life to come,

When hand in hand,

My lover and I

Shall walk in the Field of Reeds,

Love like a ring of sweet lotus

Shall ever garland our shoulders.

Young Amunhotep fidgeted with his supper and his wine cup. He had applied a liberal oil of myrrh and sandalwood to his skin, but Nefertiti could smell a sharp tang of sweat on his body, as if some restless excitement seeped from his every pore. She could guess, darkly, what he so anticipated. She recalled the night of the Hurrian's wedding feast, when he had spied upon Nefertiti and Thutmose in the garden—how he'd mocked her passion and taunted his elder brother. The thought of their wedding night to come seized her middle with a hard, clenching hand, and Nefertiti was obliged to breathe deeply to calm herself.

When at last the singer had finished her tribute and bowed her way out of the hall, Nefertiti exhaled in relief. The girl had been good—surely one of the best voices in all of Egypt. But at this moment, there was nothing Nefertiti wanted less to hear than songs of hope and love.

She glanced up at the dais, struggling to keep a frown away from her face. Had it truly been only ten days since she had sat there, at the pinnacle of those golden steps, with Thutmose alive and whole and laughing beside her? She'd had hope then, true enough—and more than hope. She'd had an unshakable certainty that she was where she belonged—that she was fortunate, destined for a life of joy, a life of beauty and pleasure as King's Great Wife to Thutmose. A bitter smile threatened to twist her mouth, and Nefertiti drank deeply of her wine to mask the slant of her lips. She would be King's Great Wife indeed, just as Ay had always wanted. But she would be tied forever to a madman—a murderer—the one who had destroyed the very love of her heart.

Recalling the singer's lyrics, Nefertiti thought viciously, *If love like a ring of lotuses ever garlands Young Amunhotep's neck, I shall take it in my fist and twist it until he strangles—just the way he killed my Thutmose.*

What a farce this feast was—this very marriage! What a gross injustice, that Young Amunhotep should be free to wed—should have for his wife the most beautiful woman in the Two Lands—when he had surely murdered his own brother. Nefertiti glanced again at the Pharaoh on his raised throne. The elder Amunhotep sat dull-eyed and slouched, his ample flesh sagging and slicked by sweat, his breaths heavy beneath the weight of his crown and his golden pectoral. Did the king know, Nefertiti wondered, that his second son had killed his heir? In his ill health, was the Pharaoh in any condition to comprehend the truth? Or was he content to believe what the priests had told him—that the killer had been apprehended, and would soon be put to death?

Nefertiti had heard the cries of the accused man as she'd left the Temple of Amun that very morning, her throat tight and her pulse pounding from the words of the ceremony she had just spoken in the dark of Amun's sanctuary. The distant, muffled wails of the man had only compounded her misery. Young Amunhotep had paused to listen to the cries, then had told her, smiling, all that he knew. It was a palace guard, he'd said. A man who was so taken with Nefertiti's beauty that he'd lost his wits and killed the King's Son out of pure, blind envy.

Of course, Nefertiti had thought. Neither the Temple of Amun nor the Pharaoh would have suffered the murder to go unsolved for much longer. It was too great an audacity— the King's Son and heir to the throne, struck down in the confines of the harem palace, on the grounds of the House of Rejoicing itself. A perpetrator was necessary, and so one was found. It sickened her—and doubly so, that her own beauty should be used as an excuse, that she should be a helpless prop in this despicable play-acting.

Young Amunhotep's calm recitation of the lie, punctuated

by the guard's faint whimpers and pleas for mercy, had raised the taste of bile in Nefertiti's throat. She had been torn by the desire to shove her new husband away from her, to scream her accusations there in the temple where everyone—court, priests, the god himself—could hear. But word had already filtered to her, that Young Amunhotep had sworn his innocence on an image of Amun. It raised just enough doubt in her heart that she kept her silence. What kind of man would glibly damn his own *ka* and *ba* with such a terrible oath? Was Young Amunhotep mad enough to cast his own soul into eternal darkness for the sake of the throne? Perhaps—although every last particle of her *ka* refused to believe it—perhaps Young Amunhotep might actually be innocent of the crime.

Young Amunhotep rose abruptly from his place at Nefertiti's side. "I find the air close," he said, extending his hand. "Would you care to stroll in the garden with me?"

Nefertiti glared at his palm, then, with an effort, straightened her face. "No, thank you," she said calmly. "I am quite enjoying the feast. I will remain."

She refused to look up at him. Instead she stared out into the crowd, leaning forward in feigned interest as a troupe of jugglers and illusionists came bounding into the hall to the accompaniment of timbrels and crashing gongs. Nefertiti watched intently as the jugglers' colored balls began to arc through the air, moving in ever-faster blurs between the performers' deft hands. At last, Young Amunhotep seemed to take her meaning. He turned from the table with a jerk of his shoulders and stalked out of the hall, into the deep blue shadows of the garden beyond the portico's umber-hued pillars. Sighing with relief, Nefertiti sat back and drained the last of her wine from her cup.

Almost at once, she heard a rustle of linen, a light and timid sound. She turned in surprise as a dark-clad figure approached. Nefertiti blinked. She had had plenty of wine tonight—how else might she be expected to cope with her misery?—and it took her several heartbeats to recognize Tadukhepa, the little Hurrian bride. She hadn't seen the new King's Wife since her own wedding feast. *How happy I was then*, she thought, feeling the threat of tears prickling behind her eyelids. Tadukhepa seemed a cruel reminder of all Nefertiti had lost, and so, although she knew it was unbecoming and ill-done, Nefertiti lashed out at her.

"Tadoo-Kiya. How nice to see you here."

"I would not miss your wedding feast, Lady. You were kind to me at my own. You sat beside me when I knew no one, and had no companions."

Nefertiti narrowed her eyes. Was the Hurrian mocking her? Despite the reassurances she'd given Mutbenret after the last feast, Nefertiti knew she had been far less than gracious to Tadukhepa. Either Tadukhepa was being subtly ironic, or the girl was dull-witted, and didn't know when she was being mocked. Tadukhepa's willingness to step into the range of Nefertiti's arrows was a welcome diversion, though—a distraction from her deep, suffocating misery. She knew that her behavior was unkind, and unworthy of a woman who would one day sit the throne of the King's Great Wife. But somehow, Nefertiti could not seem to stop herself from sticking her little barbs into Tadukhepa's skin.

"Have you companions now, Kiya?" Nefertiti asked lightly. She looked the King's Wife up and down, taking in the old-fashioned cut of her tunic-dress and its cheerless indigo hue. "Have you befriended any of the concubines or the harem ornaments? Perhaps they will teach you how to dance for the king's pleasure."

"Kiya," Tadukhepa said, meditative and prim. "It is a pretty name. If you wish to call me Kiya, I will not object."

Nefertiti stared at the woman in open shock. She said in Hurrian, "The word means 'monkey.'"

The King's Wife smiled. "I know. I am good with

languages, you see. I know Mitanni seems very far away to you—a different world entirely—but even in Mitanni, we have kings. And I am a King's Daughter. My father saw to it that I was well schooled in the Egyptian tongue, even before I came to the Two Lands to wed the Pharaoh."

"How nice for you." Nefertiti plucked up a cube of antelope meat from her supper bowl, just for the sake of some distraction from the Hurrian's placid, soft-eyed smile. The meat had gone cold. It tasted of grease and soggy onions.

"May I sit?" Tadukhepa asked.

"You are the King's Wife, not I," replied Nefertiti. When her senses caught up with the wine dizzying her head, she realized that she had been speaking with food in her mouth, and she flushed. But she refused to look toward Ay's table. *Let him see and disapprove. How can his disapproval harm me—or Mutbenret—now? My life cannot possibly be more terrible. Let Ay see and frown and make his schemes. They do not matter anymore. Nothing matters.*

"Monkeys are not so bad, after all," the Hurrian went on, sinking onto Young Amunhotep's vacated stool. Her long hair, the color of new-made bronze, was woven into an intricate braid and coiled around the back of her head. One lock had come free, and she absently tucked it behind her ear. "Monkeys are clever little things, and they chatter most warmly. There are worse things a woman can be called than Kiya."

"If you are so keen to be called a monkey, then I will not try to change your heart," Nefertiti said drily. Inwardly, she felt herself rather impressed with Kiya's unflappable grace—here was a King's Daughter indeed, sure of her place in the world and intimidated by nothing—utterly determined to be pleasant to Nefertiti, no matter what clods of mud were thrown her way. Nefertiti was not pleased with her own lashing-out, but she felt so carried

NEFERTITI

away by grief and fear that she couldn't resist.

"I don't wish any poor feelings between us." Kiya refilled Nefertiti's cup from the table's wine jar. The wine was dark and cool, its aroma rich and inviting. "We shall be together much in the future, and I would rather live with you in peace. Harmony is much better than discord. Do you not agree?"

Nefertiti sipped the wine. "What under the sun *can* you be talking about?"

"The King's Son, of course. He loves me, and intends to marry me, too, when he takes the throne."

Nefertiti burst out laughing. "Did he tell you that?" Then she recalled the way Kiya had looked at her that morning, as they'd waited outside Amun's sanctuary. No, Kiya had not merely *looked*—she had *stared*, challenging Nefertiti with those bright, green eyes. Ah—and Tiy, the displaced Great Wife, had clung to Kiya's arm like a flea in a cat's fur. "Did Young Amunhotep tell you," Nefertiti repeated, "or did his mother?" It would be like Tiy, to plant such an idea in this silly foreigner's heart. She was nearly as great a one for plotting as her brother, Ay.

Kiya blushed, a beguiling shade of pink. "The King's Son swore his love for me on the body of the god."

"Oh, ah," said Nefertiti, frowning into her cup. "I heard all about his oath. Very gallant, I'm sure, to spare you from the temple's questioners."

She peered at Kiya over the cup's rim, assessing her pretty, composed face, considering the *ka* that dwelt behind those green Hurrian eyes. She could not picture this foreign girl killing Thutmose—or any person, for that matter. Kiya was too much of a mouse. A regal, well-trained mouse, to be sure—but a mouse all the same. She couldn't even imagine Kiya as an accomplice in Thutmose's death. The girl seemed far too earnest and vulnerable, too *pure* to dissemble or scheme. Perhaps that part of Young

Amunhotep's oath had been true, if nothing else. Perhaps he did love Kiya.

She is welcome to him, Nefertiti said, giving a bitter little laugh through her nose. The expulsion of breath rippled the wine in her cup. She watched the ripples dance, shattering a faint white-and-gold blur reflected in the surface. When the ripples calmed again, Nefertiti realized she was looking at a dim reflection of Sitamun, seated on the throne of the King's Great Wife above her.

Uneasily, Nefertiti glanced over her shoulder, her head going rather dizzy at the movement. Sitamun was still and poised on her throne, straight-backed beside the sagging Pharaoh, but her face looked drawn and pale—and terribly sad. There had been no announcement of a marriage for Sitamun, no wedding feast for her—and yet there she sat, on the throne of the King's Great Wife, in the place that had once been Tiy's.

Nefertiti's eyes skated down to the swell of the girl's belly. Just who had planted that child? And Sitamun was so young...! Once the poor, framed guardsman was executed, the West Bank would forget the shock of Thutmose's death, and Sitamun and her child would be the next topic of speculation and rumor. Now that the girl was being paraded about so boldly, the court would certainly take heed, and wonder who might be the father of her child. Sitamun was a King's Daughter, and as such, there were few men who might have access to her at this tender age. One was her father. The other was her brother, Young Amunhotep. *My own husband*, Nefertiti thought in sick disbelief. She nearly asked herself whether Young Amunhotep was mad enough to lie with his sister before he held the divine office of king. Then she recalled that he had already murdered his own brother, and sworn away his soul—and the thought that he might balk at defiling his sister seemed far more amusing to her than any troupe of jugglers could be.

Nefertiti laughed loudly, sputtering over her wine. "You are most welcome to Young Amunhotep," she said to Kiya. "I wish you every happiness, if you can wring any at all from your promised union. It's certain I shall find no happiness in my marriage—you may have my helping of joy along with your own."

"But why do you think you'll get no joy from your husband?" Kiya asked.

Her eyes were wide beneath raised brows, an expression of such earnest concern that Nefertiti believed Kiya's surprise must be sincere. *She has no idea what Young Amunhotep is truly like,* Nefertiti realized through the thick, slow-moving fog of the wine. *If he truly does wed her, the poor, silly, soft-hearted fool will be blindsided.*

Kiya's presence felt suddenly threatening. Not because the Hurrian girl posed any danger, of course, but because her vulnerability felt far too poignant and awful for Nefertiti to bear. Never mind that she was a King's Wife and a King's Daughter—Kiya was nevertheless a tiny, inoffensive thing, too fine and frail for the House of Rejoicing. She truly believed that Young Amunhotep loved her—as if that man were capable of feeling love at all. Did Amunhotep know? Did he realize the sway he held over the Hurrian girl? The moment he recognized his power over this innocent's heart, he would break her like a dry twig snapping between his fingers—just for the pleasure of doing it. There would be nothing Kiya could do to save herself, once Amunhotep decided to take her heart as his plaything. The thought of it made Nefertiti feel panicked and sick—helpless, as she would ever be, from this moment on.

"Are you quite well?" Kiya asked, reaching for Nefertiti's hand. "You look so pale."

But Nefertiti calmly moved her hand away. She sampled from a small bowl of candied flower petals. She nibbled one, watching the jugglers in silence, hoping that if she ignored Kiya, the doomed little King's Wife would rise from her stool and drift away, out of Nefertiti's line of sight, out of her thoughts entirely. Then Nefertiti would no longer have any cause to dwell on the various ways this brittle creature might be shattered.

Through the mouth of the wide portico that opened onto the garden, a luminous, soft-yellow light caught Nefertiti's eye. She turned to stare at it, gazing blearily past the silhouetted pillars, out toward a patch of sky as dark-blue as Kiya's tunic. The light burned steadily, edging moment by moment past the pillars, lightening the night at its perimeter. At first, Nefertiti could not tell what the source of the light might be. A torch, perhaps? A watchman's fire along the top of the garden wall? Then she realized with a clutch of sudden fear that it was the moon. And it was setting. Soon the feast would be over, and she would be led to her chambers to meet Young Amunhotep alone, in the dark.

Will I be shattered, too? Now that he has me in his grasp, will Young Amunhotep break me as easily as he might break Kiya?

Nefertiti glanced again at her companion. Kiya had turned her gaze to the jugglers, and watched them with a focus Nefertiti had not noted on her face before, not even when the girl had stared at her in the temple. When she thought she was not being observed, the little King's Wife had a certain intensity—a thoughtfulness that was completely at odds with her previous air of wide-eyed vulnerability.

Perhaps she is not as weak as I'd imagined, Nefertiti thought. The possibility cheered her somewhat. *After all, she has survived marriage to that great lump of a Pharaoh for ten days, and she shows no signs of expiring yet.*

It was an encouraging thought. If Kiya could soldier through her wedding night, then surely Nefertiti could, as well. She turned to the Hurrian with a tremulous smile. "Kiya, what did you do on... on your first night?"

Kiya eyed her timidly, giving a small shake of her head. "My first night, Lady? I don't understand."

"With..." Nefertiti jerked her head toward the dais. The braids of her wig felt quite heavy. They seemed to swing much too slowly, and their beads clattered too loud in Nefertiti's ears.

Kiya's green eyes flicked up to the Pharaoh, then away again just as rapidly. Her face took on a pallor. "Oh. I... I haven't lain with the Pharaoh yet, Lady. He is... he is ill, you know."

Nefertiti frowned. "Yes. I know."

She felt Kiya's stare on her face, her body. She knew what the King's Wife was thinking. *Surely Nefertiti is no virgin. Surely she is not afraid of what a man has beneath his kilt.* If only she could explain—everything: her love for Thutmose, her suspicion of Young Amunhotep, the revulsion that wracked her with shudders at the thought of his hands on her flesh, his eyes on her naked, unprotected body— and her father's expectations, his cruel, iron-handed maneuvering—the way he had trapped her in sorrow and bitterness for the rest of her days, all for the sake of his own glory. The moon was setting fast, and when it did, that terrible trap would close around her. Soon she must begin the rest of her life, and oh, how she wished she could pour out her fears into a friendly, listening ear.

"I am a virgin still, myself," Kiya said apologetically, mistaking the queasy expression on Nefertiti's face, the tears that welled in her eyes against her well-trained will. "I dearly wish I had some advice to give you. But trust in the gods, and all will be well."

"Thank you," Nefertiti whispered. Beneath the table, she found Kiya's hand and squeezed it gently.

It was the final warmth Nefertiti would feel that night.

ALL TOO QUICKLY, MOONSET CAME. Nefertiti rose from the table, a picture of tranquility even though her heart raced with fear. Ay had trained her well, and she knew better than to allow her feelings to show on her face, in the set of tense shoulders or the stiffness of her gait. The palace maids who had been appointed to her service came forward to accompany her to the new, small apartments that would be hers in the House of Rejoicing until Young Amunhotep took the throne. She smiled pleasantly at the women, and even exchanged a few words with them as they gathered in a ring around her and led her from the feast hall. Cheers and well-wishes followed her as she left the hall behind and stepped into the cool, calm dimness of an interior corridor. Nefertiti smiled at the shouts from the feast hall, too. She smiled exactly as the occasion demanded, and no one, not even Ay with his keen, searching stare, could have seen in her carriage a hint of the terror that flooded her *ka*.

Young Amunhotep had not returned to the feast since she had sent him out into the garden alone. Where he might be lurking, Nefertiti could not say. As her maids swept her down the corridor, she hoped that he might have wandered to the Iteru's muddy bank, and been taken by a crocodile or a river-horse. A vain, childish wish, she knew. The gods would not be so good to her. They had allowed Young Amunhotep to commit his atrocity, after all—they clearly had no intention of punishing him, or denying him anything—not the Horus Throne, and not Nefertiti's body.

The ring of maids turned right, guiding her down a new corridor, past a great painted mural of white herons and ibis wading in a marsh. The sounds of the feast had faded away behind them, and this wing of the palace was quiet and still. It seemed many leagues away from any other person.

"Here it is," said one of the maids. She halted beside a rather plain door. Made of planked cedar and painted a simple, unadorned blue, it was much like the other doors that lined this corridor. *These must be apartments for visiting diplomats*, Nefertiti thought. She had one moment of relief, to know that even if Young Amunhotep would have access to her bed, at least she would not be required to live with him in the lavish apartments of the heir. She would have a refuge from her husband, even if it was small and rather unrefined.

The maid pushed the door open, and Nefertiti stepped inside. The chamber was dark, and smelled of river water. She could feel a faint draft stirring, brushing her bare arms with unseen fingers, raising the fine hairs of her skin. The women fanned out behind her. They lit a row of lamps that stood in tiny niches along one wall, and soon the dancing, bronze glow of many small flames illuminated the room. But despite the light's warmth, Nefertiti pulled her arms around her body, shielding herself against the chill.

The room was small indeed, though it was clean and airy, and somebody had seen to its appointments, furnishing the place with a wide, ebony-framed bed, two couches for entertaining, two ample closets, and a generous cosmetics table. The walls were adorned with bright garden scenes, flowers and vines growing in abundance, while here and there through the foliage peeked the face of a cat, or a gazelle with a ribbon tied around its long, slender neck. She could see the violet-dark entry to a tiled bath—small, too, no doubt, but at least it was private. A window on the chamber's far wall admitted a fresh breeze, which set the flames of the lamps to swaying.

"Will it do, Lady?" asked one of the maids.

"Yes," Nefertiti said, still hugging herself, distracted. "Yes, it will suffice."

"Then let us dress you. Your husband will come soon."

The maids worked quickly, removing Nefertiti's fine, blue-green gown and her ornate wig. They helped her into a robe of red, embroidered silk—easily removed again, Nefertiti noted, frowning down at the ties that secured it at her breasts and waist. The women spoke softly of the delights of marriage while they took the pins from her natural hair and unraveled its long, black braid. Nefertiti heard nothing of their words. She sat still and composed while they combed out her locks, anointing her hair with rose oil until it shone in the lamp light like the river under a moonlit sky.

Finally, the maid who seemed to be their leader inquired whether the new bride needed anything more. Mutely, Nefertiti shook her head, and the women dispersed. Alone in her new apartments, she settled on the edge of her bed, her breathing harsh and ragged, sobs gathering like a storm in her chest.

Do not weep, she told herself firmly. *You must keep your wits about you, if you're to make it through until morning.*

Her chamber door slid open. The hinges gave a slow, steady whine that sounded like the protests of some ensnared animal. Nefertiti watched the door, her jaw set resolutely, and stared into the rectangle of blackness that was the hallway beyond. For several moments, nothing stirred in that shadow. Then Young Amunhotep stepped through, intruding on the comforting glow of the lamps, his eyes wide with a fierce, avid turmoil that set Nefertiti's heart to racing. He carried something under one arm—a small, soft-woven basket—and as he stood staring at Nefertiti, licking his lips, he clutched the basket close to his body, as if she might try to take it away from him.

She willed herself to hold Amunhotep's gaze. She

would not show weakness by looking away. Nefertiti sat as immovable as the great statues in Ipet-Isut, towering, firm, self-possessed, with a face completely untouched by any concern. She waited for Amunhotep to speak, to move toward her—even to shift his weight—but he only remained, fixated on her like a leopard on its prey, staring, twitching, clinging to the basket as if it contained his *ka* and *ba*. His unnatural stillness struck an awed sort of wariness into her heart. It went beyond fear. It was the kind of stunned, disbelieving caution with which one might observe a previously unknown animal—large, powerful, and fanged, but like nothing else that existed within the reach of the sun's rays. As he continued to watch her in silence, Nefertiti's poise began to crumble. Against her will, her nostrils flared and her eyes widened; she let out one abrupt, shaking breath.

The display of fear, however slight, seemed to gratify Amunhotep. He smiled and closed the door, then advanced a few steps into the room. His confidence grew with every stride.

And he looks more predatory with each passing moment. All at once, for no reason she could discern, the image of Kiya flashed into her heart—the King's Wife staring keenly at the jugglers, her eyes flashing and bright when she thought she was not being observed. *What can Kiya see in this man? Why does she value his love?*

A strange distraction, but it gave her inspiration. Perhaps she could divert Amunhotep and spare herself from falling into his clutches.

"I would rather not lie with you," Nefertiti said calmly.

He stopped. Silence hung in the chamber, thick and foreboding.

"What?" said Amunhotep, incredulous.

"I would rather not. Because you love Kiya."

Amunhotep's brow furrowed; he looked at her with an air of genuine confusion.

"Tadukhepa," Nefertiti amended. "The King's Wife from Mitanni."

His shoulders relaxed, and he let out a little laugh—a hiss of breath between his teeth. "How do you know of my feelings for Lady Tadukhepa?"

Feelings, Nefertiti thought bitterly. *You are as incapable of feeling as a scorpion in the desert.* She said, "I know that you swore your love for her on Amun's body."

Amunhotep shrugged. He dropped the basket at his feet.

"Don't deny it," Nefertiti said. "You swore a sacred vow on Amun himself."

"Amun." Again, the King's Son exhaled his strange, breathy laugh. "This is what I think of Amun."

He bent and lifted the cover of his basket, and pulled out a long piece of white linen. He tossed the thing to Nefertiti. She did not know what it was, and found herself biting back a shriek of alarm as the fabric flew toward her. But she caught it and gingerly held it up, trying to make sense of this mystery. It was some kind of garment—simple and plain, lacking the pleats and stitching the court currently favored. Amunhotep reached into his basket again and produced a long, blue sash—the same kind of sash the priestesses wore in the Temple of Amun.

Nefertiti's hands went numb. She nearly dropped the white robe on the floor. "What is the meaning of this?"

"Put it on," Amunhotep said.

"I will not."

He took one fast, ferocious stride toward her, his presence suddenly filling and overwhelming the small chamber. Nefertiti flinched, and cursed herself for it. But she could has soon have ceased her own heart's beating as stopped herself from cringing.

"Put it on," he said, his voice grating and loud.

Trembling, Nefertiti stood. This wing of the palace was so far from the feast hall—and the celebration was no doubt growing wilder by the moment. No one would hear her if she screamed. Perhaps her maids would not even hear. She hadn't learned where they would be, whether they were even now within the range of hearing. With rising dread, she realized that she was completely at the mercy of Thutmose's killer. If she wanted to see the next sunrise, she must be meek and compliant, no matter how it galled her.

She fumbled at the ties of her red robe, blushing in mortification as it fell away, exposing her naked body to Amunhotep's eyes. But he did not seem to care—he shifted impatiently as she struggled with the priestess's smock, trying to right its tangled sleeves. At last she wrapped the thing around her prickling flesh, shielding her body within its flimsy armor. Amunhotep tossed her the blue sash; she wound it quickly around her waist and stood shivering before his eyes.

"Amun," he said harshly. "What does it matter, if I or any other man swears on Amun? The gods are nothing but lies."

Nefertiti gasped. "You cannot mean that!"

He slid toward her, his body tense with power. "There is only one god—one true force in the world. Creative force." Roughly, he seized her by the hips and pulled her body against his. She could feel his phallus, hard and straining beneath his kilt. Amunhotep crushed her against his body, and that hardness bit into her flesh, pressing insistently against her tender abdomen until she wanted to cry out in pain. "*This*," Amunhotep rasped in her ear, "is the only power—the only god. My father embodied the great power in his youth, but he has grown old. It is I who hold the power now—I who have inherited his godhood."

You have inherited his madness, Nefertiti said silently. *Madness, and nothing more.*

She tried to turn her face away, but Amunhotep kissed her, his tongue invading her mouth, his breath hot and frantic against her cheek.

"Do you want me to lie on the bed?" she asked meekly, praying he would soon spend his terrible energy and leave her in peace.

"No," he answered. "Stand there—just there, in the light, where I can see you—and do not move."

LATE THE FOLLOWING MORNING, Nefertiti ventured out of her new apartments, moving carefully in her softest-soled slippers, so that even here, in the all-but-deserted diplomats' wing, no one would hear her and come to her side. She still did not know where her cadre of new maids dwelt—it must be nearby, for they had arrived sometime after dawn to tidy her room and bring her breakfast, which was cold when she finally woke from a restless sleep—but she did not want the women crowding about her, fussing over her clothing and hair, making sly jokes about her nuptial night, or worse, asking her outright how she had fared. Nefertiti's heart was deeply troubled, her confidence shaken—and today the silly chatter of women might, she knew, be enough to break her.

She slipped out into the corridor, moving tensely along the wall with its bright-hued marsh scene, hands clasped at her waist and eyes darting. The diplomats' hall seemed entirely abandoned—a lonely and depressing place, despite its pretty colors and the peace depicted in its murals. Finally, though, she found a tiny portico—a flat, cedar roof held aloft by two slender pillars—and beyond it, warmed by inviting sunshine and rustling with a profusion of green vines, was a small, common garden. It was walled on all sides, and though it was obviously meant for the use of all who lodged within the diplomats' hall, to Nefertiti it was as good as a private sanctuary.

She sighed in relief as she stepped out into the sun, feeling the god's rays fall warm and reassuring on her face. She had been afraid, in the cold, black silence of the night—after Amunhotep had exhausted his strange lusts and left her alone at last—that the sun would never rise again. She had feared that the god was so offended that he would withhold his blessing forever, and that she was partly to blame.

The garden's serenity, the play of yellow light on foliage and bloom, seemed a divine comfort intended solely for Nefertiti's own troubled *ka*. She stood on a circular design of carved paving stones, bathed in light, and offered her palms up to the sky in gratitude, and in humble apology.

Amun, she prayed, *thou knowest that I did not wish... that I...* Her thoughts faltered, and she breathed deep, drawing in the gentle forgiveness of lotus perfume and herbs opening their leaves to the climbing sun. *Thou knowest that I truly took no part in last night's events... that it was not my desire, not my doing.* She hoped it was true, that the god saw her heart, and not merely the actions of her body—the things she had been made to do.

But if Amun had not forgiven her and she was to be punished, she would learn of it soon enough. For now, worn down by Amunhotep's games, the fears that had clutched her in the solitude afterward, and a long sleep which had brought no refreshment, it was enough to know that the sun had risen, that it still shone down on the Two Lands, and that her heart still beat within her chest. She sank onto a little bench beneath a mudbrick arbor, which was covered in purple-flowered vines. Her body ached with weariness.

She sat, absorbing the healing silence, allowing it to push away thoughts of Amunhotep. The rays of the morning replaced memories of his hands with a far gentler and warmer touch. When one strong beam of light worked its way past the tangled vines to land upon her belly, heating her skin through her green robe, Nefertiti placed a hand low on her stomach. If the gods had granted her any forgiveness at all—the smallest thread of grace—then Amunhotep's seed would take root. She would grow large, and he would avoid her bed. And if she bore a son—*Please, Mut, let it be a son!*—she would have fulfilled her duty to her husband's future throne, and she would never suffer his touch again. It was the best she could hope for, now.

Nefertiti heard low voices outside the garden's shaded entrance. She started, fearing that Amunhotep had come for her again, but relaxed when she recognized that the voices were female. A moment later, the sound of hesitant footsteps drifted around the corner. The sound was followed by Mutbenret, her narrow shoulders tense and gathered, her eyes darting cautiously around the garden.

Nefertiti sprang to her feet. "Sister!"

Mutbenret gasped, but her shock quickly turned to a grin. The sight of it sped Nefertiti's heart. They rushed into one another's arms, Mutbenret's braided sidelock swinging as she ran.

Nefertiti laughed with joy, holding her half-sister close and kissing her hair, again and again. "Oh, you can't know how glad I am to see you today."

"And I you."

"Did Father send you for a visit? No doubt he wants to know whether I am with child yet. He'll just have to be patient. It's too early even for me to know."

Mutbenret shook her head, beaming. "No—not father. Would you believe it? Auntie Sour-Face sent me. Permanently! I'm to stay here with you—live with you,

184

and tend you as your maid."

Nefertiti squealed and jumped, just like a carefree girl at a chariot race. "Oh! The gods are good, after all. It's the best news I've ever had."

"But you know, Father only agreed to it so I can act as his spy."

"I know. I wouldn't expect anything else from dear old Ay. But you're here—you're away from him. For now, that's all that matters. We'll work out how to keep you free from his clutches with time."

Mutbenret hugged her again, and Nefertiti could feel the girl's tears against her neck.

"Why would Tiy slip you into my service?" Nefertiti wondered aloud. "What does *she* stand to gain from it?"

"I don't know," Mutbenret said, pulling away and dabbing at her eyes. "She made no mention of any plan to me, on the way here. She only said, 'Your sister deserves some comfort. Gods know my son will be a trial to her.' So perhaps she only means to be kind to you."

Nefertiti raised one brow skeptically. It was not in Tiy's nature to be kind for the sake of kindness. She was Ay's sister, after all, and the two were cut from similar cloth. But never mind—Tiy's reason would make itself plain in due time, Nefertiti knew. For now, she had Mutbenret—she had happiness again.

"Holy Mother Mut," Nefertiti swore, "Amunhotep will certainly be a trial to me." She tried to keep her voice light and unconcerned, but it trembled a little, and Mutbenret looked at her sharply.

"What is it?" the girl asked. "Was he cruel to you last night?"

Nefertiti shook her head; her mouth fell open, but no words would form. How could she tell her sister what had happened? It seemed impossible—dreadfully profane. If she had not lived through it, Nefertiti would not believe it herself. She took Mutbenret's hand and led her to the bench.

"Was he cruel to me?" Nefertiti repeated, her voice choked and bitter. "He was worse than cruel. You must be brave, Mutbenret. I must tell you everything, for if you are to be my maid, you will see... *certain things* in the months and years to come. But you must never speak of this to anyone—not even to Father. Especially not to Father. The gods only know what he would do with this information. Nothing you or I would like, though—we can be sure of that."

Nefertiti spilled out her sordid tale, and moment by moment, Mutbenret's face blanched paler. She spoke in hushed tones, relating Amunhotep's strange arousal at sight of her fear, and then how he had made her stand in a posture of worship, as if she were a priestess in the Temple of Amun, while he defiled the pure white robe. He had spilled his seed upon it, then spat on it, his face twisted with such terrible loathing that Nefertiti had feared he might strike her. And then he had torn the garment from her body and trodden on it, more intent on grinding it beneath his heel than he was on Nefertiti's nakedness. She spoke of the way she had left herself, allowing her *ba* to flee the chamber when Amunhotep finally turned to her and threw her across the bed, so that she could not feel what he did to her body as he rutted and panted between her thighs. And she told of how she'd laid stiffly awake beside him, listening to Amunhotep's breathing in the stillness of her chamber, hating him more with every beat of her heart. When he finally woke from his doze and left her, sparing her neither word nor glance but only stopping to collect the soiled priestess's robe, Nefertiti had wept as she prayed, begging the gods to forgive her for the blasphemy she had done.

"It's terrible," Mutbenret whispered. "What can he be

thinking?"

Nefertiti remembered the way he had pressed his hardness painfully against her body, and her gut roiled with revulsion. "He thinks he is a god—that he is the very force of creation himself."

"But how? How can any man believe such a sacrilege?"

"I don't know," Nefertiti said. "It's clear that he's mad— yet the gods have positioned him here, and made him the last son left to the king. He is poised to claim the title of heir—and someday, he'll have the throne, too. He'll have all of the Two Lands. I don't know how the gods can countenance it."

Mutbenret shuddered. "I'm almost more afraid to be *here* than I was back at home, with Father."

"No." Nefertiti held her close again, clutching the small body against her heart, holding Mutbenret there with all her strength. "We are better off now, Mutbenret—both of us. I am clever and strong enough to survive my husband. Our father made certain of that—that I'd be clever and strong. Here, at least, we are both out from under Ay's thumb. And that's worth something, don't you think?"

Mutbenret nodded, though she looked unconvinced.

"You'll see. I'll find a way to turn our situation to our advantage."

The girl smiled timidly. "Now you sound like Father."

"Ah, but I will make this into an advantage—for us—just for you and me. Ay has no idea how well he trained me. We'll come out better in the end, Mutbenret. Trust me."

"I do trust you." She tucked herself under Nefertiti's arm, leaning her head against her shoulder.

Nefertiti kissed her sister's hair, but tears stung her eyes. Her once-perfect life had fallen into a tangle. But she was determined to unravel the knot—to find a way to make her new position in the House of Rejoicing, and even Young Amunhotep himself, a blessing instead of a curse.

She just didn't see how it could be done—yet.

Kiya

Year 36 of Amunhotep
Ruler of Waset,
Lord of Truth in the Sun,
Strong Bull Arising

THE MORNING AFTER the wedding feast dawned warm and bright, spilling an invigorating golden light into Tadukhepa's chamber. She sat before her tall, narrow stand-mirror, tying off the end of her braid with a leather lace that matched the color of her hair exactly while Nann bustled about the room, plumping cushions on the small eating-couch and muttering over the lateness of her mistress's breakfast. Outside, the garden clamored with bird song, and Tadukhepa could already hear the splashing of women in the lake as they took their morning exercise now, before the day grew unbearably hot.

"It was a fine feast," Tadukhepa said.

Nann clicked her tongue. "These Egyptians never do anything but feast."

"There are worse ways to spend one's time. Come and help me pin up my braid."

Nann lifted the heavy braid with care, arranging it in a coil around Tadukhepa's head. She reached for the hair pins in their little ivory box, but when she caught Tadukhepa's gaze in the mirror, she paused at the glint in her mistress's eye. The servant girl raised her brows in a silent question.

"I won't be stuck here in the House of Women forever,"

Tadukhepa said. "We'll get out, you and I."

Nann selected a hair pin and examined it. She said with exaggerated casualness, "I hope you don't intend to run away. We may have been wrong about the Pharaoh using geldings to guard his women, but I am certain the stories we heard in Mitanni *weren't* wrong, about women being put to death if they attempted to escape from captivity."

Tadukhepa waved a hand. "No, no—nothing like that. Honestly, Nann, I am not a fool. How would you like to attend a feast every day—to be in the center of it all, with dance and song and entertainment whenever you wanted it?"

Nann jabbed the hair pin into place, then pulled another from the box. She would not meet Tadukhepa's eyes in the mirror. "Mistress, if you think the king throws a feast every day, then I would advise you to consult a physician. You may be suffering from delusions."

"All right, not *every day*. I exaggerated. I know the king doesn't live so lavishly all the time. But wouldn't it be grand to live in the heart of the palace, among the busy stewards and the courtiers in their lovely clothes? To hear all the news of the country first-hand? Maybe even to speak to dignitaries from Mitanni, and learn how things fare back home... instead of being stuffed away here in our rooms, like some old tunic in the back of a closet?"

"It makes no matter to me," Nann said wisely. "I will still be your servant, whether we live in the House of Women or elsewhere." She fixed the last hair pin in the coils of Tadukhepa's braid, then looked down at her mistress with hands on hips. "Just how do you think you might get into the palace proper, anyhow? What put this idea into your mind?"

"Lady Tiy."

"Ah." Nann turned away, shrugging her thin, sunburned shoulders. "I should have known. I saw you and Lady Tiy together at the temple, speaking so intimately, and both of you looking so serious. But it's not my place to pry, so..."

She trailed off, leaving the temptation to gossip dangling like bait in a fisherman's net. Tadukhepa pressed her lips together. She knew it was unfitting to pour out her secrets to a servant, even if Nann was her dearest—and only—friend. But she trusted the girl completely, and the thrilling promise of the future bubbled inside her, until she felt she must blurt it out or burst from the pressure, like an overfilled wine skin.

"Young Amunhotep loves me," she said in one great rush. She finished the confession with a giggle. It made her sound so young and giddy that she blushed in embarrassment, but the tickling, bubbling sensation only grew inside her, warming her from within with a sweet, pulsing glow. It felt so good that Tadukhepa was dismayed to see horror on Nann's face when she whirled to stare at her mistress. "Oh, say something!" Tadukhepa pleaded. "Don't look at me like I've grown a second head!"

But Nann only sighed and ran a hand down her face, from forehead to chin.

"It's true," Tadukhepa said defensively. "Lady Tiy told me so, and you know he swore it on his god."

"Mistress, sometimes you can be exasperatingly naïve."

Tadukhepa glowered at Nann as the servant girl returned to fussing with the couch cushions. "I'm not as naïve as you think," she said sharply. "Just because I'm pleased about this development, that doesn't mean I'm an innocent or a fool. I spoke to Nefertiti last night at the feast."

Grudgingly interested, Nann raised a single brow.

"She isn't pleased with her marriage to Young Amunhotep. No, not in the least."

"I can't think of a single woman who *should* be pleased to marry that staring garden-creeper."

"He's not as bad as you think." Tadukhepa rose from her stool and shook the rumpled hem of her robe. It was as yellow as the sunshine pooling on the floor, and it floated merrily around her ankles as she moved. "He did save me from the questioner, after all."

"For purposes of his own."

"Tiy has made me see the way it is—the power I hold."

"Power?" Nann stared at Tadukhepa in open astonishment now, all of her dry irony burned away. "Now I truly will call a physician. Mistress, you hold no power here in Egypt, and it is far better for you if you remember that."

"That is where you're wrong. Nefertiti and Amunhotep have no love for one another. There will be no joy in their marriage."

"Do you think a king's heir requires joy?"

"No, but he *wants* joy. Young Amunhotep is a man like any other."

Nann snorted. "I have my doubts on that count."

But Tadukhepa ignored her words. "Whoever can give him happiness, and a respite from the troubles of court, will hold influence over the heir. And one day, the heir will be the king. Nefertiti will never give him happiness, or even simple peace. She will not hold him as I will hold him."

Nann looked up from the pillows, her face and hands going very still. Tadukhepa beamed at her servant, recognizing in the girl's silent, considering stare a reluctant agreement.

"Did Tiy tell you this?" Nann said at last.

"Not exactly. Tiy made me see that Amunhotep loves me, but after I spoke with Nefertiti last night, I saw the rest for myself. I can place myself in a position to win and hold Young Amunhotep's heart. And once I have it, freedom and happiness are mine for the asking—*ours*, Nann."

Nann tapped her lips with one finger, assessing Tadukhepa thoughtfully.

"You see?" Tadukhepa said. "I am not the innocent fool you think."

"Perhaps not, after all." Nann smiled, exposing the black gap of her missing tooth. "I thought you were letting your emotions carry you away, like some silly shepherd girl flirting at the well—and there I misjudged you. But you are so new to men, Mistress. You have dealt with them very little. If you're to keep this advantage and use it to your benefit, you mustn't make yourself freely available to Young Amunhotep. You must hold yourself just out of his reach—always tempting, but never satisfying... if you take my meaning."

"I suppose I do take your meaning." She felt her cheeks flush again, and though she tried to keep her mind firmly on her goal—freedom of the palace, and all the variety and excitement to be had outside the walls of the harem— Tadukhepa couldn't help but think, *He loves me!* Knowing that she, alone among all women, was of real value to the Pharaoh's heir—outshining even the beautiful Nefertiti in his esteem—filled her with warm, dizzy victory.

A tap sounded on the door frame.

"That will be your breakfast," Nann said, sweeping past the couch to answer the knock. "And not a moment too soon."

But when she opened the door, Nann gave a squeak of surprise, and dropped into a low, hasty bow.

Tadukhepa blushed as Young Amunhotep stepped past Nann. He sauntered into the room as if it were his own, then stood watching Tadukhepa in silence. He looked tired—his eyes were red-rimmed and somewhat dull—

and his body trembled faintly, with exhaustion or with excitement, Tadukhepa could not say.

"Leave us," she said to Nann.

"But, Mistress—"

"Go."

Nann held Tadukhepa's gaze for a long pause, and her eyes openly pleaded for caution. But Tadukhepa felt instinctively that there was nothing to fear. She knew she held power over this man. It was true that she was new to men, and new to power, but she recalled Lady Tiy holding tight to her elbow. She seemed to feel the little woman close beside her even now. She felt, too, a certain reassurance of her own canniness and innate ability as a King's Daughter pulsing through her veins—a solid warmth. It would be a simple thing, to handle Amunhotep, Tadukhepa told herself. She would do whatever Lady Tiy would do.

She nodded coolly to Nann. As the girl edged around the door, preparing to close it, she mouthed silently to Tadukhepa, *Tempting, never satisfying*, and Tadukhepa gave her an amused little smile.

The door shut behind Nann with a soft click.

"It is good to see you, my lord," Tadukhepa said at once. "I would offer you food and drink, but it seems my maids are lax in their duties today."

"I made them wait to bring your breakfast," Amunhotep said. His voice was harsher than usual, as if he'd spent the night panting, or shouting—and a curious, vibrating energy filled him, widening his eyes and tensing the muscles of his neck and shoulders with an agitation that seemed almost like despair.

"Why would you do that?" she asked him. "And whatever is the matter with you? You look upset."

He laughed. "I am not upset—no, far from it. How can I be upset in your presence? You are like the sun's blessed warmth to me."

Tadukhepa lowered her chin by a finger's breadth, softening her aspect to encourage his praise.

"And as for why I sent your maids away... it was so you and I might be alone together."

"You've already tired of Nefertiti?" she asked. "So soon?"

Something in his wide smile struck a chill deep in the pit of Tadukhepa's stomach. Perhaps she should have been wary, after all, and kept Nann close. But she knew that Tiy wouldn't allow any misgiving to show on her face, so she ruthlessly drove her caution away.

"Tired of Nefertiti?" Amunhotep said. "Oh, no. She will do fine as a wife—just fine. But lying with her has only inflamed me, Tadukhepa. I returned to my bed and whenever I closed my eyes, all I could see was you—your face, your tender ways, darting and soft, like a bird in the garden."

He took a step toward her, and Tadukhepa quivered, caught between excitement at her prospects and anxiety over Amunhotep's strange, wild-eyed stare. She turned her face to the side, halting him in place with a cold, Tiy-like glance from the corner of her eye.

"When I saw you in the garden," he said, "sitting alone with only your servant-woman close by—you remember; that day when you spoke to Thutmose—I thought, 'She is such a fragile thing, delicate and small, and meek, and forlord.' And then when I saw you suffering at the hands of Amun's questioner..."

A shudder wracked his frame, and his eyes slid heavily closed. Tadukhepa could not say whether it was his very evident tiredness that affected him so, or whether some darker current moved within him, deep at the center of his being. The icy touch of an unseen hand seemed to fall upon her shoulder, holding her back, urging her to caution. She wondered whether it was Tiy's touch she imagined.

"And so you thought to keep me from my breakfast—why?" she asked flippantly, even as the cold hand squeezed her tighter.

"I had to see you," he said. "As I lay with Nefertiti, I thought about you—your gentle nature, your fear in the questioner's room..."

Make yourself delicate and gentle now, Tiy's voice whispered in her ear. *If you want to rule him as Nefertiti cannot, tempt him—but do not satisfy.*

Tadukhepa let one hand flutter at her throat. She looked away shyly, tucking her chin, wilting a little, allowing her shoulders sag in a display of girlish shame. And Young Amunhotep gave a hoarse groan of longing.

He surged toward her, his arms encircling her body before she could protest. She gave a gasp of fear—not feigned, for his darting energy caught her completely off-guard—and the sound of her ragged breath only seemed to encourage his lust. He kissed her, just as he had on the day he'd saved her from Amun's questioner. His tongue flicked over hers, tracing the shape of the inside of her mouth. Heat like the unshaded sun flared within her, pounding along her limbs as her pulse raced, throbbing in the place between her legs. She wanted to go limp in his arms, to surrender to his protective power and his compelling, gratifying lust. She wanted to give herself to him entirely—but more than even that, she wanted her own power. So she summoned up the image of Tiy in the temple, and felt once more the woman's hard finger pressing beneath her chin. She heard Tiy's voice in her ear, whispering over the sound of her own panting. *You are a King's Wife. Be one.*

Tadukhepa placed her hands on Amunhotep's shoulders and pushed him firmly away. Her knees shook violently;

she wanted to collapse on her silk couch and pull him down on top of her, but she made herself stand firm. *I must give him no satisfaction. Not yet. Not until I have satisfaction of my own.*

"You cannot have me," she told him levelly. "Not yet."

Amunhotep's brow furrowed, and a ripple of darkness passed over his dry, red eyes. "What do you mean?"

"I am a King's Wife, my lord. I am not a low concubine."

He took her by the back of the neck—not roughly, but with a touch so gentle the heat leaped up twice as hot inside her. "That doesn't matter. It's not how we do things in Egypt—at least, not on the West Bank."

Tadukhepa shrugged off his hand. "I don't care how you do things in Egypt, King's Son. I am not from Egypt, and my goddess, Ishtar, demands a certain chastity from her daughters."

His chuckle was cold and deep. "Chastity."

She threw up her head, showing her full offense. "My *chastity* demands that I lie only with my husband. My goddess demands it."

"It must be a lonely kind of worship," he said, reaching for her again—but she stepped away from him, and Amunhotep frowned. "I know that old heap, that old sack of sweat and dung, hasn't touched you. Pharaoh, indeed. Your husband—*hah!* Wouldn't you rather lie with a real man than with him?"

She cast her gaze down again, bending her neck, giving him a full display of her obedient softness. "It is not for me to say who is a real man and who is not."

"I can show you. I can show you far better than *he* can, believe me. The gods know he won't be around much longer, anyway. Anupu is coming for him—coming to call him to the Duat."

"Now that is a real shame," Tadukhepa said. She broke away from him, sweeping to her garden window, gazing out into the flower beds pensively. "I have grown used to the privilege of being a King's Wife."

"Already?" His laughter sounded amused now, rid of the dangerous edge his voice had held only moments before. Tadukhepa gave a soft exhalation of relief. She wasn't aware, until that very moment, of how much his intensity frightened her.

"Yes," she said calmly. "Quite. And when your father dies, I will be nothing—a cast-off. But you will be the Pharaoh."

"And then you won't be able to refuse me." His words were playful and jesting, not threatening—but still, Tadukhepa's stomach tightened.

"When you are king, you will have the power to raise me up from nothing to a King's Wife once more." She turned to him, holding his dark eyes with a steady, unblinking gaze.

"I told you once that I would," Amunhotep said. "I said I would marry you, and make you a King's Wife alongside Nefertiti. You recall, don't you?"

"I do."

"My heart has not changed. So come to me, and relieve me of this ache. Do me a kindness, my sweet, gentle Kiya."

She smiled, unoffended. "Nefertiti's name for me?"

"Why not? You are a pet, splendid and rare and pleasing." He moved close, standing so near that she could feel the heat of his body through the fabric of her yellow robe, though he made no move to touch her. "And my pet," he whispered, his breath tickling her ear, "one day I will have you on a string, as helpless as a monkey perching on an old, fat noblewoman's shoulder."

She couldn't stop the nervous giggle bursting from her

throat.

"You laugh," Amunhotep said. Gently, slowly, he took her by the wrist and guided her hand toward his groin. "But, my little monkey, I swear that I will tame you, and one day I will make you beg for fruit."

Tadukhepa gasped when he placed her hand on the stiff thing beneath his kilt. Her face flamed, and her immediate instinct was to jerk her hand away, perhaps to slap him—to scream for Nann, for any woman who might be passing by her closed door. But Tiy's cold hand tightened on her shoulder, and Tadukhepa's hand closed on what it held, just as snugly.

Amunhotep's face went from arrogant to blissful, and then, as her grip tightened still more, surprise and pain flashed in his eyes.

"Your little monkey won't wear her string until she is King's Wife to the new Pharaoh." She whispered the words close beside his ear, as he had done to her.

She released her hold, and Amunhotep stepped back, gasping—with fear or with delight, Tadukhepa could not tell. She drew herself up, and felt the invisible presence of Tiy nod its wry approval from where it clung to her elbow.

"On your way out," she said to Amunhotep, "be so good as to send my maids with my breakfast. I am famished."

A slow, appreciative smile spread across his face. He gave her a brief, shallow bow—an appropriate courtesy from a King's Son to a King's Wife—and let himself out of her chamber, chuckling.

When Nann came stumbling back through the door, clutching at the neckline of her robe in obvious anxiety, Tadukhepa squealed and clapped her hands, then rushed to Nann and spun her around and around, until both of them collapsed, dizzy and laughing, on the couch. Tadukhepa felt as giddy as a shepherd girl at a well.

Tiy

Year 36 of Amunhotep
Ruler of Waset,
Lord of Truth in the Sun,
Strong Bull Arising

TIY WAITED IN THE SHADE of the estate's outer gate while Huya conversed in quiet tones with the gate-guard. The violent heat of mid-day had not yet arrived, and the morning's birds were still active, darting in and out of the thick vines that covered Ay's garden wall, seeking to fill their tiny bellies with ants and flies before the glaring noon sun forced them into the refuge of shade and stillness. The birds' chirruping made a constant din. Others may have found the sounds cheerful, or even soothing. But the high, incessant *chip-chip-chip* of their voices, and the rapid fluttering of their wings among the vines close at hand, only served to irritate Tiy. She strained to hear what Huya and the gate-guard said, but could catch nothing more than the words "former Great Wife." Tiy frowned.

In a few moments, though, the guard issued an order to his men, and Ay's double gate swung open. Tiy breezed past Huya and her brother's guardsmen—since Thutmose's murder, a full complement of house guards had become quite fashionable on the West Bank—and proceeded down the garden path with her steward double-stepping to catch up.

Ay's garden was flawless, as always, and laid out with a symmetry so severe and old-fashioned that even Tiy, usually a great traditionalist, found it off-putting and cold. Pin-straight paths delineated the edges of identical flower beds with fanatical precision. The paths were footed with crushed white limestone—purely, perfectly white, without a single brown or gray pebble to be found. The limestone caught the glare of the sun as it made its way toward the zenith, throwing up light so strongly from the ground that the edges of Tiy's vision glowed with reaching fingers of ethereal purple. She squinted against the glare as she walked, watching a figure bob and bend amid one of the flower beds. It was Lady Teya. She hummed as she cut lilies and placed them in a basket between her feet. Her softly aging face was fixed with the same unnerving, distantly joyous smile she always wore, beaming at nothing with her habitual vacancy. Tiy passed right before the woman's line of sight, and Teya did not blink, did not call out any greeting. She only went on about her work, caressing the lilies' golden petals without seeing the blooms at all, her voice rising and falling like the mindless singing of the birds.

Tiy stepped beneath the shade of the portico and brushed off the attentions of Ay's servants. The cool beer and fruit they offered might have been tempting on another day, when her throat was not so tight with anxiety that she could barely swallow—so fiercely constricted by the helpless, useless anger of watching from an impotent distance as years of careful, intricate work unraveled like a poorly woven rug.

"Where is your master?" she said to the servants, and when one of them pointed toward Ay's reading room, she made for the door before Huya or anyone else could tap to seek Ay's permission to enter.

Tiy pushed the heavy door open and sailed directly in. The dusty odor of old papyrus and fired clay tablets surrounded her, undercut by the earthy, toasted-barley scent coming from the bowl of cold beer resting on Ay's long, heavy reading table. The bowl stood at a precise distance from two perfectly aligned stacks of papyrus sheets. With one quick glance, Tiy could see that the uppermost sheet of each stack was turned face-down, so that not even the household servants, going about their mundane duties, might catch wind of the message it carried. Even when he was alone, Ay was always planning, always cautious, always thinking ahead.

Ay, seated behind his table with head bowed over a tablet, held up a single, peremptory finger without looking up. The blunt-trimmed edge of his thick wig swung before his eyes, obscuring his view, so he surely could not have seen that it was Tiy who had entered his study, and not some dull-witted menial.

"What a rude gesture," Tiy said.

"It would have been rude, perhaps," said Ay with languid unconcern, "if I'd done it to the King's Great Wife." He still had not looked her way, but went on with his reading.

Tiy puckered her lips, withholding further comment on his manners. When Ay was annoyed, he could be counted upon for such casual needling. He took every unforeseen shift in the sands of politics as a personal affront, and he felt entitled to make these serene little jabs at anyone who offended him. The snide remark did not ruffle Tiy— indeed, she had expected it, for she knew that Ay must be at least as vexed as Tiy was herself, to have lost her close, reliable access to the throne.

"We need to speak," Tiy said. "Urgently. Put that scroll away. It's not as important as what I've got to say, I promise you. I assume you *will* deign to speak to a fallen King's Wife?"

Ay sighed and turned the sheaf of papyrus face-down on one of his stacks. He leaned against the high, carved back of his chair. When he looked up at Tiy, a long-dead memory revived and passed through her with a chill as biting as a northern wind. Ay's face—flat cheekbones; shallow-set, hard black eyes; thin skin that clung like wet linen to every contour of muscle and bone—was so like their father's face. Old Yuya, sighing and staring with those eyes that spoke so clearly of disappointment, and of no surprise at being disappointed by Tiy yet again. And behind the uncaring, serpent-like cool of his gaze, the subtle flicker of promise—of a lesson that must be learned, and a hard and painful schooling to come.

There was a time in Tiy's life when she would have feared Ay's stare—Yuya's stare. That time was long past. In spite of all his lofty, dangerous ambitions, and not for lack of trying, Yuya had never risen above the station of Overseer of All the Horses. Neither had Ay, who was well into his middle years now, and fast approaching old age. But Tiy—well, the river had risen and receded thirty-six times while she ruled as King's Great Wife, and even now, demoted to a dim corner of the harem, she stood higher than Ay could ever hope to climb. She lifted her chin and stared her brother *and* her father down.

"What is to be done about Young Amunhotep?" she demanded.

Ay lifted his bowl of beer and sipped, long and slow. When he set the thing down, he said lightly, "He is your son. Is he truly so far beyond your control?"

"He is beyond anyone's control. He sucked the pap of his father's religious delusions eagerly as a child, but now that he is grown—now that he sees the imminence of the Pharaoh's death—he gobbles up that madness more greedily than ever, with both hands, like some bloated courtier at a feast. If I'd remained beside the throne, I might have had some hope of slipping a bit into his mouth and drawing the rein, as I did to his father long ago, but relegated to the harem as I am—"

"Ah," said Ay. "Now that she is fallen, proud Tiy is obliged to come creeping to her big brother for help."

Tiy advanced on him, bracing her hands on his table, leaning across its breadth to stare fearlessly into his eyes. "Don't think to spite me, you envious scorpion, you bottom-feeder from the river's muck. And don't speak to me of *falling*, of rank. It was you who maneuvered me into the court when I was hardly more than a child—you who placed me before Amunhotep's eye—"

"It was Father who wished it," Ay interjected smoothly. "It was Yuya who thought of making you King's Great Wife."

"But it was *you* who enacted the scheme, and you who tried to rule me. Don't be bitter, Ay. I did everything you and Father wished me to do. You have no cause for complaint. You should be proud of all I've achieved. I did my task so well that I slipped beyond your reach. It's unbecoming, for a brother to resent his sister's great success."

Ay lifted his brows in amusement, tenting his fingers below his chin. But he did not mock her again. He waited for Tiy to speak on.

"Relegated to the harem as I am," Tiy repeated, straightening her spine and watching her brother with regal calm, "my resources are limited in the extreme. I am working to influence Sitamun, but she has always been a timid, fearful child, and I doubt whether she'll give me leverage over the Pharaoh. It is the king we must worry about now. If we can convince him to name any man other than Young Amunhotep as the heir—"

A coarse laugh burst from Ay's throat. "You must be mad! After I've just put my daughter in his bed? No, I'll see Nefertiti on the throne of the King's Great Wife. I've worked too hard to suffer any other outcome."

"Divorce is a simple matter," said Tiy. "And if you will agree to it, I'll see that Nefertiti is wed to whichever man the Pharaoh names heir in Young Amunhotep's place."

"*You'll* see to it? Relegated to the harem, with your resources limited in the extreme? I think not, Tiy. Nefertiti will stay where she is."

Tiy scowled at him as he sipped again from his bowl. "I know what you're thinking, Ay—that through your daughter, you'll enjoy the same tight hold over the Horus Throne that I once had. But I tell you, it's not as simple as that. Young Amunhotep is far more complicated and strange than his father ever was. And Nefertiti does not love him."

"That is no trouble to me. Nefertiti was raised to serve this family; she will do as I tell her. Whether she loves her husband or hates him is immaterial."

Tiy's wry smile made her brother blink and the corners of his mouth twitch—as much an expression of surprise as Ay ever showed. "Is that what you think?" she said. "That Nefertiti's feelings for my son will make no difference in your schemes? What a fool you are, Ay. Even if your plans succeed, and Nefertiti ascends to the throne as King's Great Wife, she will be useless to you if the man who sits the Horus Throne is Young Amunhotep. A woman who hates and fears the king will never grow close to his heart. Nefertiti loathes him, and so she will give you no purchase on my son. You'll have more luck clinging to a slickrock cliff in a high wind than you will with Nefertiti in Young Amunhotep's bed."

"Unnatural, for a mother to speak so ill of her son."

"By all means, attack my femininity if it makes you feel better. I promise your assault on my character will wound me terribly, and I shall weep as many tears as you'd like— *later*, Ay, when this crisis is averted. Just now, I have no time to be hurt by your barbs. I've more important matters to think about, and so have you."

Ay smiled, and to Tiy's amusement, it seemed an expression of genuine appreciation for her wit, not the scorpion-cold, calculated maneuver his smiles usually were. Tiy pressed her advantage: "You know that what I say of my son is true. I'd praise the gods a hundred times a day if they could turn Young Amunhotep into something else, a person with feeling, with some regard for *maat*. But he is what he is, and only the gods know the reason why. Don't let your desire to control the throne lead you into an atrocity. We must stop the Pharaoh from proclaiming Young Amunhotep the heir, or the Two Lands will suffer."

"Why? Young Amunhotep may be cold and strange, but—"

"*He killed Thutmose*, Ay. You would see a brother-killer on the Horus Throne? You'd see Set himself proclaimed king?"

"Your grief has unhinged your wits. It's only natural, I suppose—losing two sons at once, as you did. Amun's questioners found Thutmose's killer, Tiy—the guardsman they apprehended. Justice has been served. *Maat* is satisfied. Young Amunhotep is no threat to the Two Lands."

Tiy stepped back, caught so short by the conviction in Ay's words that for a moment she could hardly breathe. "You cannot possibly believe it. Come, Ay. A *guardsman*, strangling Thutmose in the harem? It's only a story, to satisfy the court, to hide the truth. You don't believe it. I know you aren't such a fool as that."

Ay's shrug was sinuous, unconcerned. "It satisfies well enough. Nefertiti is a very lovely woman. Her beauty is surely enough to drive any man to madness, don't you think?"

"It's not enough to drive Young Amunhotep to madness, or to anything else. I tell you, the only passion that exists between them is hatred—at least on your daughter's part. And it will soon spark into a fire that burns in my son's heart, too. This match was a mistake, Ay, but it's not too late to undo it.

"Help me exert pressure on the court, so that the Pharaoh's favorite nobles press for a change. Help me influence the king to choose some other man as heir—*anyone.* You may pick your favorite candidate, for all I care. We'll wed Nefertiti to that man instead, and I will gladly yield all the influence I still have over the Horus Throne to your daughter—to *you.*

"I'll go far away—as far as you like. I'll never approach the court again. With me out of the way, you can wrap your fist around the throne as you've always wanted to do, and forget that your sister ever outshone you. You can pass a new law, so that no one may speak my name on the West Bank again. I don't care—I'll suffer it all gladly. Only don't damn Egypt by placing a brother-killer on the throne."

Ay leaned comfortably into his chair's scarab-carved back. Laughter rumbled deep inside his chest. "Tiy, my dear sister. If I'd ever wanted you out of the way, it would have been a simple thing to be rid of you. Do you think I've never killed before?"

She narrowed her eyes at him, at the way his skin wrapped the angles of his thin face, like the shrunken skin of a mummy clinging to its skull.

"Nefertiti will stay where she is," Ay said again. "Your concern for Egypt is noble, but unnecessary. My daughter is my hand on the throne, and my hand is steady. When I control the Two Lands, there will be no need for fear."

Tiy jerked her sun-shawl tight around her shoulders. "Don't count the chicks in your nest before the eggs have hatched. My influence over the throne hasn't dried up yet, Ay, and I'm still better positioned than you are to place a steady hand on Egypt's rein."

Ay's silent stare was eloquent with doubt.

"If you won't assist me in influencing the Pharaoh, then my heart shan't break. I have other resources—

other means, I assure you, and more carefully laid plans than you and Father together ever could have concocted between you. Beware *my* sting, Ay. It is fast and sharp."

She turned and stalked from the reading room, collecting Huya from his position outside the door. Tiy ignored the bows of Ay's servants as she marched from beneath the estate's portico, out into the searing, limestone-white glare of the garden. She felt Huya's curious glance as she made her way down the wide central path toward the double gate, but she was too furious to speak. The garden was empty; her fast, angry steps crunched on the path's gravel and reverberated from the high stone walls. Tiy barked a command for the guards to open the gateway long before she had reached the shade of its arch, and she did not look back, or acknowledge the guards' courtesies, as she left Ay's estate behind.

When she and Huya were out on the road, a furious hiss escaped her teeth. They rounded the corner of Ay's outer wall, and Tiy halted in the green, vine-rustling shade, reaching for her skin of wine without a word. She closed her eyes as she took a long swallow of the bitter stuff, and would have drained the skin completely if Huya hadn't cleared his throat and said in an urgent whisper, "My lady, look—who is that?"

Tiy capped the wine skin quickly, wiping the corner of her mouth with the back of one hand. Down the long, shaded lane between Ay's estate and another, she saw a timid rustling among the vines, a brief flash of red linen and the drift of a wispy sun-shawl. Then a figure stepped from an alcove in Ay's wall—evidently a small, side entryway to the estate—and hurried up the lane toward Tiy and her steward. It was clear from the figure's clothing and long wig that it was a woman, but the direct, confident way she moved prevented Tiy from recognizing her until she had drawn very near.

"It's Lady Teya," Tiy muttered to Huya. He nodded, and

stepped warily between Tiy and her sister-by-marriage when Lady Teya approached.

Teya gave the steward a sharp, piercing look, flattening her lips into an angry line. Then she turned to Tiy, holding her wondering gaze for a long, silent moment. Tiy felt utterly confounded. Lady Teya's typical vague, misty aspect was gone, that unaware happiness replaced by a stark, purposeful frown. Intelligence glimmered in her wide eyes—the first hint of it Tiy had ever detected in Ay's wife—and those eyes were as hard and sharp as obsidian.

Tiy greeted her by name, but Teya said nothing. She only held out one hand, reaching a closed fist past Huya's body, toward Tiy.

Tiy looked at the hand. It hung steady in the air, never trembling or wavering. She made no move to approach, though, taken aback by this unexpected change in Teya's personality.

"How does Mutbenret fare?" Teya said in a clear, almost harsh voice.

"Well," Tiy stammered. "She is well, and seems happy."

"Thank you for getting her out."

Tiy could think of nothing to say. She only nodded in acknowledgment of the thanks. Teya shook her outstretched fist, once, insistently, and Tiy stepped forward, reaching for whatever the woman held.

She felt something light and sinuous drop into her palm.

"I found this in Ay's reading room," Lady Teya said. Then, without another word, she turned and walked briskly back toward the hidden gate.

Tiy looked at the object in her hand. It was a leather cord, and at least a dozen thick, hard knots showed along its length, tied at regular intervals.

For one long, cold moment her heart was blank, stripped

of all thought, shocked out of any consciousness, save for a dim awareness of the chattering of birds in the vines. Then her eyes lifted slowly from the cord, and she met Huya's disbelieving stare.

"Gods," the steward said. "It was Ay. Ay killed Thutmose."

Nefertiti

Year 36 of Amunhotep
Ruler of Waset,
Lord of Truth in the Sun,
Strong Bull Arising

I N THE DESCENDING HOURS of afternoon, when the boat of the sun was gliding down the slope of the sky toward its nighttime mooring, the steward of the former King's Great Wife made his way in to the small, shade-cooled privacy of Nefertiti's garden. Nefertiti looked up from the blanket where she and Mutbenret reclined on piles of soft cushions with a *senet* board laid between them. The steward Huya halted and bowed. He was not an unusual sight anywhere in the House of Rejoicing, but there was something in his manner—a certain slow, cautious slide of his observant eyes over Nefertiti's features—that filled her with sudden apprehension.

She looked across the *senet* board at Mutbenret. The girl had paid the steward no heed, but had risen from her cushions to sit cross-legged, bending over the game board to study her next move. The childish softness of Mutbenret's face, the innocence of her swinging side-lock braid, sent a poignant stab of loss deep into Nefertiti's stomach. She couldn't say just why. Did Huya come bearing some news that would scour away the last of Mutbenret's precious youth? The gods knew, Nefertiti herself was much older now than her seventeen years. Life in the House of Rejoicing—and four weeks of marriage to Young Amunhotep—had stripped away the last bright pleasures and innocence of life.

Nefertiti clapped her hands, dismissing the musicians who plucked out their quiet, soothing refrains in the garden's far corner.

Mutbenret glanced up from the *senet* board, frowning as the musicians and Nefertiti's few maids filed past Huya into the enclosed hall of the diplomats' wing.

"What is it?" Mutbenret said.

"I don't know," Nefertiti replied, gesturing for Huya to approach. "But you had better go, as well."

"Why? I would rather stay with you."

"It might be news you'd rather not hear, Little Sister."

"I am brave enough to hear any news."

Nefertiti took her hand and squeezed it gently. "I know you are. All the same, be a good girl and run along. I'll find you at supper time, and we'll eat together."

When the garden was empty, save for Nefertiti and Huya, the man bowed again. "Lady Tiy wishes to speak with you," he said.

The sensation of grim foreboding had not abated. In fact, it had only grown stronger. Nefertiti wanted to refuse the audience, but she owed Tiy a good turn, for having brought Mutbenret out of their father's house. So although it made her stomach clench with fear, she nodded. Huya vanished from the garden, and several moments later, Tiy took his place, drifting from the shadows beneath the portico like a bird sailing down to the river, her path straight, direct, and true. She halted at the edge of Nefertiti's spread blanket, scowling down at the scattered pillows and the *senet* board with its pieces still arranged, mid-play.

Nefertiti rose to her feet with well-practiced grace. She bowed to Tiy, but not as low as she once had. "Aunt. It is good of you to visit."

Tiy tossed her head, and the shoulder-length braids of her wig lashed in the air like the tail of an angry horse. "Visit, *pah!* I've come on business."

"Of course. Please, sit down. I'm sorry I can't offer you a chair, but the cushions are comfortable, if they aren't very formal."

Tiy sank down on the blanket, arranging the skirt of her flowing robe carefully. She picked up one of the *senet* pawns and rolled it between her fingers, considering the smooth, luminescent alabaster in thoughtful silence.

After what felt like far too long and heavy a pause, Nefertiti prompted, "What business brings you here?"

Tiy dropped the game piece back on the board. It bounced and rolled across the polished, lapis-and-ivory squares with a noisy rattle. "I went to see your father today."

Nefertiti hummed in sour disappointment. In the month since her forced marriage, she had managed to think of Ay only when occasion made it unavoidable. She waited for Tiy to speak on, but the old lady gazed off into the garden's foliage, watching in detached silence as a stray breeze stirred the glossy leaves of a nearby flower bed. The wind's soft rustle seemed to mock Nefertiti's anxiety.

"I suppose he wants to know whether I am pregnant yet," Nefertiti snapped when Tiy showed no sign of coming out of her reverie. "You can tell him I'm not. I only just found out yesterday. I cursed Mother Mut for it, you can be sure. My husband has visited me several times since our wedding night, and each time, I've prayed that his seed will take root." She clenched her jaw, too angry to say more. His seed—his foul, watery seed, dripping down her thighs. It was a sensation she'd felt more times now than any woman ought to suffer in a lifetime. A thrill of disgust raced up her spine, making her scalp prickle beneath the weight of her wig. "Tell Ay," she finally managed, "that I have done my best, but there is only so much he can expect in such a short time."

Slowly, Tiy's misty gaze focused on Nefertiti's face. She wondered whether the old lady had heard her words at all.

"Your father," Tiy muttered. Her voice was faint—so whisper-thin that Nefertiti almost didn't hear it, though only the space of a *senet* board separated them. Then Tiy sat up straight with an abrupt air of setting to work, and said, "I have found evidence, child, that it was not Young Amunhotep who killed Thutmose after all."

Nefertiti blinked rapidly, shaking her head—not in denial, but to clear the fog of confusion from her heart. "What?"

"It wasn't your husband who killed your lover. It was your father. Ay."

A great, unseen fist closed around Nefertiti's chest, squeezing tight, cutting off her breath. She gaped at her aunt as a ringing filled her ears, followed by a silence so deep and complete that Nefertiti wondered, with a kind of light, hysterical curiosity, whether she had gone deaf from shock. But then Tiy shifted on her cushions, and the sound of linen rustling against silk was so obtrusive that Nefertiti flinched.

"Why would he do it?" she asked. Her voice sounded much too plaintive, childish and high. But she couldn't modulate it, couldn't bring her racing heart under control. "What reason would he have? Why should he wish Thutmose dead?"

"I don't know," Tiy admitted. "I've asked myself that same question a thousand times in the last hour, since I learned the news—and I can find no answer that satisfies. Perhaps he thinks Young Amunhotep a weakling, easier for him to control than Thutmose would have been. If that is what he thinks, then he's worse than a fool."

Nefertiti's shoulders shook with a tiny, bitter laugh. "You don't know the half of it, Aunt, I promise you."

"I suspect, though, that Ay's motive matters very little. He is one removed from the palace—from the throne—and from your husband."

Nefertiti's brow furrowed; she stared at her aunt, uncomprehending, so astounded by the unexpected news that it was all she could do to sit upright on her cushions, and not collapse into the grass with bones as weak as water.

"It is still you and I," Tiy said, weighting her voice with significance, "who have the necessary access."

"Access? To what?"

Tiy's hand darted across the *senet* board, seizing Nefertiti's wrist with a grip so sudden and tight that Nefertiti cried out in alarm. Tiy squeezed; her nails bit like the talons of a falcon, and Nefertiti's gasp snuffed out the sound of the breeze among the garden's beds. "*Control,*" Tiy said, lifting Nefertiti's arm into the air. She tried to free herself from the old lady's grasp, but Tiy's grip was as cold and unbreakable as bronze. "Power," Tiy said. Her black eyes glittered with intensity—and, Nefertiti thought, the merest hint of desperation.

Nefertiti tried again to free her arm, for now the position was growing uncomfortable. Her fingertips had begun to itch with bursts of tingling as the blood drained away, or was choked off by Tiy's tight-clenched hand. "Power over what?" she said, twisting and pulling against Tiy's grip.

Tiy released Nefertiti just as she gave a great wrench of her arm; she toppled back on her cushions, catching herself from falling with her prickling hand braced in the grass.

"Don't be a fool," Tiy growled. "You're Ay's daughter, may the gods pity you. You don't need to ask that question. Power over what, indeed! What were you raised for, girl?"

Tiy rose, tugging her skirts straight, smoothing the pleats over her thighs. She frowned down at Nefertiti. The sun sank lower, dipping behind Tiy's head and shoulders, so that her dim, deep-lined face and the backlit halo of her braided wig seemed to fill the whole evening sky. "My strength is limited now, Nefertiti. I'm not the woman I once was—I don't have the power I had, when I was younger and in the king's favor. The sun is setting on my strength. But it has not yet begun to rise on yours."

Nefertiti clutched her sore wrist, rubbing it with care. She gazed up at her aunt in sullen silence.

"I've told you what you need to know," Tiy said. "And now the only question is what you will do with the knowledge. You can let your father maintain his hold on you—" her eyes flicked down to Nefertiti's wrist—"or you can break his grip, and use the power the gods have given you for your own ends. It is your choice to make now— your decision entirely. At least, that is, as long as Young Amunhotep is still poised to become the heir."

Tiy turned and swept from the garden, gathering the ends of her sun-shawl around her bony shoulders. Nefertiti watched as Huya the steward scrambled out of the portico's shadows, following his mistress like a lap-dog into the black depths of the diplomats' wing.

Trembling, Nefertiti climbed to her feet. The sun was halfway behind the wall now, throwing a long, blue swath of shade across the small patch of lawn. The garden was chilly, now that the sun had set. In a daze, Nefertiti stooped, took the corner of the blanket, and pulled it up, scattering the cushions and upsetting the *senet* board with a stony clatter. She wrapped the blanket around her body, holding herself tight as she shivered.

As the sun sank lower and the shadows grew, the blanket soon filled with the warmth of Nefertiti's own body. Her shaking slowed, then stopped. Tiy's voice filled her ears, the words repeating in her aunt's age-smoked voice. *What were you raised for, girl?*

Ay may have raised her to be a pawn, but Nefertiti was no fool. She squared her shoulders in her blanket, and stood tall in the face of the gathering dusk. *Let me show you just how well you've raised me, Father,* she thought wryly. *Oh, won't I make you proud? Won't you be glad for the schooling you gave me—and Mutbenret—when I turn you into my pawn, and show you how the game is truly played?*

Nefertiti dropped the blanket from her shoulders, welcoming the chill of the oncoming night. The sun was setting, but what did it matter? Soon a new dawn would rise, and for Thutmose's sake as much as for her own, Nefertiti would be ready to stand in its light.

Nefertiti

Year 37 of Amunhotep
Ruler of Waset,
Lord of Truth in the Sun,
Strong Bull Arising

T HE CIRCUIT OF THE SUN spread, pale and well-worn, across the flattened top of the rise. The chariot track was a dust-white scar encircling the earth's breast, marring the blanket of sprouting foliage that covered the sloped feet of the western cliffs with a fresh tint of golden-green. The hill on which the Circuit stood was high enough that from where she sat on a wide, limestone platform—the vantage point from which spectators normally watched horse races—it seemed to Nefertiti that she could see the whole of Upper Egypt.

At the base of the hill, the estates of West Bank nobles were clustered together like fine stones set in a pectoral of new-polished gold. Their gardens grew in lush, almost frantic proliferation, waving banners of new leaves above high stone walls, for the annual flood was close at hand, and all the green things up and down the great length of the Iteru's narrow valley responded to the promise of water with energy and jubilation. Amid the gleaming estates, the House of Rejoicing stood tall and proud, a vast sprawl of white stone indented with the thick, dark shadows of its pocket gardens and private lakes, its shaded walkways and secret courtyards.

The Iteru River had just begun to change its colors, casting off the pale, silvery blue of the late harvest season, taking on the first hints of the deep, red-brown blush that signified the Inundation to come. Across its broad expanse, a few canals shone brightly in the mid-day sun as they tracked back into the fields and orchards surrounding the city of Waset, transporting the first of the season's water—and the rich, nourishing silt it carried—to the farms that fed the privileged nobles of the West Bank. Waset itself was a gray-brown stain soiling the far shore, spreading its squalor across the land, dulling the bright effect of the citrus-green weeds that would sprout, flower, seed, and die in the few weeks of moisture before the river peaked and covered the earth with its sacred water.

A wind rose from the river, carrying the rich, mineral scent of the silt-laden water up to the Circuit of the Sun. It stirred the great, waxed-linen canopies that shaded the viewing platforms, flapping the fabric high above Nefertiti's head. The women on the limestone platform exclaimed as one, breathing in the fresh gust with smiles of satisfaction, lifting the locks of their wigs away from their necks so that the breeze might cool their skin. The day was unusually hot. Typically the early days of the flood brought cooler weather, and a refreshing moisture in the air that relieved tight skin and dry eyes. But this day was as fiery as the middle of Shemu. Nefertiti worked her hand-fan vigorously, as if she might maintain the breeze's dying momentum by sheer force of will.

Tiy leaned close to catch the benefit of the fan's swishing feathers. The former Great Wife was seated on a folding leather stool that creaked beneath her slight weight.

"Look," Tiy said, nodding toward the small dais that had been erected near the middle of the Circuit. "The High Priest of Amun is nearly finished with his prayers. Thank Mut. Perhaps we'll soon have done with this spectacle."

Nefertiti sighed. If only this charade *would* conclude. She would be grateful, and not only because she had long since tired of the heat. Today marked the *heb-sed*—

the long, arduous renewal ceremony that was meant to reinvigorate the king and reassure his watching subjects that he would continue to rule well, as strong and capable as ever. In the two months since Nefertiti's marriage, the Pharaoh had only grown fatter and weaker, the last vestiges of his long-gone power eroding day by day as the abscesses in his jaw and the delusions in his heart tightened their grip on his *ka*. The *heb-sed* was meant to be a display of kingly strength. But this felt like something else entirely. To watch the king sweating and struggling in the bare field of the Circuit, quaking beneath the weight of his golden ornaments, swaying under the glare of the sun, felt faintly embarrassing to Nefertiti—and shameful, as if she witnessed an open mockery of the gods.

At the uncomfortable thought, her eyes flicked down from the women's shaded platform to the half-circle of chairs that faced the nearest curve of the Circuit. There, among a handful of stewards and priests—and, Nefertiti noted with wry approval, two physicians, in case the Pharaoh collapsed in the midst of his glorious renewal— Young Amunhotep stood with his arms folded across his chest, watching the High Priest's prayer with narrowed eyes. Even from the distance of the women's platform, Nefertiti recognized the quiet, speculative intensity in her husband's face, the eager tension in his shoulders and neck, and she knew that he would soon act—would soon put into motion whatever game he had planned. The gods knew she had seen his blasphemous scheming enough times already to recognize it at a glance.

And she had no doubt that Young Amunhotep had planned *something* for this day. It was only a matter of time before he made his intentions known. The entire spectacle of the *heb-sed* had been his idea—his insidious seed, planted carefully in the Pharaoh's heart and nurtured with quiet words, with remarks that seemed off-handed to anyone who didn't know Young Amunhotep—and

Nefertiti, the gods take pity on her, had come to know him all too well. Once the old Pharaoh had warmed to the idea, it had taken root and flourished—as Young Amunhotep had known it would—until the king could think of nothing else, and would not be satisfied until preparations for the *heb-sed* were underway. When the renewal festival was formally announced, Nefertiti had noted the pleasure in Young Amunhotep's face, the way his thick, almost feminine lips had curled in satisfaction. Now, she eyed her husband over the edge of her fan with mingled expectation and suspicion.

But Young Amunhotep made no move as the High Priest concluded his prayer. He only watched as the priest lifted a bowl of beer to the high sun in salute, then poured it into the dust of the Circuit. Beer and flecks of mud splashed up to speckle the tawny edge of his leopard-skin robe. Then he handed the empty bowl to a waiting *we'eb* priest, and bowed toward the shaded dais where the Pharaoh hunched over his own lap.

Amunhotep stood slowly, bracing his hands against the arms of his throne to lever himself to his swollen feet. Kiya, seated to Nefertiti's right, leaned forward on her stool, watching the Pharaoh descend the steps of the dais with bright, questioning eyes.

Nefertiti spoke close to Kiya's ear. "Next comes the raising of the bull's back."

"Why?" Kiya asked.

In the Circuit below, Amunhotep accepted a bright white bone from the High Priest. It was about as long as his forearm and flat as a dining bowl, and came from the lower end of a bull's spine, from the place just above the creature's tail.

"It symbolizes the base of his strength," Nefertiti said, "the source from which his inner power springs."

Kiya gave her a grateful nod.

Over the past two months, Nefertiti had found herself often Kiya's company, seated beside her at feasts or standing with her on the rare occasions when the King's Wife attended court. She suspected it was Kiya herself who arranged this proximity—the girl had not given up on her desire to marry Young Amunhotep, it seemed, and perhaps she thought that Nefertiti might help her achieve this mad aim. The possibility ought to have annoyed Nefertiti, she knew. But to her surprise, she had learned to like Kiya. Or rather, she did not *dislike* the Hurrian as much as she once had. Kiya's wide-eyed innocence still filled Nefertiti with a sense of danger—a terrible reminder of how little control any of them had over Young Amunhotep—but Kiya was amusing, quick with jokes and eager to share subtle, knowing glances when court proceedings became too dull to bear, or when drunken nobles disgraced themselves at festivals.

As their cautious friendship developed, Kiya had persisted in asserting that Young Amunhotep loved her, and that she hoped to become his wife when he claimed the throne. On occasion, this did raise Nefertiti's ire—for if she, Nefertiti, was to find some grip on her husband, any woman whom he loved might pose a real threat to her designs.

But despite her sense of caution toward the Hurrian, Nefertiti thought that under different circumstances, they might have become close friends. She had taken on the task of educating Kiya about traditions and customs, helping her better assimilate into Egyptian life, and she found that she enjoyed explaining the *heb-sed* to the girl, if she enjoyed nothing else about the day.

Nefertiti had witnessed two *heb-sed* festivals already— one jubilee to mark the traditional first thirty years of the Pharaoh's reign, and another for continued renewal, three years later, as was the custom. She had come to feel like something of an expert, more than equal to the task of guiding a foreign King's Wife through the events of the *heb-sed* day. More difficult to explain than the rituals, though, was the fact that there had been no *heb-sed* the year before, three years after the prior rejuvenation rite. Last year, the Pharaoh had simply been too ill to complete the arduous tasks the festival required. His health was poorer this year, and truly no *heb-sed* should have been attempted, for if the king failed to perform any of the physical rites, it would be a perilously ill omen for the Two Lands.

Yet how can he do anything but fail? Nefertiti asked herself. She picked at the handle of her fan with trembling fingers, and hoped that her worry did not show on her face. *Is that what my husband wants? To place a curse on Egypt? Is that why he planted this doomed idea in the Pharaoh's heart?*

Out in the Circuit, under the direct force of the mid-day sun, the Pharaoh swayed on his feet. The bull's sacrum hung in his limp hands, and his face was devoid of all expression, blanked by exhaustion and long-suffered pain. On Nefertiti's left, Tiy went very still, staring down at the king with fierce, dark eyes, with a look that shot like a javelin straight to the Pharaoh's heart. It was, Nefertiti thought, as if Tiy sought to pierce the king's body with her stare, and inject her own strength into her husband's failing body.

Lift the bone, Nefertiti pleaded silently. *Please, gods, let our king not fail now, when the ceremony has only begun!*

The king gave a sudden jerk. *Perhaps he can feel the force of Tiy's stare, after all.* And then, with arms that shook like papyrus fronds in the wind, he raised the sacred bone of power above his head.

The women's viewing platform sent up one great gust of exhaled breath—one sigh of alleviation, in perfect unison. Nefertiti plied her fan again, chasing the flush from her cheeks. She looked beyond the cluster of stewards in their half-circle to the men's viewing platform, where at least two dozen noblemen sagged in sudden relief, leaning on the supports of their shade canopy or patting one other on the back with an air of fellow-feeling.

One among them stood apart, watching the proceedings with such a striking avidity that he leaned over the gilded cedar railing, his head and shoulders protruding from the shade and lit brightly by the sun. Nefertiti's lips tensed; she frowned, recognizing her father's hawkish intensity even with a quarter of the Circuit standing between them. Ay's stare traveled from the Pharaoh to his son—Young Amunhotep still remained among the stewards, his arms folded in a display of perfect aplomb.

Nefertiti could not keep the scowl from her face. She lifted her fan higher, covering all but her eyes so that none of the other women could see how she glowered. *You can't have him,* she told her father silently. *I'll take control of my husband before you will, Father, and then you'll see who truly holds the power. Then you'll reap a rich harvest of all the seeds you've sown.*

"What comes next?" Kiya sat back on her stool, accepting a small, faience-enameled cup of beer from one of the servants who moved about the platform, offering dainties and drinks from their silver platters.

Out on the Circuit, the High Priest offered his arm to guide the Pharaoh back to his dais. Amunhotep climbed the low steps with a trudging, shambling gait, then sank dully onto his throne once more.

Nefertiti sighed in dismay. "Running the four pillars," she said, "though I confess I can't see how the king will manage it. Did you note those four little obelisks placed around the track?"

Kiya nodded.

"He must run the circuit once on his own, and then again, guiding a black bull around the ring with only his

224

voice and a single shepherd's prod."

The Hurrian nearly choked on her beer. "Surely he can't. Why, he can barely walk!"

Tiy leaned across Nefertiti to address Kiya. "He *cannot* manage it. This whole thing is one great, gaudy folly—an insult to the gods."

"Hush," Nefertiti whispered. "It won't do any good if the court ladies hear you speaking that way. You know what they'll do with a rumor."

Tiy only spoke all the louder. "I don't care. Let them gossip. It's no rumor, anyhow. Anyone can see that this is folly, and a curse to Egypt besides, if the Pharaoh should fail. I shan't be surprised if—"

She cut off abruptly, for the little knot of stewards stirred into sudden action on the edge of the Circuit's broad, golden-pale track. Young Amunhotep stepped out of their midst, holding himself apart, his arms thrown up in a gesture of appeasement—though whether he was addressing the High Priest of Amun, the Pharaoh, or the crowd of onlookers, Nefertiti could not say. He seemed to speak to all of them at once, confident and bold, his voice carrying to the platform where the women settled into uneasy silence.

"My body is young and strong," he called. "Let me run the pillars in my father's place."

Tiy and Nefertiti shared a sharp, wary look. The High Priest hesitated, and turned to the Pharaoh to seek his approval—but Amunhotep only huddled on his throne, his lips twitching as he murmured ceaselessly to himself. The king seemed unaware of all, save for his own thoughts. After a moment, the High Priest beckoned to Young Amunhotep, indicating his approval.

From amid the stewards, a burly soldier came forward, square-jawed and flat-eyed. Nefertiti recognized Mahu at once, for he was often in Young Amunhotep's company, lurking about the King's Son, a personal bodyguard. Mahu's tense but quiet ways, his sharp-eyed, silent observation, had always struck Nefertiti as rather inhuman, as if he were more scorpion than man.

Mahu held something long, thin, and dark in his hands. Kiya watched with interest as the soldier approached Young Amunhotep and tied the object around his waist.

"The bull's tail," Nefertiti supplied. "He must run the four pillars with the bull's tail in place, to unite his strength with that of the sacred bull, the one we call Hapi-Ankh."

Tiy gave an indelicate snort, and grabbed a handful of dates from a passing servant's tray. "It's not the place of a King's Son to wear the bull's tail. Even the heir has no right to wear the tail. It is for the Pharaoh only."

"I don't disagree," Nefertiti said, "but what else can anyone do? The Pharaoh is in no condition to run the pillars. He could barely lift the bone! But shall we curse Egypt, by letting the rites go unfinished?"

"Madness," Tiy muttered sourly, stuffing her dates into her mouth. "This whole day is madness, and the gods will curse us no matter what we do."

Kiya blanched. "Curse us?"

"Don't be afraid," Nefertiti said, giving her hand a gentle squeeze. "All will be well, as long as we see through all the rites."

When Mahu finished his work and stepped back among the stewards, Young Amunhotep sprang into an energetic run. His legs pumped steadily, kicking up the hem of his white, knee-length kilt, fluttering the red-and-blue ends of his waist sash. Puffs of golden dust rose into the air and hung there, glimmering in the sun, marking each of his long, even strides as he sped around the track. He rounded the first pillar and turned north, heading away from the women's platform. Nefertiti squinted after him, watching the black bull's tail bob and slash through the streamers of dust as Young Amunhotep grew smaller in the distance.

"He is fast," Kiya said. "And vigorous."

As thoroughly vigorous as the Pharaoh is not. So this was Young Amunhotep's plan all along: to take over the rites for his father, to prove himself strong and capable before the eyes of the court—to make himself the obvious, unanimous choice, and secure his place as heir.

Young Amunhotep passed the northern pillar and struck out for the next. His pace did not flag in the terrible heat. If anything, he seemed to grow more energetic as his trial wore on. Nefertiti watched him for a long, silent moment, ignoring Kiya's questions, lost in her own thoughts.

Then she looked across to the men's platform, where Ay stood at the railing, his eyes trained on Young Amunhotep's progress. Nefertiti could sense her father's speculative mood, could practically feel his air of self-congratulatory glee. *He thinks he made the right choice, by forcing me into marriage with this man. He thinks that I am the good, obedient daughter, that I will yield access to the power he desires.* Oh, Nefertiti would see to it that her husband was appointed heir. Even if Young Amunhotep had possessed no ambitions of his own, Nefertiti would climb the ranks of power herself, dragging her husband behind, and seat him on the Horus Throne with her own two hands, just so that she could gain the upper hand, and give Ay exactly what he deserved for taking Thutmose away.

She considered the Pharaoh, drooping on his throne while his young, robust son dashed easily around the four pillars, as strong as the bull he represented. Did the old king regret his passion now—his blind insistence that the *heb-sed* be held? For surely Amunhotep now realized how his son had maneuvered him, setting him up for a display of staggering impotence before the eyes of the entire court.

The Pharaoh should have been wiser, Nefertiti thought, shaking her head at the shame of it. Then she checked, leaning back slowly on her stool. Realization broke over her heart like a fresh, rosy dawn. *My husband maneuvered his father by appealing to his religious zeal.*

She considered her wedding night—she could do that now, recall the strange and frightening things that had transpired in the isolation of her bed chamber, without shuddering in revulsion. Young Amunhotep was more like the old Pharaoh than anyone realized. Nefertiti might be the only person in the whole length and breadth of the Two Lands who understood just how zealous Young Amunhotep could be. She recalled his words as he'd pressed himself against her, remembered the way his voice had grated in her ear, hoarse with the intoxication of his own perceived might. *My father embodied the great power in his youth,* Young Amunhotep had said, *but he is growing old. It is I who hold the power now—I who have inherited his godhood.*

The warmth of absolute assurance flooded Nefertiti's limbs, and she smiled serenely in her father's direction. She knew *just* how to fit Young Amunhotep into her hand. Ay certainly could not do it—he wasn't close enough to the King's Son, didn't have the access, or the insight, Nefertiti now possessed. Ay had thought to use Nefertiti for his own ends, but when he next attempted to pick up her puppet-strings, he would find that the complacent tool he had so carefully honed had sharpened into a dagger, and that its point was leveled directly at his own heart.

Young Amunhotep rounded the final pillar and glided to a stop before the Pharaoh's dais. He bowed low to his father, then turned to receive the shouts of acclaim that rang from both of the viewing platforms. He lifted his arms as if to embrace the men and women of the court— to embrace all of Egypt, or to scoop it against his chest like a greedy child snatching sweets from a basket.

The women around her raised their voices in ululating cries of approval, but Nefertiti sat calmly on her stool, stirring the air with the gentle sway of her fan. Tiy and Kiya remained seated, too, and both women watched Young Amunhotep with rapt attention. What either of them might be thinking, Nefertiti could only guess.

While the stewards and soldiers prepared to usher the black bull of Hapi-Ankh from his holding pen onto the Circuit of the Sun, Young Amunhotep sauntered toward the women's platform, shrugging off the cheers of the court as though the people's acclaim was no more to him than the whining of evening gnats. Nefertiti could see the wide grin on his face long before he reached the foot of the platform. It was clear that he was pleased, smugly congratulating himself on the brilliance of his scheme.

He leaned one hand on the limestone platform, bracing the other on his hip. His bare, sweat-slicked chest heaved slowly as his breath returned to him with ease. Young Amunhotep gave Nefertiti a nod of polite acknowledgment, and she found it was easy to return the greeting with a warm smile—now that she knew how she must proceed— now that she knew how to beat Ay at his own game.

But Young Amunhotep turned away from her, and looked up at Kiya with adoring eyes.

The Hurrian flushed, hiding her mouth behind her hand so that no one would see the silly, overly pleased smile that broke across her face. She was, after all, still the wife of the Pharaoh, and until Young Amunhotep succeeded to the throne, her infatuation was a scandal in the making.

Nefertiti cut a sharp glance in Kiya's direction, her thoughts and her stomach churning while the Hurrian and the King's Son conversed. Perhaps Kiya would prove problematic after all—for if Nefertiti's plan was to succeed, she must be able to command Young

Amunhotep's attention. No woman must be allowed to stand higher in his affections than Nefertiti herself. An unaccustomed hollowness seemed to tear open inside her, and immediately a well of bitterness bubbled into that empty space. She let her fan fall into her lap, staring dazedly into the distance as she examined this strange new feeling, trying to identify it, to control it by finding its proper name.

Tiy leaned close, indicating Kiya and Young Amunhotep with a subtle nod. "There is a problem for you, I think." Tiy did not sound particularly concerned. In fact, she seemed rather amused.

Nefertiti tossed the braids of her wig. "It certainly is not a problem for me."

But as Young Amunhotep went on speaking to the Hurrian, laughing at her wit, praising her beauty, ignoring the rest of the women who called down their approval of his performance on the Circuit, Nefertiti found the correct name for the acrimonious flutter that choked off the breath in her chest.

Ridiculous, she thought, taking up her fan again and whisking it busily, turning her face away from Young Amunhotep. Ridiculous—unthinkable—that a woman as beautiful as she ought to have any cause for jealousy.

But there was no denying the truth. Nefertiti was envious, and as the black bull was herded onto the field and Young Amunhotep finally turned away from the Hurrian—as Kiya shifted her stool, her lashes fluttering in a giddy display of delicacy—the envy welled up stronger inside, threatening to spill over the banks of Nefertiti's *ka*.

Sitamun

Year 37 of Amunhotep
Ruler of Waset,
Lord of Truth in the Sun,
Strong Bull Arising

THE NOISE AND CLAMOR of the Feast of the Tail rose up to the great, soaring ceiling of the pillared hall. Sitamun pressed her back against tall, gilded throne of the King's Great Wife. The commotion made her head spin, and slicked her body with sweat—an after-effect, she felt sure, of the day's brutal heat, and the necessity of enduring the long *heb-sed* ceremony with proper, rigid composure. The smells of the feast—rich, roasted duck, the cloying honey of delicate cakes, and the salty tang of stewed fish—sickened her almost as much as the noise. The child had grown large inside her, leaving little room in her stomach for feasting. Yet even if she had any appetite, her persistent dizziness would have prevented her from eating anything at all.

There was nothing she wanted less in that moment than to sit still on her throne, watching as the Feast of the Tail raged throughout the great hall below her. She ached, both physically and deep within her worn-down heart, for the comfort of her bed, the dim stillness of her chamber, and the soothing sounds of her maid-servants whispering, their plain linen dresses rustling like reeds beside the river as they went about their light, easy duties. But she was resolved to play the part of the King's Great Wife as well as her mother Tiy had ever played it. And that meant suffering through yet another feast, sitting silent and complacent at the Pharaoh's side, displayed like a vase on a plinth, an unthinking, unfeeling bauble set up for the admiration of the court.

Though Amunhotep had only succeeded in performing one rite during his renewal ceremony—the raising of the spine—still the heat of the day seemed to have taken its toll on the king. He was just as hunched and dazed as he had been in the Circuit of the Sun, slouching in his throne, oblivious to everything that went on around him. But now and then, between the crashing of the musicians' cymbals or the high, sudden bursts of laughter from the guests below, Sitamun heard the Pharaoh mutter beneath his breath.

"Renewal," he whispered, his lips twitching and beaded with sweat. "I must renew."

And each time he muttered, the child twisted inside Sitamun's belly. Despite the gaiety of the music—despite the brightness of the women's fine dresses, the colors bleeding into one another as the court ladies milled about the hall—despite the pervasive sound of laughter, Sitamun was afraid, and trembled.

Gripping the arms of her throne, she looked down into the midst of the hall. Nefertiti was there, clad in a golden robe, drifting from table to table with a bright, confident smile. Something had pleased Young Amunhotep's wife, though Sitamun couldn't imagine what new delight, what lucky twist of fate had Nefertiti grinning like a cat over a dish of cream. Nefertiti had been sullen in the months since her marriage, a reaction Sitamun could not understand. Didn't she have Young Amunhotep? What more could any woman want? And now, following his brilliant display of strength and vigor throughout the *heb-sed* ceremony, Young Amunhotep was sure to be named the heir. Nefertiti's prospects continued to look up, while Sitamun's future seemed ever more uncertain.

Between the fish course and the salads, the nobles of the West Bank and the ladies of the harem drifted about the great hall, chatting merrily, discussing the display Young Amunhotep had given in the Circuit of the Sun. The performance was certainly inspirational—and a striking counterpoint to the current Pharaoh's obviously fading strength. The King's Son had cut a dashing figure, guiding the bull around the four posts with skill, driving a chariot as well as his warrior brother Thutmose ever had, and erecting a stone pillar in the center of the Circuit as easily as a boy plants a stick in the river's mud, the muscles in his sun-darkened arms standing out, chiseled and firm, like those of a soldier on the battlefield. He was beautiful to watch, and as he performed the feats of renewal on behalf of the king, Sitamun had stroked the swell of her belly, whispering her hope deep in her heart.

Silent and smooth-faced, sitting as regally still as Tiy ever did on her throne, Sitamun moved only her eyes as she watched Young Amunhotep drift through the festival crowd, following in Nefertiti's wake. There was no doubt in Sitamun's heart. Her brother would be proclaimed the heir soon—how could he not, after today's performance?— and after that, he would be the Pharaoh. The child kicked hard at Sitamun's belly, making her gasp, and she soothed it with her hand. Young Amunhotep would come to appreciate the gift Sitamun had given him. He must surely appreciate it already.

"Renew," Amunhotep muttered. "My *ka*... renew."

A servant dressed in a gold-belted tunic approach the dais, bowing. She woman held out a platter filled with curved, pale-green lettuce leaves, heaped with chopped dates and the white crumbs of goat cheese. Sitamun's throat tightened at the sight of the delicacy. She waved the woman away. With each word the Pharaoh spoke, her tension and nausea increased, and the very thought of food filled her dread. She peered at the trembling, whispering

Pharaoh from the tail of her eye. His breath was heavy, rasping, rattling in his great, fat-softened chest. Sweat still covered his skin, though the evening was cool, in spite of the liveliness of the celebration and the bodies that crowded the great hall.

As the servants made their way around the tables, offering the next course, Sitamun's eyes tracked Young Amunhotep's progress through the feasting hall. He visited each table to graciously accept congratulations and praise, and the glow of his smile, the force of his pride, filled Sitamun with a warm throb of success. *For you*, she told him silently. *All of this—the Feast of the Tail, the* heb-sed *festival, the Horus throne—it is all for you.*

Again the baby twisted, pressing hard against her lungs until her breath came shallow and short. *And this is for you, too*, she thought, holding the great, obscene swell of her belly in both hands as she watched her brother bend and smile over each table in turn, receiving his well-deserved praise.

"Renew," the Pharaoh whispered again, his voice thick with lust and power, darkened by desperation.

Sitamun's belly clenched. The sudden tension was like nothing she had felt before, forceful and strong, as if the child inside her resisted the Pharaoh's words. The nagging, tickling fear that had plagued her for months flared up with a sudden, furious heat.

My baby is not yours, she thought viciously in the king's direction. *It cannot be. Please, gods, make it so.*

Ever since the day when she had displaced her mother as King's Great Wife, Sitamun had feared the Pharaoh's prophecy, his promise that he would regenerate himself in the body of her child. Her dreams had been haunted by images of the baby coming forth from her womb, looking up at her from its mask of blood, leering with her father's face, staring with her father's small, commanding eyes. In the cold, fertile corners of her nightmares, she had heard a baby's cry turn to the Pharaoh's voice, the slithering force of his orders sliding about her heart, his harsh breath rasping in her ear.

As the king went on muttering beside her, her heart beat faster. *I don't want to be his vessel,* Sitamun thought desperately. *I don't want to make him live forever. I only want to go on, and be happy, and love.*

Tears blurred her eyes. She blinked them away, refusing to wipe with her fingers, lest anyone should notice the movement and see her distress. She gripped the arms of her throne tighter to lock her hands in place. She would not weep before Nefertiti, whom the gods had given to Young Amunhotep. Nor would she weep before Kiya, whom her brother loved so well. Oh, yes, Sitamun knew about his passion for the Hurrian. For though she was as quiet and still as Tiy, she was also as observant as Tiy, and whenever they were within one another's sight, Sitamun's gaze never left Young Amunhotep's face. She saw the way he looked at Kiya, the way his stare sharpened and focused like a falcon on the hunt. She saw the slowness of his smile, the lazy pleasure of his anticipation. Sitamun knew better than anyone what those looks meant.

When the servants had done their work and the guests settled at their tables again, the main doors were thrown wide, and a troop of acrobats were ushered in. They sprang hands-over-feet down the aisles between tables, tumbling and shouting their cues over the lively piping of the musicians. Dull-eyed, Sitamun watched with little interest. Their oiled, gold-dusted bodies flashed in and out of the pools of lamplight, raising cries of admiration from the crowd, but Sitamun kept her lips pressed tightly together. Her belly tensed again, and something unseen clutched at her throat with a dry, scratchy fist. The acrobats worked their way forward, converging on the great circle of lamplight that illuminated the bright-tiled floor in front of the dais. The tumblers stacked themselves into a tall pyramid, their shining limbs entangling in intricate knots. A small woman vaulted and climbed to the peak, but just as she reached her perch, her foot slipped, and she nearly fell to the floor. The guests in the hall sent up a loud gasp with a single voice, but one of the male tumblers caught the woman by her wrist, saving her from the fall.

Sitamun gasped, too, but not because of the drama unfolding below the dais. She was no longer aware of the acrobats at all, nor even of Young Amunhotep. Her belly clenched hard, the muscles of her abdomen clamping down with such violence that her eyes widened, and the force of the contraction jerked her halfway out of the throne.

Sitamun's distress seemed to reach into the Pharaoh's stupor. Slowly, he turned his head and gazed at her, his small, jackal-dark eyes sharpening on her face. Beneath the heavy double crown and the banded braids of his wig, his jowly face was wet with perspiration, but all the unfeeling dullness was burned out of his eyes by the sudden fire of his zeal.

"It is time," he said.

Sitamun shook her head, trying to steady herself, easing herself back onto the throne. "No."

"Yes. My hour is at hand."

Sitamun stared around feasting hall, searching for her mother's face. Her chin quivered, and she felt the tears rise again. The pyramid of acrobats disassembled itself; the performers made their way out of the hall, howling at their applause, stooping to pick up the chains of gold and the precious stones the king's stewards tossed out as their payment. Sitamun peered through the press of bodies, her panic increasing with each beat of her heart.

"Like the sun rising at dawn," the Pharaoh said, "I shall

soon be born again."

Wordless—beyond all hope of words—Sitamun shook her head. The only word she might have spoken just then was her mother's name, and she was tempted to scream it, to cry out from the throne, to reach for Tiy like a helpless child.

"Oh Re-Harakhty," the Pharaoh said, his thick voice rising over the cheers of the crowd, "god of the high sun, your blessing is upon me! I have been patient; I have been vigilant; I have suffered long. But now, like the god I am, I shall resurrect."

Sitamun shook her head frantically, setting the curls of her wig flying like the wings of a black bird, beating in a hunter's net. "The child is not yours," she said aloud, though she did not dare to look into the king's face.

"The child is *me*," the King insisted. "I have seen to it. I have willed it. It will be so."

He stirred himself, marshaling his faded strength, seeking to pull himself up from his own throne. But worn down as he was by the demands of the *heb-sed*—even if he had only performed a single, simple rite—he was weaker than Sitamun. She clambered to her feet first, swaying, holding her huge belly. The Pharaoh reached out a hand, his clammy, slick fingers wrapping tight and hard around her wrist. She didn't know whether he intended to use her as a lever to pull himself to his feet, or whether he sought to restrain her. Ordinarily, with a superstitious terror of his holy power, she would have done exactly what he wanted. But a force she did not understand seemed to have taken her over, body and heart. With a panicked strength that shocked her, she jerked away from his grip. She was dimly aware of the guests murmuring as they looked up the dais, shocked by the sight of the King's Great Wife defying the Pharaoh so openly. She gasped and looked out over the crowd, and far at the back of the hall, pushing and fighting her way between the tables and the milling bodies, Sitamun saw the small, dark figure of her mother, dressed in a gown as red as Hathor's robe.

"Mother!" Sitamun shrieked. Her voice split the air of the feasting hall, shivering among the high pillars, stunning the guests to absolute silence.

Tiy pushed past the final row of tables, bowling her way beyond Young Amunhotep and Nefertiti. The former Great Wife snapped her fingers at a pair of guards and pointed up to the peak of the dais where Sitamun stood swaying.

"Get her down from there," Ty said. "Get her down, and follow me."

The guards hesitated, glancing uneasily at the panting, muttering king who still strained against the arms of his throne.

"Never mind him," Tiy said. "Do as I say, or I'll have your heads."

Still the guards hesitated. It was an ill thing, to cross the Pharaoh, and it was obvious that the Pharaoh intended Sitamun to remain on the dais. *Does he expect me to give birth here, where everyone can see? Does he wish the entire court to witness his transformation?* She would have fled down the steps of the dais herself, if she had been able to control her legs. But it seemed all she could do was stand and shake in fear, staring down desperately into the dark, powerful eyes of her mother.

"Do as I say, Amun damn you," Tiy shouted. Nefertiti jumped from her seat, taking Tiy's elbow, tugging at her, trying to restrain her anger. But Tiy pushed her niece away. She started for the dais herself, but before she could set her sandaled feet on the first step, Sitamun's belly and back seized with one long, drawn-out pain. A piercing wail ripped from her throat, setting the watching courtiers to shouting as they reached for the protective talismans that hung from their necks and wigs.

Tiy lunged at the soldiers, cuffing the nearest one over his ear. "Now," she barked.

The soldiers scrambled to the top of the dais, lifting Sitamun's arms, supporting her weight down the steps. They followed Tiy briskly from the hall.

As the soldiers helped her past the head table, Sitamun, gasping with pain and fear, reached one trembling hand toward Young Amunhotep. But Tiy stepped between them, slapping Sitamun's touch away, and a moment later Nefertiti slid her soft, slender hand into the crook of her husband's elbow, pulling him back. Sitamun's final impression of the Feast of the Tail was of Kiya, the Hurrian foreigner, peering at her over Young Amunhotep's shoulder, her face pale with pity.

Tiy led them from the hall, out into the open, pillared corridors of the House of Rejoicing. The night's cool breezes poured along Sitamun's skin. The gusts dried her sweat and soothed the feverish heat of the pains that wracked her belly and back, but did nothing to quench the fire of her fear. She blinked at Tiy's back, dazed and bleary, as the soldiers bore her onward. Her mother cleaved the darkness like a falling star, her path direct, her ornaments and fine linens shining bright against the dimness of the night, her will hard and unstoppable. But she did not turn to look back at Sitamun as they went. She led the way to the apartments of the King's Great Wife, throwing open the door herself, scattering Sitamun's servants with a brisk flutter of her hands.

"Out into the garden," Tiy commanded.

Women and soldiers alike followed her obediently. Sitamun hung like a sack of barley between the men, her heavy body swaying and bumping with their unsynchronized steps.

Tiy led them through the lavishly decorated antechamber,

then to the bed chamber that had once been her own, and onward to the garden's open door. Beyond, the paths and beds of the garden were transformed to an unfamiliar landscape by the cool blue of night.

According to the usual custom, Sitamun's women had set up the birthing pavilion weeks ago in the garden, to await the first pains of her labor. It was best that a woman should give birth out-of-doors, where the air was cooler, where the breezes could soothe her laboring body and welcome the child to the world with sweet, wholesome odors. Outdoors, too, the gods could be of greater assistance, unhindered by the stone and mudbrick walls of men. Sitamun shuddered with fear as the guards ducked into her birthing pavilion, lowering her onto the bed of soft cushions that had been made ready for this moment. No gods would come to aid *this* birth, Sitamun felt sure. Not even gentle Hathor, who assisted mothers in labor, nor Bes, the lion-maned dwarf god who chased away the evil spirits that would steal a new child's *ka* if they could. As her belly clenched again, wracking her lower back with pain, Sitamun feared this child would be an abomination, and that the gods had already turned their faces away, abandoning her to the trial of birth without hope for survival.

The guards left the garden—it was ill luck, for men to remain in the place of birth—and Tiy crouched on the cushions beside Sitamun. Her hands were cool and sure as they lifted Sitamun's wig away, casting it out of the pavilion onto the grass, then smoothing her brow with a touch so gentle it startled the girl.

"I have sent for the midwife," Tiy said. "She will be here soon. There is nothing to fear."

There is everything to fear, Sitamun thought. She groaned with the force of a contraction, clutching her mother's hand. When the pain abated, Sitamun sagged back on the cushions, trembling.

"It is happening," she gasped.

"It is only a birth," said Tiy sensibly. "You are small, it is true—but so am I, and I gave birth to seven children. The gods never took me. You will come through it, too, child."

"No," Sitamun said. "Not that. I mean... the Pharaoh."

Tiy grunted in disgust. "*Nothing* is happening to the Pharaoh," she said with vicious emphasis. "Nothing, except that he gets fatter and sicker by the day."

Sitamun panted and pulled a cushion over her face, hiding her eyes so she would not see her mother's hard, angry scowl. "He will renew," she cried into the cushion, her voice muffled in her ears but raw and harsh in her throat.

"He will *not* renew," Tiy said. "He will expire, and *good riddance.*"

"He is coming now!" Sitamun shrieked. Another pain gripped her, and the cry turned to a wordless scream. It left her gagging as her stomach tried in vain to vomit up her fear.

Tiy turned, staring out of the shadowed depths of the pavilion into the garden. "Where is the midwife?" she shouted at Sitamun's women.

She turned back to Sitamun, stroking her brow. "Listen, child. The baby is your own. It has nothing to do with the Pharaoh."

Sitamun shook her head in a weak denial.

"Listen to what I say. Your baby will have its own *ka*, not his."

"He is the Pharaoh," Sitamun panted. "He is a god."

"He is *not* a god. Not until he dies. As long as he still lives, his *ka* remains inside him, and therefore it cannot go into your child."

The pain mercifully abated. Sitamun rubbed her belly,

gasping with relief, then allowed Tiy to pile cushions behind her back until she was nearly sitting upright. Tiy undid the knots of Sitamun's dress, stripping her naked. The garden breezes raised her bared skin into gooseflesh, but the chill was a relief. She cast a wordless, teary gaze of thanks at her mother, her lips trembling.

"You shall see," Tiy said. "The baby will not be him. You are safe, and the child is safe. You shall see."

At last, after two more pains had gripped Sitamun and receded, the midwife and her two assistants arrived. The midwife made Sitamun rise and walk through the night-dark garden, supported sometimes by the assistants and sometimes by her maid-servants. In those long hours of endless pacing and gripping pains, Tiy never offered her shoulder for Sitamun to lean on. She only stood at a distance, a violet shadow in the darkness of the garden, her wiry arms folded across her small, sagging breasts. She watched her daughter's labor with thin-pressed lips, with a cool, speculative silence.

The pains came closer, and sharper. Whenever one receded, Sitamun listened to Tiy's soothing words, eager to believe her reassurances the child would not bear the Pharaoh's *ka*. But whenever a pain took her again, squeezing and twisting, battering her bones and flesh, its force burst behind her tight-shut eyelids and flared there, as bright as the sun. And in those long, drawn-out, unending intervals, the only words Sitamun could hear were her father's—his endless lectures about the power of the sun, about the way its potency filled him—and all she could see was the terrifying zeal in his eyes as he commanded her to lay across his bed or sink to her knees beside his couch.

"The sun," she moaned. "The sun is rising."

Tiy bent close to her ear. Her breath was a cool whisper. "The sun is not rising. It is night."

"The sun is resurrecting. The sun is renewing! The sun has come again, and I am destroyed! The gods have turned their back on me! The gods have thrown me away, and made me useless!"

"No daughter of mine is useless," Tiy said, emphatic and low.

The fire flared in Sitamun's belly, burnt behind her eyes. "*The sun!*" she wailed.

"Open your eyes," Tiy commanded.

Sitamun shook her head.

"Do as I tell you. Open your eyes."

Fighting through the pain, Sitamun opened her eyes, and stared out at the dim, purple traces of the garden. Women moved around her like unanchored *kas* drifting through a tomb. Their faces, their flesh, the fabric of their tunics, all were rendered colorless by the shadows of the night. The air was cool, not fiery, and the voices of insects rang over the flower beds and around the edges of the pond. All the birds of daytime were asleep.

"It is night," Tiy said. "Do you see?"

Sitamun blinked, wiping tears and sweat from her eyes with the knuckles of her hand. Through the mobile, whispering branches of a sycamore, she watched the moon dance, dappled in leaf-shadow, looking down at her with a gentle, golden face.

"This is the moon's child," Tiy said, cupping Sitamun's belly with one strong, firm hand. "Your child. This is no child of the sun. Whatever Amunhotep may think, you and the gods have outwitted him. How can this baby be the child of the sun, if you bring it forth by night?"

The midwife's fingers pressed low on Sitamun's belly, digging into her taut flesh. She moved Sitamun's thighs apart, feeling the door to her womb. Then the midwife straightened, nodding to her to assistants, and the women hurried to set the bricks on which Sitamun would stand.

"This child will be the very opposite of the sun," Tiy said quietly. "The very opposite—I swear it. I swear it, my girl."

The words were a pillar of strength, and Sitamun clung to it tightly as she set first one foot, then the other on the birthing bricks, and crouched in the moon's soft light.

W ITH ONE FINAL RUSH of pain and blood, Sitamun brought forth the child at last, just as the moon was setting.

"A girl," the midwife exclaimed.

A sob of relief burst from Sitamun's chest. "A girl?" she said, choking on her tears.

The midwife cleaned the baby vigorously, and it let out a sharp, robust cry. The sound seemed to strike Sitamun's heart, as a priestess strikes a gong in the deep of the temple. She reached out insistent arms for her child, so eagerly that the midwife's assistants chided her as they struggled to balance her atop the birthing bricks.

"Patience," the midwife said. "Let me examine the baby. And it will be several minutes yet until I can cut the cord."

Tiy held a bowl of strong beer to Sitamun's lips, and she drank, deeply and gratefully.

"A girl," Tiy said. "And so you see." But Sitamun could read the note of relief in her mother's voice, the hint of a grave danger averted.

Tiy's relief was nothing next to Sitamun's own. The baby certainly could not be the king's resurrection if it was female. She had brought no abomination into the world, had done no dark magic, no evil. The gods would have no cause to abandon her now, nor to destroy her. She gestured for the bowl of beer again, drinking just to feel the sensation of it sliding down her throat, just to know that she was alive, that she still existed, that she had been spared.

"Your daughter is quite perfect," the midwife said. The baby went on squalling, and the midwife's assistants laughed with pleasure. "She is aggressively healthy. This one will certainly survive. Well done, little mother!"

"Well done, indeed," Tiy said. Her voice and bearing were as cool as ever, but all the same, Sitamun detected the barest hint of unaccustomed pride in her mother's words. "What will you name the girl?"

"I know the perfect name already," Sitamun said weakly. "Nebetah."

"*Ruling lady of the moon*," Tiy said, musing. "A fitting name."

May she be a ruling lady indeed, Sitamun thought as the midwife sliced the cord and tied it off with a bit of beeswaxed string. *May she be stronger than I have been. May she rule herself more wisely than her mother. May she give in to no man, not even to a king.*

The midwife wrapped the baby in a blanket of soft wool, and placed it in Sitamun's arms. Sitamun cradled that precious weight against her heart, and as she looked down into the crinkled, red face, as she peered into the new, dark eyes, she saw no trace of her father—none at all. Tears of relief matted her lashes and slid down her cheeks. *I thank thee, gods*, she whispered in her heart. *Thou hast preserved me after all—spared me and forgiven me.*

Across the darkness of the garden, a commotion rose up from the direction of Sitamun's chambers. She heard several voices speaking at once, and one of them, low and dark, familiar and beloved, pulled forcefully at her heart.

Tiy scowled. She turned to Sitamun's women and barked, "It's the King's Son. Send him away. Tell him I say—"

"No," Sitamun said. "I will see him."

"You will do no such thing."

Sitamun clutched her baby closer. "It is I who am King's Great Wife, Mother, not you."

The words were true enough, but Tiy ignored them. She snapped her fingers at Sitamun's waiting women. "Do as I say," she told them, and the women hastened off at Tiy's command.

"You're unkind," Sitamun told her mother. "He only wishes to see his daughter."

Tiy's stare was level and cold. "Don't speak of such things. He had no right to you."

"He is the heir."

"Not yet," Tiy said with emphasis. "And in any case, an heir is not a king. He had no right."

The voices came closer. It seemed that Young Amunhotep had made his way through Sitamun's bed chamber, despite the protests of her maids. She could see his silhouette in the lamplit door to her bedroom, his tall, lean, beautiful body as stark against the bright light as an obelisk against the sun. He was on the verge of stepping out into the garden, but another shape caught at him, holding him, pulling him away. Sitamun recognized the slender, lithe form of Nefertiti. Nefertiti's voice rose, and Sitamun could just make out, over the buzz of night insects, the protestations of her brother's wife.

"You mustn't." Nefertiti's voice came faintly across the flower beds. "You must not even acknowledge that the child is yours. If indeed it *is* yours. You can't say for sure. It will lead to nothing but gossip and ill feeling among the courtiers. It will undo everything you accomplished today at the *heb-sed*, and endanger your bid for the throne."

Young Amunhotep made some low reply. Sitamun could not catch the words. But Nefertiti responded, "Don't be a fool. It's only one child. You will have more. And as for your sister—we know she is well. She survived the birth. What more assurance do you need? What is she to you? You will have other women, as well as other children. You *have* other women already."

Breathless, Sitamun waited for Young Amunhotep to shake off Nefertiti's hand, to cross the darkness of the garden and come to her side. But he hesitated a moment longer, and then turned, and followed Nefertiti back through the door, back into the House of Rejoicing.

A terrible, hollow cold settled deep in Sitamun's chest. She pressed her trembling lips against Nebetah's soft forehead, but even the feel of her baby in her arms couldn't drive away her sorrow.

"Are those tears in your eyes, child?" Tiy frowned at her.

"Yes," Sitamun said defiantly. "Why shouldn't I weep?"

"You have a healthy child, for one thing. For another, you came through your first birth intact, and avoided going to your tomb. That's cause for celebration, not for tears."

Sitamun looked down at her daughter's face. Nebetah rested peacefully, content in her mother's arms. But already, Sitamun could see the future written on the child's soft cheeks, inscribed in the tiny lines of her perfect lashes, just as if Sitamun were a priestess reading omens in the temple. "This child will cause strife," she murmured.

"How not?" Ty said wryly. "It seems everyone born to this family causes strife of one kind or another."

Sitamun looked up quickly, clutched by a sudden fear. "Does the Pharaoh still live?"

"Of course," Ty said in surprise. And then added, "More's the pity."

He'll be angry, Sitamun realized. The initial spark of fear fanned itself to a flame of dread, and then a conflagration of panic. "He'll be expecting some change. He thought he would transform. If word has reached Young Amunhotep that my baby is born, then it has reached the Pharaoh, too. He'll see that he is the same—he'll know that his spell has failed."

"Good. Let him wallow in defeat."

"He will blame me!" Sitamun sat up on her bed of pillows. A wave of dizziness caught at her head, but she ignored it, trying to clamber to her feet with the baby still in her arms.

Tiy pushed her back down onto the cushions. "You need to rest."

"I can't," Sitamun cried. "He will blame me. He will kill me—and my baby, because she is not a boy!"

When she tried to rise again, Tiy held Sitamun down with stiff, forceful hands. "I tell you, you must rest. You came through the birth all right, but the days following even an easy birth are critical. You mustn't tax yourself, or worry yourself. That only invites demons. You aren't out of danger yet, Sitamun."

"Her words are true," the midwife chimed in as she packed a few of her implements into her bag—copper knives, reeds, and potions. "As soon as you feel well enough to walk, you may return to your bed indoors, but you must stay there for two full days."

"I won't!" Again Sitamun tried to rise, struggling against her mother's grip. "I cannot rest. I cannot stay here! I must get away from him, and take my baby with me. Otherwise he'll have us both killed!"

"I won't allow him to harm you," Tiy said.

Sitamun almost spat her words at her mother. "You can't stop him!"

And in her desperation—in the certain knowledge that both she and her baby were condemned, that she could do nothing to save the precious child in her arms— Sitamun began to weep in earnest. The tears poured from her, choking off her breath, and she sobbed and wailed wordlessly, unable to do any more than keen out her helpless fear like an animal in a trap.

"Gods," Tiy muttered. "Quiet yourself, child. Carrying on so will only invite evil spirits!"

Sitamun went on crying. She clutch Nebetah so close to her that the baby began to scream, too, and Tiy, fearful the child would be hurt, tried to wrest her from Sitamun's grasp. The attempt to separate her from the child only deepened Sitamun's panic. She screamed and thrashed, and Nebetah shrieked helplessly in her arms.

Tiy seized Sitamun's shoulders. "Stop, child. You must stop!"

The midwife clutched Sitamun's ankles to cease her kicking. "Please, great lady," she begged. "You'll only invite demons!"

But no demons could have frightened Sitamun more than the Pharaoh, who she knew was waiting even now in the depths of the House of Rejoicing—waiting like a spider in its web, to use Sitamun and her baby for his own insidious ends. She struggled and wept, wishing for a boat to carry her north, like the one that had carried Smenkhkare away. If only she had gone with her brother. Perhaps then she would be out of the king's reach, and she and her child would be safe.

She remembered the Pharaoh's clammy, cold touch, his grip on her wrist when she had pushed herself up from her throne only hours before. That had not been the grip of a dying man. It was strong and insistent. And Sitamun new that no matter what Tiy thought or hoped, the Pharaoh was no closer to death than he had been yesterday, or the day before—or the year before that.

But she, Sitamun, was. She saw those thick, grasping hands reaching from the shadows of the garden, stretching out to catch her up in her hour of helplessness—and to catch Nebetah, too.

"No!" she cried. "Save me!"

A shadow bent over her in that moment, but even through her terror, she perceived at once that it was not the grasping shadow of the king. It was soft, and moved with a gentle, deliberate care. A cool hand caressed her for head, her cheek. A soft voice murmured close to her ear, speaking words she did not understand—a language she barely knew. She opened her eyes and looked up into the face of the Hurrian.

"There," Kiya whispered in Egyptian. "All is well."

"Where did you come from?" Tiy snapped.

"I met Nefertiti and Young Amunhotep in the hall," Kiya said. "They told me Sitamun had birthed her child. I came to offer my help, if it is needed."

"It seems it is needed," the midwife said quietly.

Kiya sank onto a cushion beside Sitamun's bed. Murmuring in her soft Hurrian tongue, she loosened Sitamun's arms, releasing the hard grip on the baby. Nebetah's frightened cries settled into a low whimper, and then into contented silence.

"All is well," Kiya said. "You have a fine baby, you came through the birth, and all is well."

There was no reason, Sitamun knew, why she ought to believe this foreign King's Wife. But something in Kiya's voice, in her very bearing, soothed Sitamun's fears as her mother and the midwife could not. She panted, catching her breath, and felt the terror drain from her body and heart as she gazed up into Kiya's face, just like an infant herself, tucked into its mother's arms.

"Now," Kiya said softly, "let me hold the child—your dear little daughter. I shall carry her inside for you, and I shall tuck you into bed, and lay her down beside you. And you shall sleep soundly while I watch over you, and all will be well."

Sitamun relinquished the baby, trusting her to Kiya's arms. Then, fighting the waves of dizziness that threatened to consume her senses, she allowed Tiy and the midwife to help her to her feet. Staggering and weak, still trailing the cord from Nebetah's birth, and naked and vulnerable to the cold of the night, Sitamun made her way into her bed chamber, with the Hurrian walking steadily, peacefully, at her side.

Kiya

Year 37 of Amunhotep
Ruler of Waset,
Lord of Truth in the Sun,
Strong Bull Arising

SITAMUN STIRRED FITFULLY in the silence of her bed chamber, mumbling faint but emphatic words of protest. The newborn baby fussed where she lay against Sitamun's shoulder. The swaddling had come untucked, and the baby weakly waved one soft, pink fist in the air. Kiya tucked the soft linen back into place, then placed her hand on Sitamun's brow. The girl's face was hot, flushed with the effort of her labor and the trial she faced now as she wrestled with her dark, unknowable dreams. Kiya stroked the soft skin gently, brushing back the sweat-matted curls of her natural hair, smoothing Sitamun's fears away. She prayed that he girl would not wake again. Kiya had only just coaxed her back into sleep, an arduous task that she had repeated several times already, for nearly every time Sitamun began to drift off, she started up again, eyes wide and fearful, staring into the dim corners of her grand bedchamber and muttering about the Pharaoh and the sun.

Kiya began to hum again, repeating the soft, gentle strains of the Hurrian lullaby. She had sung it so many times already that her voice felt cracked and used up, as dry as a long-dead well. She had sung it so often the words no longer made sense to her. She might as well have been as oblivious to their meaning as Sitamun was herself. But despite her incomprehension, the cradle song did seem to comfort Sitamun. Even in her restless sleep, the tension relaxed from her young face, and she settled once more into her mattress. The baby at her side, wrapped tightly once more, kept its eyes closed.

Kiya let the lullaby die away, trailing off into weary silence. The bronze-red glow of lamplight flickered against the wall, illuminating for a moment Sitamun's ornate cosmetics table with its neat rows of paint pots and brushes, and the huge electrum mirror that hung on the painted wall above it. Kiya caught sight of her own reflection in that mirror, a tiny, pale shape standing out against the vast darkness of the chamber of the King's Great Wife. She sat very still on the stool beside the girl-queen's bed. She was a lone, frail force against the night, the only light and bright thing in Sitamun's chamber.

Kiya thought back with an ironic smile on all the tears of anger and fear she had shed when her father had announced her marriage to the King of Egypt. In her wildest and most terrible imaginings, Kiya had never dreamed what darkness lay at Egypt's heart. When she had just been a silly, innocent girl in the Mitanni court, the fact that Egyptian kings married their close relations had seemed amusing—just another strange, exotically thrilling story of the far-off land, just one more salacious detail of a place so distant that it might as well exist in the realm of gods or dreams. But Egypt wasn't far away any longer. It was Kiya who was far from home. And there was nothing amusing about Sitamun's plight.

She is just a little girl, Kiya thought, gently stroking Sitamun's shoulder as she whispered in her sleep. *She is defenseless, and frightened, even if she is the greatest queen in the land*.

By the time she had helped Sitamun inside from the birthing pavilion, the contractions had begun again. The midwife made Sitamun kneel on a rug and coached her through the expulsion of the afterbirth. Tears of terror had welled up fresh on the girl's cheeks, and she had babbled again about the sun—always the sun—crying that now, at last, the Pharaoh was coming to claim her *ka*. Kiya had distracted Sitamun she pushed, as she cried out against the pain in her raw womb and torn vulva, by showing her the gift Kiya had brought to celebrate the birth of her first child.

It was a necklace, very fine and lovely, made in the wide, collar style that was so popular with the ladies of the court. As broad as Kiya's hand, it was stitched with tiny blue beads of lapis lazuli, and rondels of carnelian softly draped between intricate, beaten-and-carved leaves of purest gold. The workmanship was enough to impress even the King's Great Wife. Kiya had noted Sitamun's low-slung belly and slow, halting gait at the *heb-sed* festival. She had understood then that the girl's time to give birth was drawing near, and had spent the hours before the Feast of the Tail rummaging through the special storeroom of the House of Women—the one reserved only for King's Wives—choosing just the right gift to bring to Sitamun. She had searched as avidly as if the perfect bauble or the most precious gem she could unearth in those many baskets of hidden finery might guarantee that Sitamun would come through her trial alive. Kiya had no special reason to care for Sitamun—she was one among many wives of the Pharaoh. But something about the girl's demeanor—her quiet, serious face, or perhaps just her startling youth—touched Kiya deep in her spirit, and filled her with an ache of pity.

She had not dreamed, before the feast, how accurate her prediction of Sitamun's impending labor had been. After all, Kiya was no midwife. She was just as shocked as anyone when Sitamun had lurched, screaming, from the throne. She had chanced to glance at Young Amunhotep in that moment, and had seen the keen interest break over his face. The King's Son had watched the guards carry his sister from the feasting hall with a curiously triumphant stare. In that moment, Kiya had realized what Young Amunhotep's interest had signified, and it had sent a chill lancing into her heart.

The soft rush of Kiya's breath mingled with the sounds of Sitamun and the baby murmuring in their shared dreams. She pressed her fingers to her temples, trying to massage the dull ache out of her head. There was nothing—no song, no potion she could think of, that would chase the ache from her spirit. Her future and her hope lay tangled with Young Amunhotep. She must maintain his love for her, if she was to have any hope of freeing herself from the confines of the harem and building any sort of acceptable life here in Egypt. But how could she love—or even accept—a man who impregnated his own young, frail sister? And how could the gods of Egypt allow such an offense to occur in the very royal family they favored? It was one thing to titter with her sisters over the shocking customs of a far-off land. It was another thing entirely to be confronted with the stark, bruising reality of those same customs. Kiya glanced down at the baby, and a frown pulled at her mouth, and a terrible, dragging weight pulled at her heart.

Outside the bed chamber, far across the broad, lush expanse of the Great Wife's anteroom, Kiya heard a familiar voice at the door of Sitamun's apartments. It was Nefertiti, speaking in her lush, low tones to Sitamun's serving women. Had Nefertiti brought the King's Son again? Kiya trembled, dreading the prospect of facing Young Amunhotep over Sitamun's bed, with his child tucked against the sleeping girl's breast. What could she possibly say to him? Congratulate him? Show her scorn for his carnal greed, and scold him—thus ruining her hope of freedom forever? Knowing what she knew now, how could Kiya ever hope to maintain the air of intoxicating appeal she had worked so hard to cultivate in Young

Amunhotep's presence?

And then, swallowing hard as her cheeks heated with an unwelcome flush, Kiya thought of Young Amunhotep's beauty—his catlike grace as he had run the four pillars, his strength and masculine appeal as he had guided the great, snorting, dust-spangled bull around the Circuit of the Sun. She wondered whether she would have to work to maintain a façade at all. Even as she loathed him for what he done to his sister—even as she hated his terrible sin—she longed for his affection, his touch. She remembered the heat of his kiss, and the way he had come to her in her bed chamber, eager and demanding. She recalled with a shiver the way he had trembled with the delight of anticipation when she had sent him away, unfulfilled.

But when the maids' voices finally subsided, it was only one set of footsteps that Kiya could hear crossing the great, tiled length of the antechamber's floor. Nefertiti came alone into Sitamun's bedroom. She hesitated on the threshold, her eyes going wide at the unexpected sight of Kiya waiting, stoic and alone, beside the Great Wife's bed. But after a moment, she approached, gazing down at Sitamun with a carefully detached curiosity.

"Good evening," Kiya said. "Or I suppose I must say good morning. The sun will soon rise."

Sitamun tossed her head in the half-moon of her padded ivory head rest, muttering darkly.

"A new day is dawning already," Nefertiti said. Her voice was smooth, mellow, musical as always. As she spoke, the first notes of early bird song sounded in the garden.

Kiya nodded wearily. "I've stayed by her bed since we put her in it, just as I promised her."

"You are a loyal friend," Nefertiti observed. She did not sound impressed, or disapproving, either. She was merely... observing.

"Young Amunhotep is not with you?" Kiya asked tremulously.

Nefertiti eyed her sharply, the lamplight playing over her high cheekbones, her full lips, her narrowed, river-dark eyes. She did not answer the question directly, but said, "He wanted me to look at the baby, to verify that it is truly healthy."

"Healthy and whole, as you can see," Kiya said. "Praises to Ishtar."

Nefertiti raised one kohl-drawn brow. "Praises to Mut," she said with a faint note of correction.

"It is kind of the King's Son, to be concerned for his sister's child." Kiya said it carefully, watching Nefertiti's face with a steady gaze, gauging her reaction.

"Kind," Nefertiti said drily. "Indeed. I will reassure him that the child is well. And let us pray," she muttered almost under her breath, "that he is satisfied with that."

Nefertiti glanced at the table beside Sitamun's bed. A bowl of herbed wine stood there, which the midwife had left with instructions for Sitamun to sip it if she awoke again. Beside the bowl, spread out like the wings of a felled bird, Kiya's gift caught the flickering lamplight, sending little stars of reflected gold pattering and playing over the walls. Nefertiti's eyes widened.

"What is this?" She asked, approaching the necklace with a quick, graceful stride, reaching out one slender hand to touch the golden leaves.

"A gift for Sitamun," Kiya said slowly.

"From whom?"

Kiya drew herself up, squaring her shoulders. "From me."

Nefertiti's frown was deep and dark. Kiya did not understand the source of her displeasure. Why should a

King's Wife not give a gift when a new child was born into the Pharaoh's household? Was it a thing not done in Egypt, perhaps?

"Where did you get a necklace so fine?"

"In the harem," Kiya said. "In the storeroom reserved for Kings' Wives."

"I see." Nefertiti scowled down at the necklace and picked up its edge, rolling the beads of lapis between her finger and thumb. Then she let it fall with a clatter. She turned away in disgust. "You King's Wives certainly have lovely treasures."

"You will be a King's Wife soon," Kiya said, offering it like a banner of truce between them. "And then all the finest things will be yours to enjoy, too."

Nefertiti turned back to her, tapping her pointed chin with her henna-dyed nails, but her smile was bitter, not friendly. "Do you think that's what I want? The finest things? Simple treasures to hang about my neck?"

"What woman doesn't appreciate finery?"

Nefertiti's black eyes slid across to Sitamun, to her slack, childish face, all the girl's awareness lost in the mercy of dreams. "I would wager that Sitamun, for one, wants more than just finery," Nefertiti said. "She is King's Great Wife. Any beautiful thing in the world could be hers for the asking." Nefertiti's voice dropped low. Kiya had the instant, uncomfortable awareness that Nefertiti didn't truly wish for her to hear the words she spoke next, but Kiya caught them all the same, heard them slither through the dark of the room like serpents in tall grass. "And yet what does she want? What, indeed."

Nefertiti did not supply the answer to her own question, and Kiya would not venture her guess aloud. She had seen the desperation on Sitamun's face as she had reached for Young Amunhotep, and then the unmistakable, wrenching pain in the girl's eyes when Tiy had slapped her hand away. *The poor child*, Kiya thought. *The poor, sad, helpless little thing.*

Nefertiti moved close to Sitamun's bed and stood frowning down at her, her face still undeniably beautiful—Nefertiti could never be anything but lovely, even while scowling— but that innate loveliness turned to something twisted and strange in the harsh, red angles of the lamplight. Kiya had the sudden, fearful notion that Nefertiti meant to harm Sitamun. Was it envy, she wondered? Did Nefertiti so love her husband that she might stand at the bedside of a helpless girl and think evil thoughts about her and her newborn baby? If so, then despite their months of wary but blossoming friendship, Nefertiti could be dangerous. Thoughts were intentions—Kiya had always believed that. And if Nefertiti could feel no pity for Sitamun's plight, if she could let an abused, sad little child raise her ire, then she would certainly look on Kiya with feelings far less kindly. For Young Amunhotep showed no signs of relinquishing his professed love. He lavished ever more attention on Kiya with every opportunity he found, even taking special pains to speak to her at the *heb-sed* festival, singling her out among all the women for his smiles, his praises, his smoldering, promising stares. With a sick twist in her gut, Kiya wondered what evil thoughts Nefertiti might already have for her. She felt suddenly defensive— of Sitamun, and of herself.

"You and I have been friends, I think," Kiya said. She stood abruptly from the stool. Her legs tingled with a rush of blood, but she ignored the sharp, sudden pain. "However, Nefertiti, I will not allow you to cast any ill over Sitamun. I have sworn that I will protect her tonight, and I will protect her, even from you."

Nefertiti drew back, her pretty lips curling, her eyes flashing with surprise. "Cast ill over her? Whatever do you mean?"

Kiya clenched her fists. Then she said, "I will not let you

cast ill over me, either. I will have my place in the world, at any cost."

"Your *place* in the world?" Nefertiti sounded baffled.

"You can't imagine what my life has been like," Kiya said. The threat of tears squeezed her throat, but she pushed them away, determined to show no weakness before Nefertiti. Dry-eyed, she said, "You cannot comprehend what it's like to leave your home, your family—to go so far away and marry into a place as strange as Egypt." Kiya frown down at Sitamun, and took the girl's hand.

"Ah," Nefertiti said, "aren't you the martyr. Perhaps *you* can't imagine what *my* life has been like."

Kiya narrowed her eyes, her mouth twisting wryly. "I'm sure it's been just terrible for you, as beautiful and privileged as you are. And you are married to the man who will soon be heir. One day, you will be King's Wife. King's *Great* Wife, I shouldn't doubt. Terrible and difficult, indeed."

Nefertiti gazed at Kiya for a long moment, her expression caught somewhere between shocked offense and hysterical amusement. Then a serene smile curled on her lips. She said nothing, but a flicker of pain flared in her dark eyes, and vanished again, deliberately quenched.

"I *will* be King's Great Wife, one day," Nefertiti said levelly. "You would be wise to remember that, Kiya."

Perhaps it was only the strain of the long vigil Kiya had kept at Sitamun's side, or perhaps it was a deeper, longer strain—her absence from far Mitanni, and the disorientation of being cast into a strange, dangerous culture, so unlike her own. But an unaccustomed boldness swept over Kiya's soul, straightening her spine and hardening her heart as she faced Nefertiti, unafraid.

"Perhaps," she said. "But as strange as Egypt is, I think it is not so very unlike many other lands. The greatest wife of all will be the one who can give the king his sons." And she laid a hand low on her abdomen, though the gods knew it was empty.

Nefertiti, though, did *not* know. She glanced down to where Kiya's hand rested, and her eyes narrowed, then widened. She stared into Kiya's face again, her long, slender neck trembling as her whole body tensed. It made the beads in her wig chatter faintly in the silence of Sitamun's chamber. Then her serene smile returned. It did not shake or waver, and Kiya had no hope of reading the flat, dark expression in Nefertiti's eyes.

Kiya opened her mouth, ready to recall the lie, unsure what had possessed her to tell it in the first place. But before she could speak, Nefertiti turned, and slipped out of Sitamun's chamber with her back straight and poised, her chin lifted high.

Shuddering, Kiya sank back onto the stool. Dawn broke outside. The garden was alive with bird song, and the sky, peeking through the sycamore branches and the frame of Sitamun's garden door, bloomed with a rosy-golden hue. Sitamun seem to respond unconsciously to the rising sun, tossing in her fretful sleep until the baby, Nebetah, twitched and whimpered. Little by little, the light of the sun beat back the light of the lamps, illuminating the chamber with a dusty warmth. The chamber's brilliant walls, painted with murals of gardens and riverside wild-places, resolved out of the darkness, asserting themselves in a tangle of foliage and flowers as the night's gloom receded. Kiya stared into the depths of the riotous, clamoring paintings, her eyes unfocusing as they lost themselves in an endless forest of curves and stalks and vines.

She lifted Sitamun's hand again, and was surprised to feel the girl's fingers curl around her own.

"Father," Kiya muttered, knowing the King of Mitanni could not hear the words, "what danger have you sent me into?"

And what deeper danger have I made for myself? Kiya thought, remembering Nefertiti's flat, unfeeling smile.

Nefertiti

*Year 37 of Amunhotep
Ruler of Waset,
Lord of Truth in the Sun,
Strong Bull Arising*

NEFERTITI STALKED ALONG THE WALLS of her little private garden, pacing its modest length, retreading the traces of her own furious footsteps as the sun climbed into the morning sky. The encounter with Kiya had shocked her, and filled her gut with the weight of a hundred dry stones. Never would she have expected the little Hurrian mouse to rise up and roar, and the news that she might carry Young Amunhotep's child already had sent a jolt of terrible, new awareness through Nefertiti's *ka*.

She marched again along the garden wall, kicking the hem of her best blue robe until it was stiff and stained with the dust of her sandals. *Kiya, indeed.* To think she had begun to consider the foreigner a friend. Nefertiti could see her folly now, could count all the ways she had been complacent—a weakness Ay would have scolded her for, or worse. Far worse.

Young Amunhotep's influence was increasing—his clever scheme to turn his father's *heb-sed* into his own display of youthful glory had worked, right enough. There was no doubt in Nefertiti's heart that the courtiers would soon begin pressing the king to make his proclamation, and would push for him to select Young Amunhotep as the true heir. His name would be engraved on official stone scarabs and sent out to every *sepat* in the Two Lands. If

Nefertiti was to have any hope of enacting her vengeance on Ay, she must win her husband's heart before that time came—for she knew Young Amunhotep well enough by now to predict how the heady rush of that new power would muddle his senses, sinking him in a deep pool of self-satisfaction, and making him cast all caution—and all his courtly resources, of which Nefertiti was one—aside.

For now, she remained Young Amunhotep's only wife. But despite her shocking display of complacency where Kiya was concerned, Nefertiti accounted herself no fool. She knew her husband would move quickly the moment the law of the Two Lands allowed it, and gather up a flock of appealing wives like a child stealing dates from the kitchen. He'd shown his propensity and impatience already—hadn't he already taken Sitamun, long before he could claim any right to the divine act of sister-marriage?

As long as Nefertiti remained his sole wife, she still had reason to hope that she might corral Young Amunhotep's wild heart—might work her way close enough into his confidences to use the same subtleties he had used on his own father. Each day the Pharaoh lingered was another day that Nefertiti's slim advantage held. But once the king went to the Field of Reeds—and the gods knew it could happen at any time; old Amunhotep stood in the very mouth of his deep, black tomb—the King's Son would move quickly, taking all the wives he pleased. Unless she could make Young Amunhotep love her as he evidently loved Kiya, Nefertiti's superior position would be lost in the blink of an eye.

That eye would blink all the sooner if children were involved—sons. For the Hurrian had been right: whoever was the first to bear a son would stand highest in Young Amunhotep's regard—despite his strange predilections and blasphemous bed-chamber games, he was a man like any other, and where sons were concerned, all men's hearts were the same. Helpless and hot with fury, Nefertiti struck a fist against her stomach, beating at the womb that remained stubbornly empty. If Kiya's child was a boy, then Nefertiti had no doubt that she, Kiya, would be named King's Great Wife just as soon as the old Pharaoh was safely buried. And Nefertiti, despite her famed beauty, despite Ay's long years of maneuvering and her own attempts to catch the power of the Horus Throne in her fist, would find herself relegated to the forgotten, distant chambers of the harem, just like old Aunt Tiy.

A stiff, breezy flapping sounded high above her head, near the rooftops of the diplomats' wing. Nefertiti glanced up in time to see an ibis alight on the edge of the garden's wall. She stilled herself, body and heart, and bit her lip, watching the ibis with reverent expectation. The sacred birds seldom strayed into cities, preferring the peace of the reed forests and the tall papyrus fronds at the river's edge. The ibis shook its wings, settling its pale flight feathers with a satisfied air, then darted its long neck this way and that, peering down at Nefertiti with its bead-like eyes. She remained quiet, blinking at the bright blaze of the sun as it rose to silhouette the sacred bird. The ibis turned, showing the profile of its long, downcurved beak, and took a few steps along the wall, strutting with a short, confident stride.

The ibis was a symbol of luck and wisdom. Had it appeared just for Nefertiti, showing itself only to her eyes, a signal from the gods? She clasped her hands at her throat, wondering.

If I want to assert myself over Kiya--and yes, even little Sitamun--then I must give my husband something more valuable than children. Something even more valuable than a son.

There was one thing Young Amunhotep still lacked— one great and glorious gift that could still come to him through Nefertiti's hands. But she must act quickly. There, too, her advantage would fade with each passing day. *And I've lost enough ground already*, Nefertiti thought with grim determination.

With one last, grateful glance at the ibis, she strode from the garden and back into the diplomats' hall, making for her small chamber and calling to rouse her maids from their sleep. She threw open her door and went directly for her bath, pulling off last night's wig and casting it on her cosmetics table as she passed it.

Mutbenret was the first of her maids to respond to her call.

"Set out the most beautiful gown you can find," Nefertiti said from the little bath chamber. She pried open the bath's sluice, and the small sunken tub filled with a bright rush of cold water.

She submerged herself, washing quickly and oiling her limbs even before the water had dried on her skin. Mutbenret peeked inside the bath, holding up a fine, red dress with a question on her sleep-creased face. But the red dress wasn't fine enough—not for this day's purpose.

"Something better that that," Nefertiti said, running a comb through her hair and hissing as it snagged in a tangle. "Something with a much finer weave. Something that's almost as clear as water."

When her hair was braided and wound tight against her head, when her face was freshly painted and her skin perfumed with myrrh, Nefertiti finally approved the fourth dress Mutbenret brought before her. It was a white gown as light and pale as a moth's wing, with a weave so open that it left not a hair or freckle unseen. Mutbenret helped tie it at Nefertiti's shoulder and waist, and the girl's eyes widened at the effect of the moon-white fabric sliding over the dark shadow of Nefertiti's navel, the perfect, high-set circles of the nipples on her round, firm breasts.

"Excellent," Nefertiti said. "Now bring my longest wig. It still has the silver beads on its braids, I believe. Silver will look very well with this gown."

Nefertiti's wig and jewels were in place well before the sun had reached its height. She rose from the stool at her cosmetics table with a grace that would have gratified Ay, smiling at herself in the mirror, well pleased with her fresh, captivating beauty and the lush temptation of her near-naked skin.

"I'm ready," she told Mutbenret.

"Shall I accompany you? Will you need me to serve?"

Nefertiti patted her little sister's head. "No, darling. This is a mission best carried out alone. Wait for me here until I return, and you'll know by the smile on my face that I've accomplished what I set out to do."

Mutbenret's brow creased in confusion, but Nefertiti only laughed lightly. Bolstered by the luck of the ibis, she swept from her small room, breezing through the diplomats' hall toward the heart of the House of Rejoicing, where the Pharaoh lay waiting in his chambers.

N EFERTITI HAD SUSPECTED that she might be obliged to wait—perhaps for several hours—until the Pharaoh would deign to see her. She was prepared for such an eventuality, resolved to sit quietly in his receiving room until Amunhotep finally grew bored enough with whatever entertainments he had arranged in an attempt to distract himself from his ever-present pain, and from the specter of his tomb, which, Nefertiti assumed, must loom greater in his heart with every sunset.

But to her surprise, almost as soon as the king's steward had ducked into the royal bed chamber to announce her arrival, the man reappeared again, beckoning Nefertiti forward.

"The king wishes to see you at once," the steward said.

Nefertiti graced him with her best and brightest smile, sending up silent thanks to the ibis for its blessing on her day's work.

She had never been inside the Pharaoh's personal chamber before. The room was vast, edged in massive pillars painted in red and white, their lotus-carved crowns soaring high above her head, where the light streaming in from a wall of windows cast them in sharp, sideways relief. The floor was tiled in pale blue, with here and there the shapes of fish picked out in mosaics of precious stone, each piece fine enough to grace the throat or wrist of a noble lady. It felt delightfully shameful—heady and wasteful—to scuff the carnelians and pieces of turquoise beneath the soles of her sandals as she made her way across the room to the massive bed where the king of Egypt sprawled.

A few servants moved about him, waving plumed fans to stir the air with a constant, gentle ripple, cooling his great, sweating hide. A lithe slip of a girl knelt on a cushion near the king's shoulder, offering up a tray of cakes and cheeses, while another waited with a jug of strong beer poised on her hip, ready to pour the moment Amunhotep complained of thirst.

Across from the great, sloped bed, backlit by the row of windows, a circular stone platform stood a foot above the floor. This plinth was covered with woven rugs and scattered with cushions—a small, private stage, and Nefertiti could well guess the spectacles that were performed there for the Pharaoh's private delight. A woman's veil was half-draped from the platform's edge, dropped and forgotten, and Nefertiti caught the glint of a little silver bell amid the cushions, as if it had fallen from the adorned ankle of a dancer.

Nefertiti swept into the Pharaoh's view. She bowed low, presenting her palms—and lingering as she bent, presenting, too, the ripeness of her curves and her other charms, which her open-weave gown displayed admirably before the king's squinting, shining eyes.

"Nefertiti," Amunhotep said.

There was a thickness to his voice, a rough, hoarse note that Nefertiti that heard too many times before when her husband had spoken her name in the privacy of her chamber—always before he instructed her to don the priestess's robe, before his perverse games began. Nefertiti's eyes narrowed, considering the king's flushed face, the sweat that stuck the linen sheets to his pale body. Yes, she recognized the king's panting urgency, too—the expectant, staring stillness, the shiver of barely controlled need that made his soft flesh quiver like yellow fat carved from a steer's carcass as his eyes roved down the length of her body. His lust was just the same as Young Amunhotep's—familiar and repellent in every respect.

Ay once told me that my task and duty were to work my charms on the king, she mused. *Well, here I am, Father, as you'd intended. But it's not for your designs that I do my duty.*

She had expected to cajole the Pharaoh into a state of arousal, plying her charms so subtly that his desire surprised him and was well enflamed before he realized it. She had not expected to find him already damp with eagerness, leering at her from his bed, devouring her bit by bit with his greedy, possessive eyes.

It is just as well, she thought. *My task will be finished all the sooner.*

"I am happy to see you looking so well, my lord," Nefertiti said, training a playful note into her voice.

"Yes," he grated. "Yes, *well*—very well. Any time now, any moment—ah, Re-Harakhty, I feel you descending!"

He sagged back on his cushions, panting, and Nefertiti noted the fearful glances his servants shared. Was the Pharaoh in some distress? Or even, she wondered with a clutch of panic, on the verge of expiring? But why weren't the servants calling for priests and magicians, if that were the case? No, Nefertiti decided—such fits must be commonplace in the king's private chambers. She took a few steps toward his bed.

Amunhotep righted himself again, grinning so wide at Nefertiti that she could see the brown ruin of his rearmost teeth. "The child," he said. "My *ka* will soon go into it."

Nefertiti stumbled to a halt, struggling to keep the frown of confusion from her face. *What child? Sitamun's?* She couldn't imagine what Amunhotep might mean, so she said smoothly, "Is that so, Mighty Horus? You must tell me more."

"I ensured it..." He trailed off and squeezed his eyes shut, gasping—with pain or lust, Nefertiti could not tell—then seemed to marshal himself with an effort. He went on, "I bred it. I made it my own, with the right spells, the right words. My vessel. My resurrection."

Cold seeped into Nefertiti's limbs. She made herself move with grace, not the leaden, thick-mud stiffness that threatened to overcome her body. With a force of will that would have put Ay to shame, Nefertiti banished the shudder of disgust from her body. She stood poised and serene, gazing down at the Pharaoh with feigned admiration. "How fascinating."

"I shall move into him—my son, my vessel—and like a god, I shall go on forever."

Nefertiti allowed one eyebrow to twitch, lifting by a hair's breadth. *He doesn't know that Sitamun's baby is a girl. He hasn't yet heard the news.* Perhaps no one had yet dared to tell him. Perhaps every steward and courtier in the palace feared that terrible duty, for the king was so enveloped in lust over the thought of his own impending renewal, so consumed with the expectation of godly powers, that there was no telling what he might do to the man who shattered his beautiful delusion. Nefertiti would certainly not risk it herself.

"I congratulate you, my lord, most sincerely. Every man and woman in the Two Lands looks forward to your continued, glorious reign."

The Pharaoh gave a long, drawn-out grunt, not unlike the sound his son made when he surrendered to his release. The morning light glinted from Amunhotep's sweat as he strained against his lust, as his bestial heat rippled along his large, flaccid gut and the bulge of his thighs.

Nefertiti drifted closer, hoping the scent of her fresh myrrh oil carried to the king. "As much as we all anticipate your continued good health, Mighty Horus, I have come to ask a personal favor. I would ask that you send out the proclamation now to all the *sepats* of your kingdom, naming my husband, your son, the true and accepted heir."

Amunhotep's laugh shook the frame of his bed. "Heir? What use have *I* for an heir?"

"None, surely," Nefertiti said quickly. "I will be as blessed as any humble subject by your godly renewal. It is a formality only, my lord..." She trailed one hand along the plunging neckline of her gown, allowing her fingers to play lightly over the swell of her breast. "A favor to me, to give me greater status."

"Status. Women always chase it, like dogs chase bitches in heat."

Nefertiti giggled, tossing her braids, and the silver beads rang their beguiling chimes. "It's true—we women are such silly, flighty things. But it's so easy for a king as great as you to please us, my lord—so easy to please *me*."

Amunhotep went still and silent, staring at her with sudden, focused intensity, his feverish anticipation of resurrection evidently forgotten—for the moment, at least. Nefertiti resisted the urge to step back, quailing from the force of his eyes.

"Go, all of you," the Pharaoh barked, and his servants fled the room with alacrity. "Not you," he said, just as the girl with the tray was on the verge of slipping from the room. "You will remain." She bowed and crept hesitantly back into the room, then pressed her back against a pillar, as if hoping she might meld her body with the stone.

The Pharaoh smiled up at Nefertiti. "So it's easy to please you, is it, wife of my son?"

Nefertiti glanced at the door through which the servants had scattered. It was firmly shut. Her throat went dry, but she smiled serenely and lowered her lashes.

"Perhaps you should learn how easy it is to please *me*," the Pharaoh said.

Nefertiti's heart pounded loud in her ears. *Mother Mut, what trap have I walked into?*

The king gestured for Nefertiti to approach. She took one more step toward him, but remained out of the range of his hands.

"I'll do this thing you ask," Amunhotep said, quivering with suppressed laughter, "if you do for me what Sitamun does."

Nefertiti could not stop her eyes from widening with shock, nor her nostrils from flaring with fear. She had no need to ask what sort of tasks Sitamun performed. That newborn brat hadn't come into the world by some miraculous act of the gods.

She covered her mouth with her fingers, pretending coyness. "Oh, Mighty Horus, you flatter me too much with your desire." But as she spoke her bowels clenched, and her knees turned to water. When the king gave a command, it could not be disregarded. Her thoughts fluttered and battered against her heart, her ribs, tumbling over one another and tangling as she sought some plausible way out of this ever-tightening snare.

As Nefertiti's gaze darted around the king's bedchamber, searching for any means to loose his treacherous hold over her *ka*, the servant girl gave an ill-timed twitch where she stood with her back pressed against the red base of the pillar. Nefertiti caught the girl's eye and summoned her with a jerk of her head. Trembling, cringing like a beaten slave, the girl crept forward. Nefertiti took her firmly by the shoulder and pushed her toward Amunhotep.

At once the Pharaoh, his desire like a fever in his heart, seized the servant's thigh and pushed up the hem of her skirt, stroking and prodding as the girl turned her face away, gritting her teeth against the desire to scream.

"Let me dance for you," Nefertiti said. "Let me entertain you while you take your pleasure."

The servant gasped, staring at Nefertiti in desperate shock. But she only cut the girl a stern glare and moved to the foot of the king's bed, twisting to unheard music, stepping her feet and rolling her hips in time to the frantic, frightened, self-loathing beat of her heart.

The Pharaoh grunted and pushed the servant down, directing her toward his plump loins. Nefertiti closed her eyes so she would not see the humiliation in the servant's face, or the shivers of fear that wracked her slender body as she bent to the unsavory task. But Nefertiti could not shut her ears to the girl's miserable sniffling, nor to the sobs which she fought to strangle in her chest.

Gods, forgive me, Nefertiti prayed as she twisted and spun, displaying first her breasts, then her buttocks, then the smooth curve of hip and waist before the Pharaoh's eyes. *I had no real choice.* But though she felt the cold, hard glare of the gods' judgment, their all-seeing eyes watching her cavort and simper like a painted whore for the king's delectation, she felt none of their absolution, and she knew that she would not be pardoned for this wrongdoing.

Then at least let this not be in vain, she pleaded. *Soften the king's heart. Make him do as I say, so that I will need to harm no one else.*

Amunhotep gave a loud bark of pleasure as the force of his release built. Nefertiti opened her eyes, willing herself not to see the servant girl, and glided to the head of the bed, where the king lay with his head thrown back, grunting in wordless bliss.

"You are all-powerful," she whispered in his ear, breathing in the sour scent of his sweat, the stench of the illness that clung to him. "What does it matter if you indulge one woman's heart, oh Mighty Horus? What will the naming of an heir matter, after all, when you renew yourself, and rise again like the sun in the sky?"

Amunhotep growled as the wave of his pleasure washed over him, rolling and shuddering like a beast wallowing in mud. Nefertiti flinched away, frightened that he would touch her in that moment, afraid that his hands would contaminate her, soiling her *ka* worse than she had already stained it herself. He opened his bleary eyes, and smiled up at Nefertiti almost tenderly.

Then he snapped his fingers at the servant girl who huddled on the floor beside his bed, hugging her thin body and shivering as she cried. "You," he said. "Go and fetch a scribe. I have a proclamation to make."

"Be quick," Nefertiti called after the girl as she ran, sobbing, from the room.

Tiy

Year 37 of Amunhotep
Ruler of Waset,
Lord of Truth in the Sun,
Strong Bull Arising

T IY'S ANGER RIPPLED AND BOILED before her, rolling like a fierce, towering storm as she sped down the halls of the House of Rejoicing. Her rage was a palpable force, a thing of teeth and sharp edges, and with satisfaction she sensed the way it tore and scraped at the painted walls and bright floors of the palace, as if it sought to tear up the murals of gardens and rivers of mosaic, making a ruin of Amunhotep's reign, leaving nothing but scattered shards and refuse in her wake. Huya panted as he scuttled behind her, struggling to keep up. A dull but insistent pain throbbed behind Tiy's forehead, spreading across her skull with each beat of her heart, as the flames of a metal-caster's forge build and spread and burn hotter with each blast from the bellows.

Servants in their plain white tunics, who ordinarily would have bowed to honor a King's Wife, looked at the stark, fuming murder masking Tiy's face and forgot their courtesies, turning to run from her path. Guards offered their salutes, but she did not acknowledge them with even a flick of her eyes, so intent was she on her wrath—on the way it bore her like the Iteru's flood-swollen current toward the object of her rage and hatred.

Amunhotep thought to make me a goddess, once, Tiy mused darkly, *and set his southern subjects to worshipping me in a temple built in my name.* Well, now he had done the impossible, and converted her to a goddess in truth—into two roaring, bestial goddesses, screaming their female rage from deep within Tiy's *ka*: Sekhmet, the blood-thirsty warrior; and Pakhet, the ravening lioness with claws that tore like obsidian blades. Now he would feel the bite of her teeth, the powerful grip of her jaw. Now her claws would sink into his loose, sagging flesh, and he would know what it meant to stand in the presence of divinity, and he would *fear*.

She rounded the corner of one great, columned hall. The Pharaoh's chambers stood before her. The twin figures of Bes carved upon their surfaces leered down at her with a grotesque, mocking grin.

"Stand aside," Tiy shouted to the guards at Amunhotep's doorway.

The men glanced at one another, concern and hesitation clear on their faces.

Tiy did not deign to repeat her command. She swept toward them, borne on the inexorable force of her anger, and when one mumbled his apologies and tried to block her entry with his spear, she flung his arm and his weapon aside with a force that staggered the man, and seized the handle of the door in her own small but powerful hand. She shoved it open, making it scream on its hinges, and together with Huya, she stormed through the knot of startled servants within, parting them like a blade ripping through linen as she made for the king's bed chamber.

Amunhotep, alerted to Tiy's presence by the surprised exclamations of his servants, was already waiting on his bed, his bulk propped on one elbow, his face twisted into a smile as ugly and amused as that of the dwarf god he favored. Tiy's lips tightened with disgust at the sight of him—at the bloated, useless waste of his power-fed greed. But when she noted Sitamun, pale, blank-eyed, and weakly trembling on a stool beside the Pharaoh's bed, Tiy's furious stride was hobbled at last. She stumbled to a halt, staring first at her daughter, then at the king, quivering with brutal loathing.

"What in the name of Hathor's teats is *this*?" Tiy demanded, jabbing one dagger-sharp finger at Sitamun. "She gave birth only the night before last!"

"What's your worry?" Amunhotep wheezed with laughter. "She has spent her two days in bed. It's time she was up, and back to her duties."

Sitamun said nothing, trembling miserably, huddled on the seat of the stool.

Tiy rolled her eyes, sighing as if at the wearying antics of a child. "She is not healed. Her flesh is still torn, and her body is painful. I know. I have been in her place seven times before. What can she even *do* for you in this state, you twisted old fool?"

The Pharaoh sank back comfortably on his cushions. "She has hands, does she not? And her mouth is not torn."

Sitamun gave a loud sniff, and Tiy glanced at the girl's face. There was a frantic desolation there, a wide-eyed, instinctive fear, and a sick trembling in her limbs that Tiy recognized at once. *The poor child is distraught at being separated from her baby.* Tiy had chosen her grand-daughter's wet nurse herself, and knew that Nebetah was in capable hands. But that deep, instinctive dread a mother felt at being out of sight of her newborn could not be assuaged with comforting words or common sense. Sitamun was rattled by the need to hold her child, and no doubt still exhausted from the birth, despite her two days of rest.

Tiy gestured curtly for Huya without taking her eyes off the king. "Take Sitamun back to her chambers."

Huya moved at once to do as his mistress commanded, extending a hand to help Sitamun up from her stool. The

Pharaoh lurched toward him, roaring in anger. He could not countenance the thought of his favorite toy being placed beyond easy reach.

"Leave her be," Amunhotep shouted. He grunted, straining to spring up and stop Huya from carrying out Tiy's orders.

"Do as I say," Tiy commanded her steward—though there was never any danger that Huya would disobey Tiy, not even if the Pharaoh himself countermanded her.

Amunhotep turned a desperate, demanding glare on Tiy, his jowls quivering, his wig slipping comically askew. "Leave her where she is! I won't have her taken away!"

Tiy folded her arms and regarded the Pharaoh's distress with cool satisfaction. "Then get up, oh renewed and rejuvenated god! Get up, and stop her—stop *me*—if you can!"

Amunhotep subsided, a slow, ponderous sinking into the depth of his groaning bed. His small, narrow eyes never left Tiy's face. The look of hatred he gave her—the way his rage shivered down the length of his body—might have made her cautious once. But not anymore. The two lionesses roared inside her, and she faced the king with bold assurance, steady on her own feet while he sagged and faded into his sweat-stained linens.

"What were you thinking, Amunhotep?"

The Pharaoh's leer of hatred remained on his face, but he lifted his brows in a lazy, unspoken question.

"Proclaiming Young Amunhotep your heir," Tiy said. "I just heard the news."

The king's chest rattled with his laughter. "Aren't you pleased? Your son will inherit the throne one day."

Tiy couldn't resist needling the king. "Oh, will he inherit after all? I thought all of Egypt was to wait in breathless expectation for your imminent renewal."

Amunhotep scowled, refusing to respond to her mockery.

"It was the worst choice you could have made," she said. Even if she now knew Young Amunhotep to be innocent of Thutmose's murder, still the thought of him on the Horus Throne—commanding the Two Lands to do his twisted will—filled her with revulsion. "Your country will suffer under Young Amunhotep's control. He is just as decadent and selfish as you are—the gods cast him in your exact mold, though Mut knows I can't say *why*. But his vigor and youth make his greed far more dangerous for us all, Amunhotep. He can reach beyond where you can, dream the kind of foul dreams you cannot even imagine—and with the wealth and power of the Horus Throne, nothing will stop him from making his dreams realities. Egypt will be forever changed, all to suit the grasping desires of one man. But *you* will be the one to answer to the gods, for it was you who was mad enough to make him the heir. Did that truly never occur to you?"

Amunhotep gave a lazy, unconcerned shrug.

Bile rose in the back of Tiy's throat, and she resisted the urge to spit the bitter taste out onto Amunhotep's floor—not because she felt any need to respect the Pharaoh, but because such a display would diminish her superior dignity.

"What put the idea into your head, I wonder?" Tiy mused. "There you were, on the verge of 'renewing,' according to your foul magic. And yet you named him heir. Why?"

Amunhotep's slick, oily chuckle sounded again, sliding into the corners of his vast chamber, where it echoed back at Tiy and seemed to mock her from every angle. "Take it up with Nefertiti," he said.

Tiy blinked. "Nefertiti?"

"Yes, that one—and her *dancing*." He closed his eyes in remembered bliss, and Tiy gave a quick, involuntary shudder. What had the girl done? Tiy would have asked herself what the girl had been thinking, but she could guess easily enough. Nefertiti had been activated by her father, sparked to life at just the right moment to make Ay's own fantasies of power a reality. *Dancing?* Could Ay truly have commanded his own daughter to stoop to the level of a bed slave, working upon the Pharaoh's lusts with her young, tender body?

Why not? Tiy thought with bitter clarity. *Ay did the same with his sister, did he not? Led and cajoled and pushed me into Amunhotep's bed, all for the chance that I might tie a thread to the man who would become the Pharaoh, and place that thread in Ay's hand to control.*

But look, Tiy said to herself, beating back the bleakness of memory. *Look where fate and the gods have led us, after all. Here I stand, the lioness rearing up to strike, free to move and act of my own will. And there lies the king, the wellspring of divinity, the power of the Two Lands—the crook and flail Ay desires for his own clever hands. He is a bloated bag of dying flesh, fading from the world moment by moment, and taking Ay's threads of control with him. But I am a lioness stalking the desert. I go on living, as vital—as capable—as ever.*

And whatever else happened, whatever mad follies the Pharaoh and his grasping, scheming son could dream up between them, Tiy still held her secret pawn. Smenkhkare still dwelt in guarded seclusion, far to the north. She could recall him at any time, and make his bid for the throne. But she must wait until the time was right, until Young Amunhotep could be safely and permanently removed. Otherwise, Tiy had no doubt that her littlest boy would meet the same fate as Thutmose. Ay would not balk at taking the life of another of Tiy's sons—not if Smenkhkare stood in his way, in his crooked path to power.

She turned away from the sight of her husband, from his smug grin and his panting remembrance of a once-great might.

"Very well," Tiy said coolly. "I shall take it up with Nefertiti."

Or with Ay, at any rate, she amended silently. And as she strode from the Pharaoh's bed chamber, her brows lowered and her dark gaze sharpened like the eyes of a falcon speeding toward its prey.

Kiya

Year 1 of Amunhotep
Beautiful Are the Manifestations,
Great of Kingship,
Who Upholds the Sun

S HE DREAMED OF MITANNI.

High on the green, salt-scented cliffs, she clung to the bough of a pine tree and leaned to look over the promontory's edge, to see the surf pounding, white as Egyptian alabaster, far below.

A quiet, unseen presence moved behind her, twisting its dark way through the pine forest. Kiya tensed, and her hand tightened on the branch. The presence drew up behind her—she could feel the sudden warmth of a body, intruding on her privacy, on the sweet memories of home. For a moment she was frightened, certain all at once that the watcher would push her from the cliff, and she would spiral down, down to the jagged rocks, and break among their hard, black points. The blood rushed in her ears with a sound like the roaring waves.

But then the dark presence reached arms around her waist, pulling her back from the edge, holding her tight against firm, hard, masculine flesh. She sighed and leaned back into the embrace, and a warmth gathered in her middle, and spread, throbbing and insistent, along her limbs. She heated in her secret place, and desire bloomed within her as the grasses beneath her feet sent up tall, slender stalks, and the stalks burst into great, round flowers of every imaginable color. Their spicy perfume filled her head, and her heart beat faster.

Something brushed Kiya's cheek, scattering the misty image of her dream. The flowers tumbled across her vision, their petals dispersing on the wind, bright and bobbing, evading her grasping fingertips.

Kiya woke, one hand bunched in the cushion beneath her head. She had adapted to the Egyptian nickname Nefertiti had given her, and had even grown used to other foreign oddities, such as bathing daily in standing water— but she had never taken to the hard, curved headrests the Egyptians used for sleeping. She squeezed her eyes shut and turned her cheek into the pillow, resisting the morning, wishing only to return to the dream, to the strong arms that had held her and the heat that had tempted her.

The touch came again, this time tickling her ear, and spreading a warm thrill down the length of her back.

Kiya's eyelids fluttered open. She looked up.

And lurched upright in her bed, screaming, clutching her bed linens about her naked body. A man stood over her, broad-shouldered, dark-skinned, the white of his kilt gleaming forcefully in the slant of dawn light that burst through her chamber's window.

"Hush," the man laughed, reaching out a hand to soothe her.

Kiya flinched away.

But she recognized his voice, and blinked the sleep from her eyes, rubbing with one knuckle. "Young Amunhotep?"

Kiya looked around her room. Nann stood pressed against the far wall, her slender, white legs shivering below the hem of her short tunic-dress. Her face was frightened and pale, her eyes wide with affront.

"I tried to send him away," Nann said indignantly, "but

he forced his way in. What could I do, Mistress? I couldn't stop him."

Despite her anger and obvious fear, Nann seemed unhurt. Kiya glanced up at Young Amunhotep, opening her mouth to speak, but no words would come.

"I'll send for the harem guards," Nann said briskly, turning for the door.

Kiya held up a hand to stall her. "Wait." She recalled the safe, protective embrace of the unseen man in her dreams, and she knew that Young Amunhotep meant no harm. "It's all right, Nann."

Her servant scowled at her from beyond Young Amunhotep's shoulder. "Let me go fetch someone," Nann said quietly.

But Kiya shook her head. The spicy intoxication of the dream-flowers' petals was still blowing through her, and the heat still hung inside her, the way the echo of the sun's image hangs against the inside of closed eyelids, darting, half-formed, and bright. She stared up into Young Amunhotep's face, at his long, elegant features and the sensitive curve of his mouth—and the softness of his smile caught her. All his typical bravado was gone, his casual boldness, his air of dark, slinking confidence. Gone, too, was the compelling eagerness he had shown the last time he'd come to her chambers, when she had kissed him and then withdrawn the thing he had wanted. He beamed down at her, eyes shining with simple, grateful gladness.

Kiya gave her servant a quick nod of dismissal. "Leave us, Nann."

"What? Mistress, no!"

"Go on—it's all right, I swear it."

Still Nann hesitated, and Kiya laughed at her good-naturedly. "Look at me, Nann. Am I afraid?"

Nann's green eyes slid toward Young Amunhotep's back. Her lips pressed into a pale line and her fingers tangled at her waist as she regarding the King's Son with infinite suspicion. But when Kiya laughed again, Nann turned and reluctantly walked from the room.

Kiya pulled the linens up closer around her body. "Why are you here? I don't understand."

Young Amunhotep seated himself on the edge of the bed, leaning toward her with a happy, buoyant joy that reminded Kiya of a child among his toys. His smile was wide and bright, and soothed away any small anxieties Kiya still felt. She returned his grin, shaking her head in wonder.

"The first thought I had when I heard the news," he said, "was that I must come to see you. I must come and look upon my wife—my King's Wife."

Kiya's smile fell away. "I don't understand," she said again.

"He's gone, Kiya. The old king is dead—your old husband has departed for the Field of Reeds. The Horus Throne is mine. I am the Pharaoh now, and you belong to me."

Kiya's breath left her chest with one sharp gasp. Her fists clutched the linens tighter as Young Amunhotep's demeanor shifted from that of a happy child to the towering confidence of a conquering warlord. A tiny worm of caution coiled inside her stomach. She looked at Young Amunhotep with a wary, assessing glance, and beneath the linens, her body felt quite vulnerable and bare.

"But what happened?" she asked him. "How did he die?"

Young Amunhotep shook his head impatiently, leaning closer still. "Who knows? Only the gods. It was due to his illness, no doubt. He'd been sick for so long, after all."

"But so soon after he named you heir? It has been only a few days since he made the proclamation, Amunhotep.

The court will suspect you."

He gave one short, quiet laugh, a huff of confident amusement that made Kiya's scalp prickle. "Let them suspect whatever they will. The proclamation has already been made, carved into the stone of the holy scarabs. It cannot be undone now. And besides, my conscience is clean. I did not harm my father—I can swear to that."

You swore once, Kiya told him silently. *You swore that we were lovers, although we were not.*

Kiya knew that oaths meant little to this man—this slinking lion of the desert. And yet he had promised to make her a King's Wife as soon as he obtained the throne, and here he was, raising her out of her dreams, and calling her his queen. Here he was, smiling at her with gentle eyes that seemed to mean her no harm. He had the power now to shape the world to his whim. And he had come for her first, to fulfill the promise he had given her.

Kiya's eyes grew heavy with relief, with the unbearable joy of knowing that her confinement would soon be at an end. The dark fringe of her lashes obscured Young Amunhotep from her sight; she sighed as she felt the burden of her terrible months in Egypt lift a little from her shoulders.

He seemed to mistake her reaction for desire, for at once he closed the distance between them and kissed her, his mouth falling against her own with a hunger and a passion that frightened her. But she recalled that he had come to save her, just like the unseen watcher in her dream—pulling her back from the cliff, holding her close, sheltering her in his arms. And so, even as his teeth scraped her lip and his tongue pushed forcefully into her mouth, she chided away her fear. She banished it from her body, and as it went, it left nothing but the heat of desire in its place.

His lips moved to the taut, white line of her neck, where

her pulse beat fast and hard. The linens slipped from her trembling hands, and Kiya fumbled for a moment to regain them, until Young Amunhotep's hand found her small, firm breast, stroking the soft skin with gentle fingers. She arched her back, moaning in welcome, in gladness that her isolation was ended.

Nann's advice fought its way past the throbbing in her body, the rush of blood in her ears. *Tempting, never satisfying.* Kiya summoned her strength, fighting back against the languid weakness that suffused her limbs, the compelling fire that melted the resistance within her.

She pushed feebly against Amunhotep's shoulders.

He drew back from her neck, casting her a confused, faintly irritated look.

"You must," she panted, "make me a wife."

His low, soft laugh pulled at the heat inside her, and she ached between her legs, at the tips of her breasts, along her neck where his kisses had trailed.

"Didn't I say I would?"

Kiya pressed against him, digging her nails into the skin of his shoulders. His eyes widened in surprise.

"I want my own estate," she insisted. "My own home. Not a room in the harem, or anywhere else."

He tapped his chin. "I shall have to do the same for Nefertiti, then."

Kiya tossed her head. "Whatever you give to Nefertiti, you must give to me, too."

"Is that so?" His lips curved with amusement, with the indulgent pleasure a man shows for his quarreling, competitive wives.

Kiya wanted those lips on her neck again, and lower—on her breasts, on the flat, sensitive plane of her stomach. "Yes," she said impatiently. "You must give me *more* than you give her."

Suddenly, and so roughly that it made her cry out, he seized her by the back of her neck. "I already do give you more," he whispered. And his hand tangled in her braid, pulling backward, exposing her throat to his lips. He pulled harder; her back arched, and the breath rasped helplessly in her chest. The fear returned, sending ice along her fast-throbbing veins. But when his lips descended on her breast, Kiya cried out with the force of her pleasure, and the ice flashed all in a moment to fire. She shuddered and twisted against the restraint of his fist in her hair, her body bent and exposed, helpless to his exploration, his mastery. She wanted to break away and flee from him, to cover herself against the shame. And she wanted him to go on, to take from her whatever he wanted, to make the fire rushing inside her burn on and on like the heat of the Egyptian sun.

"I won't..." Her voice was faint, weak in her tight-stretched throat. "I won't be..." The words were lost in a moan as he moved to her other breast, his tongue circling her nipple, his teeth grazing her with a flare of sweet pain. "I won't be shut up here... in the harem."

Amunhotep released her breast, leaning back to eye her where she hung in his grip, pinioned by his power. At once she regretted speaking, regretted distracting him from that singular, compelling pleasure.

"Please," she whispered.

"Please?" Bent backward as she was, she couldn't see his slow, satisfied smile. But she could hear it in the confidence of his voice, as rich and dark as the Iteru's silt.

She twisted, thrusting her chest up toward him again. "Please... give me more."

"You shall have more. More, King's Wife, and *more*."

He released her braid, and rose up from the bed. Kiya

nearly cried out in loss, and her hands stretched out, reaching for him, not willing to let the flame die away.

But before she could touch Amunhotep, his hands found her body first. He took her hard by the hips, dragging her toward the edge of the bed where he stood, and her linens fell away. Kiya was dimly, briefly aware of a flash of bright, quivering shame, as her entire body was exposed to his eyes, spread before him with nothing concealed. Roughly, he parted her thighs. Kiya gasped, darting her hands down to cover herself, but he took her wrists in a grip like bronze, tight and unbreakable, and pinned her hands at her sides.

He entered her with one hard thrust. Kiya's shout of pain turned at once into a long, shivering, breaking cry of pleasure, and she stared up at him while he worked with a furious energy, each forceful movement of his body increasing her heat with relentless pressure. He towered over her like a monument to a god, imposing and stark, a force of will that Kiya knew could never be denied.

Tiy

T HE NEXT TIME TIY RETURNED to her brother's estate, it was at his request—his *summons*, as if he believed himself inexorable, already hung with the golden trappings of a god-king.

Tiy longed to resist Ay's request, just to prove to him that he did not yet hold the power he craved. And in fact she did tear up the papyrus Ay's messenger had brought, scattering its thin, pale fragments across her chamber and shattering Ay's blue wax seal beneath the toe of her sandal. The gesture—and the sight of the family's leaping antelope symbol cracked in waxy bits against the tiles of her floor—brought a few precious moments of vindication, and a tight, vicious smile to Tiy's lips. But curiosity—her never-ending need to know all, to see all—ruled her *ka* as ever, and with a growl of frustration she summoned Huya and told him to prepare for the walk to Ay's estate.

Ay was waiting to receive her, standing straight-backed and still in the shadow of his outer portico, his hands locked behind his back, his obvious pleasure rising like a stink from his body, making Tiy's nose wrinkle in distaste as she made her way down the unforgivingly straight, white-limestone path of his garden. Ay had bedecked himself as if for a festival, the long, pleated folds of a formal kilt falling all the way to his feet, his chest covered by an electrum pectoral made in the image of the family's proud, running antelope. Its slender legs were jointed with wire-thin loops, so that they shivered and swung with the faint stirring of Ay's breath.

"Sister," he said in greeting. His voice was rich with triumph.

Tiy halted with her steward in the sunshine, refusing to step into Ay's blue shade. She looked at him expectantly, but did not speak.

Ay's shoulders shook with one short bark of self-satisfied laughter. The antelope's legs kicked. "Well," he said, "it seems the sun has risen on a new regime. And my daughter is King's Wife."

"How proud you must be," Tiy said drily.

Ay tested the sound of the new title that was his by rights. "'Father of the God.' Fitting, don't you think?"

"Timely," Tiy conceded. "Well done, you clever, clever man."

Ay raised his brows, amused at the chagrin Tiy could not conceal, no matter how she wrestled with her anger. "I was diligent in raising Nefertiti to be an effective King's Wife, and worked hard to maneuver her into position. But I had nothing to do with the *timing.*"

"I am sure." *Just as you had nothing to do with Thutmose's death.*

Tiy still had not confronted Ay with the evidence of the knotted cord. But now, musing on the new title that so delighted her brother, her frown eased as realization dawned in her heart. *I have a new title, too.* King's Mother—an especially potent position in the court. Not nearly as powerful as Great Wife, but certainly antelope-leaps ahead of the Pharaoh's father-by-marriage.

Tiy smiled fractionally, and her helpless anger receded a little. As a discarded King's Wife, she had no real potency to accuse Ay of the murder—not unless she stood in especially great favor with the Pharaoh, and there had been no love lost between Tiy and Amunhotep.

But the King's Mother could press her case to the Pharaoh himself, and if Tiy was careful—accommodating and patient—she might sway Young Amunhotep's heart, and find a place of favor within his circle of closest advisors.

Then I'll give you cause to grin, Brother, Tiy promised silently as Ay accepted a cup of wine from a bowing servant. The thought cheered Tiy enough that she reached out a hand for a drink, too, and savored the sweet vintage while she and Ay locked eyes over the rims of their cups.

"Dancing," Tiy said at last, as she swallowed the last drop of her wine. "I wouldn't have suspected it from you."

Ay tilted his head. "Dancing?"

"The theme of your plots usually run to the cunning, not the openly carnal. After all, even when we were young you never set me to dance seductively for the king. But any old trick to seal the deal—is that the way you operate these days, now that old age is fast approaching?"

Ay chuckled. "Tiy, what *are* you talking about?"

"Nefertiti. What she did to convince my husband to make the proclamation in the days before he died."

Ay's dark brows knit in a frown of consternation, a change of expression so instantaneous that Tiy knew at once it was genuine, and not a part of Ay's usual games.

He doesn't know, she thought. *He has no idea that Nefertiti acted without his knowledge, or his consent—that she took her fate into her own hands, and did not wait on his directive.*

The realization of all that this implied crashed upon Tiy's heart like a gong struck full in her face. Any other woman would have reeled in sudden fear for her own carefully laid designs, or crowed in victory over Ay's helplessness— at the way his power drained away right before his eyes, though he didn't yet recognize that relentless trickle. But Tiy only pulled herself a little straighter, folding her arms and feeling the full warmth of the morning sun, its reassuring, life-giving caress.

Lightly, happily, Tiy smiled. "Ay. You old, blind fool."

He peered at her sharply, the skin tightening over the subtle curves of his flat, staring face. But he said nothing.

"You raised Nefertiti well, indeed," Tiy said. "You put the stone in her spine, and no mistake. And now she has turned on you, it seems."

"Turned on me? Why in the name of Amun would she do that? You're babbling, Tiy. Come out of the sun. An old lady like you needs shade and rest. Let me call for a chair."

Tiy rolled her eyes, ignoring his taunts. "Nefertiti is operating on her own. She struck before you could, and acted of her own volition, to ensure her husband was named heir before it was too late." As Tiy spoke, the details of Nefertiti's plan unfurled before her, the motives and methods writing themselves plainly before her heart's eye. Tiy was certain she wasn't wrong. Nefertiti was an intelligent young woman, and had, after all, received the benefit of observing Ay all her life. She was certain that she understood Nefertiti now—and just as certain that both she and the girl's father had underestimated her ambition and ability. "Nefertiti ensured that Young Amunhotep received the heirship *through her*—by *her* hand, through *her* doing. He now owes his throne to his wife."

Ay grunted in satisfaction. "All the better."

"All the worse for you. She severed the hold you had on her, Ay, neat and clean. And all it took for her to break your grasp was a little..." Tiy rotated her hips suggestively, and Ay turned his flat stare away with a moue of dignified disgust.

And all the worse for me, too. Tiy's thoughts warred

somewhere between bitterness and grudging respect for her niece. A King's Mother had power, but no one would have as much pull with the new Pharaoh as the woman who had managed, at last—even against the old king's staunch belief in his own immortality—to effect the proclamation of the heir. Tiy had to admit that it was an impressive feat, for she knew what a stone-hard will one must have to break free from Ay's insidious, lifelong influence. *Nefertiti is stronger than I know—a force far greater than Ay can imagine.* To think Tiy had once pitied the girl for her loveless marriage. *Hah!* Would Nefertiti pity Tiy, or her pathetic, grasping father, when she reshaped the world to her own desires?

"You have no tool any longer. Your hand is empty, Ay." She tossed the locks of her wig over her shoulder and turned, ready to leave her brother to lurk alone in his shadows and his defeat. "Don't count on making use of Nefertiti anymore. You have no hold on the throne. Your daughter's hand is no one's but her own."

"Is that what you think?" His voice was sly and cold.

Despite her conviction, Tiy hesitated, and glanced back at Ay. The sun was bright on her face, and Tiy blinked as she peered beneath the portico. Ay had stepped backward, receding into the darkness, so that veils of blue-black rippled shadowed his face, casting his form in silhouette.

"My influence goes deeper than you know, Tiy. Don't dismiss my power yet. Nefertiti might think herself beyond my reach, but she is wrong. Utterly wrong. And so are you."

Tiy spun away from him and marched past Huya, lifting her skirts in shaking fists as she went, so that her stride would be strong and unhindered. At first, she couldn't name the blunt, driving fury that propelled her down the path until she was nearly running from Ay's presence. She slowed herself with monumental effort, forcing herself to consider her brother's scorn, his words; the rapid, sick-tremble beat of her own heart.

Did he ever speak of me that way? she wondered. *Did he ever tell another person—our father, perhaps—that I was helpless in his grip, no matter how free and clear-thinking I believed myself to be?*

She thought of Sitamun, pale-faced and red-eyed with the need to hold her baby, and her stomach clenched with sour disgust. *It's abominable—inhuman—for Ay to use his children in this way, to think of them with so little regard.*

But as the gates to Ay's estate closed behind her, Tiy's appalled revulsion turned inward. She had used her children in the same despicable manner, placing them like pawns on a *senet* board, skipping them one over another, capturing and bargaining, sending them into danger with a sharp word and a black glance, to do the duty she had set for them. She had always used them thus.

I am just like Ay. Her vision danced around her as the truth of her *ka* beset her with a dizzy force. *Just like him—and I am as much in his power now as ever I was before, because he has made me... made me into* him.

Tiy clapped a hand to her temple, fighting back against the pounding heat. She was dimly aware of Huya rushing to her side, taking her arm with solicitous care. "My lady?"

Tiy turned to her steward, peering desperately into his ever-calm face, hoping to see some grace of the gods, some redemption in his eyes. But all she could see reflected there were two tiny images of herself, one in each of his pupils, backlit by the sun, but tiny and trembling.

"Oh!" Tiy cried. She reeled away from Huya, but the morning's growing heat battered her, and she lurched back toward him again, stumbling as her sandals caught in the road.

Huya caught her as she fell, pulling her close, tucking

her face against his shoulder so that no chance passers-by would see the great, unflappable Tiy weeping.

"My lady," he said quietly, "please."

But Tiy went on crying, her fists clenched against Huya's back, while behind her burning eyes, Ay's face and Nefertiti's coalesced and floated, circled one another in a slow, wary dance.

"I am just like him," Tiy wailed, "and the gods will curse me for it."

"Curse you, lady? Never! Please, you must pull yourself together. Don't do this here, where there are eyes to see."

But there were always eyes to see—everywhere, in the privacy of her chamber, in the dark of the temple, in the flickering lamplight in a filthy alleyway, where a boy lay sprawled as if in sleep. There were eyes in the shadows that surrounded her brother. There were eyes on the river, glowing in the darkness, slipping beneath the surface with a sly, deliberate glide.

The gods' eyes saw her, and Tiy's heart froze in terror.

I don't know how to save myself. She mouthed the words silently against her steward's chest. *Myself—or anyone else.*

Sitamun

Year 1 of Amunhotep
Beautiful Are the Manifestations,
Great of Kingship,
Who Upholds the Sun

THE KING HAD NOT SUMMONED Sitamun, but she was through with waiting on commands. As she made her way toward the great, painted doors decorated with the fearful, disapproving scowl of Bes, she lifted her chin higher, moving with the directness and assurance of King's Wife Tiy. She did not know whether her timidity had died with old Amunhotep, or whether her bravery had been birthed under the golden moon, as she'd labored to bring Nebetah into the cold and fearful world. But either way, it made no difference. Sitamun was through with being a flitting moth, a quivering mouse. She had been a King's Great Wife, and if the gods had any mercy at all, any shred of pity or kindness, she would be again. She had no cause to slink through the halls of the House of Rejoicing with her eyes downcast. Those days were gone, and she would not suffer them to return again.

Sitamun let herself into Young Amunhotep's new chambers, and only the lightest shiver of loathing prickled her flesh as she crossed into the apartments where she had once been the object of base humiliations. Now, after the trials her body and heart had faced, she knew herself to be powerful—no one could take that knowledge away. Whatever had happened in the past was done. Sitamun moved fearlessly toward her own bright horizon.

She was pleased to see that her brother had moved quickly, clearing out the old Pharaoh's furnishings and stripping his gods from the niches in the wall. A cadre of servants moved briskly through the wide, nearly bare apartment, sweeping, scouring, fetching baskets of Young Amunhotep's goods, burning incense to drive away the sour stink of the king that was.

The servants bowed low as she passed, trailing the long hem of a red gown behind her. She moved like a desert wind toward the bed chamber, a route she knew all too well, but she did not hesitate before she threw the door open and strode inside.

Here, too, everything was changed, save for the murals on the walls and the river scene of the tiled floor. The old closets and tables had been whisked away, and the wide bed where the old king had breathed his was last no more than a bad memory. Even the stone plinth where Sitamun had often been made to perform was dissasembled, gone— only a ring of discoloration remained on the floor to mark its former location..

Young Amunhotep looked up from a table scattered with the remains of his breakfast. Goose bones, picked bare, and a few crumbs of bread lay in a bowl beside a stack of scrolls. Amunhotep held one of the scrolls open on his lap, examining its contents. When he saw that it was Sitamun who had interrupted him, he cast her a dark, brooding frown, and went back to his reading. "What do you want, you little flea?"

Sitamun's nostrils flared in anger, a fury almost equal to the hollow pain that yawned inside her at his harsh words, his rejection. But she would not allow these weak emotions to show on her face, nor permit them to color her voice.

She glanced again at the table, and noted a small statue beside the breakfast bowl—a seated woman worked in alabaster, pink granite, and jet. Sitamun squinted at the thing, trying to puzzle out which goddess it represented. She drifted closer, and lifted the statue in her hand. The figure didn't wear the typical, straight-sided wig of an Egyptian—or of a goddess of the Two Lands—but her hair was coiled around her head in a thick, pink-granite braid. *Kiya.* Sitamun let the statue drop back onto the table, thumping heavily from her fingers.

Amunhotep looked at the figure with a stupid, dewy grin. "Lovely, isn't it? Now my little pet, my little monkey can watch over me even while I'm here in my new chambers."

"*I* could have watched over you," she said bitterly.

Amunhotep sighed, letting the scroll snap closed in his lap. He looked up at her with a slow, long-suffering twist of his neck. "This again?"

Sitamun's *ka* quivered inside her chest, but she folded her arms, and pinched the soft skin inside her elbow to keep from crying. "You can't just cast me off like some rind of fruit, tossed onto a refuse heap." He stared at her blankly, and she added, "I won't allow it."

"You won't *allow* it? Remember who you speak to, Little Sister. I am the king now."

"Then behave like one," she retorted. "You used to be kind to me. You used to value what we had—"

"What?" Amunhotep flared, rising from his chair. His thigh bumped the edge of his table as he stood, and his pile of scrolls scattered, rolling across the tabletop and onto the floor, but Amunhotep took no notice. He stepped toward her with a menacing glower, his shoulders tight with anger. "What did we have? A little wetness between the thighs? Some panting and whimpering in the garden? That was *all* we had, Sitamun—nothing more. Now get out."

"We had a bond," she shot back at him, refusing to be

intimidated. "We are more than just lovers. We are brother and sister. That makes us stronger—that makes our ties closer and better than your ties to other women." She felt the Kiya statue staring at her from the tabletop, but she would not meet its tiny, jet-black eyes.

Amunhotep grunted in disgust and brushed past her, then rummagjed in one of his expensive cedar chests for a brush and ink. "I have work to do. Begone. Your prattling annoys me."

Sitamun stood her ground. "Who else has done as much for you—all the things I've done for you? I gave you a child!"

"You gave *me* a child?"

"Nebetah is your daughter. I am sure of it."

"Well, I'm sorry I can't share your certainty," he said, returning to his table with the brush and ink, casually unrolling one of the scrolls again. "You certainly enjoyed cavorting with Father, so—"

"I did *not* enjoy that," she spat. She tore the stroll out of his hands and crumpled it, flinging it across the room. "How dare you even say so! I only did what I was commanded to do—commanded by the Pharaoh himself."

"And now the Pharaoh commands you to leave, and to stop harassing him with your unreasonable demands. Besides," he added as he calmly selected another scroll, "I've heard from the concubines all about Father's little spell—the magics he laid on you to turn your child into his, no matter who originally sired it."

Sitamun's eyes stung with shock. She blinked the tears away.

"Oh, yes," Amunhotep chuckled, "it's no secret."

"Father also swore the child would be a boy," Sitamun said. She was proud that her voice was low and cold, smoothly amused, just like Tiy's. "So you can see how well his magical spells worked. Everything he did was in vain. And he is gone now, anyway—drying out beneath the salts in the House of Death, just as he deserves. But you are here—and I am here."

Amunhotep stroked his chin as he read, evidently absorbed in the scroll, paying no heed to Sitamun's words.

Desperation surged up like a cold well below her heart, and she tried again, fighting to keep the fear from her voice. "My daughter is *yours*, Amunhotep. I swear it."

He gave no sign of having heard her.

The bold façade of Tiy began to crumble, and Sitamun's old, fearful self showed tender and raw through the cracks. She clasped her hands in a gesture of pleading, and hated herself for doing it. But she could not let her love go as easily as that. "Amunhotep—Brother—after all I've done for you—"

This time, he crumpled the scroll himself and threw it, all in one fast, tight, furious movement. It hit Sitamun in the face; she jerked her head aside, holding her cheek with a trembling hand as if he had slapped her.

"Gods damn you," Amunhotep roared, "what do you want, then? Tell me, and get out of my sight! I'm *tired* of you, Sitamun—utterly through with you! Can't you see that?"

She remembered the bright face of the moon smiling down at her through the sycamore branches as she lay in the birth pavilion. With a firm, deliberate hand, Sitamun shoved her fear and timidity away. She had worn the cobra crown, when she had reigned as King's Great Wife. She would be a cobra now—for now, and forever more.

She dropped her hand from her cheek and faced her brother squarely. "I won't be cast aside," she said, steady and calm. "Remember this, Amunhotep: no other woman in the harem has the royal blood. No one at all, save for me. Not Nefertiti, and not your precious pet Kiya. I am your key—your *only* key—to godly heirs. No other woman has the power to breed your divine offspring."

"I have other sisters," he muttered.

"Oh, indeed. Recall them from the temples, if you can. They will not come, not even at a king's command—not if that king is *you*. I am the only one, of all your sisters, who will obey the divine will. I am the only one who never recoiled from your touch. I am your only hope for a legacy."

His face went very smooth, very still. His eyes traveled down the length of her body, assessing her rigid posture, her rich gown and regal jewels, the familial carriage of absolute confidence and power. He pursed his lips, and Sitamun could read his thoughts as clearly as he read his scrolls. His other sisters—Iset and Henuttaneb, who had fled the West Bank at the first opportunity—were beyond his reach now, and would certainly not return, even if he issued a divine order.

"You had best treat me well," Sitamun said, "for the sake of your divine progeny. And it *is* divine progeny you want, I know. Now you are the force of creation in the world— the inheritor of our father's power. You will be satisfied with no less than the children I can provide—the children *only* I can provide."

He did not speak then, but his look softened, the tension leaving his back and neck, his wide lips almost curving into a smile. He nodded, once—and that was all.

Sitamun accepted his acquiescence with an abrupt lift of her chin that would have done Tiy proud.

"You will marry me," she told him. "I will not be cast off. You will make me a King's Wife."

"But not Great Wife," he interjected.

"That is all one to me. I have no desire to wear that title

again—but I won't live out my days as a cast-off. I'll be a wife of standing, and anything you give the others, you must give me, too."

He sighed. "Women—always so jealous, so grasping."

Sitamun ignored the taunt. "I've heard you're planning to give Kiya her own little palace in the great garden. I shall have one, too—exactly like hers."

Amunhotep waved his hand briskly in the air, his attention already drifting back to his scrolls. "Fine. It's as good as done. Is there anything else you demand, oh mighty King's Wife?"

"Just this," she said, her stomach writhing as anxiety and victory tangled tight around one another. "I'll have *everything* Kiya has—Kiya and Nefertiti both. If one of them sits beside you at a feast, I shall sit on your other side. If you spend a night in one of their beds, you'll spend a night in mine, too."

Amunhotep shrugged. "A simple enough request."

She nodded briskly, like a trader completing a transaction. "I am glad we are agreed."

She turned and marched from the king's bed chamber. It had once been the place where humiliations had once piled upon her small, yielding body, until she had felt sure she would suffocate, or crumble like the old mudbrick of an abandoned house. But it wasn't the same chamber anymore, and this Pharaoh wasn't the last.

Mother would be proud, Sitamun told herself, biting back a triumphant grin as she breezed by the servants who still rustled about the outer room. They bowed in the wake of her passage, then returned to their work, dusting away the last, dry remnants of the king that was—the king who, Sitamun knew, would never come again.

Nefertiti

Year 1 of Amunhotep
Beautiful Are the Manifestations,
Great of Kingship,
Who Upholds the Sun

THE CURTAINS OF THE LITTER were tightly drawn to block the worst of the pre-dawn chill. The Inundation had reached its peak, flooding the Black Land with long, still, clean-smelling swaths of water, rich with silt. The increased moisture meant a sharp bite of cold against the skin—at least in the dark hours, when the sun god was entrenched in his nightly battle through the black caverns of the Duat. When the sun rose again, the silver pools and new-made marshes that blanketed the farmers' fields would warm beneath the god's benevolent gaze, and the water would yield its eternal blessing in a thick, fragranced vapor, filling Egypt with the sweet perfume of black mud and green leaves—the promise of life renewed.

But morning was still some distance off, and Nefertiti kept the wool curtains shut as her litter made its way out of the lanes and roadways of the West Bank estates and began the long climb up to the flat-topped hill where the Circuit of the Sun lay, reaching the loop of its long, pale arms out beyond the empty viewing platforms.

Nefertiti pulled her thick cloak tighter around her shoulders, huddling against her cushions in silence. Beside her, Mutbenret peered from side to side, as if she could see past the curtains, out into the chill, dark-gray world.

"What is this all about, Nefertiti?" her little sister asked, not for the first time.

Patiently, Nefertiti answered as she had before. "I don't know. Sit-Hathor, my night-maid, woke me an hour ago and told me to dress, because the king had summoned me here." She smiled confidently at her sister in the litter's gloom. "That's all I can tell you. I suppose we'll soon find out—Sit-Hathor said the king's messenger told me to meet him at the Circuit of the Sun, and we're nearly there now."

Mutbenret stared darkly at the curtains. "I don't like it. It's strange."

"Everything is strange with Young Amunhotep." She found Mutbenret's hand among the cushions and squeezed it. "But there's nothing to be afraid of. I'm solidly in his favor now. He knows it was I who finally convinced his father to issue the proclamation. He has told me so, and he seemed genuinely grateful. I think I shall have an easier time managing him, now that he owes me a debt of gratitude."

I hope I shall. If Nefertiti had grown certain of anything in the months following her marriage, it was that Young Amunhotep's moods were impossible to predict. *I may as well try to guess what sort of creatures might be lurking at the bottom of a muddy pool.* Possibilities ran an endless and terrifying gamut. *And whatever assumption I make*, Nefertiti though, *I'm almost certainly in for a nasty surprise when I dip my toe into the water.*

Still, in spite of his mercurial nature, Young Amunhotep was logical and observant. Only two days ago, he had called Nefertiti to his chamber, where he was engaged with scrolls and tablets and stewards, planning the Opening of the Mouth ceremony, which would seal his father's mummy in his tomb and officially raise Young Amunhotep to the Horus Throne, making him the legitimate king in the eyes of his subject and the gods. With a distracted air, he had beckoned Nefertiti to approach as he frowned down at calculations of costs and directives from the Temple of Amun, which stipulated what he must wear at the ceremony, and even the words he must speak. Nefertiti had waited quietly beside the arm of his chair, thinking he had forgotten her—but then he had suddenly taken her hand and smiled up at her. "I owe it all to this one," he'd said to his stewards. "Not only beautiful, but clever, too. If she hadn't acted in just the right moment, we would be wrestling Tiy right now, trying to fend off *her* choice of an heir." Then he had risen and kissed her on the cheek. It was the first embrace of any real warmth that Nefertiti had ever received from her husband.

But he knows the part I played, she told herself as the litter continued its long, swaying climb through the darkness. He couldn't possibly know the specifics—how she had gone to the old king dressed like a whore from a Waset dockside, and then allowed herself to be trapped in a degrading performance. Or how she had forced the servant girl to take her place. The girl's sobs still drifted through Nefertiti's dreams, and when she woke she still tasted the salt of the servant's tears on her own tongue. *I only did what was necessary*, she insisted, repeating the words with every beat of her heart. *For myself, for Thutmose, for Mutbenret—for my father—him, most of all. Soon he will reap what he has sown.*

Nefertiti had neither seen nor heard from her husband since that summons to his chamber. She suspected he was entrenched in preparation for the Opening of the Mouth, and in any case, every night she spent without him was a relief—every night she was not required to spend dressed in a stiff, reeking priestess's smock, or gritting her teeth through the pain as Young Amunhotep rutted her uncooperative body with a predatory intensity in his eyes, with his teeth bared in an expression that was more animal snarl than rictus of pleasure.

Still, despite the welcome peace of the past two nights, she was growing impatient. Nefertiti had done all she could to learn more about Kiya's condition—how long she had carried the child, when it might be due—but the Hurrian's servants were remarkably tight-lipped. Even the Egyptian girls who waited on the mouse wouldn't give a word of gossip to any of the women Nefertiti sent their way, and the foreign maid with the missing tooth would pull the spindle from her waist-sash, brandishing the thing like a weapon, if anyone mentioned *Kiya* and *pregnancy* in the same breath.

Kiya already had Young Amunhotep's heart—and welcome to it, for all Nefertiti cared. But if she gave him a son...? Nefertiti couldn't lose her weak grasp on her husband. Justice for Thutmose depended on it.

Kiya doesn't matter, she told herself firmly, jerking the edge of her cloak up to her chin. *If she had a dozen sons, she would still stand in my shadow. I gave him a throne. A king may need sons to inherit, but without a throne, he is no king at all.*

The litter shifted as its bearers reached the crest of the hill. Nefertiti and Mutbenret shared a look—the girl wide-eyed and anxious, Nefertiti fixing a placid, unconcerned smile to her lips. When the litter lowered to the ground, Mutbenret gathered up her own cloak as if she meant to venture outside its curtains, but Nefertiti stayed her with a gentle hand on her shoulder. "Wait here. He summoned only me, and we mustn't upset him."

"But what if you need me?"

She kissed Mutbenret's forehead. "You good, dear thing. I'll be well. We have the soldiers who carried us here, and I'm not afraid of the Pharaoh."

Nevertiti rose and dropped the curtains back into place, but as she straightened and turned, the smile slid from her lips.

Her litter-bearers had deposited her in the trampled,

dusty ground between the large limestone viewing platforms at the edge of the Circuit of the Sun. As the Two Lands waited in respect to inter their former king, there were no chariot races scheduled for a week or more to come, and so the waxed-linen shade canopies had been removed from the limestone platforms. The long, flat shapes of the platforms, like pale barges stripped of their sails, stood out in bright, almost glowing contrast against the cold, formless gray of the pre-dawn landscape. Two more litters stood waiting beside the nearest platform, their ornate bearing-poles and lotus-carved drapery columns vivid, cruelly sharp, against the beached barges of white stone.

As Nefertiti stood blinking in surprise, the curtains of one litter shifted. The guards who milled around it moved quickly to hold the drapery aside, and the slender, white figure of Kiya emerged from its depths. She stood gazing about her with her habitually timid air, and Nefertiti imagined she could see the little mouse trembling from across the trampled yard.

Movement around the other litter shifted Nefertiti's attention. Its guards, too, held the curtains aside, and Nefertiti gave an undignified grunt of shock when little Sitamun stood, tugging her dress straight and brushing wrinkles from its skirt. Sitamun glanced up, noticed Nefertiti staring at her, and held the look with a still, direct gaze that reminded Nefertiti uncomfortably of Tiy.

Kiya gave a hesitant wave and started toward Nefertiti— then stopped, bunching up her cloak as if in indecision, and finally looked around at Sitamun, waiting for the younger girl's lead.

"You sickly kitten," Nefertiti muttered under her breath, then turned away from the girls and their litters, and walked alone out into the Circuit of the Sun.

She stood alone in the bare, stone-scattered place beyond

the chariot track. Had it truly been a just few months ago, she wondered, that the old Pharaoh had sat here, raised on his throne before the eyes of the court with the sun beating down its fierce, insistent blessing? Nefertiti remembered how she had warmed to Kiya, sitting with her on the viewing platform, leaning close to whisper in her ear as Young Amunhotep had put his strong, graceful body gracefully through its paces, handling all the required rites of the king with capability and ease. And all the while, the old Pharaoh had sagged on his throne, his weakness and incapacity on full, shocking display.

There was no throne here now. The dais where it had stood was long gone. The Circuit of the Sun reached out toward the western cliffs, the shallow ruts of its track like old, fading scars in the earth's skin. Beyond the cliffs, the sky-goddess Nut was tucking her black, shimmering body away, fading herself into the horizon and winking shut the eyes of her stars, one by one, as dawn came ever nearer.

Nefertiti squinted toward the cliffs, wondering which secret cleft or cavern held the entrance to old Amunhotep's tomb. She would find out soon enough, when all the residents of the West Bank joined his funeral procession, carrying the ornate, nested coffins up the dusty trail to the place of his eternal rest. There, once Young Amunhotep had performed the ceremony to raise the old king into the afterlife, the stone of his grave would be sealed and no one in the living world would look upon the old Pharaoh again. No one could have seen Nefertiti's tight, wry grimace of anticipation, there in the gray-shrouded dawn of the Circuit. Perhaps when the old king was locked in darkness, the memory of her dance—and the weeping servant girl—would finally leave her in peace.

Sandals scuffed on the earth behind her, but Nefertiti did not turn. She sensed Kiya's shrinking, tentative presence, and felt, like the creep of an insect walking on her skin, the other woman's nervous desire for Nefertiti to speak first, to break the silence and lead the way. Nefertiti kept her mouth closed.

Sitamun drew up on Nefertiti's other side, her cloak thrown back as if she welcomed the morning's chill. The girl's breasts were still quite full and round from her recent pregnancy, though the baby had been passed off to a wet-nurse for feeding. Sitamun's sharp chin and narrow, assessing stare gave her a stronger resemblance to Tiy than Nefertiti had ever noted in the girl before. She could almost see the permanent frown-lines inscribing themselves on Sitamun's face as they regarded one another in silence.

"Did the Pharaoh summon both of you, too?" It was Kiya who spoke first, to Nefertiti's surprise. Her voice was friendly and high, as if the three of them had chanced upon one another in a *rekhet* marketplace, and she wished to share the day's gossip.

Nefertiti's eyes flicked down to Kiya's flat belly, but she forced herself to look away again, considering the western horizon and the dying stars with an air of calm composure. "No," she said. "I always go traipsing about the chariot track before the sun is up, just for the fun of it."

"Leave her alone." Sitamun's quick, quiet command cut through the dark space between them. "I won't have Kiya harassed."

"I beg your pardon?" Nefertiti gaped at Sitamun. "You won't have...? You are speaking to a King's Wife. You'd do well to remember that."

"I was King's *Great* Wife," Sitamun reminded her.

Nefertiti shrugged. "Once. No more."

She thought Sitamun might argue, or try to defend her fallen status. The girl, however, only curled her lips in a slow, cool smile.

"Where is the king?" Nefertiti asked sharply, as if

the other two women might know already, and were deliberately concealing his whereabouts. The cold, and the mystery of the summons, were both growing quite unbearable.

"Is that him?" Kiya pointed west, out toward the cliffs. "Look."

Nefertiti peered into the darkness, but for a long moment she saw nothing, save for a faint, pale mist that moved low across the ground, the vagabond moisture of the Inundation wandering the hills to leave its dew among the rocks and thorns below the cliff faces. Then, as she continued to stare, she caught movement and form—disjointed, fragmented by the banks of moving vapor. The swing of an arm, the high angle of a strong shoulder, the long, sure stride of a man—and all at once, as if the gods had breathed his shape into sudden being, Young Amunhotep was there, crossing the stony ground within the ring of the Circuit, dropping shadow from his skin.

Kiya clasped her foolish hands below her chin. Sitamun folded her arms, firm and expectant. Nefertiti wanted to shrink away, to retreat beyond the track, as if its pale border might suddenly become as impassable to Amunhotep as a wall. But neither of the other women moved to greet him, and so she resolved to press whatever advantage she could find in their stillness.

She stepped forward, smiling and reaching out both hands. "Husband."

He took her hands in his own, pausing to stare deep into her eyes. With so little light from above, Nefertiti could make out neither iris nor pupil; his *ka* regarded her out of two black, bottomless pits, and she was grateful for the morning's chill to excuse her sudden shiver.

But his words, when he spoke, were kind. "I am so glad you have come. All of you. This is a great day—great and momentous, and we shall all remember it for the whole of our lives. And after, too, when we are together in the Field of Reeds."

Kiya rustled forward, her grin wide and childish in her slim, white face. "What is it? Oh, tell us! We're all so eager to know why you've called us, Lord Horus."

He laughed indulgently. "My eager, grasping little monkey—my pet—my plaything."

Nefertiti's stomach lurched. Even in the gray half-light, she could see how Kiya blushed, turning her eyes down to the rocky earth as her cheeks colored like blood on linen. Somehow, Nefertiti kept her benign, welcoming smile in its place. "It's true—we are all very curious," she said.

"You shall know soon—*soon*. But for now, let us be silent. The sun is about to appear. I would enjoy the moment with all three of you." He took Kiya under one arm, and held the other out for Sitamun. Despite the girl's cold demeanor, she came eagerly enough, and pressed herself close to Young Amunhotep's body, her eyes half-closing as his hand found her shoulder and pulled her tight against his side.

"Nefertiti," he said, "stand before me. Face the sun—watch it as it rises. And lean back against me, so I can feel your nearness—ah, that's the way."

Thus entangled, so close that Nefertiti thought she could almost hear the mingled heartbeats of Kiya and Sitamun, they gazed together over the river, past the dark sprawl of Waset with its few pinpoints of flickering light to the far western hills beyond. There the horizon had already faded to a soft, pearlescent gray, and while Nefertiti willed herself to remain pressed against the king, refusing to allow the slightest shudder, light broke over the edge of the world with a petal-red glow. It spread along the jagged line of the hills, unfurling its banners in shades of violet and orange. It reached with the long, slow, deliberate motion of a sleeper just rising from a dream, stretching

NEFERTITI

its languid limbs.

"Here," Amunhotep whispered in Nefertiti's ear. The muscles in his chest tensed as he pulled Kiya and Sitamun closer, and Kiya gave a tiny, unconscious purr of delight. "Now..."

The first fiery rays of the sun itself lifted from behind the hills, rising in a gleaming curve over the horizon. Its brilliance dazzled Nefertiti's eyes, so that she blinked and turned her face away, but Amunhotep chided her with a soft whisper. "Don't look away—you must see it."

He cannot see my face, Nefertiti realized, so she shut her eyes tightly and faced the sunrise, just to appease her husband. Her eyelids flared as bright as flame, and for a moment she could see a tracery of fine, purple veins cutting across her inner vision, intricate and laced like cracks in long-dried mud. Then the flame-orange flared to a golden dazzle, so that, even with her eyes closed, tears dampened her lashes.

Young Amunhotep's breath rasped in her ear. "Yes," he panted faintly. His body shook with eagerness—a vibration of energy Nefertiti knew all to well—and as he pressed himself more firmly against her buttocks, she felt his phallus begin to harden.

Oh, gods, she thought frantically. *What will I do if he wants to take me here—to play his little games in the open? Or if he wants to take all three of us...?* She could formulate no good answer to her own panicked questions. She struggled to control her breathing. Her chest burned and threatened to heave like the gills of a fish freshly hauled out of water.

Just as a hysterical, terrified laugh began to claw at Nefertiti's throat, Young Amunhotep abruptly broke the strange, trebled embrace. He spun away from the women so quickly that Nefertiti was thrown off-balance. She stumbled, and might have fallen, if Kiya had not reached out a quick hand to steady Nefertiti by the elbow.

"Come," Amunhotep said.

He stepped a few paces away and reached into a small, beaded-leather pouch that hung from his kilt's sash. He withdrew two tiny packets, concealing them in his palm.

Nefertiti approached cautiously. "What is that? What do you have there?"

The rising sun drove back the night's lingering gray. Color began to bloom all around, and the flat, stony hilltop of the Circuit of the Sun transformed into a stage of pinks and golds. Amunhotep, his face glowing with the gathering light, opened his hand to show Nefertiti what he carried. With deft fingers, he unpicked the knots that bound the two packets. The soft leather that encased them fell away, revealing a pile of salt and a flat, delicate-looking pottery flask, no longer than Nefertiti's smallest finger.

"What is this?" She stared at the opened packets in confusion.

Amunhotep beckoned to Sitamun and Kiya. When they had drawn up close beside Nefertiti, he gave each of the women in turn a long, pride-filled look, breathing deeply as if to drink in their individual perfumes.

Salt and oil. Suddenly, the significance of Amunhotep's packets became clear.

"Wait," she said, glancing suspiciously at Kiya. "This isn't the correct place for wedding rites. We must go to the Temple of Amun."

It was the wrong thing to say—the very worst words she could have spoken—and Nefertiti knew it even before Amunhotep lowered his brows to glared at her. With a hot, shameful rush, she recalled every detail of her husband's bed-chamber games, the stench of the unwashed priestess's robe, its stiff, thick feel against her skin. She opened her mouth to apologize, but no words would come.

But even the king's dislike for the chief god of Egypt

couldn't dampen his joy on this day. He said cheerily, as if explaining a simple concept to an especially dull young child, "I am the Pharaoh, Nefertiti. I'm endowed with ceremonial power. Wherever I go is a temple, and I have the right to perform any ceremony I please. Whatever I do is good before the eyes of divinity."

He turned to the rising sun once more, beaming at its red face as if it had just praised him. "Besides, there could be no place more sacred than here, where the sun's rays touch us, without any man-made object to interfere or cast its light away. See how the rays reach out toward us, even from the eastern sky? No temple's darkness can compare with that blessing."

I must not lose his favor now, Nefertiti told herself sharply, thinking fast. It was not unusual, of course, for a king to take many wives. Nefertiti had expected it, even back when she'd had that golden, peaceful hope of wedding Thutmose. But if she was to sit higher in Amunhotep's regard—in his heart—than Kiya, she must be careful to approve of his whims, to laud his beliefs, even if they ran counter to her own.

So she beamed at him, hoping her smile looked as bright and approving to the king as the rays of the newborn sun. "How right you are," she said warmly. "Nothing could be better—certainly not the dark of Amun's temple." She closed her eyes and inhaled deeply. "Why," she said with a happy sigh, "those gentle rays—they smell as good as the Breath of Life, don't they?"

Amunhotep paused, glancing up from the salt and oil in his hand to eye Nefertiti with searching speculation.

He sees my falsehood, she thought, her pulse fluttering in her throat. *He knows what I'm trying to do.*

But then a wide grin broke over his face, and to Nefertiti's dazed surprise, true affection warmed his dark eyes. "That's the way of it," he whispered. "That's it, *exactly.*"

Nefertiti looked on with a determined smile as Amunhotep performed his own marriage rites, dropping a pinch of salt onto Kiya's tongue and drizzling the golden oil on the crown of her braided, bronze hair. She still could not fathom why the king was so drawn to this timid, quiet foreigner, who had so little to offer, save for her blinking green eyes. But Nefertiti had assumed he would eventually make Kiya a King's Wife, ever since news of the old Pharaoh's death had reached her.

Sitamun was an entirely different mystery, but as the girl came forward eagerly, opening her mouth to receive the salt before Amunhotep had finished reciting the ceremony's words, a chill of understanding rippled up Nefertiti's spine. Sitamun had already proven herself capable of birthing healthy children—always a risky gamble in any potential King's Wife. And although not all Pharaohs chose to practice the divine marriage, breeding doubly royal children from their own sisters, as the gods before them had done, Amunhotep clearly had no reservations about the ancient rite.

Their first child was a girl, she told herself, fighting to soothe away her fears. *Perhaps all Sitamun's children will be girls—and Kiya's, too—every last one of them.*

When the rites were concluded, Nefertiti joined hands with Sitamun and Kiya while Amunhotep prayed, offering up words of thanksgiving to the sun itself. He spoke not to any of the sun-god's familiar aspects, but to its warmth and generosity, so its life-giving rays, to its potent power of creation. Nefertiti's palms tingled and twitched, but she resisted the urge to dig her nails into the backs of the other girls' hands, gripping them like a merciless falcon until they cried out and ran from her in terror and pain. When the prayer was finished, she made herself stroll back to the three waiting litters with light, even steps, laughing and chatting with Sitamun and Kiya, sharing in their joy—and each time the morning sun glimmered off the oil that still dripped from their hair, Nefertiti's jaw clenched a little tighter.

She waved to the new Kings' Wives as they climbed back into their litters. Then she kissed Amunhotep warmly on the cheek, promising to see him again soon. Regally, in no rush, she seated herself on the cushions beside Mutbenret, issued a soft command to the litter-bearers, and lazily pulled her draperies shut.

But when she turned to face Mutbenret in the privacy of the blue curtains, she knew the look on her face was terrible with desperation.

"In the name of Iset, what happened?" Mutbenret said.

She reached for Nefertiti's hand, but Nefertiti tugged her fingers out of her sister's grip, pressing the heels of her hands against her eyes. "Oh, gods," she moaned.

"Nefertiti, what is the matter?"

"He married them, Mutbenret—right there in the open, without a temple, without a priest!"

Mutbenret was silent for a moment, but at last she said, "Well, he is the Pharaoh now, after all. He can do whatever a priest does."

"Yes, I *know*. And I knew he would take more wives. For Amun's sake, I don't care about *that*—they are both welcome to him, and however many more wives he takes are welcome, too. Only he *loves* Kiya, don't you see? And Sitamun—he can breed divine children on her, as he can't on me."

All the fine, well-trained control she had exercised on the Circuit of the Sun shattered, and tears poured down Nefertiti's cheeks, smearing her kohl, wracking her body with hard, heavy sobs.

"Oh!" Mutbenret wrapped her arms around Nefertiti's neck. "Please don't weep! It will be all right—I know it will."

"How? How will it be all right if I can't capture his heart? No man has endless room in his heart. The walls are closing in around me, and soon I will be pushed right out. Kiya is his now, completely. If her child is a boy, there will be nothing I can do to compete. And Sitamun—any children she gives him—any *more* children, that is—will be as good as gods. How can I do better? What can I give him that they cannot? His accursed seed won't take root in my womb—I cannot even give him a daughter!"

All down the length of the hill, as the litter made its way toward the House of Rejoicing, Nefertiti sobbed and choked against Mutbenret's shoulder. Every miserable, dark thought she'd ever had went dancing through her heart; every terrible memory came lurching out of the shadows to needle and taunt her. The sound of the servant-girl's misery rang in her ears like a temple's chimes, and no matter how she tried to push the sound away, the sway of the litter felt to Nefertiti like the sway of her own hips, the roll of her shoulders as she had danced, eyes shut, while the old Pharaoh had gasped and grunted in the throes of his foul pleasure.

Be still, a voice whispered in her heart. Nefertiti swallowed hard, wiping her smeared kohl on the back of her hand. The voice sounded like her own. She listened. *You knew just what to do to move one Pharaoh's heart, did you not?*

Yes, she said in bitter reply to her own question. *And I regret it now—oh, Mut, how I regret it!*

If you moved one Pharaoh, you can move another. You need only give him what he wants—what he truly wants.

Nefertiti sniffed, and dabbed at her eyes again. The litter reached the foot of the hill and rocked as it came level. The curtains swayed, parting just enough that a bright dazzle of morning light spilled inside, making her blink and throw up a hand to shield her eyes from the sun's force.

The sun's force.

The desperation fell away from her. Mutbenret gazed at her a moment, noting that her tears had dried, and the fear had left her face.

"What is it?" Mutbenret asked, hopeful.

"I see how it's to be done," Nefertiti said. "Yes, it *can* be done, after all—and I see it now."

"What, then? Oh, tell me!"

Nefertiti smiled at her sister, and dabbed the wet kohl from her cheeks with the corner of a silk cushion. "Not yet, Little Sister. We must wait for the right moment to act, but the right moment will come—I know the king as no one else does, not even Sitamun, not even Kiya. Our moment will come, sooner or later."

Sitamun

Year 1 of Amunhotep
Beautiful Are the Manifestations,
Great of Kingship,
Who Upholds the Sun

A BASIN STOOD ON A TALL plinth under the Pharaoh's window. Sitamun dipped her rag in it, relaxing her hand, allowing the scrap of linen to fill with the clear, tepid water. She made no move to withdraw either cloth or hand from the basin, but only stood in silence, watching the rings on the water's surface ripple and spread. The reflection of the room shivered and broke; high pillars, garden murals, and empty niches in the walls where once gods had stood tumbled into one great confusion of line and color, movement and shadow.

The water felt soothing on her skin, rinsing away the sheen of sweat that had formed on her forearm and wrist. Sitamun stared at her arm as it hung limp in the basin, fascinated by the way the light broke its image, so that the bones beneath her flesh did not quite align. She shifted, pulling out by a finger's breadth, smiling at the way the bend in her forearm healed as it left the water, then broke when it submerged again. Each time she disturbed the water's surface, the reflection of the Pharaoh's bed chamber fell into its patterns of confusion. She liked that, too.

It's only from the surface that I seem broken. But underneath the water, I am me—I am whole.

"What are you doing?" Amunhotep's voice was brisk and

impatient, even though he was still sprawled on his bed in the curious exhaustion that always fells men after they love.

"Washing."

"Be quick about it." He rolled over, so that all she could see of him when she glanced up from the basin was the blank wall of his back, the downhill slide of his body from one sullen, tense shoulder to his narrow hips.

Sitamun took up her rag and squeezed the excess water back into the basin. It made a quiet, gentle music as it fell, a soft murmur like the sounds of the birds settling in their evening roosts outside. She washed between her legs, then dropped the cloth on the floor. The Pharaoh's servants would see to it later, when they brought in his evening meal.

Her gown and wig lay atop the nearby ebony-wood table; her small sandals, embroidered with gold, rested side by side below. The days were long gone when Amunhotep had torn at her clothing, keen to take her in his rough, demanding arms. Now when she came to his chambers, she undressed in businesslike silence, lay on his bed staring up into the dim, pillared heights of the ceiling, and waited for him to muster the energy or the inspiration to do his duty, and plant another child of the divine blood inside her.

At least he *did* call her to his chambers. Every three days, more or less—and so Sitamun had the satisfaction of knowing that the king kept his word, and gave her all that he gave to Kiya and Nefertiti, in full and equal measure. All except his love, of course. She did not have an equal share of her brother's heart, and the knowledge of that bitter truth broke her own heart in two.

Sitamun dressed slowly, stepping into her long, red skirt and snugging its beaded belt high on her ribs, just below her breasts. She took her time pulling the straps up to her shoulders and adjusting their knots so the gown hung just so. Amunhotep sighed emphatically without deigning to glance her way.

It's strange, Sitamun thought, gazing around the chamber as she picked up her sandals and lowered herself to her brother's chair. *Everything in this chamber is different—or nearly everything, save for the murals on the walls and the tiles of the floor.*

Sunset light, as ruddy and glowing as the best carnelians, angled in through the garden window. It played in soft, warm tones over the surface of the table, the high-backed chair, the line of costly cedarwood closets and the harps and drums standing in the corner, waiting for the king's musicians to take them up and make them sing for his divine pleasure. Every stick of furnishing, every vase and mirror was new, changed from her father's coarser tastes to the elegant sophistication Young Amunhotep enjoyed. Even the great double doors of the outer apartments had been changed, the images of Bes replaced by twin golden circles of the sun-disc, its long, life-giving rays reaching down with dainty little hands to caress the world, to coax life from the still, black earth.

The king in the bed was different from the one who had lain there before, allowing the garden breezes to dry the sweat from his skin—and yet Sitamun's sadness had not changed. Sitamun realized as she stooped to fasten her sandals, bending around the aching hollow of her heart, that her sorrow was far worse now. For the brother she had always loved had no affection for her—no warmth to return—only this brisk, unfeeling duty, and when he had finished his work and delivered his seed, he had no words for her but *get out*.

She finished tying on her sandals and stood from the chair.

"Get out," Amunhotep said.

Sitamun brushed past his bed, the beads of her wig pattering faintly as she moved, like water falling into a basin. She touched his shoulder gently. He did not move or speak. "Until next time," she said, and left the bed chamber behind.

Outside, in the Pharaoh's sweeping anteroom, Sitamun passed the furnished alcoves and reclining couches, empty and quiet in the shaded, dusky gloom. She smiled in sympathy at the sight of two servants leaning on one another's shoulders, their mouths slack in sleep, the flickering flame of their small, lone, clay lamp illuminating their faces from where it sat on a nearby table. Not even a week had passed since the Opening of the Mouth, and Sitamun had no doubt that the king's personal servants had been run ragged, tending to his preparations for the unending feasts of celebration, the audiences with great nobles and high priests of every god's temple, the court formalities in the great hall, for which Amunhotep's appearance must be impeccable, with every last, tiny cabochon of his ornaments polished to a sheen, and every braid of his wig hanging in flawless order. Surely his body servants had little time for sleep, except in these intervals when the Pharaoh entertained one of his three wives.

She ought to wake them, perhaps—to warn them that the king was no longer occupied, and might call for them to draw a bath or lay out a fresh kilt at any time.

She had just made up her mind to approach the sleeping women and shake one gently by the shoulder, when the little statue of Kiya caught Sitamun's eye. The seated figure of the King's Wife gazed out at Sitamun from the circle of lamplight. Her tiny, stone eyes looked mocking, as the real Kiya's never did.

Sitamun paused, folding her hands at her waist, staring back at the statue. In the days since Sitamun had realized that the Pharaoh no longer loved her, she had often wished she could hate Kiya. She certainly envied the beautiful, soft-eyed Hurrian—how not? But she couldn't seem to turn her envy to loathing, nor even to the simple, cold dislike that Nefertiti showed to everyone. Kiya had been kind to her—she had given Sitamun peace when no one else could. Everything would make more sense if she could hate the Hurrian for claiming Amunhotep's heart so easily—the one thing in all the world Sitamun desired. But it simply could not be done. She could not muster anything but kind feelings for Kiya.

I must win back by brother's favor, Sitamun decided, giving the little statue a confident nod. *Perhaps if I am more like Kiya—if I can learn her ways, and shape myself after her pattern...*

If it *could* be done, Sitamun would achieve it. Over the course of the preceding year, her own inner strength had surprised her. She was a stronger woman than anyone knew—almost stronger than she herself could comprehend.

I will earn his heart once more, she told herself, and, feeling greatly cheered, she slipped from the room.

Amunhotep had sworn to give her a palace, equal to the one he had built for Kiya, and that promise, too, he had kept. The twin mudbrick homes stood, separated by some two dozen yards, at the far end of the House of Rejoicing's largest garden. In truth, they were no palaces—just small, private houses with a modest number of rooms, but the king had spared no expense in their construction, and they were designed with meticulous attention to detail, the painted murals of their interior walls so fresh that when she was inside, Sitamun could still smell the earthy minerals and the rich oils the artists had used.

She made her way slowly through the garden toward her newly built home, in no rush to leave the gentle calm of the sunset world. Red light hung like a canopy over the garden, tinting banks of white flowers to lotus-pink, making the insects that buzzed over the blooms glow like tiny suns themselves.

Sitamun lingered on the garden path, toeing the gravel with the edge of her sandal. Lamplight flickered in Kiya's home, a cheery counterpoint to the dark windows of Sitamun's own house. She would like to go to Kiya tonight, she thought, and learn what she could of her ways. But she felt suddenly shy at the prospect, and her eyes drifted away from Kiya's warm, bright house as she plucked absently at the petals of the white flowers.

It would be a challenge to regain what she had lost to Kiya, Sitamun had no doubt. But at least she had only one wife to contend with for Amunhotep's affections. Sitamun was quite certain that Nefertiti would pose no obstacle— at least, not where the Pharaoh's heart was concerned. Nefertiti had her charms and graces, but Amunhotep could surely tell, as easily as Sitamun could, that his lovely first wife was a schemer—a dangerous intruder in the House of Rejoicing, encroaching on their beautiful, self-contained, half-divine world.

Nefertiti was Ay's creature, and Sitamun had never trusted the Overseer of All the Horses.

Sitamun recalled the time—years ago, when she was just a little girl—when she had first met Nefertiti and her father. It was the Feast of Wag, when all the temples of the Two Lands were crowned with little, model boats, and by night the people went from tomb to tomb, laughing and singing in the light of their torches, leaving bread and beer for sustenance at the graves of the departed.

Ay was determined to push Nefertiti under Thutmose's nose—for in those days, Thutmose was the obvious choice as the heir to the Horus Throne. Sitamun, crouching beside a bread offering in the shadowed entrance to a tomb, had seen young Nefertiti toss her head in defiance when her father had whispered his instructions in her ear. But Ay had gripped the girl hard by her upper arm, and at once Nefertiti had subsided, smoothing her recalcitrance away with a sweet, obedient smile. Ay had pointed toward Thutmose, and off Nefertiti had gone, just like a trained hound on the hunt. She had simpered at Thutmose, and batted her eyes, and within minutes the two were holding hands, Nefertiti looking down at the torch-lit earth in feigned, bashful submission, and Thutmose grinning as if he'd just caught a fine, golden fish.

Sitamun had watched Ay carefully as the Feast of Wag wore on. His gaze was always on his daughter, his dark eyes keen and speculative and his face coolly unmoved, even while his hands fidgeted with the knotted cord he kept in the band of his kilt, a counting-cord used for tallies. As his daughter whispered in Thutmose's ear, or spun with him in a childish dance beneath the silvery stars, Ay's fingers had slipped up and down the knots of his cord, counting his victories, tallying his costs, planning his next move.

Now that they were all grown, Sitamun recognized that same eerie deliberation in Nefertiti's mien. Ay had shaped her—carved her out of the granite from which he himself was made. And Sitamun had never forgotten the sight of Ay's hard fingers locked in the tender flesh of Nefertiti's arm—the way she had winced away from his grip. Nefertiti's self-control might be sublime—how else could she wear such a flawlessly calm expression, even in the face of surprises like Amunhotep's startling marriage ceremony at the Circuit of the Sun? But deep in her heart, Nefertiti was as jealous and volatile as Ay. Sitamun was resolved never to trust her.

A loud crunch of gravel sounded from the direction of the House of Rejoicing. Sitamun turned quickly from the bank of white flowers. Tiy was making her way down the path, her feet catching now and then as she stumbled and then held out her hands for balance with exaggerated care. Sitamun eyed her mother warily as Tiy approached. Tiy's face was more deeply lined than ever, and despite a clever application of paints, bags hung below her eyes, weighted by many sleepless nights. Tiy's normally perfect wig sat just barely askew, so that its fringe lay unevenly across her dark brow.

Drunk? Sitamun wondered. It was no secret that Tiy was fond of wine, but she never indulged to the point of intoxication.

"Well," Tiy said, her voice rasping and low, as if she had spent far too much time breathing the smoky air at the heart of a temple.

Sitamun nodded in greeting. "Mother."

"What a mess," Tiy spat, glaring at Sitamun in the gathering dusk.

Eyeing her mother's disgraceful state, Sitamun could not help but agree, but she kept her thoughts to herself.

"You failed at the *one task* I set for you."

Sitamun squared her shoulders. "Failed?"

"Yes. Failed. I told you to work upon your father, to use your... your *charms*. To remove Young Amunhotep's hope for the throne. And here we are—here Egypt is—with Young Amunhotep resting his Amun-be-cursed balls on the very seat I worked to keep him out of."

Sitamun's face flushed at her mother's coarse language. "But the Temple of Amun found Thutmose's killer. They put the man to death."

"*Hah,*" Tiy croaked. "Did they? I wonder."

Sitamun swallowed hard, stepping away from her mother's sharp, bitter stare.

"There is no need to fear for Egypt," Sitamun tried again. "Amunhotep didn't kill Thutmose, Mother. He isn't cursed—he won't bring ill luck to the Two Lands."

"He may not be a brother-killer, but he is no good for the throne—no good for Egypt—or for the world. He is a wild animal loosed, Sitamun—a force more selfish and volatile than your father ever was. And you had *one* task: to bar that beast from the succession."

Sitamun's fists clenched. "Easier said than done, I think! If it was such a simple task, why didn't you handle it yourself?"

"I have my reasons."

"Because your power is gone—that's why. It faded away with your youth, and left you with nothing."

"Watch your tongue, you dockside whore. My power is greater than you know."

Sitamun advanced on her mother, the stones of the path grinding beneath her soles. "Perhaps you ought to watch *your* tongue. Perhaps it's *my* power that's greater."

Tiy gave an undignified squawk of laughter.

"Look at yourself," Sitamun said, glancing down at her mother's wrinkled dress, its hem trailing in the dust. "Is this how a King's Mother comports herself?"

"I comport myself as needs must," Tiy said loftily.

Sitamun caught a whiff of herbed wine on her breath. *She must have drank an entire skin in one draft.*

"You don't know the things I've done..." Tiy's voice went suddenly soft, all her stiff bravado falling away. Her shoulders sagged with the weight of regret. "You don't know what I've become, Sitamun—the sacrifices I've made."

But Sitamun was in no mood to pity Tiy. They were both former Great Wives, and both rejected by kings. They should be fellows—friends, if not as close as normal mothers and daughters were. But instead, Tiy insisted on maintaining her usual air of cold superiority, on setting herself apart and above, like a goddess in the sky.

Sitamun's brows knit in a fierce frown. "What *you've*

done? The sacrifices *you've* made? I've done more, given more, than you can ever know. What have my efforts earned me?"

Taken aback by Sitamun's fury, Tiy only blinked at her, mouth agape.

"You don't know the meaning of sacrifice, Mother," Sitamun whispered fiercely.

"What are you talking about?" The wine seemed to evaporate from Tiy's heart. She peered at Sitamun in the purple twilight, eyes sharp and clear.

"And what has it earned me?" Sitamun said again. Tears stung her eyes. Before Tiy could see them fall, she whirled on the path and sped toward her little palace, leaving her mother to stand alone in the emptiness of the garden.

Nefertiti

Year 2 of Amunhotep
Beautiful Are the Manifestations,
Great of Kingship,
Who Upholds the Sun

NEFERTITI THREW HER HEAD BACK as the midwife's assistants braced her shoulders and back, supporting the weight of her body over the two large, gold-leafed bricks. A great, long wail of triumph and relief wrenched from her chest, rising to the height of the birthing pavilion's roof, escaping past the linen drapes that lifted and rippled on the garden's breeze. The sound of her victory carried out across the sunlit flower beds, the lazy pond with its carpeting of lotus blooms. It silenced the birds in the trees who were just beginning to settle into their roosts as the sun descended toward the western hills.

In the same moment, the baby cried—a loud, healthy shout that sent a fierce warmth spreading outward from Nefertiti's heart, reinvigorating her tired, shaking limbs. All the women in the pavilion exclaimed over the child's health, its red, robust body and the energetic kicking of its legs.

Someone wiped Nefertiti's forehead and neck with a cool, damp cloth, then eased her back from the bricks, one foot and then the other. Women's hands coaxed her down onto the great bed of cushions. The midwife herself—a stooped and brown-toothed woman who was nevertheless quick and confident with her commands, and sure with her hands and knives—followed closely with the baby bundled against her bony, slack-breasted chest, for the child's slick, white cord still trailed from Nefertiti's womb, and pulsed lightly with the beat of her heart.

"You are both bright and well-colored," the midwife said over the baby's cries. She smiled down, exposing her darkened teeth in a wide grin, as Nefertiti reclined on the makeshift bed. "I have no fear for either of you, King's Wife. Egypt has much to celebrate today!"

"Thank Mut," Nefertiti sighed. "Thank Hathor, thank Bes, thank Tawaret, and all the good gods who protect mothers." She stretched out her arms for her child, eager—*desperate* to hold the baby, her chest and throat constricting with a need she had never felt before.

The midwife obliged, tucking the screaming bundle close beside Nefertiti's swollen breast, even as her assistants wiped the blood and the debris of birth from the baby's face. Nefertiti gasped in wonder—at the child's perfection, and at the churning of her heart, for she had never known that she could love so fiercely, nor that she could feel so powerful and complete. *I never even knew I was missing you*, she told the baby silently, her eyes filling with tears of gratitude and worship as she took in the wet, black curls on the little head, the tight-squeezed eyes with their dark lashes, the angry, red, adorable mouth that opened and shut as the baby made its loud displeasure known to the whole of the Two Lands. *A piece of my heart had never existed until now. And now that you're here, I know I cannot truly have lived before you existed.*

"A lively and beautiful girl," the midwife said.

Stunned, Nefertiti looked up from the baby's face. "A girl?" The child's cries still rang loud in her ears, still pulled at her heart with an unbreakable grip.

"Yes, my lady." Still the midwife grinned, and Nefertiti's

dazed eyes drifted down to the corruption of her teeth. "A King's Daughter to please the gods."

One of the assistants offered Nefertiti a bowl of strong beer, and babbled cheerily while Nefertiti sipped. "You can tell already that she'll be a great beauty, just like you, King's Wife. I've seen dozens of newborns, but none as pretty as this one."

Nefertiti relinquished her hold on the baby when the midwife declared that it was time to cut the cord. She watched in a helpless, trembling terror as the knife flashed beside her daughter's vulnerable stomach, and if her wracked body had been capable in that moment, she would have thrown herself across the pavilion, naked and sweat-slicked as she was, to shield her child from harm. And yet... *A girl.* When they returned the baby to her arms—now tightly swaddled in the softest, finest linen, dyed red to invoke the protection of Hathor—Nefertiti stared down at her child, confounded by the emotions battling within her chest. The most soaring, all-encompassing, dagger-sharp adoration she had ever known warred with the suffocating crush of utter disappointment.

A girl—how can it be? How, after all the time I tried to conceive, after all the prayers and offerings I made to Mut and Hathor? To say nothing of the daily offerings I made to Khnum, begging him to shape my child as a male on his potter's wheel.

Nine months of offerings. Two hundred and forty-nine visits to the shrines on the east bank—she had counted every one, kept a tally on a scroll in her bedside cabinet. She had crossed the river faithfully to present her gifts to the gods, each and every day since she first learned that she was with child. Even in the early weeks of her pregnancy, when sickness and headaches plagued her and she would rather have remained in bed, listening to soothing harps and flutes—and later, when her belly had grown so large and heavy, and her ankles had swollen so that she could only move with a slow, graceless waddle—even then, she had made the crossing with her gifts of meat and honeyed milk, lotus flowers and gold. Two hundred and forty-nine offerings, and the gods had thrown every one back in her face.

But she couldn't be displeased. The baby girl was perfect in her eyes—perfect in her heart. A son would have made everything right. A son would have guaranteed Amunhotep's favor, and rid Nefertiti of the necessity of ever lying with her husband again. A son would have made the whole world right, but a son could not be more perfect than this small, red, angrily squalling daughter. Nefertiti cuddled the baby close, and hoped that none of the gathered women saw the tears she dropped onto the child's still-wet head. Or if they did see, she prayed that they would take them for tears of pure, unconflicted joy.

Later, when the sun had left the world for its nightly trek through the Duat's caverns of darkness, Nefertiti lay on the gentle slope of her own bed, watching through her garden window. The splash of stars across the night sky grew denser and more silver-bright as the evening advanced. When she had announced her pregnancy to Amunhotep, he'd been quick to provide her with a little mudbrick palace of her own, whitewashed and painted and elegant in its design, alike to Kiya's and Sitamun's in every way. Hers stood at the opposite end of the grounds from the other two, and across the violet darkness of the great garden, she could see the small, dancing flicker of lights in the little twin houses of her rivals. She wondered whether Sitamun and Kiya had heard the news, that Nefertiti's child had turned out to be a daughter, after all. And if they had heard, did they rejoice?

Of course they rejoiced, Nefertiti thought dismally, stroking the baby's soft cheek as she whimpered sweetly in her sleep. *I would, if I were in their places.*

Nefertiti heard a furtive scrape outside the arched, doorless entryway to her bed chamber. A moment later,

Hrere, her maidservant, peeked around the doorframe. Nefertiti twisted carefully against her padded head-rest, tearing her gaze away from the stars and from the lamplight in the distant windows. She spoke quietly, so as not to wake the baby. "I'm awake, Hrere. What is it?"

"Pardon, my lady. Your sister is here to see you, if you are well enough to receive her."

Despite her brooding thoughts, Nefertiti smiled. "Send her in."

Even in the deep shade of night, Mutbenret's face glowed with wonder and joy as she tip-toed across the tile floor. The girl seemed to be holding her breath as she bent over the baby, sidelock swinging, to examine the round face that peeked out from its swaddling of red.

"Oh!" Mutbenret whispered. "Isn't she perfectly lovely?"

Nefertiti beamed; the pride and love she felt for her daughter won out over disappointment and fear. "She is. There has never been a more beautiful creature, since Atum flicked the world from his hand."

Mutbenret eased herself down, slowly and with meticulous care, on the edge of Nefertiti's bed. She brushed the baby's cheek with a tentative finger, feather-light. "She's so pretty and sweet, I can hardly believe she came from the Pharaoh's seed."

Nefertiti allowed herself one quick, quiet laugh. The mattress shook and the baby's little brow furrowed in disapproval, but she returned quickly enough to untroubled sleep.

"News has reached him, I suppose—that my child is a girl?"

Mutbenret glanced up at Nefertiti, noting the mingled joy and disappointment on her face. She took Nefertiti's hand. "Oh, Sister—don't fret. I know you wanted a son, but one never knows what the gods have in store."

"I'm not fretting—much," Nefertiti said. She looked down at her daughter again, and she couldn't help but smile. It felt like a soft and foolish smile, fuzzy and wistful and weak in its soft-kneed warmth, but Nefertiti couldn't manage a more regal expression just then—not when she looked at her child. "It's just that I know how useful a son would have been."

"Useful?"

"Of course. In climbing higher into Amunhotep's favor—in taking the throne of the Great Wife."

Mutbenret looked down at the baby again, with a slow, troubled frown. "It's strange, isn't it, how he still hasn't named any of you the King's Great Wife? Why, I wonder?"

"Who knows why Amunhotep does anything. We've been married for nearly two years, the gods help me, and I've only found him more puzzling with each passing day. But it would have been useful, to have a son—to take the throne. It would have given me power over Ay, and maybe even over my husband."

"You mustn't rebuke yourself. Even without a son, you've worked your way into his heart."

Nefertiti nodded in the ivory cradle of her headrest. She *had* worked her way into Amunhotep's heart—as much way as could be made in a heart as dense and black as his. Kiya used simpers and sighs, and the eagerness of her body; Sitamun held the intoxicating lure of divinity within her very blood. But Nefertiti had placed a far more subtle hook into Amunhotep's *ka*—subtle, but infinitely stronger, she hoped, than any wiles her rivals used. She had built a pathway, stone by stone, into the only cavern of the king's heart where he was truly vulnerable to influence: his religion.

Nefertiti had never forgotten Amunhotep's strange arousal on the Circuit of the Sun, that cold, mist-shrouded morning when his rapture had boiled over at the sight of the new dawn. Nor had she forgotten—she never could!—her wedding night, when he had shown her how little regard he had for the gods of Egypt. *There is only one true force in the world—creative force,* he had said, pressing the instrument of his godhood against her, bruising her flesh with the force of his zeal.

As the months of their ill-matched marriage turned to years, she had kept a keen eye on her husband, had turned an ever-eager ear to whatever words he said in passing or at court, from his throne or in Nefertiti's bed. And as Amunhotep swelled with the power he now commanded, becoming ever more a canny, jealous master of the Horus Throne, Nefertiti had kept pace with his interests, quietly encouraging his enthusiasm for the very creative force he so revered, and reinforcing his belief that he was the master of it all, more completely than his father ever had been, and more a force of potency than any living man could ever hope to be.

It was the only grip she could maintain on his *ka*—the only way she could set herself apart, and hope to receive from him the title that would make her a force in her own right—no longer beholden in any way to Ay's insidious influence, the undisputed mistress of her own fate.

Nefertiti had learned that the force Amunhotep revered had a name. It was called Aten—or, as Amunhotep preferred, *the* Aten. It had no whims, no real will, as the other gods had. It had no needs, no desires, no personality at all. It was the sun, and yet... *not* the sun. It bore no resemblance to the sun as Nefertiti—or any other good Egyptian—knew it. It was not the benevolent creator Amun, with his double plumes of golden light and his sanctuary of peace in darkness. It was not Re-Harakhty, the fearsome heat-warrior, flying high in the mid-day on falcon's wings. It was not the Ram of the West, settling boldly into the horizon, preparing at each sunset for the routine battle through the Underworld; nor Khepri, the benevolent ball of fire pushed from the eastern horizon by the sacred scarab at the dawning of each day. The Aten was only what it seemed to be: a disc of golden fire, moving from one horizon to the other, staring down in mute observation on a world that was small and removed, and far below its reaching rays.

But the rays—those were the force itself, the warmth and light that made green things grow and coaxed beasts from slumber, and filled the world with activity and vigor when they arced across the sky. The rays were the force that robbed from the world all that was good and inspiring when they faded away with the sunset, replacing the world's gentle peace with the terrors of the dark. The sun's rays made life—they were the force of creation Amunhotep held so much in awe, without the jealousy other gods possessed, or the demands they placed on their worshippers.

In truth, the Aten frightened Nefertiti. She did not know what to make of its faceless, uncaring aspect; the other gods' petty demands and capricious cruelties were at least emotions she could understand. What was she to make of a god who didn't even care for her prayers? The Aten made her feel weak and small—as helpless as ever Ay had made her feel—and since Nefertiti had learned the truth of Thutmose's murder, she had resolved never to be weak or small again.

But, for all its strange and frightening anonymity, the Aten gave Nefertiti that precious, rare hand-hold with which she clung to her husband's heart. A son would have been better—a son would have freed her from the need to lie with Amunhotep ever again, and would have given her an excuse to disregard the Aten, too. But she did not have a son. She had a daughter now, and she had the Aten. And so she would make do.

Again, Mutbenret noted the troubled, distant expression on Nefertiti's face. "Be glad for your daughter. She is still the only royal child, born of a King's Wife—even if she is a girl."

Nefertiti smiled. "That's true." Nebetah, Sitamun's girl, was healthy and growing bigger. But she had been born before the marriage—and no one could be certain of her parentage, in any case.

"Poor Kiya," Mutbenret said. "She must have miscarried early, and she never breathed a word again of falling pregnant... though," she added after a thoughtful pause, "I know the king visits her bed often."

Nefertiti arched one eyebrow and hummed wryly. She had her doubts that the Hurrian had ever fallen pregnant in the first place. But that was immaterial. She certainly had not conceived since that strange wedding ceremony at the Circuit of the Sun, or if she had, she'd kept the news to herself.

"And Sitamun hasn't had another child, either," Mutbenret said. "Why, do you suppose?"

Nefertiti shrugged. "Too tender an age for her first—it must be. I've heard it happens that way sometimes—when the mother is so young, the first child saps all the strength from her womb, and is her last child, as well."

Mutbenret tilted her head, considering, and the braid of her sidelock brushed her smooth, young shoulder. "Do you think it is Sitamun's fault? Or is it the king's?"

"Better not let *him* hear you say that," Nefertiti warned. "Don't even hint it. He places much store in the idea of his own potency, believe me."

"Well, I know he has visited the harem often enough. I've heard your servants gossiping about it. But none of his concubines or ornaments have announced a pregnancy, either. Not one."

Nefertiti squinted out her window, considering the spray of stars once more. They poured across the sky in a great, white, glowing cascade, like milk spilled from a broken jug. But below that broad and lovely light, the two little flames still flickered across the garden—one in Kiya's window, the other in Sitamun's.

Nefertiti frowned at the twin houses. Their dark, blocky shapes stood out clearly against the far garden wall, which seemed to pulse faintly with the pallid reflection of the starlight. *Kiya and Sitamun both keep a vigil tonight, though the hours march on, and the night grows older.* Were they praying for their wombs to fill again? Were they praying for sons, that they might succeed where Nefertiti had failed?

She considered those empty bellies, far across the garden, and the others, too, out in the distant harem palace. Perhaps some priest—or some god—had laid a curse on Amunhotep, a vengeance for his zealous allegiance to the Aten. Perhaps his seed was doomed to wither, no matter where it was planted.

If so, then Nefertiti's daughter—the only royal child, for now and perhaps for all time—was more precious than even she believed.

T EN DAYS LATER, NEFERTITI LAY on the low stone retaining wall of the garden's sparkling blue lake, bathing in the warmth of the sun. It was just the right sort of day—the sun had a nurturing sort of heat, insistent but not brutal, and the air was rich with the spicy, languid odors of warmed leaf and blossom. Despite the fact that exposure would deepen her complexion to an unfashionably dark shade, Nefertiti luxuriated. The golden rays pressed down upon her chest and stomach, which was still rather slack from the baby—and the heat of the flat stone wall radiated up into her back and legs, smoothing away the lingering aches of birth better than any bath-maid's massaging hands could do. One of Nefertiti's hands trailed in the tepid water, nibbled at now and then by the gentle kisses of minnows. The other stroked her daughter's cheek on the blanket where she lay, kicking and gurgling in the shade of two fans, which Nefertiti's servants kept poised assiduously over the infant's silky skin. Mutbenret sat on one corner of the blanket, humming dreamy cradle songs while she tickled the baby's toes with a blade of grass.

Nefertiti sighed deeply, not for the first time that afternoon. In the two years since she had moved to the House of Rejoicing, she had seldom enjoyed a day of such simple leisure. Mutbenret's humming worked its way deep into her heart, lulling Nefertiti as much as the baby. *I must do this more often*, she thought lazily, swirling her hand among the flat, glossy leaves of the lotuses.

Rapid footsteps pattered along the path, heading doggedly in Nefertiti's direction. She opened one reluctant eye, squinting toward her little white-brick house. Hrere was hurrying toward her, lifting the hem of her white linen smock in hard-bunched fists.

"My lady!" Hrere spoke even as she bowed, and Nefertiti could see that the woman's cheeks were flushed with agitation. "The Father of the God is here. He has asked to speak with you."

Ay. Nefertiti sat up so abruptly that the baby fussed. The quick movement sent a ripple of dizziness through her head, and Nefertiti frowned down at Mutbenret, whose eyes had gone wide and fearful at the news.

"What shall I tell him?" Hrere panted.

Nefertiti would have been within her rights to send him away. She was a King's Wife now, and although King's Wives had little political pull, they could at least refuse audiences if they did not wish to speak. Nefertiti had no desire to shatter the peace of the only pleasant day she'd enjoyed in two long years. But after all, she might find it useful to know Ay's thoughts, to gauge his attitude. She had seen her father little, praise the gods, since she'd left his household, and if she was to obtain power over him, she must at least maintain some familiarity with his ways.

She straightened her wig. "Send him to me." She glanced at Mutbenret. The girl had never stopped going home to Ay's estate, ostensibly to visit her mother, but Nefertiti knew that Ay pressed her for information about the House of Rejoicing—about Nefertiti herself. She did not know just how strong Ay's hold still was over her little sister. Better to be cautious in Ay's presence. "Mutbenret," she said, "you had better go. No, not back toward my house— he may be there. Run along across the garden to visit with Kiya and Sitamun."

When the girl had gone, Nefertiti arranged her skirts and brushed the dust of the wall from her shoulders, nodding a dismissal to Hrere. The woman was hardly gone from Nefertiti's presence a moment, when Ay appeared around a distant bend on the garden path, striding with his usual precision and purpose, the folds of a long, formal kilt swinging around his ankles.

Nefertiti received her father's bow in silence, as cool and poised as if she sat on the throne of the King's Great Wife, and not on the limestone edge of a lake.

When Ay straightened, his thin-skinned, flat-cheeked face tightened in a grimace that might have passed for a smile. "I came to pay my respects to you and your new child." He looked down at the shaded blanket, and the baby peered blearily at her grandfather, then opened her little lotus-bud mouth in a scream of disapproval.

Nefertiti motioned for the wet-nurse. The woman came forward quickly, scooping up the child and soothing her with soft murmurs and a heavy breast to suck.

"A healthy King's Daughter," Ay said, betraying no hint of pride or joy at the sight of his granddaughter, but no disappointment, either. His voice and expression were calculated to a flawless neutrality. "What do you call her?"

"Meritaten is her name."

Ay's neutral expression broke. His dark brows lifted in surprise. "You named her for Aten?"

"*The* Aten," Nefertiti corrected smoothly. "The Pharaoh prefers."

"It's a rather untraditional name."

"My husband is a rather untraditional king. He is not a lover of old-fashioned things."

"Yes, but... the Aten? A cold god—a cold name, to bestow upon a child."

Nefertiti gave a tiny shrug. What did a name matter, after all? Nefertiti had the kindest, warmest name any girl could hope for—*the beautiful one has come*—but her name hadn't softened her childhood, nor warded away any of her father's coldness.

"The king," she told her father, "was most pleased with the name I selected."

Greatly pleased, in fact. Amunhotep had made no secret of how Nefertiti's choice had impressed him. He had come to her the evening after Meritaten's naming ceremony, at the head of a procession of stewards who bore all sorts of rich gifts: fine, thick carpets for her floors; gold for her neck and wrists; alabaster vases so finely worked that the stone was as translucent as river mist. And he had knelt before Nefertiti as she'd sat in her little chair beside the garden window—the king, actually kneeling to *her!*—and kissed her hands, and looked up at her, his dark eyes alight with a gratitude and joy so clear that Nefertiti shrank away from the force of his unaccustomed warmth. "You *understand*," he said. "You see what I see, when you look upon the sun." Nefertiti, sensing a rare moment of advantage, had only smiled serenely and stood, pulling him up from the floor, and kissed his cheek reverently, as if in worship of a god.

"It seems you're doing your work quite well," Ay said. "Pleasing the Pharaoh."

Nefertiti pursed her lips. *Better than you know, Father— and that's a certainty.* But she made no response.

"Are you much in his confidence?"

"As befits a King's Wife," she said evasively. She cut her eyes toward Meritaten's two fan-bearers, who stood nearby with their dark ostrich plumes stilled above their heads. Nefertiti clapped briskly, and all her women—wet-nurse, fan-bearers, and servants with food and drink—headed at once for the white brick house.

When she and Ay were alone, Nefertiti leveled a flat glare at her father. "What do you want? You didn't come to pay your respects to your granddaughter, or to me— that was only an excuse. I can see that much clearly. So ask me whatever question you came to ask, and be done with it."

Ay frowned, but he did not deny her accusation. "There is new construction just outside the temple complex of Ipet-Isut."

Nefertiti cast him a mysterious little smile.

"What do you know about it?" Ay asked casually.

"Amunhotep is building a new temple. There is nothing unusual in that. Pharaohs do such things."

Ay made as if to sit on the wall of the lake beside her, but as he settled into place, Nefertiti stood, and moved a few paces away from him.

"There is nothing unusual in a king building a new temple," Ay agreed, "but *now*? During Shemu? The time for building is during the season of Akhet, when the Inundation floods the fields and no *rekhet* can work the land."

343

It was true. The very fact that Amunhotep's building campaign had begun during the season of growing made it conspicuously strange—even suspicious. It was not an economical time for building; the *rekhet* were put to better use planting and tending crops, not hauling bricks and stone. But the king, Nefertiti knew, was eager. He wished to see his vision come to life, and like a child anticipating some great reward, he could not wait patiently, until the Inundation came again.

"The floods were plentiful, and the fields are very fertile this year," Nefertiti said. "He has not diverted many *rekhet* from field work, and besides, the temple is almost finished. The workers will return to their farms soon enough."

"Still," Ay said, "I don't like anything about this work. The timing... the pace of construction... What do you know about the temple itself?"

Nefertiti knew quite a lot about the temple. She had planted the seed of the idea into Amunhotep's heart herself, just as he had once planted the idea of the *heb-sed* in his father's thoughts. She had already given him the heirship and his only royal-born child. Now she had given him the encouragement to build a temple, too. Gempaaten, it was to be called: *The Sun is Found.*

But she kept her counsel where Gempaaten was concerned, and only shrugged again. "It's only a temple, Father. Why are you allowing it to plague your thoughts?"

"It's a dangerous risk."

Nefertiti burst into bright laughter. She picked a flower from a nearby shrub and sniffed at its ruffled petals without the slightest display of concern.

"I've seen where the temple is placed," Ay insisted. "Too near to Amun's great house. It's encroaching upon the chief god's territory. The priests of Amun won't be pleased, and neither will the god himself."

Do you think the Pharaoh cares about that?

Nefertiti resisted the urge to speak those words aloud. It was true; though Gempaaten's plans called for a wall to separate it from the eyes of the Amun priests—Nefertiti had wisely pressed for that measure of prudence—it lay so close to the rear of Amun's temple that the priesthood would certainly feel as if their god's territory were being impinged. Worse, it lay directly to the east, so that the rays of the rising sun would fall on its long rows of blocky pylons and its wide, spacious courts before they ever reached Amun's holy house.

Ay wasn't wrong. Gempaaten *was* a risk; everything about it, from its out-of-season construction to its treacherous placement, flaunted Amunhotep's disregard for the traditional gods of Egypt. But what could Nefertiti do? Once she had suggested that he build a temple, the Pharaoh had whirled away with the idea, roaring ahead with his extravagant plans like the demon-winds of the far north. Nefertiti accounted herself lucky that she'd been able to retain a hand in the planning and construction at all.

She sniffed again at her flower, batting her lashes as if she cared not a whit for Ay's concerns.

"Be careful," he growled. "Don't get over-confident. I taught you how to use caution."

"You have taught me many things, Father."

"Remember your caution. You haven't achieved your goal yet."

"My goal?" *What do you know of my goals, old man?*

"You aren't King's Great Wife."

"I will be. Give it time."

"You've had two years already, and still you do not hold the throne. I am growing impatient, Nefertiti."

You are growing anxious, and insecure. And that is no concern of mine.

"You may never hold the throne," Ay went on, "if the way your husband stares at that Hurrian wife is any indication."

Nefertiti tossed her flower into the lake. "Kiya? What do I have to fear from that one? She's barren, evidently. And so is everyone else, as far as I can tell—even the women in the harem. I've given Amunhotep his only child—I alone have borne his offspring."

"What about Sitamun's girl—Nebetah?"

Nefertiti tossed her head in defiance. "If Nebetah is the daughter of *this* Amunhotep, and not the one who came before, then she was born before my husband accepted Sitamun as a wife. Nebetah is illegitimate, and Sitamun will likely never conceive again."

She turned away from him, taking a few slow, languid steps toward her home, hoping her father did not see how her knees trembled with the sudden rush of anger that sped along her limbs. "And now, Father, I've grown weary of your company. It's time for you to return to your estate."

She heard Ay rise from the lake's edge. She remained gazing out into the depths of the Shemu-green garden, refusing to acknowledge her father as he stepped slowly toward her along the limestone path.

"You may have given the Pharaoh his only royal offspring," Ay said, "but don't get careless, Nefertiti. Meritaten is only a girl, after all."

Then she did look at him, fixing Ay with a long, dark stare that pinned him to silence and melted the confident half-smile from his dry, thin face.

"Oh, Father," she said quietly, "you shouldn't be so quick to disregard a daughter's worth."

THE GROWING SEASON PASSED, its lush, dense greens making way for the golden-browns of the harvest. The fields across the river that had lain all Shemu long like rich, verdant rugs strewn across a palace floor bared their earth-black skin as the harvest was gathered in. Nefertiti watched the dark swaths of the newly reaped fields grow larger and wider from the bow of her little traveling barque. As her boat neared the docks outside the temple complex of Ipet-Isut, the warm, dusty fragrance of earth bared to the sun reached out its unseen hands, clinging to the locks of her wig, where it remained to whisper in her ears, speaking of the ongoing wealth and stability of the Two Lands.

The boat moored, and her little contingent of three palace guards escorted her across the quay. As they made their way around the outer wall of Ipet-Isut, Nefertiti kept her gaze fixed on the sparkling cloud of golden dust that rose up behind the complex's eastern wall. There, she knew, Gempaaten was flourishing, rising out of Amunhotep's fevered, wide-eyed visions into a final, undeniable reality. Construction was in its final days, and Amunhotep had called for Nefertiti to join him as he inspected the last artistic touches of his temple, the great work of his heart.

She rounded the northeast corner of Ipet-Isut, and there the new temple stood, stretched long and great across the brown earth, like a cobra warming itself in the sun. Over the edge of its high, mudbrick wall, Nefertiti could see an astonishing array of squared, pylon-like pillars, standing rank upon rank, a force as mighty and plentiful as the armies of Egypt. They ran all down the length of Gempaaten, their shapes repeating in a seemingly endless display of rhythm, strength, and regularity.

Nefertiti found the front entrance, flanked by two impressive pylons. Artists were busy on a series of scaffolds and high sand ramps, bringing the gate to life in bright colors and pleasing designs, each motif worked about the round, faceless disc of the sun. The artists could not bow in the midst of their labors, but they called down their praises to the King's Wife, and Nefertiti raised a hand in acknowledgement. She smiled broadly, keeping her eyes satisfied and serene, though as she crossed through the band of shadow beneath the great gate, a quiver of cold ran along her limbs.

"Nefertiti!" Amunhotep cried out her name with a blissful shout. He came to greet her on light, buoyant feet, nearly skipping for joy as he emerged from between two of the high, blocky pylons, the very heads of the long ranks that stood to either side of the temple.

Nefertiti stepped forward, reaching out for his hands. Amunhotep laced his fingers with hers, laughing with pleasure in the bright sun.

"I'm so pleased that you've come," he said. "I can't wait to show you what I've built."

He led her by the hand down the long central aisle of Gempaaten. It was floored by soft, deep sand, as golden-bright as the sunlight that streamed down from above. Neither stone nor precious cedar roofed the spaces between the pillars' queues. There was nothing overhead but open sky, hot and emphatic with the rays of the high, staring sun. The tap of chisels echoed all about them as they walked through the sun-heated sand. From deep within the ranks of pylons, she heard the scrape of planes smoothing mudbrick, and the air between the columns was filled with dazzling, sun-struck dust.

When at last they reached the temple's main sanctuary— no more than a sand-filled courtyard, in truth, for it, too, was open to the sky—Nefertiti gasped and dropped Amunhotep's hand. Four huge statues towered over her head—six times the height of a man, at least. They were positioned with their backs to the outer walls of

Gempaaten, so that they stared coolly down on the great, sandy expanse of the sanctuary with Amunhotep's unmistakable long, faintly amused face—and yet, the statues did *not* bear Amunhotep's face. Oh, they wore the red-and-white Double Crown of Egypt, poised above the striped folds of the Nemes headdress. And the colossal figures held the crook and flail crossed over their chests in the classic attitude of a king. But although the large, soft, gently curving lips were Amunhotep's, and the heavy-lidded eyes, as well, all else in the great stone figures was distorted almost beyond recognition. The real man's chin was long and pointed, his face narrow and severe—but the proportion in the faces of the statues was exaggerated, every curve of cheekbone and slant of feature dizzyingly overstated.

Worse still were the statues' bodies. Nefertiti could not quite tell whether they were intended to be male bodies, or female—or perhaps both at once. Behind the fists that clutched the staffs of the Pharaoh's office, Amunhotep's statues seemed to have the suggestion of breasts, and the hips were dramatically swollen, the belly soft and protuberant, like the lower body of a woman who has borne many children.

Even the paint that adorned the statues was exaggerated, the colors more vibrant than she had ever seen on a king's statue before, and although the shading which gave the illusion of curves of flesh and folds of cloth was clever, it made the statues seem disconcertingly real, as if they might come to life at any moment, step from their massive plinths, and crush Nefertiti beneath their uncaring heels without ever changing the sly, satisfied, mystically distant expressions on their faces.

They were unlike anything Egypt had seen before.

"What do you think of my statues?" Amunhotep said, beaming up at them with hands on hips.

"They're..." Nefertiti swallowed hard as she searched for the appropriate description. "Distinctive."

"Quite! And I'll have many more, too." He gestured toward the empty plinths running down the sides of the sanctuary. There was room for a dozen more of the massive things.

"I've... I've never seen anything like them before."

"The style pleases me. I'll have none of the stiff formality one sees in the other temples—not here. Gempaaten is a truly sacred place, where we shall celebrate life and creation and *reality*. These look so much more like a true depiction of flesh and bone—don't you think?—compared to the usual style."

Nefertiti could only nod. The huge statues peered down at her from their real-yet-unreal faces, their mouths curved in cold, silent smiles.

Amunhotep went on explaining the wonders of Gempaaten as Nefertiti twitched and shivered, trying to ignore the palpable stares of her husband's monuments. "Open to the sky," he said, "to let the sun's rays caress us as we worship—just as you suggested."

Nefertiti gave herself a little shake. *Pay attention. Don't give him any reason to doubt your enthusiasm—not now, not when you've come so far.* "It's wonderful," she said emphatically. "It's like nothing the world has ever known."

She left his side, walking out into the center of the vast, sandy courtyard. There, with the sun beating mercilessly upon her head and shoulders, Nefertiti tipped her face to the sky and held her hands aloft, palms up, in a posture of ecstatic worship. She held the pose for as long as she could, while beads of sweat gathered on her arms and neck, and trickled down the sides of her face to dampen the locks of her heavy wig. At last, she felt Amunhotep draw up close beside her.

"Beautiful," he whispered.

Relieved, Nefertiti dropped her arms and smiled at him.

"You love the sun, do you not?" His voice was almost pleading, as if he sought reassurance or erasure of doubts.

"More than anything," she said. "It is the giver of life."

He took her hand again. "I have something special for you. A great surprise."

Amunhotep tugged her along the length of the courtyard, until they reached the cool relief of shadows between the last ranks of pillars. The rearmost portion of Gempaaten's outer wall rose above them, and at its foot, a little mud-brick manse waited in sunlit solitude.

"Oh!" Nefertiti exclaimed. "What is it?"

"Your own temple." Amunhotep pulled her toward the arched doorway. "I made it just for you, because you, of all women, *understand*. I must admit, Nefertiti, I never thought you would understand. I thought you too haughty, too cold. I thought you too devoted to the old gods to ever adopt a new and better way."

She could not keep her brow from creasing. *Adopt a new way? 'Old' gods? Surely he doesn't mean...*

But he mistook her frown for displeasure at the criticism, and he laughed and stroked her cheek, as if soothing a fussy child. "Ah, but I was wrong—wrong!" Amunhotep said. "You named our daughter Meritaten, to honor the greatest god of them all—the force of creation—the source of all life. You *do* understand."

She nodded, glancing down at the sand, as if suddenly shy of his affections. "I do."

They crossed the threshold of the manse. The interior was not yet painted—the walls were freshly plastered with pale lime; bare of all ornament, they shone fiercely from the sunlight pouring in through the open roof. In the center of the tiny temple, a raw chunk of granite stood, about as tall as Nefertiti, columnar, and naturally shaped rather like a man's phallus. The stone was embedded with tiny flecks of mica; it glittered in the bright, direct light. Nefertiti blinked at it, uncertain just how Amunhotep expected her to react to this strange gift. She waited for him to speak.

"I call this place the Hawet Ben-ben," he said in an awed whisper. *"The House of the Holy Stone."* He lurched forward, brushing the phallic rock with an appreciative hand. "See how virile it is? It rises up just like the great mound of creation, where the sun brought the first life into being from out of the Iteru's waters."

So that's what I'm to make of it. Nefertiti rose to the occasion readily. She came forward to join him, stroking the stone with both hands, then, with a show of sighing affection, pressing her cheek against it in a loving embrace.

"It's beautiful," she assured him. "An everlasting reminder of the true force of creation."

Amunhotep fell silent, holding her in place with a darkly approving half-smile. As Nefertiti continued to fondle the Ben-ben, he said quietly, "I wish you to be the High Priestess of the Sun."

She looked up, startled, from her impromptu ministrations. "Me? You honor me too much! I'm not worthy of such a high office."

"There is none more worthy. Kiya is dear to me—the Aten knows she is. But she is such a simple, delicate little thing."

On that, we are agreed, Nefertiti thought wryly.

"She doesn't understand, Nefertiti—not like you. She can't grasp my passions, can't feel them as you do. I have never forgotten your delight on that glorious morning when we stood—you and I, and Kiya and Sitamun, and watched the sun rise. Do you remember how you breathed in the rays of the sun?"

She lowered her eyes, hoping she looked like a woman swept away by a fond memory. "And," she said after a moment, "I alone, of all your women, have proven fertile."

"That's true." Amunhotep's face darkened, and he turned away.

Nefertiti reached for his hand. "Don't let sorrow take you. More women will yet bear children to you."

He sighed. "How do you know? The gods know I've tried, but all my efforts are in vain."

"They are not in vain. Don't we have little Meritaten? And she's so healthy and strong. Your seed is robust, Amunhotep. It will take root again, in the gods' time."

He turned back to her, gripping both her hands in his own. "Yes," he said, his voice hoarse with intensity. "Yes, it is a good plan—yes, you must join me, here at Gempaaten, and become a leader of worship."

Worship of the Aten. From the direction of Ipet-Isut, Nefertiti could feel a great black cloud of disapproval welling, like a column of smoke boiling into the sky. *Is Amun angry with me? But how can I stop what has already begun?*

"Still," she said, thinking quickly, "I am only a woman, after all. Perhaps it's too much, to name me High Priestess of the Sun. Perhaps I would do better on the throne of King's Great Wife."

Amunhotep gave a dry snort of disgust. He dropped Nefertiti's hands as if they were the coils of an asp.

"You women—you King's Wives—always pressing me to raise you to the throne. What does it matter to any of you, which if you is Great Wife, or even *whether* any of you will rule at all?"

It matters because it's the only real *power any of us can have,* she thought.

She was not fool enough to expect that any substantial influence over the throne—over Ay—would come from her place in the Hawet Ben-ben. Yet she knew it was the best she could expect from her husband. *For now.* And she remembered her promise to Mutbenret, that morning as they'd ridden in the litter, back to the West Bank from the Circuit of the Sun. *The time will come,* she had told her sister. *Soon.*

She reached out to him, caressed his face with a grateful hand. "I shall be pleased—honored—to act as your priestess, my husband. My king."

He nodded, folding his arms in satisfaction. "I must return to the House of Rejoicing," he said. "I've court matters to see to. Will you join me on my barque?"

She pressed a hand to her heart, as if overwhelmed by the honor of the invitation. "Oh, how lovely—but I had hoped to stay here a while longer, and worship the glories of the sun."

That excuse pleased him—far more, Nefertiti knew, than her company would have done. He bade her farewell with a kiss, then strode off through the heat and sand of Gempaaten, the sun beating down on his back, making his golden ornaments shine so fiercely that Nefertiti was obliged to shield her eyes from the sight.

She waited, leaning on the outer wall of the Hawet Ben-ben in its narrow strip of shade, until she was certain Amunhotep must be aboard his barque and sailing for the western shore. Then she strode back down the length of Gempaaten alone, kicking the sand as she went, hissing at the throbbing heat of the sun overhead.

Nefertiti gathered her guards from their place outside the temple. They sensed her dark mood, and trailed her in wary silence as she skirted Ipet-Isut and found the entry pylons to the massive temple complex—the traditional home of Egypt's oldest, truest gods.

At the shrine of Mut, goddess of motherhood, Nefertiti sank to her knees in the mercy of the dark-blue shade. The stones of Mut's little temple were cool beneath her hands as she bent forward to leave her kisses at the goddess's feet, for she had brought nothing else to offer. She sat back on her heels, allowing the shadows to soothe the memory of Gempaaten's throbbing heat from her body. Mut smiled down at her with her white vulture's wings stretched wide, offering the shelter and benevolence of her embrace. The statue was made in the traditional style, stiff and formal—familiar and safe.

Nefertiti placed her hand low on her belly.

Please, Mother Mut, she prayed. *Forgive my transgressions against thee, and make this new child I carry a son.*

Kiya

Year 2 of Amunhotep
Beautiful Are the Manifestations,
Great of Kingship,
Who Upholds the Sun

NANN RETURNED TO THE HOUSE of Rejoicing just as the cool of evening set in. The sky was drawing up its cloak of indigo blue as the last rays of the sun faded to the west, and here and there the earliest stars shimmered, soft and white, against the dusk. Kiya, idling at the lakeside, watched her servant approach from the great garden's main gate. Nann carried a basket on her head with one hand raised to balance it. In the gathering starlight, her simple white smock looked as soft and luminous as a moth's wing.

Kiya dabbled her bare toes in the lake, tapping the wide, flat lotus leaves that lay cool and inviting on the water's surface, as Nann eased the basket down to the lake's edge.

"You were gone to the market all day!" Kiya said in mock reproach.

"My mistress had so many requests."

Kiya eyed Nann with a sudden sharpness, withdrawing her toes from the water and pulling her knees tight against her chest. Usually on market days, Nann was in the mood to banter and play. But today the girl bent over her basket in silence, removing the goods Kiya had requested with a sober, distracted air.

Kiya picked up one of the citrus fruits she always

craved and began working at it with her nails. Its plump peel released a burst of fragrant oils into the air, and for a moment the night was perfumed with the cheery, bracing notes of the tangy fruit. Nann did not stop to sniff appreciatively, as she usually did, but only worked on.

"Whatever is the matter, Nann? You look positively depressed!"

Nann unpacked the final goods from her basket, laying the combs, hair pins, and fruits along the lake's wall for Kiya's inspection. Then she sat heavily beside her mistress, sighing. "The mood in the marketplace was awful, Mistress. The streets of Waset are thick and stinking with tension."

"Waset always has a bad smell."

"No—I mean it truly. You can *smell* the anger, a terrible, rotten stink. You can almost touch it, the feeling is so heavy and dense."

"Anger?"

"And fear, too, I think."

Kiya tossed the citrus peel into the nearest flower bed, then split the fruit in half, offering some to her maid. "What are the *rekhet* angry about? And what has anyone to fear?"

Nann took the citrus, but held it absently in her cupped palms, making no move to peel up one of the juicy, sour sections and pop it into her mouth. "It isn't just the *rekhet*, Mistress. It's the priests of Amun, too. Or at least, the *rekhet* say it's the priests. I heard the same rumors everywhere, and oh, *everyone* I spoke to was simply *livid*. After the first hour—after the sellers in their stalls began casting terrible glowers at me—I thought it wisest not to admit I came from the West Bank at all, and never mind that I'm from the Pharaoh's own household. No, I told them my mistress lived in one of the grape farms to the east of the city, and I—"

"Nann," Kiya pleaded, "tell me!"

"Well, it's Mahu, Mistress."

"Mahu?" Kiya frowned.

She was familiar with the burly soldier, of course. Over the past several months he had become a special favorite of the Pharaoh, rising from the station of a palace guard to a kind of unofficial shieldman of the king's own body. Amunhotep had increased his activity on the eastern bank, overseeing the final work on his new temple, and he had found it prudent to keep a strong arm close at hand, for Waset and its surrounding districts were always unpredictable.

But despite the good service the man did for the king, Kiya had never been able to make herself like Mahu. His eyes were flat and beady, and devoid of all warmth, just like a fish pulled up from the river's deep. The bodyguard had always seemed quick to anger, his face flashing from calm to jaw-clenching fury at the smallest provocation. Mahu even displayed these steep swings of temper and this tendency toward violence to the King's Wives, if they ever displeased Amunhotep in his presence. To be sure, he had never struck any of the women. But the way his hand would flash to the hilt of his dagger at any hint of the king's anger was more terrifying to Kiya than any slap or shove. She often feared that Mahu's influence would transfer to Amunhotep, scouring away all of the Pharaoh's kind consideration, turning him into a harsh, cold warlord of a king.

"It seems Mahu has been hanging about the temple precinct." Nann said. "He tries to intimidate the people who come to worship at the old gods' shrines, and threatens them with his eyes—or sometimes even with dire promises—if they refuse to visit Gempaaten."

"Ah." Kiya's frown deepened. She bit into her half of the citrus, but its puckering sweetness couldn't lift her mood.

Does Mahu do these things at Amunhotep's command? Kiya wondered. No—that couldn't be. Amunhotep was proud of his innovative new temple—Kiya had often heard him speak of it, and had sat with him in the garden as he composed the lines of a hymn which he intended to recite at every ceremony held within the walls of Gempaaten. The hymn was beautiful and gentle, full of bliss and happy praise. That alone would have convinced her that Amunhotep would never compel his subjects to worship the Aten, if her husband's loving nature hadn't spoken well of his intentions.

Amunhotep is always kind, always loving... even if his love was often fierce and intense.

"Gempaaten." Kiya repeated the name slowly, sucking on a slice of her fruit. "Gempaaten... and the Hawet Benben."

Nann nodded, giving Kiya a long stare, heavy with significance. Night insects chorused all around them, and above the lake the tiny cries of bats sparkled in the air like stars. But Nann and Kiya remained silent, mulling over the news from Waset with hunched shoulders and somber faces.

"Nefertiti," Nann finally said, barely louder than a whisper, as if she feared to upset the songs of the night— or perhaps she feared that Nefertiti herself might hear her name spoken from clear across the wide, dark garden. "She's High Priestess of the Sun now."

"I know," Kiya said lightly. "But what is that to me?"

"She's one step closer to the throne. I'm sure of it."

"I don't care a bit for that." Kiya flicked a citrus pip into the lake. It landed well beyond the lotuses, and the ripple of its landing spread in smooth, dark rings. "I don't want the throne. I only want Amunhotep's heart, and I have that. I am content. Let Nefertiti have her Hawet Ben-ben. It's all one to me."

Nann, ever practical, said, "If she has a temple from the king, and such a lofty station, too, then she might well steal his heart away."

Kiya rolled her eyes.

"And," Nann pushed on relentlessly, "she has already given him one child."

"A girl."

"Rumor has it that Nefertiti has another child on the way."

At that unexpected news, Kiya felt her face drain of blood. Her hands went suddenly cold; she folded them beneath her armpits for warmth. Her loving heart and genuine, pleasant nature had been enough to win Amunhotep's affections—and, Kiya admitted to herself, her constant readiness to take the king into her bed. With his favor had come the free rein Kiya had craved ever since she'd arrived in Egypt. She had worked Amunhotep to her benefit, won her pretty little house, the title of King's Wife, and the freedom to go about Egypt as she would—within reason, of course.

But now she found herself wanting more. She was still desperately lonely. True, she had Nann and Sitamun for company, but her longing for Mitanni had never left her. Even after two years as a queen in Egypt, the land still felt foreign to her, the culture and people strange, and not even her little white palace in the garden truly felt like home. She was still uprooted, blown on the winds of fickle gods like a soft white puff of seed.

Often she had watched Sitamun playing in the garden with little Nebetah. The girl had grown strong and sun-browned, running about the white pathways and exploring the flower beds on plump, energetic legs. Sometimes Kiya would join them, playing chasing games with the child, or tickling her soft skin until they both collapsed against the roots of the tall, shady sycamore, laughing.

Kiya wanted a child—a darling little cub just like Nebetah, who would fill the days with purpose and joy, and who would love her—only her—who would grow up to be devoted and tender and attentive, with time in each day for Kiya alone. Even the kindest Pharaoh could never give her the company and love she desired.

Nann reached out to take Kiya's hand. "Mistress, you look sorrowful."

Kiya smiled and shook her head. "I'm not," she promised. "All is well. Come, now—let's gather up these things you've bought and take them inside. The gnats are starting to bite."

They walked back to the little brick house slowly, enjoying the crisp, fresh bite of the night-time air.

"Well," Kiya said, as if their conversation had never diverted from its original path, "if things are so bad in Waset just now, perhaps it's better if you stay on the West Bank for a while. I won't send you out next week for market day—not until we hear that Waset has settled, and accepted the new temple."

"I don't know if the *rekhet* ever will accept it, Mistress, but I'll do as you think best."

"Has Lady Tiy gone to Waset lately?" Kiya asked suddenly. "She's a clever one, always so quick to puzzle out the mood of the people. I wonder what she makes of the rumors about Mahu and Gempaaten."

"Tiy?" Nann shrugged. "I haven't seen her at all in many a long week. I assumed she'd gone north, to one of her old estates in the countryside, and retired from court life."

"She never would. Not Tiy; the court is too much in her blood. No, she is still here in the House of Rejoicing, living in the harem, as before."

"Do you see her, then?"

Kiya nodded as they reached the door of her little house.

She opened it for Nann, whose arms were full of the basket and the goods from Waset. One of the house maids had lit a clay lamp, and its flame greeted them with a cheery red flicker. "I see her now and then. She talks to me sometimes, here in the garden. I'm surprised you've never noticed her, Nann."

"I have my duties," Nann said, rather shortly. "I don't have time to moon about the garden, day and night." She let the basket slide to the floor, then regarded her mistress with hands on hips as Kiya removed the sandals from her feet. "What does Tiy want with you? Why is she creeping about the garden, whispering in your ear, when I am nowhere near?"

Kiya laughed. "It's not like that!"

"It most certainly is. Sly old Tiy—she has always been a mover in the shadows. Now tell me—what does she want with you?"

When Kiya had kicked her sandals from her feet, she untied the knots of her gown and let the linen fall lightly to the floor. Nann stooped to pick it up, shaking out the day's wrinkles.

"Well," Kiya said with an amused, conspiratorial note in her voice, "I must confess that Tiy has been trying to impress me with certain... *ideas*."

Nann paused in the act of draping Kiya's discarded linen over the back of a chair. Her frown was deep and wary; Kiya saw at once that her maid found no humor in this news. "Ideas?" Nann said sharply. "What ideas?"

"Oh, Nann, it's all silliness—the fears and desperation of an old woman whose best days are behind her. Don't fret over Tiy. Besides, I think she drinks too much wine, and it has made her rather pathetic."

"What ideas?" Nann persisted.

Kiya sighed, unpinning the coil of her golden-brown

braid. She sat on the stool before her cosmetics table, and looked placidly into the mirror while Nann unraveled the braid, working through Kiya's long, wavy locks first with her fingers, then with the teeth of an ivory comb.

"Tiy is trying to convince me," Kiya said slowly, "that Amunhotep is... potentially dangerous."

The comb stilled. Nann's green eyes met Kiya's in the mirror.

"Perhaps wine and age haven't made Tiy as pathetic as my Mistress thinks," Nann muttered.

"Tiy thinks her son needs 'firm control.' She is worried about..." she hesitated, recalling Nann's sober face after a day spent among the *rekhet* of Waset with their rumors and agitation. But finally she admitted, "She is worried about the temple, and what it may mean for Egypt."

"I find myself liking Tiy more and more, much to my surprise."

"But it's silliness, Nann—all a lot of needless fear. Amunhotep is not a man to be feared."

Nann dropped the comb on the cosmetics table with a noisy clatter. "*There* you are wrong. And I've always told you so."

"He has always been good to me. Why should I think of him as dangerous, or a threat to Egypt? He has never given me cause. I'd be unjust, to mistrust him on the basis of rumor when he has only ever shown me kindness and love."

"Love." Nann rubbed rose oil between her palms, then worked it carefully through Kiya's hair. "I'm not convinced that man *can* feel love, Mistress."

"Well, *I* am. It's I who takes him into my bed, not you. I know his heart better than anyone."

Nann made no response, but Kiya could see in the girl's

reflection that her mouth was tense and her eyes were troubled.

"Tiy tells me I'm the only one who can truly *control* the Pharaoh. But I don't know what she expects of me, or what she means. Naturally, I'm flattered that a lady as intelligent as Tiy thinks so highly of me, but I don't think half so highly of my own abilities. Even if I thought Amunhotep needed someone to control him—*and I don't*—how could I, of all people, do it? I'm only a woman, and a young one, at that. And worse, I'm a foreigner. I still know so little of Egyptian ways and politics. I'm about as useless as anyone can be."

Nann sighed in sympathy, taking Kiya's hand to raise her from the table. She draped her shoulders with a robe, just substantial enough to ward off the evening's subtle chill. Then she led Kiya to her couch and eased her down onto the cushions. Nann sat beside her.

"Mistress, you mustn't dismiss your own abilities."

Kiya wrinkled up her nose in a frown of confusion.

"You are stronger than you realize," Nann insisted. The gap from her missing tooth showed plainly as she spoke, and Kiya remembered her first sight of the girl, as she sat trembling and alone on the litter that would carry her onto Waset's shore, and into her destiny.

Impulsively, Kiya threw her arms around Nann, tucking her head against her maid's shoulder.

"I wish we were in Mitanni," Kiya whispered.

"I know. I do, too."

"I don't want any of this, Nann. I don't want to be stronger than I realize. I don't want to be the only one who can control the Pharaoh. I don't want to be of any use to anyone—I only want my husband's love, and a child of my own. I want to live my life in peace. I just want to be happy."

Nann made no reply, except to wrap her arms around Kiya in a fiercely protective embrace.

There was nothing Nann could say, Kiya knew. The boat that had carried her from Mitanni to Egypt had long since sailed. Kiya was an Egyptian now—and in two years, she was twice a queen. There was no going back, and, if the gods decreed it, no living in peace. Ishtar and the stern gods of Egypt had arranged her fate, and she had no choice but to live out her appointed destiny.

Sitamun

Year 2 of Amunhotep
Beautiful Are the Manifestations,
Great of Kingship,
Who Upholds the Sun

SITAMUN WAS THE FIRST of all the King's Wives to step from the wide central corridor into Gempaaten's vast, roofless sanctuary. She threw her head back, allowing the sun to strike her full in the face, heating her cheeks and forehead until the sweat gathered on her skin. She could bear the sun well enough. It was the closing of the calendar—the festival of the New Year would begin in just a few days' time—and even the mid-day sun at the tail end of the harvest was not as merciless as the heat of Shemu.

She stared up in wonder at the double rows of her brother's massive statues. The paint on their stone skins looked as warm and nuanced as living flesh, and the artistic distortion of their features captivated her, sending a thrill up her spine as she imagined each one coming to life, raising their arms to praise the bright light overhead. The monuments seemed to smile down at her alone. She saw herself as if from their great height—from their wise, slitted eyes—a small thing, even if she was a King's Wife, delicate and awed in the swath of sand below. Everything looked small to those giants, Sitamun realized. The mightiest men in all the world were like ants to the statues—to her brother's *ka*, which now dwelt in each and every one—and to the sun that rode bright above them, in the winter-pale sky.

Kiya drew up beside Sitamun, carrying Nebetah on

her hip. She, too, gazed up at the statues, and her white brow furrowed at the sight of their odd proportions and exaggerated features. Little Nebetah gasped and clung to Kiya's neck, hiding her face from the stone giants.

Nefertiti was the last to make her way into the vast open courtyard. Her hand lay on the swell of her four-month belly, and she moved to stand near Sitamun and Kiya, but made no attempt to speak to the other King's Wives. Meritaten's nurse trailed a few steps behind, toting the child in her arms.

As the women waited in expectant silence, a rumble of male shouts rose up from the direction of the Temple of Amun. It was a distant sound, muffled by the depth of Gempaaten's walls, and the walls of Ipet-Isut, too, which were far older and thicker. Still, there was no mistaking the outrage in the priests' voices. The priests of all the local temples had converged on Ipet-Isut, endlessly discussing their disapproval of Gempaaten and the insult of its favorable placement, where the rays of the morning would strike its walls before blessing any other temple.

The unrest made Sitamun fearful.

She was glad for Amunhotep's accomplishment— Gempaaten was a marvel, unique in all the Two Lands, from its open-air construction to the compelling, dreamlike style of its adornments. With the completion of this great house of worship, the Pharaoh had achieved what no king in all the land had ever done before: he had made something *new*, something entirely without equal. Even if he never won a war, or expanded the boundaries of the Two Lands—even if he never found new routes of trade to further enrich Egypt's treasuries—his reign would be remembered forever, thanks to the stunning singularity of Gempaaten.

But as the wave of shouts reared again—a soft but bitter moan blowing over the ranks of Gempaaten's pillars—

Sitamun wondered at the cost of Amunhotep's monument.

Egypt has always gone on and on, because of the blessings of the gods. The traditional gods—the ones whose shrines and temples stood within the walls of Ipet-Isut. The gods whose priests had bristled in offense at Gempaaten, and the disregard for traditional ways which the new temple, with its bizarre art and its glaring light, so clearly represented.

Sitamun glanced up again at the nearest statue of Amunhotep. She peered past the swell of its belly and the crook and flail held across its chest, past its impossibly long chin and curving mouth, to the dark slits of its eyes. What would it mean, she wondered with a quiver of anxiety, if old traditions were cast away? If the gods-that-had-always-been were brushed aside and a new, faceless god set in their place, just what would become of Egypt? Would it no longer go on?

The winter sun, which had seemed gentle and bearable only moments before, beat down on her with a sudden, stern force. Sitamun squeezed her eyes shut. Her ears rang loudly, and her heart beat hard and fast as a vision coalesced before her inner eye—the darkness of the Duat, rising like the river in flood, creeping ever higher until it swallowed Egypt beneath its dense blanket of night. The whole of Egypt was gone, vanished into the black, save for Amunhotep's great statues.They towered from that suffocating depth, staring down with their satisfied smiles at the world that had been, but was no more.

Sitamun swayed, then stumbled. A hand caught her by the shoulder, and she opened her eyes to find Nefertiti beside her, righting her balance on the uneven sand.

"Don't let the heat affect you," Nefertiti said quietly.

In that moment, a glad, wordless shout carried across the sand from the pillars shadowing the other end of the courtyard. Despite her sudden misgiving, Sitamun's heart gave a hopeful lurch at the sound of Amunhotep's voice.

They approached him, making their way carefully across the deep, hot sand while the sun glared down from above. The children began to fuss. Amunhotep stood at the head of a single stone table. It was piled with offerings of meat and jars of milk, and the heaped, crushed petals of wilting flowers. The offerings gave off a rank smell in the direct sunlight. Flies had gathered, buzzing in a spiral over the table, walking along the raw, red surfaces of the meat, their quick legs tapping greedily.

"Do you like it?" Amunhotep indicated the table. "Soon this space will be filled with altars just like this one—dozens of them, reaching all the way across the courtyard. And every one will be heaped with offerings to the Aten."

Sitamun eyed the inelegant cloud of flies rather dubiously, but Nefertiti spoke before anyone else could. "It's a marvelous idea," she said smoothly. "Room enough for all the offerings the Aten could ever desire."

But the Aten desires no offerings. Sitamun bit her lip. Amunhotep often spoke of his lone, curiously detached god when he called Sitamun to his chambers for his regular attempts to make her pregnant again. She had learned much about the Aten in those times, the cheerful minutes before Amunhotep began his work, when his mood was still light and his hopes still high. Sitamun feigned interest every time, praying that enthusiasm for the Aten might be enough to restore her former place in her brother's heart.

She knew well that the Aten was unlike other gods—that no offerings could appease it, nor win its glorious favor, for it held itself above the base, human-like desires of other, lesser deities. She waited for Amunhotep to correct Nefertiti's erroneous statement, but he only nodded over his altar of spoiled goods.

"That's right—very true—that is good," he muttered,

beaming down at the table.

Then he clapped his hands, so quick and loud that little Meritaten cried out in fear and Nebetah hid her eyes again.

"At last you've seen my temple in all its glory," he said, dodging around the table to kiss first Kiya, then Sitamun on their cheeks. "I've been waiting to show it to you, my ladies, to impress you with its beauty—and finally, it is done. Well," he amended, chuckling at his own enthusiasm, "all but the altar tables. What do you think? Tell me truthfully, now."

Sitamun's scalp prickled as Kiya turned a quick, urgent glance in her direction. But Sitamun refused to meet Kiya's eye, afraid Amunhotep would see her hesitation, or read the worry in her face. "It's extraordinary," she said. "It's unlike any other temple in all the world."

That seemed to please the Pharaoh. He brushed Sitamun's chin with gentle fingers, smiling down at her—and her breath caught painfully in her throat.

"Go now," the king told them gently. "Go with Nefertiti, into the Hawet Ben-ben. The year is drawing to a close— this glorious year, when I have done so much for Egypt. I would have the High Priestess of the Sun bless you both, to make your wombs fertile. The Hawet Ben-ben is a sacred place, you know. The power of creation lives there."

Without another word, Amunhotep left them, striding away down the length of the courtyard, his step proud and sure, as if he stood as tall as the statues that lined the sanctuary.

Nefertiti watched him go for a long, silent moment, her mouth pressed into a thin line, her dark eyes thoughtful. Then she sighed lightly, and led the way past the altar table without a glance at its rotting, fly-specked offerings.

"Come," she called over her shoulder as she pressed on toward the little, white-sided temple that crouched against Gempaaten's rear wall. "The force of creation waits to bless you."

W HEN THE BLESSINGS were concluded—a ceremony which Nefertiti seemed to restrict to the barest minimum of prayer and chanting—the King's Wives and their attendants made their way back to the barque that would return them to the House of Rejoicing. A stout contingent of West Bank guards encircled the women as they walked from Gempaaten, past the massive outer walls of Ipet-Isut.

Sitamun could hear the priests' objections more readily here, beyond Gempaaten's confines. Now and then as they hurried toward the quay, the dull, formless clamor of debate and riled passion shaped itself, and a single shouted word carried clearly through the air. *Outrage*, cried one man, and another shouted, *Blasphemy!* And each time the protestations rang out, the guards that surrounded the Pharaoh's women tightened hard hands on the grips of their daggers.

The quay was littered with the servants and stewards of priests, men with suspicious eyes who leaned against stone pillars, muttering to one another behind the shields of their hands as Sitamun and her companions passed by. Some of the men paced like restless dogs, stalking between the great mooring blocks where the priests' ships were tied, perking up when the shouts behind Ipet-Isut's walls soared up to the sky on a crest of anger.

Sitamun exhaled in relief when she reached the top of their boat's ramp, followed by the final West Bank soldier. The lines were cast off, and soon Ipet-Isut—and Gempaaten beyond—were diminishing as the barque pulled away from the shore. The barque's musicians lifted their instruments, plucking soothing melodies from the strings of their gilded harps. The discord at Ipet-Isut lost itself in distance and in the refrains of gentle song.

Sitamun leaned on the boat's rail, watching Waset and the temples dwindle. Someone approached, leaning likewise a precise distance away—not near enough to seem friendly, but not far enough to imply isolation, or that Sitamun was being ignored. She did not need to look around to know that Nefertiti had joined her. That rigid aloofness and aristocratic silence were as characteristic of Nefertiti as her grace and remarkable beauty.

"High Priestess," Sitamun said in greeting. Only a little irony peeked through her words.

"What did you think of the ceremony?"

Sitamun shrugged. "You invented it on your own, I suppose."

"Of course. I have no traditions to go by, and no other priestesses from which to learn. The Aten is an old god, but so very old that no one recalls how best to worship it. I did my best."

Sitamun did look at Nefertiti then, for the admission of insecurity caught her completely off guard. The winter sun was sliding fast and low toward the west, and the surface of the Iteru sparked and flashed with a pale-white glimmer that seemed to cast a halo of washed-out light around Nefertiti's face. The other woman smiled, and lifted her hand—and Sitamun saw that she offered a cup of cold, watered beer.

"You looked thirsty in the temple," Nefertiti said.

Sitamun took it with a nod of thanks, and drained the cup in one long draft. The beer did seem to brace her, driving away a little of the sun's previous harshness.

"Thank you. The heat took me unaware, I suppose."

"It's easy to be taken unaware in Gempaaten."

"I thought your ceremony was well-done," Sitamun said. "It seemed... sincere." Her mouth twisted in a self-deprecatory smile, and she tipped the cup to her lips again, just to hide the bitterness on her face, though only a drop of beer remained.

Nefertiti, at least, had a fertile womb. One daughter already, and now she was growing larger with a second child. *It will be a boy for certain*, Sitamun thought in bleak surrender. *She is the only one among us who can still conceive. Perhaps the old gods have cursed our wombs, one by one, just to spite Amunhotep. But it's we who suffer, not the king.*

"I am glad you approved," Nefertiti said.

From across the boat, Kiya's light, musical laughter rang like a bell on a morning breeze. Nefertiti and Sitamun both turned from their moody study of the Iteru to gaze at their companion. Kiya sat on the deck of the boat with Nebetah and baby Meritaten, trying to show the little girls how to play some clapping game Sitamun did not recognize. No doubt it was a Mitanni importation.

"I think Kiya was best pleased with your ceremony," Sitamun told Nefertiti. "She wants a child of her own so desperately. I already have Nebetah, but she... Well, I saw tears in her eyes as you chanted over the Ben-ben stone. For her sake, I hope the Aten hears your prayers."

Nefertiti frowned in contemplation as the clapping game, and Kiya's airy giggles, went on. At last she said, "I think the Pharaoh is far more concerned about *your* womb than Kiya's."

As she spoke, Nefertiti's hands closed protectively over the swelling that pushed out the pleats of her white robe. Her finely-made face, so delicate and harmonious in its features, was shadowed by a thick veil of anxiety.

Sitamun glanced at Nefertiti's belly, then turned once more to lean on the rail. Far across the blue-white dazzle of the river, Waset was a thin smudge of gray against the slope of the low eastern hills. And just to the north, the massive limestone monuments of the temple district seemed no more than a freckle on the earth's skin. From this distance, the Hawet Ben-ben, Nefertiti's own place of distinct and new-wrought power, was tinier than a gnat.

If only I can be the one to give my brother a divine son, Sitamun thought wistfully, *I shall be closer to Amunhotep's heart than Nefertiti—or even Kiya, if the gods are good.*

But the memory of her strange vision returned to her—the darkness rising up to bury Egypt's old gods, leaving only Amunhotep to smile down on the world—and her stomach turned sick and sour.

If the gods are good... The sound of the discord within Ipet-Isut carried deep into her heart like a whisper, like a hiss, and Sitamun's hands tightened on the barque's wooden rail.

If there are any gods left at all, to give me their blessing of mercy.

Tiy

Year 2 of Amunhotep
Beautiful Are the Manifestations,
Great of Kingship,
Who Upholds the Sun

TIY WAS WAITING IN THE GARDEN, still and
secluded beneath the blue-green shade of the great,
tall sycamore, when Kiya returned from the temple. She
pressed herself close to the tree's rough bole, watching
with narrowed eyes as Kiya handed Nebetah off to
Sitamun. The Hurrian then kissed Sitamun on the cheek
in farewell, and started up the limestone path to her little
house, alone.

Kiya's arms were folded tight beneath her breasts, her
eyes downcast as she made her way slowly through
the garden. The shrubs of the flowerless beds had been
trimmed back for the winter, cut into pleasing shapes to
delight the eye until the season of Akhet came again to
call the blossoms from vine and branch with dampness
and warmth. But Kiya took no heed of the fanciful curves
of the flower beds, nor of the birds skipping and fluttering
along the path before her.

She did not look up at all, until Tiy came briskly from
her concealment. Kiya startled at the movement, then,
noting with tight mouth and sparking eyes that it was Tiy
who approached across the beds, she seized her skirt in
both hands and nearly ran for the door of her house.

"I think not," Tiy muttered. She, too, picked up her hem.
She glided rapidly to intercept Kiya. It was just one of the

many skills she had honed in her long years at the House of Rejoicing—moving fast enough to be everywhere at once, and to appear at a fleeing subject's elbow composed and serene, utterly unruffled.

When she caught up to Kiya, the girl jumped and squeaked, but ceased her scampering and offered Tiy a correct bow. "King's Mother."

Tiy very nearly rolled her eyes. King's Mother may be her title now, but whenever she heard those words they seemed pedantic to the point of mockery. Young Amunhotep had no love for Tiy, and the title meant little to *him*—and so it meant little to anyone else, Tiy especially. The Pharaoh was content to keep Tiy stuffed away in a dark, dusty corner of the harem, never sparing her a thought, and all but barring her from court affairs and matters of the throne room. *King's Mother, indeed. Anupu take my useless title and cart it off to the Underworld, where it belongs.* It gave her no leverage over the throne, and so it meant nothing to her.

"How was your visit to the new temple?" Tiy asked.

Kiya swallowed hard, and her pale, pretty cheeks flushed.

"Come," Tiy suggested. "Let's go inside. We have much to speak of, you and I."

Kiya held the door for Tiy, but would not meet her eyes. Inside, Kiya's foreign, gap-toothed maid came sailing around a bright-painted corner, chattering in her native tongue. When she saw Tiy lingering near the door, the maid bowed deeply, but when she straightened, her green Hurrian eyes held a cautious, darkly amused glimmer.

"So," the maid said to Kiya, "Lady Tiy *is* still in the House of Rejoicing, after all."

"Lady Tiy speaks Hurrian quite well," Tiy informed her.

The maid-servant blushed.

Kiya laid a hand on her servant's shoulder. "Wine and

dates from our little cellar, Nann. And let us all speak Egyptian here."

When the servant had turned to do Kiya's bidding, the King's Wife sighed and sank onto her ebony-wood couch.

"You know why I'm here, I suppose," Tiy said, choosing a high-backed chair near the window. She liked the way its tall arms and towering straightness held her body upright, and reminded her of the Great Wife's throne.

"Now, as ever, there is nothing I can do," Kiya said wearily. "The Pharaoh is not a man I can control, Lady Tiy."

"You underestimate your own abilities. You sell yourself short."

Kiya shook her head, squeezing her eyes shut. "He forges ahead without me—without anyone, save for Nefertiti. He remakes the world to suit his desires. He is not a force I can master."

Tiy narrowed her eyes at mention of Nefertiti's name. Her niece had certainly been clever, making herself an intrinsic part of Amunhotep's religion as he built it from the ground up, brick by brick like his temple across the Iteru.

"You must do what Nefertiti has done," Tiy said. "Ingratiate yourself to the king by devoting yourself to his god."

Kiya gasped. "Surely you're jesting."

The Hurrian servant returned with a laden tray. Tiy watched in silence as the girl set a bowl of dates beside herself and Kiya, then filled two polished horn cups with wine as dark-red as blood. The servant vanished into the depths of the house as Tiy sampled the wine. It was good—a fine, northern vintage, sweet and robust.

"I am not jesting," Tiy finally said. "You say Nefertiti goes along with him—well, then, so must you. If he wants

reinforcement of his beliefs—even of his own divinity—
then let him have such things from the lips of his own
sweet Kiya. Every day you hesitate to put the king under
your spell is another day Nefertiti's power grows. The
more interest she shows in the Aten, the sooner she will
eclipse you, Kiya. And not only in standing; I know you
care little for that. But in Amunhotep's love."

The girl's green eyes widened. Evidently, she had not
considered the possibility that Amunhotep might weary
of her affections. But it was possible—likely, even, Tiy felt
sure. For all his maundering divinity, Amunhotep was
more *human* a man than any Tiy had ever known. He was
base and selfish, grasping and keen. And it was only a
matter of time before he noted that among all his women,
it was the most beautiful one of them all—ethereal, regal
Nefertiti—who seemed to share the desires of his heart.

When that sun finally dawned on Amunhotep, Tiy
mused as she drearily chewed on a date, Kiya's potential
would be spent, and all her use exhausted.

"Amunhotep's love." Kiya's brows furrowed as she sipped
her wine, and for a moment, Tiy thought the girl would
weep. But she controlled herself with an obvious effort,
smoothing the worry from her face, lifting her chin like a
King's Wife of Egypt.

"But the Aten," Kiya said with no hint of tears or
weakness. "Such a strange and lonely god..."

"What can it matter, if you make noises of praise in the
Aten's direction?"

Tiy jerked her head toward Kiya's indoor shrine, and the
goddess statue that stood on its well-shined, malechite
platform. Golden Ishtar was raised up on her clawed feet,
proud and erect, draped in the majesty of her eagle's
wings.

"You are still a devotee of Ishtar, through and through,"
Tiy said. "Your heart is Ishtar's. So what does it matter to

your *ka*, which Egyptian god you might promote? To you, all our gods may as well be the same, and the Aten is as good as Amun, Sobek, or Khonsu."

For a moment, Kiya seemed to consider this. The girl's head tilted slightly, as if in acceptance of Tiy's assertion. But then a veil of memory passed over Kiya's face. Her eyes unfocused, and whatever she saw as she gazed sightlessly past the brick walls of her home pulled her mouth into a deep, troubled frown.

Is my son's new temple really so strange? Few West Bank courtiers had seen Gempaaten as yet, and Tiy had been unable to gather any reliable information about the controversial new construction.

"It makes sense, to reach Amunhotep through his god." Tiy, sensing that Kiya had nearly agreed with her, pushed all the harder against the girl's defenses. "His father became obsessed with the idea of his own divintiy early in our marriage—that is, divinity-on-earth, which a Pharaoh does not attain—not until he is dead. The only way I ever could control my husband was by appealing to his vanity—his obsession. But I learned to do it well, Kiya. Very well. And so can you."

The veil over Kiya's eyes suddenly parted, and she stared at Tiy with sudden clarity. "Did you ever love your husband, Lady Tiy?"

Tiy blinked. "*Love* him?"

"Yes," Kiya hissed. "*Love* him. Did you ever want his affection, or crave his touch, or pray that he would come to you to alleviate your loneliness? Did you ever beg the gods to plant a child in your womb, so that you wouldn't be so dreadfully *alone*?"

Tiy gaped, aware that she looked as elegant as a carp in a net, but so startled by this sharp bend in the road of Kiya that she was powerless to close her own mouth.

"I didn't think so," Kiya said with mounting scorn. She set her wine cup on a nearby table and folded her hands primly in her lap. "I am not the woman you think I am. I do not *think* the way you do—of control and obsession, and power and manipulation. You cannot judge my ability to play your despicable power games, because you cannot know me. You cannot know me, Lady Tiy, because you cannot understand me. I don't want the throne of King's Great Wife. I don't want a temple, as Nefertiti has, or a position as High Priestess of the Sun. I only want..."

Her tirade broke, and Kiya seemed to choke on the bitterness of her words. Tiy kept very still in her chair, gripping her wine cup tightly, watching in observant silence as Kiya struggled with her emotions.

"I only want to be happy," Kiya said at last. Tears spilled from her eyes, and she buried her face in her hands. "I want a child—someone who is mine alone, and loves me, and always will. I only want to be happy in love!"

Tiy's exasperation exploded from her lips. "*Pah!* Love? Wake up, girl. Amunhotep is incapable of love."

Kiya's anger flared in her eyes; she shook her head in a fierce denial. At the sound of her mistress's sniffling, the Hurrian servant crept from hiding and stood staring at Tiy with her arms folded across her thin chest, but Tiy made no move to leave.

"*Incapable*," she said with cruel emphasis. "He killed his own father! What greater proof of his coldness do you need?"

"He did not kill his father," Kiya insisted. "I know he did not. He came to see me the morning of his father's death, and he was good to me, and kind. No one who had just killed would behave that way."

"You poor, innocent little thing," Tiy said with relentless scorn. "Do you truly believe that?"

Kiya's voice rose nearly to a shout. "And anyhow, you've always told me—*told me all along*—that I have power over Amunhotep because he *loves me*. If he is incapable of love, then why have you tried so hard to make me into your tool?"

"There is a difference between real love and base, animal lust," Tiy said coolly. "If you were too naïve to see that on your own, and too besotted to tell that Amunhotep's lust for your body is not love for your heart, then I cannot help you."

Kiya leaped to her feet, her white fists balled. "I am not naïve."

Tiy rose more regally. The only response she made was to lift one eyebrow.

"Do you think I am naïve?" Kiya aid. "I'm not so naïve that I can't see what would happen to *you* if I told Amunhotep everything—how you've been coming to see me, trying to train me to be your creature, to place the Pharaoh under your control."

A terrible, metallic crash sounded inside Tiy's head, louder than a hundred rattles in the depths of Amun's temple. She felt her face blanch, and the skin around her lips went cold and tight as her heart raced with sudden fear. But she controlled herself, as ever, and the only satisfaction she gave to Kiya's bluff was to blink once, slowly, as calm and distant as an owl perched high in a sycamore.

"Try it," Tiy finally said, when Kiya, trembling, sank back onto her couch. Her gap-toothed servant rushed to soothe her, patting her hand and glaring up at Tiy like a pet cat upset from its cushion. "Try it, and find out how the Pharaoh rewards those who speak against his divine family." She turned and swept toward the door. But on its threshold she paused, and cast one final word over her shoulder. "Incapable."

Tiy departed Kiya's little palace with a controlled, stately step, drifting over the garden's paths as serenely as a woman who had only gone out to the garden to enjoy the fresh air. But as she put more distance between herself and the Hurrian, she found her fists clenched in her skirts, and the hem of her skirt lifting above her ankles. She noted how her pace quickened, how her sandals scuffed over stone, and by the time she reached the House of Women, she was out of breath and wide-eyed, her heart pounding hard in her ears.

She climbed the narrow stairway to the rooftop of the House of Women. There, alone with her racing thoughts and her quivering knees, she stood looking over the West Bank estates, across the silver-gray expanse of the Iteru to the temples in the far distance. Ipet-Isut was pale and small, but even so, Tiy fancied that she could see the tense, milling bodies of the angry priests who gathered there in protestation, and imagined their shouts drifting over the river, carried on the cool winter winds.

Amunhotep did not love her. Unlike Kiya, Tiy was no naif. She knew how little the Pharaoh's *ka* would be troubled if she gave him any excuse to banish her to some isolated estate—or worse. He would do it as soon as blink, and think nothing of it—all in a day's work, he would wipe Tiy's blood from his palms like a stonecarver brushes away the dust of his routine labors.

But does Kiya know? Does Kiya see the advantage she would have, even over me, if she betrayed me to the king?

Despite Tiy's insulting words, she still believed that Kiya was no fool—not truly, not deep within her *ka*. And the girl was stronger than she realized. But she did not know whether Kiya would awaken to her own potential—and her aptitude for these 'despicable power games'—until it was too late for Egypt, too late for Tiy, and too late for Kiya herself.

Staring out at Waset, Tiy thought achingly of Smenkhkare. He would be thirteen years old now—nearly fourteen. Perhaps he was just old enough to place on the throne, assuming Tiy could rally the nobles of the West Bank to her cause. But nearly three years shut away in the harem had stripped away so much of the influence she had once possessed, and uncertain as she now was of her place in the world, she feared that to recall Smenkhkare would be to send him straight to his tomb.

Kiya was still the best—the *only* hope she had, but that hope had worn ragged and thin.

As the sun settled into the weak flame of a winter sunset, Tiy watched the pale smudge of Ipet-Isut with shaded eyes. *Gods*, she prayed, *Amun, Mut, Sobek—is this impotence and fear the price I must pay for my sins?* The gods had not forgiven her for making her own children pawns on the *senet* board. Tiy knew it was so. And if they did not exact their punishment now, then the day of reckoning was soon coming.

Tiy

Year 3 of Amunhotep
Beautiful Are the Manifestations,
Great of Kingship,
Who Upholds the Sun

THE FEAST OF THE VALLEY opened with ritual song. A chorus of girls arrayed themselves below the dais in the great hall, their palms lifted as they sang a hymn of praise to the sun. The girls were dressed in wisps of brightly colored, yet transparent, silk—draped from their wide, golden collars and flowing down around their not-quite-nubile bodies. Their voices were as sweet as the flowers braided into their sidelocks and twined around their wrists and ankles.

Flowers, the last of the harvest season's blooms, filled the hall in riotous profusion. Long, shallow dishes of water stretched down the center of every feasting table, and the spikes of white and bright-violet lotuses floated there like jewels set in silver. A trio of floor vases surrounded each of the hall's many pillars, and vines with blossoms like dancing flames spilled over their sides. Both men and women of the West Bank estates wore garlands of waxy flowers, and the Pharaoh's dais was covered in a thick, pink carpet of rose petals, those garden favorites imported from the lands far across the northern sea.

When the feast wore to its natural close, the nobles would gather up the flowers and the remains of the meal, and carry them up into the western hills. There, in the dark of night, when the *kas* of their ancestors walked again, they would leave the gifts as offerings at their loved ones' tombs.

The Pharaoh, though, would not join them. Amunhotep had let it be known weeks before that he had no intention of joining the celebrants in their tomb-worship after the Feast of the Valley. Nor had he joined the priests of Amun earlier that day, as they'd carried the god's statue, veiled against the encroachment of light, up among the tombs in its boat-shaped shrine. His absence from the annual Visitation of Amun had been noted by the priests. They were displeased, but they were not surprised.

Amunhotep allowed this feast in the great hall only because he saw an opportunity to publicly stress his allegiance to the Aten. Tiy had to admit with a grudging frown that the show was effective. The chorus of girls was a pretty and innocent display—one might even suspect from their sweet, gentle voices that the Aten, and Amunhotep himself, were forces entirely benign. The words of the hymn had been carefully chosen. Despite Tiy's efforts to maintain a cynical distance and to focus on her wine, a thrill of awe ran up her reluctant spine as now and then a particularly lovely phrase soared across the hall.

Amunhotep smiled down at the singers from the height of his dais as they sang their final verse. Nefertiti's features were as placid and unmoved as those of a carven statue. She sat straight-backed and regal on the throne beside the Pharaoh, with the cobra circlet of a King's Wife glittering on her brow.

So Nefertiti has the honor of the Great Wife's chair this evening. It was not always so. At some feasts, Amunhotep allowed Kiya to claim the place of honor, and occasionally—though far less often—he gave the seat to Sitamun. None of the three women had yet found a way to seize the title of King's Great Wife—Nefertiti's second baby, now a few months old and thriving, was another girl—but Tiy kept careful track of how the women were placed at feasts and in the proceedings of the court. Nefertiti's turns on the throne of the Great Wife had now exceeded Kiya's by half. It made Tiy purse her lips in bleak contemplation. She reached for her wine cup again.

The corner of Ay's thin mouth tensed as he watched Tiy sip her wine. "It won't do to get sodden," he said. "Not so early in the evening."

"When have I ever been *sodden?*" Tiy flicked one swift glance toward Lady Teya, whose mask of dazed, misty bliss was as firmly in place as ever.

Tiy could not say just who had arranged for her to sit with Ay and his wife, so near the dais and the table where Kiya and Sitamun gathered with their attendants and guards and a few select ladies of the court who were favored by the King's Wives. She peered over the edge of her wine cup, considering the pair on the dais. Amunhotep certainly had not placed her here—a Pharaoh had grander thoughts to occupy his heart than where his guests should sit at a feast. Was it Nefertiti, then? Tiy wondered. If so, the girl had meant no kindness to her aunt, but had done it with purpose. *Does she wish me to spy on her father, and carry news of his plots to her chamber when the feast is done?*

Or perhaps Kiya was behind this strange table arrangement. It would be like soft, silly Kiya to think she was doing Tiy a kindness, finding her a place at a higher table than those she'd grown accustomed to since her fall from grace. Thank the gods, Tiy's threat that day in Kiya's little garden palace seemed to have worked. Kiya had never breathed a word of Tiy's scheming to the Pharaoh. If she had, Tiy had no doubt that she'd be receiving her wine tonight as an offering at her tomb, and not sipping it from an alabaster cup, enjoying its sweetness on her intact and living tongue.

It hardly matters who seated me here, Tiy mused. *If I owe Nefertiti a report later, then she shall have it, and gladly. And meanwhile, I shall make the most of my good fortune.*

The hymn concluded on a swell of golden harmony, and applause and shouts of praise broke out across the hall. The acclaim seemed genuine to Tiy—not the usual, sycophantic show of enthusiasm the West Bank nobles always showed for Amunhotep's strange endeavors. The music had been a genuine delight. Tiy even set her wine cup aside to offer two or three lazy claps of her hands.

"Your son has quite the talent for music," Ay said.

"Who knew?"

"If only he had an equal talent for managing the country."

"We must make do with what the gods have given us," Tiy said flatly. *I would bring Smenkhkare back, Brother, and put a true, good-hearted king upon the throne, if I could be sure you wouldn't strangle another of my sons with your scorpion claws.*

As the chorus took their bows and made their way from the hall, each little girl receiving a golden chain from the king's own hands in payment for her performance, servants presented the first course on brightly glazed platters. Tiy chose a dish of her favorite fish stew and sipped its spicy, salty broth, watching her brother from the tail of her eye. What a shame that her rise to King's Mother had brought her no closer to power. She would give nearly anything to bring Ay to justice, but not at the cost of her own life. She could not move against him until she was certain of enjoying the king's protection. Perhaps, she thought, staring across the hall at the Hurrian, there was still a drop of hope left in Kiya's cup. More likely, she must make an alliance with Nefertiti—a prospect that appealed to Tiy about as much as sticking her hand into a sack full of asps. Anything raised in the viper's-nest of Ay's home was not a creature Tiy would care to clutch against her bosom—but as Kiya descended further into her childish fantasies of love and gentle motherhood, Nefertiti might soon become Tiy's last refuge.

Ay noted the direction of Tiy's thoughtful gaze. "Still hanging your hopes on that foreign King's Wife?"

Tiy's toes curled in her sandals, but she kept her face still. *You've no right to be shocked that he has learned of your alliance with Kiya.* Maids were fearful gossips, and Ay had never accounted himself too lofty to listen to servants' stories. Certainly tales of Tiy's visits to Kiya had made the rounds among the palace maids—particularly the story of Tiy's angry exit from the garden estate.

She nibbled a piece of stewed fish. "My hopes are more stable than your own, Father of the God. Kiya is pregnant."

He shrugged. "What does that matter? Pregnancies are lost all the time."

"She has passed the weeks when such losses normally occur. But after all, you are right—it matters little. Kiya, too, might produce only girls—just like your daughter."

Ay would not be needled. He turned away from Tiy, watching with flat-eyed aloofness as a troupe of dancers filed into the hall, trailing veils like wisps of cloud.

"Do you think the priests of Amun have come down from the hills yet?" he asked casually. "Toting their god on their shoulders?"

"*Their* god? Are you becoming an Atenist, too, Ay?"

"A timely conversion might be prudent. I shall keep my options open. You know how tense things have become on the east bank."

Indeed, Tiy did know. She supped her fish stew in a misery of helpless frustration as the dancers whirled gaily around the room. Once the temple protests had settled to a simmer, the soldier Mahu returned to his efforts on the Aten's behalf, lounging around the great pylon gates of Ipet-Isut with his pack of paid men, pressuring Waset's citizens to pay their respects in the open-air halls of Gempaaten. The priests of Amun could do little about

388

it—they were not military men, after all—and their attempts to hire guards of their own, to drive Mahu and his feral dogs away, had proved unsuccessful. Either Mahu or Amunhotep was exerting influence on the soldiers of the area, forbidding them from serving the Amun cult no matter what price was offered. Or, Tiy thought with sudden misgiving, perhaps Ay was the one pulling those particular strings. He was still the Overseer of All the Horses, after all—a position that afforded him considerable weight with the generals and charioteers. Was Mahu Ay's reserve? His backup plan in case his carefully groomed daughter failed at her life's purpose, and denied him a hold on the Horus Throne? Tiy squinted at her brother with a new, slow-twisting wariness.

"Mahu's harassments have crossed over into outrages, I hear," Tiy said lightly. "I heard that only a week ago that a handful of young priests attacked him, trying to drive him away from the gates of Ipet-Isut."

Ay chuckled, a sound like dry stones rattling in a desert gulch. "Foolish. The boys were sent packing back to Amun, considerably worse for wear."

"The king ought to put a stop to this," Tiy said. "These tensions are unnecessary, and will soon escalate into more violence. Chaos at the temples is the last thing Egypt needs."

Ay shrugged.

"Careful, Ay," she said under her breath, so that no one could hear, save for him. "If Mahu's outrages aren't controlled, someone might slip hints to the High Priest of Amun that the world would be a better place without Mahu in it." She cast a narrow-eyed stare up at the dais, at her own son slouching back on his throne. The double crown of the Two Lands stood tall upon his brow, and his grin was slow and self-satisfied. "Better without Mahu— and without the one who controls him."

Ay raised his brows in real curiosity. "Oh? You'd willingly part with your last remaining son?"

"You mistake my meaning," Tiy said smoothly, knowing that Ay did not, in fact, mistake anything. He rarely did. "Though, if anyone were to suggest an assassination of Mahu to the High Priest, you would be the ideal man. You have the contacts among the military to recommend a person capable of the job—someone who could make better work of it than a handful of skinny, youthful apprentice-priests."

"But," Ay said, "if I were to put such an idea into the High Priest's heart, he would hardly stop at Mahu. Amun's anger has seethed in the darkness of his shrine for two years, Tiy. One act of violence—one strike against the Pharaoh's entourage—would unleash a chain of events that no one could control. Not you, and," he added with a wry laugh, spreading his hands in a mockery of helplessness, "certainly not me."

Tiy lifted one kohl-blackened brow.

"An heir to the throne was already killed, within the vary walls of the House of Rejoicing," Ay went on. He sampled a handful of fire-roasted dates, sucking their sticky sweetness from his fingers as if they discussed the price of fish or turquoise, and not crimes against divinity. "And my source inside the palace tells me that *you* suspect the old Pharaoh was murdered, too—even though he was about as robust as a drought-stricken goat."

"And so you think, if Mahu were to be assassinated—"

"Like a baying hound, the rage of Waset would be set loose. The priests and the *rekhet* would fall upon our peaceful little enclave, here on the West Bank. They would remove your son from this world. Their anger has burned like banked coals for far too long. One gust of air, and it will roar into a terrible conflagration."

Good, Tiy thought. *Let the* rekhet *clear the way for*

Smenkhkare's return.

"But I will not let it happen, Tiy."

Ay did not speak as if to comfort her, soothing a mother's fear for her son. Rather, his words were laced with dark promise, as if he had read the thoughts in her secret heart.

He turned to regard Nefertiti on the dais. She smiled at something the laughing Pharaoh whispered into her ear, then looked out over the feasting hall with an air of self-possessed dignity. Ay grunted in approval at his daughter's untouchable, regal mien.

"Destroy Mahu," he said contemptutously, "and make my daughter a widow? A fool's errand. Besides, who would then be king, once Amunhotep met his inevitable death at the point of the High Priest's blade? The Pharaoh has no sons."

Who would be king? Tiy had a very good notion of just who would take the Horus Throne when Amunhotep was kicked off to his tomb where he belonged, to join his father in the Field of Reeds. At least in the afterlife, neither of the Amunhoteps could do Egypt any harm. But she said only, "Who would be king? *Anybody* else! Lovely hymns aside, you can't truly believe that my son is a capable Pharaoh. Who, indeed! *You*, Ay, for all I care."

For one small, shivering moment, one breathless space between two beats of her heart, Tiy saw a black spark of ambition flare in her brother's *ka*, illuminating the spare angles of his face with a fiery glow. But then Ay quenched it, and sipped unconcernedly at his wine.

"Or me," Tiy offered.

Ay sputtered. "You! Don't become pathetic in your old age, Sister. Ambition doesn't suit you—not anymore."

"Why not?" Tiy said. "Didn't Hatshepsut rule as Pharaoh for two decades?"

"You are no Hatshepsut. For one thing, you haven't got

two decades left. For another, you've been languishing in some musty corner of the harem, and all your old influence has turned to dust along with your wit and physical charms. You could never rally the people behind such an absurd bid for the throne."

A thrill of inspiration tingled in Tiy's palms. She watched Ay's face carefully as she said, "Nefertiti, then."

He looked at her sharply over the rim of his silver cup.

Yes, she felt tempted to say. *Place your daughter on the throne, and there would be no one who stood between you and power, Ay. You could sink your claws into the king herself, instead of just a King's Wife.* But she must not taunt him now—must not crack the fragile idea before it had time to fire and harden in the kiln of Ay's heart.

Finally, Ay shook his head and turned his face scornfully away from Tiy. "Madness. It's foolish to place a woman on the throne."

"What is it, then?" Tiy asked with venom. "Are you afraid that if you set your daughter on the throne, you won't be able to control her?"

"How well it's worked for *you*," he rejoined, nodding casually toward the Pharaoh.

"I have news for you, Ay. You've lost control of Nefertiti already. Whatever game she's playing, with this business of the Hawet Ben-ben and her enthusiasm for the Aten, she's playing it for herself, and for no one else. Not even for you. You've lost her entirely—she has become her own woman, a force unto herself. She is not your tool any longer, Father of the God."

Ay's mask of thoughtful stillness broke with an amused grin. "We'll see wether I still have my hold on Nefertiti."

He nodded across the hall, to the table where the King's Wives sat chattering with their favored guests. A slender, brown form rose from one of the stools, carrying a dish of some delicacy in her palms as she climbed the steps of the dais and bent at Nefertiti's elbow. Tiy hadn't visited Nefertiti's private quarters for quite some time— it took her a long moment to recognize Mutbenret, for the girl had grown into the first flush of womanhood. Her childish hips had just begun to widen and curve, and where her chest had once been flat, small breasts now swelled. Tiy blinked in disbelief—for in spite of the girl's obvious advancement into womanhood, her hair was still fixed in the braid of youth, swinging over her shoulder as she stooped beside the King's Wife, and she was dressed in a wisp of silk as flimsy and transparent as those the chorus girls had worn, arranged in a tantalizing mockery of a child's traditional linen tunic.

Tiy shook her head in confusion. "Mutbenret is old enough to wear a woman's wig, and to dress like a grown lady. What is this, Ay?"

"You may have spirited her out of my home, Sister, but that girl, at least, still does exactly as I say."

With a chill, Tiy remembered the casual words he had uttered, just minutes before. *My source inside the palace.*

"Let Nefertiti fancy herself beyond my reach," Ay said quietly. "I have set my hook where it counts, and when the time is right, I will draw upon my line."

"But why?" Tiy gestured helplessly at Mutbenret, as her twisted simulation of youth. "Why make her go about so? It's—"

In that moment, the Pharaoh leaned across Nefertiti to smile at his little sister-by-marriage. Tiy watched as Amunhotep's eyes skated from Mutbenret's face to her neckline, and down to her small, tender breasts beneath their insufficient covering of silk. The king's smile turned to a leer, and his eyes flashed with black fire.

Tiy's heart gave a tight, painful wrench of guilt. She thought of Sitamun at the same age—Sitamun in her father's chamber, huddled pale and stricken at the Pharaoh's bedside.

She turned on Ay, her cheeks flushed with rage. "I didn't take Mutbenret out of your home so that you could continue torturing her."

"She is not your daughter," Ay said coolly. "Mind the morality of your own children, Sister, and leave me to tend my garden in peace."

Tiy pushed herself away from the table and rose on trembling legs.

"What," Ay said, "leaving the feast so soon?"

"I find I have small appetite," Tiy said. "And no liking for my present company." She turned away, but paused—then reached for her wine cup and finished off its contents in one long draft. She dropped the cup into Ay's bowl of stew; the red-spiced broth spattered his face and chest, and he gasped in offense.

Tiy spun away and swept from the hall. The wine throbbed warm along her arms and curled in her belly as she walked, and under its soothing influence, the pounding of her heart steadied, then slowed.

If I am to save innocent Mutbenret from becoming the Pharaoh's plaything—and keep Ay's bloody talons well away from Nefertiti and the throne—then I must act now. Kiya must act now.

The time had come to put the Hurrian to the test, and to pray night and day that she would live up to the intelligence Tiy saw shining in her eyes, far behind the glaze of wistful hope and foolish dreams. Kiya was her final hope for victory—for control. More fates than Tiy's alone hung in the balance, and Kiya was the only stone Tiy had left to cast upon the scales.

Nefertiti

Year 4 of Amunhotep
Beautiful Are the Manifestations,
Great of Kingship,
Who Upholds the Sun

NEFERTITI KNELT IN THE DEEP sand of her little, white-walled temple. The sun-scorched floor stung her knees and shins, but she did not shift or fidget against the discomfort. Light poured in from the open roof, and the reflective specks in the surface of the Ben-ben's granite shimmered and danced before her eyes. She lifted her palms in prayer, but it was not to the great, erect stone—or to the Aten—that she prayed.

Mother Mut, dost thou hear me? Canst thou find my voice, even here?

Ten days had passed since the birth of Nefertiti's third child. Another girl—and although the baby had cried so faintly in the birthing pavilion that the midwives had predicted she would not live to see the next sunrise, the child had pulled through, growing pinker and fatter by the day, until at last Nefertiti felt safe in giving her a name. Ankhesenpaaten—*She Lives for the Aten.* The new baby had joined her sisters, Meritaten and Meketaten, in the House of Women. There wet-nurses and royal caregivers could bring them up in peace, beneath the protection of many women's arms, stretched above their heads like Mut's gentle vulture wings.

I thank thee, Mut, for another healthy daughter. I thank thee for sparing her, even though she was weak.

And even as she prayed these words—so sincere, for the love Nefertiti had experienced at the birth of her first child only increased with each new daughter's arrival—a small, frail portion of her heart whispered, *And I curse you, Mut, for not sending me a son.*

Nefertiti hunched her shoulders as the unworthy thought twisted from her heart like a worm from a blossom, writhing its way up past the Ben-ben, into the sky.

I thank thee, most humbly, Nefertiti prayed with greater force. And then, dreading the consequences of her moment of dark weakness, she pleaded: *Do not take my children away.*

She held herself still, no longer conscious of the sand's heat as she strained all her senses toward the heavens. But she could detect no response from Mut—none at all, not even a distant disapproval of Nefertiti's curses.

Perhaps Mut simply did not hear Nefertiti's prayer, for although Gempaaten and the Hawet Ben-ben were nearer to the goddess's shrine than was the House of Rejoicing, a rumbling clamor rose up from Ipet-Isut, tumbling over the towering walls of the great temple complex and spilling as freely down into the heart of the Hawet Ben-ben as the sun's golden light. The priests were unsettled again, debating and shouting and fighting in the courtyards of Ipet-Isut. The unrest had been so fierce—and the presence of Mahu and his soldiers so distressing—that Nefertiti had forgone her plans to make her thanksgiving in Mut's shrine, and opted for the relative safety of the Hawet Ben-ben instead.

But Mut does not hear me, she realized sadly. *Perhaps she will never hear me again.* Was it only the noise of the restless priests that barred Nefertiti from the Mother-goddess's embrace? Or had Mut forsaken Nefertiti altogether, offended once too often by her ministrations to the Ben-ben stone and her professed enthusiasms for the Aten?

Her pleading, upraised arms had begun to ache and

tremble. Nefertiti sighed and lowered her hands, then slowly climbed to her feet. She brushed the clinging sand from her skin.

"It's beautiful, to see you worshiping here."

Nefertiti gasped and spun. Amunhotep stood, long-faced with his hands clasped at his kilt, in the entrance to the Hawet Ben-ben.

"You frightened me!"

"I didn't mean it."

"How long have you been there?"

He smiled rather sadly. "Long enough to see you at worship. You have never looked lovelier than you do now—here—offering your praises to the sun."

Thank all the gods I prayed silently, she thought in desperation, pressing a hand to her racing heart. If the Pharaoh suspected that she'd been searching for Mut's embrace, diluting the sacred purpose of his precious temple by inviting another god in, Nefertiti likely would have found herself jerked to her feet by Mahu.

She made herself smile at him, and reached for his hand. "Why do you look so sad, my husband?"

"Kiya's baby has arrived. It came fast, for a first birth— just after you left the House of Rejoicing in your barque."

Nefertiti held her breath, waiting.

"A girl," Amunhotep said in a quiet, defeated voice.

Relief and gratitude surged within her heart, striking Nefertiti with a force so great, she nearly cried out from it.

"Praises to the Aten," she managed, smiling. "How is the baby's health?"

"Very well. Another strong daughter, and Kiya is well, too."

"Kiya must be so pleased. She has wanted a child for so long." Now that Nefertiti had no need to fear a son from Kiya's womb—for now, at any rate—she discovered with some surprise that she could feel real happiness for the Hurrian. *We were friends once—almost friends. I am glad for her.*

Amunhotep tugged his hand out of Nefertiti's grasp. He pressed his eyes and turned away, the striped folds of the royal Nemes head-cloth hiding his expression. "What if I..." He faltered.

Gently, Nefertiti touched his shoulder, and turned the Pharaoh to face her once more. His eyes were pink-rimmed. Nefertiti had never seen him closer to weeping.

He swallowed hard, then said in a level, calm voice, "What if I can't conceive a son at all? What if I am incapable?"

"Incapable?"

"What if the..." He glanced upward, through the Hawet Ben-ben's roof to the swath of blue above. The sun was nothing more than a patch of terrible, white glare, clinging to the edge of the sky.

Wryly, Nefertiti finished his unspoken thought. *What if the gods have cursed you?*

But she knew the Pharaoh would never speak such words—never utter those sentiments which he had declared blasphemy. In nearly three years, since Meritaten's birth, Amunhotep had drawn progressively nearer to his lone, unknowable god, and frighteningly convinced of his own priestly power. Now he seemed more oblivious than ever to the unrest brewing at Ipet-Isut. To him, the demands of those who represented the old and faded ways might as well have been the demands of spoiled children, as far as the Pharaoh was concerned. To hear him speak so uncertainly—to see him look up to the heavens in fear—dizzied Nefertiti with wonder and disorientation.

"Perhaps I ought to..." He cupped his chin with a hand, and the sorrow fled his face, replaced on the instant with a look of predatory calculation that sent a chill deep into Nefertiti's heart. "Kiya's girl..." he muttered, and turned to gaze from the Hawet Ben-ben's doorway, into the open sanctuary of Gempaaten where stone altar tables crouched, row upon row, like desert cats waiting to spring. Suddenly the buzzing of the flies over the sun-rotted milk and meat roared in Nefertiti's ears, drowning out the clamor of the priests of Amun.

She gasped.

And then, in a flash of inspiration—did Mut, the protector of children and mothers, hear her after all? Did the goddess fill Nefertiti's heart with the courage to do what she did, for Kiya's sake, and for the baby's?—she took the Pharaoh's long, almost feminine face in her hands. She beamed at him with the gentle love of a goddess, and laughed lightly at his fears.

"Amunhotep—king. You have nothing to fear."

His eyes lifted from the sandy ground, and met her own with a wide, harried expression, somewhere between worship and fear.

Nefertiti released him and stepped back, so that the light of the Hawet Ben-ben fell upon her in its force. She reached her arms wide, as if to embrace the king. She knew that the white linen of her robe glowed in the sun, and that the metallic beads weighting her braids must glitter in the hot, potent glare, sparkling like the Ben-ben stone itself.

"Look at me, Amunhotep."

He did. She watched as his eyes traveled from her face to her breasts, still round and heavy from Ankhesenpaaten's birth. They lingered on her waist, narrow and fine, then took in the soft protrusion of her belly and the width of her hips.

"I am a living symbol of fertility," she said, her thoughts racing in her heart. "Of *your* fertility, for I was given to you by the Aten."

She could see his eyes go distant, unfocusing on her form as he was borne away on a current of rising zeal.

"Do not mourn the birth of daughters," she said. "Neither cast them away, nor give them back to the god. They are precious gifts: a sign of your own potency, and of the Aten's great favor. For females are life-givers, just like the sun. Like the Aten, they create what is new."

"Yes," Amunhotep muttered. "That is good—that is true."

"The more females you sire, and the more daughters you gather around you, the greater is your proof of the Aten's satisfaction."

"Yes. His satisfaction—and his potency."

Nefertiti shifted in the sand, turning slightly so that the light spilling from above bounced and reflected off her body from new angles. Amunhotep squinted against her brightness, and his lips moved rapidly in silent revelation or prayer.

"*Your* potency," Nefertiti said.

"My own—my godlike power!"

Nefertiti let her arms fall. A frown pinched her brow, but Amunhotep, caught up in his own vision now, did not notice. *His godlike power.* The words did not surprise her— hadn't he claimed, on their long-ago wedding night, that he possessed the generative force of the gods? But there was something different about those same words now—a simple conviction, a totality of belief that made Nefertiti's skin crawl with fear.

But you have him, she told herself. *Don't stop now.*

"I am a promise from the Aten," Nefertiti said. "My fertility—and my three daughters—are a promise to you, from the great god that shines down on us all. I speak as the High Priestess of the Sun: *all* your daughters are vows from the god. When the time is right—when the world is prepared for your glory—then you shall have your sons, Amunhotep. All the sons you could ever desire. But only when the way is prepared and the Two Lands are ready to accept your glorious truths."

"Many sons?" he asked weakly, his eyes streaming with tears as he stared at Nefertiti's sunlit brilliance.

"Many. And through them, your reign will go on eternally. But it is not time yet—for sons are heirs, and heirs are only required when a Pharaoh has passed the height of his power. You have not yet reached your height, my king, and a son would only distract from your greatness. Only be patient, and your sons will be granted, when you've climbed to a pinnacle as lofty as the sun itself."

Amunhotep dropped to his knees in the sand, shuddering with ecstasy, then fell flat at Nefertiti's feet, writhing and moaning like a woman in the grip of sexual release. Instinctively, she stepped back, remaining just out of the reach of his grasping hands. She could not bear the thought of his hands on her at that moment. Not while that terrible vision still burst and smoldered inside her heart—of a baby laid on an altar, of flies circling its flesh.

Gods, let me be right, she prayed. *Let a son arrive, and sooner rather than later—for if my promise never comes true...*

His anger would be unavoidable. Sooner or later, if he did not receive the heir he expected, his fury would break, and with her words, her promises, Nefertiti had guaranteed that *she* would be the focus of that rage—that slowly building storm. *I will be the one to suffer...* Then, with a fear so cold and terrible that her heart stopped beating, *Or my daughters.*

As the Pharaoh lay gasping on the floor of the Hawet Ben-ben, struggling to master his own unrest, the shouts of anger rose up from the walls of Ipet-Isut, louder and harsher than before. Nefertiti stilled her shaking, and turned her face once more to the sun.

Amun, she pleaded silently, *send the king a son. Let his ka be settled—let the madness that rules him heal. For if thou will not soothe his desires, more than his innocent daughters will suffer. I fear the Two Lands will tear themselves apart. I am only one woman. I cannot manage him alone.*

NEFERTITI RETURNED ALONE to the House of Rejoicing, insisting gently to the king that as High Priestess, she must remain in privacy with the sacred visions the Aten had granted her. He gripped her wrist as they parted ways on the quay. She recognized the trembling in his hand, the forceful darkness of his stare, the shallowness of his breath. His encounter with the Aten's word had aroused him, stirring his mild intoxication with his own power to a frantic, shivering drunkenness.

"Come to see me when you've returned to the West Bank," he murmured. He spoke very close to her ear, and droplets of his spittle landed cold on her cheek.

According to ritual, Nefertiti still had ten days remaining until she was cleansed of the magic of childbirth, and could safely lie with a man again. But Amunhotep cared nothing for ritual—unless he had created the ritual himself. She knew he would allow her no excuse.

"As you wish," she said, smiling.

The return trip across the river was at once unbearably long and mercilessly short. Nefertiti's dark, desperate thoughts dragged at her *ka*, so that the efforts of the oarsmen seemed to haul *her* through the sideways current, as much as the barque with its gilded rails and pointed prow. Twisting her hands in her lap, watching the House of Rejoicing loom larger by the moment on the western shore, she breathed deep of the river's bright, cool, water-blue scent, hoping it would chase away the threat of tears.

Tears. Useless, she told herself bitterly. Yet still, they threatened to come. *To think there was a time when my father thought Amunhotep could be controlled. When Tiy thought it. When I thought it!* Nefertiti had barely managed to divert his sickening impulses in the Hawet Ben-ben. It had only been Mut's divine intervention that had spared Kiya—and everyone else in the House of Rejoicing—an unimaginable horror. Nefertiti could not be everywhere at once, always at the king's side. Even if he named her Great Wife, she could not expect luck and the gods' grace to favor her forever.

He is farther lost to madness than ever the old king was. What sort of monster contemplated killing a child—exposing it to the sun's relentless glare? For all the old Pharaoh's sins, all his reckless self-indulgence, he had never wasted an innocent life, so far as Nefertiti knew.

There is no way to control Amunhotep. Not reliably. Not anymore. He is a force beyond all reckoning—a flood waiting to scour the world away.

For one moment, one sharp, black beat of Nefertiti's heart, she considered the unthinkable. Egypt had had plenty of disappointing and even dangerous Pharaohs. But never had any man or woman dared to take a king's life. To do so would be to defy the gods—to spurn their grand design, to account one's self more knowledgeable and capable than they. The implications of such an act turned Nefertiti's bowels to water. Her own *ka* would be damned forever; the afterlife would be an eternity of torment. But worse, the Two Lands would be thrown into chaos. The river would never rise again; the fields would lie barren, cracking beneath the sun; the sun itself might fail to rise, or might track backward across the sky, or fall altogether, plunging into the river and expiring, like an ember dropped in a pot of water.

No. To kill the king would only invite more evil into the world—an evil darker than Amunhotep's heart.

When the barque docked on the western shore, Nefertiti walked slowly back to her miniature palace in the garden. She saw nothing of the world around her—not the bright, glossy leaves of the flower beds, open beneath the sun like hands offering gifts. She heard nothing of the birds, gaily singing in the shade trees or piping as they waded among the reeds and lotuses of the lake. She saw only the rows of stone altars in Gempaaten's courtyard, and the sound that filled her ears was the harsh, black buzzing of flies.

Nefertiti shut herself inside her house and leaned against the door, fighting to keep her dark thoughts away, to shut out the memory of Amunhotep writhing and moaning in the sand. But it was no use. He crowded in upon her heart, and she pressed quaking hands to her face, sobbing without the relief of tears.

The gentle scrape of a sandal's sole distracted her from her misery. Nefertiti looked up to find Mutbenret gazing back at her, wide-eyed and solemn, dressed in the light, transparent tunic that was half childish, half womanly. The sight of that strange costume, and of Mutbenret's ever-present sidelock, sent Nefertiti's anger boiling over.

"Why do you wear that?" she demanded.

Mutbenret drifted toward her, hesitant and shy. "What's the matter? Why are you crying?"

"I am not crying."

"Did something happen at Ipet-Isut?"

"I said, why do you *wear* that? And your hair—you're long past your first blood; you look like a fool."

Mutbenret hung her head. "I know."

"Then why?"

The girl's lips quivered, and her eyes filled with frightened tears. And in that moment, her stomach sinking in dismay at her own gods-cursed blindness, Nefertiti knew. *Ay. Ay still has her.*

She wanted to scream, but her throat closed. She wanted to tear the linen of her gown in rage, but her hands, limp and nerveless, hung still at her sides. *All this time, I've thought she was safe. But she is as much in Ay's hands as ever before, and I have done nothing to protect her.*

Mutbenret sniffled, shifting uncomfortably on her feet, waiting for Nefertiti to speak.

But she could say nothing. The gods had ripped the words from her throat and scattered them on the wind.

I can't control the Pharaoh alone, she told herself. *The gods know this—they surely must. Perhaps it is not Ay who holds Mutbenret after all. Perhaps the gods have put her within* my *reach—*my *control. Perhaps she has a purpose here, in the House of Rejoicing.*

But there was only one purpose a woman might have in Amunhotep's court.

Nefertiti narrowed her eyes at Mutbenret, coolly assessing her childish garb, the way burgeoning womanhood sat light and fresh upon her body.

The Pharaoh liked Sitamun well enough, when she was a girl of just this age.

And *someone* must give the Pharaoh a son, before it was too late—before the stone altars in Gempaaten filled, one by one.

Nefertiti straightened from where she leaned against the door. She hardened herself, drawing the regal detachment of a King's Great Wife around her, pulling indifference like a shield across her heart.

"The king wants company," she said.

Mutbenret looked up from the floor, her large, soft eyes

blinking in surprise.

"But you still have ten days—"

"Not me. You."

Mutbenret trembled. Her chest with its small, new-raised breasts heaved beneath the slip of silk she wore, but she made no sound.

"It must be done," Nefertiti said, lifting her chin, refusing to weep.

"But... But he'll do to me what he did to Sitamun."

"He will. And you will be complacent, and give him whatever he wants."

Mutbenret rushed forward, clinging to Nefertiti's hands, her neck—then falling to her knees and weeping into the hem of her gown. "Please, Sister. Don't do this! Don't make me!"

Gently, Nefertiti raised her to her feet. "There is no use crying over it. The king must have a son, and if you are the one to give him his heir, then you will be blessed beyond measure." *And my daughters and I will be safe.*

"But you are his wife!"

"And it seems I can produce only girls."

"Nefertiti, please!"

A bitter memory returned to Nefertiti—the servant girl pressed against the pillar in the king's bed chamber, trying to make herself invisible beneath Nefertiti's sharp, searching gaze. And she remembered the sound of the servant's tears, her humiliation and shame, as Nefertiti danced with her eyes closed to music no one could hear.

The gods will damn me, she thought, weak-kneed and faint. *They have damned me already.* She would face their judgment gladly on the day of her death, when Anupu came to claim her, when the blackness of the Duat yawned its mouth and swallowed her into its never-ending heart. *As long as my daughters are safe, I do not care.*

"Go," she said harshly to Mutbenret. "Do as I've instructed you, and stop your crying. We all must do our duty in the House of Rejoicing. You do not suffer more than anybody else."

I do not care, she told herself as Mutbenret, hugging her thin frame with trembling arms, stumbled out the door, toward the Pharaoh's quarters. *As long as the gods give the king a son, then nothing else matters. Let them damn my* ka *forever. I do not care.*

Kiya

Year 5 of Amunhotep
Beautiful Are the Manifestations,
Great of Kingship,
Who Upholds the Sun

T HE NEW YEAR CELEBRATIONS were over, and
Kiya's cares lay far behind her. The gilded cage of
the House of Rejoicing dwindled to a pinprick on the
southern horizon as the Pharaoh's massive pleasure barge
sailed downriver, carrying Kiya into realms of Egypt she
had not seen since she first arrived in Waset as a young
and frightened bride, seven years before.

The clamor and stink of Waset faded away, too—as did
the high, gleaming walls of Ipet-Isut, where day by day
unrest and violence grew as the priests of Amun clashed
with the Pharaoh's most devoted followers. They had never
ceased to fight the rise of the Aten, but even Kiya, confined
as she was to the western shore and inclined to keep only
the company of Nann and Sitamun, could see that the
priests' battle was a lost cause. The nobles of the West
Bank lived in Amunhotep's shadow; none of them were
foolish enough to seek the king's disfavor. They turned, one
by one, to Atenism—leaving old gods and rituals behind—
and their influence spread through Waset, through its
farms and merchants' shops, its barracks and cellars.

It is no matter to me, Kiya mused. She stood in the bow of
the ship, head thrown back and eyes closed, feeling the
bracing, damp river wind rush through her hair and press
its cool fingers through the linen of her gown, caressing

her skin. *Let these Egyptians worship any fool gods they please.* Ishtar was her only concern, and Ishtar had granted Kiya's prayers at last, and given her a child.

Kayet was only four months old, a soft, pink miracle of coos and milky smiles and curling brown hair. It was not the Egyptian way to nurse one's own child—at least, it was not the way of a King's Wife. And so Kiya had surrendered her daughter to a wet-nurse to rear, but she insisted on keeping both nurse and baby close, summoning them each morning and keeping their company until well after sunset. She whiled away her days in bliss, adoring her daughter in the cool of the little white-brick house, or singing to the baby as she and the nurse lounged in the sunlit garden. Kayet was ever on hand for kissing and cuddling, whenever the urge struck Kiya—and it struck often.

This adventure, this trip down the Iteru, was the first time Kiya had been away from her daughter for more than a few hours. Although she knew Kayet was in capable, loving hands, still each beat of her heart pained her, burning her chest with the agony of separation.

My child is healthy and whole, she told herself firmly. *I will not mourn the fact that we are apart. I will give thanks to Ishtar for the blessing, and enjoy myself while I can.*

For only the great goddess knew when Kiya would experience such a grand occasion again. Kiya well knew that the very idea of this trip was Tiy's. The old shadow-dweller had made the same comments to both Kiya and Sitamun—they had confided in one another, and laughed to discover that Tiy was still trying to work through them both—pressuring each of them to slip the suggestion of a grand, downriver excursion into Amunhotep's ear.

The king should remove himself from the House of Rejoicing for a spell, Tiy had told them both. *Even a Pharaoh needs to replenish his ka when his burdens grow too heavy, and perhaps*

if Amunhotep takes in the beauty of the countryside, he will find
some reason to appreciate the old gods again.

Sitamun swore she never mentioned a grand progression
to Amunhotep—he was not likely to listen to her
suggestions, anyway. For Kiya's part, she only brought it
up once, when Amunhotep lay with his arms wrapped
around her waist and the linens of her bed twisted around
one leg, catching his breath when their lovemaking was
through.

Kiya was certain that Tiy intended this trip to be much
more than a simple, *ka*-replenishing pleasure excursion.
She had no doubt, in fact, that Tiy intended Kiya to finally
stake her place in Amunhotep's heart, to use the magic of
river and starlight and unfettered movement to wreath
the king about with all her charms and bring him neatly
to heel. This adventure was, Kiya knew, meant to secure
her hold over the Pharaoh and save Egypt from the doom
Tiy feared.

Kiya had no intention of playing into Lady Tiy's hands.
Let the Pharaoh do as he would; Amunhotep remained
the kind and considerate lover, the stern but just king she
had always known. It was not for Kiya to control him, to
leash him with her wiles and train him to Tiy's liking.

She wished only to enjoy the exhilaration of travel; the
thrill of riding the king's stately, luxurious barge—its
cabins plush with fine appointments, its complements of
cooks and musicians. She intended to soak up and revel
in every moment of freedom and variety, to cherish all
the novel sensations she could not obtain in the House of
Rejoicing. She drank in the rich, full scent of river water.
She watched the lazy turn and glide of crocodiles as they
drifted in the shallows near the shore. She felt her scalp
prickle with a sweet thrill as a flight of ducks soared up
from a patch of reeds, crying in their harsh, nasal voices.
The ducks circled the barge once, then hung parallel to
its progress for one breathtaking moment, their feathers

whistling as they beat their wings in a clamorous fury. Then they settled on the water, each one tucking its body into the V of its own little wake, and rapidly, the barge left them behind.

Let Amunhotep do what he will, she thought, turning from the boat's prow as the servants laid out the mid-day meal beneath a canopy of blue linen. *He is a good man, a good king—and the only care I have now is to live these days of freedom to their fullest.*

She joined the other King's Wives beneath the canopy. Sitamun and Nefertiti were already enjoying spiced nuts and tart, dried fruits in little silver bowls. Their low conversation did not carry over the rhythmic plunge, slap and chatter of the oars through the water. The two women wore guarded, if peaceful, smiles—Nefertiti and Sitamun had never lost their mistrust of one another, and the rivalry to birth an heir continued—but they seemed determined to put their differences aside, and enjoy the rare excursion and the rich, verdant scenery, too.

"What a brilliant day," Kiya gushed. She sat on an overstuffed cushion and sampled from her bowl of nuts, then licked spice and honey from her fingers. She smiled across the low, heavy table at Nefertiti, and caught a flash of anger on the woman's face before Nefertiti blanked her expression once more in a neutral mask.

Kiya hesitated as she reached for the fruit. It was not the first time she had seen a rapid flicker of regret or some other, stranger pain cross Nefertiti's features. Ever since Kayet's birth, the beautiful King's Wife seemed altered from deep within, no longer able to maintain her icy, flawless control, and the pale face of some terrible weakness peeked through these shabby rents in Nefertiti's exterior.

"Where is our husband?" Kiya asked.

Sitamun nodded toward the large on-deck cabins, which

stood like shrines to the gods, painted in blues and reds, their flat roofs carved with lotuses and bees, with scarabs and frogs.

"He is resting," Sitamun said.

"Is he so very tired? Perhaps Lady Tiy was right after all, and this excursion is sorely needed."

"Tired," Nefertiti blurted. Then she huffed a coarse laugh, quite unlike her usual, musically light tittering. "Exhausted by his own zeal."

Servants approached from the stern of the boat, where the smoky sting of char drifted from the cooking braziers. They laid a platter on the table, laden with white cheese, grilled fish, and fire-blackened duck. Nefertiti ripped the leg from the duck's body and bit into it with a flat stare toward the cabins.

"I am glad he approved the journey," Sitamun said. "It's good to be away, to have a change of scenery."

"I'm surprised Amunhotep agreed to leave the West Bank at all," Nefertiti said. "Or I should say, the *east* bank. He doesn't like to be far from Gempaaten anymore. I believe he would visit that temple daily, if not for the unrest at Ipet-Isut."

"It *would* please him to visit the temple more," Kiya said. "He speaks of it so often when we are together."

"Please him," Nefertiti muttered darkly. "Yes, we must all be mindful of the Pharaoh's pleasure. All of us." The half-eaten duck's leg dropped from her fingers into her bowl, and she turned to regard a stand of reeds and tall, silk-tufted papyrus plants as the ship slid by. Nefertiti's gaze was misted, and Kiya had the sense that she saw nothing of that patch of bright wilderness, nor the flock of white ibis that rose piping from among the green.

She almost asked, *Are you well?* But experience with Nefertiti had taught her that the woman would admit to no weakness, and any show of concern would only be brushed off or mocked away.

Kiya turned to Sitamun, who was always loyal with her friendship, ever since Kiya had come to her on the night of Nebetah's birth. They chatted on as they worked through the fish and cheese, smiling over the water-green vistas and reveling in the freshness of the wind. But Nefertiti never joined in their happiness. She only picked at her meal in pensive silence, and whenever she looked at Kiya, that same expression of regret—of loathing—rippled below Nefertiti's crystalline surface, until Kiya felt all her joy begin to run out of her, drop after rapid drop.

She was just considering excusing herself from the table and returning to her place in the ship's bow, where she could cling to her remaining happiness and fill up her spirit once more with the simple pleasures of movement and the ever-changing delights that danced before her eyes. But before Kiya could act, Nefertiti rose abruptly from her cushion and stalked away across the deck without a word of excuse.

Kiya and Sitamun watched her go in silence. Finally, when Nefertiti vanished into her little cabin, Kiya said, "She hates me."

Sitamun shook her head with a wry smile. "She doesn't. I think she quite likes you, actually. Or at least, she respects you."

Kiya laughed. "Even for an Egyptian, she has strange ways of showing favor. Did you see the way she looked at me? She does it all time, now—ever since my Kayet was born. I think perhaps she is angry at me for not having a son."

"If she is angry with anyone on *that* count, it is herself. Three girls—no wonder Amunhotep hasn't named anyone King's Great Wife. He is waiting to see which of us gives him a son. I am sure of it."

Kiya tossed the end of her braid over her shoulder. "I don't want to be Great Wife, anyhow. I don't want anything at all—nothing but to feel the river breeze on my face." She inhaled, savoring the sweet, earthy scent of current and bank. "Isn't it divine?"

Sitamun gave her an amused look, head tilted and both eyebrows raised.

"Don't look at me like I have a job to do, like I'm shirking some duty," Kiya said comfortably. The inside of her bowl was littered with crumbs of the soft, white cheese. She tamped them with her fingertip, then licked the cheese away. "Whatever work Tiy intended to set before me, whatever her schemes for this trip, I'll have none of it. This adventure is all my own, Sitamun, my darling. Let the gods bring what they will; I am only drifting downriver, like a twig on the waves."

Night came, waving a white banner of starlight high across the sky. The barque's captain anchored in the shallows, for the river could not be safely navigated in the dark, and as the musicians began their lively, skirling river songs, Amunhotep emerged from the seclusion of his cabin, eating everything that was laid before him like a man who had starved in the desert, laughing loud and long at the antics of the jugglers and acrobats, and swaying with blissful abandon to the rhythm of pipe and drum.

Kiya adored him as he clapped and grinned on the deck, lit by an ethereal, pale-silver moon. Not even in their love-making had he seemed so energetic, so bursting with rough, human joy. *Perhaps Tiy had no secret motive after all,* she thought as she watched him cheer on the jugglers. *Perhaps he truly did need a restoration of his ka—and perhaps Nefertiti, too, will find relief from whatever worries plague her.*

Another golden day passed—more precious hours of smooth movement, of lazy joys, of the constant ripple and flash of the sun on the river. Amunhotep was often on the deck now, watching his kingdom slide by like two great, green scrolls unrolling down the length of the valley, lush and fertile between the high, yellow cliffs far to the east and west. As the sun set he pulled Kiya into his cabin, and kissed her and stroked her thighs beneath her gown. But he seemed to want nothing more, content merely to revel in her presence, and to talk of the sights they'd seen from the ship's deck. Kiya found the simple, quiet companionship of her husband even more agreeable than his lovemaking, and she was sorry when he stretched and yawned and sent her off to her own bed.

The third day passed like the one before. Kiya and Sitamun stood side by side at the ship's rail, and waved to the tiny villages set like a child's blocks among the far, green fields. It was likely, she knew, that no one could see them. The river was quite broad here, and she and Sitamun must seem little larger than ants from the shore. But they giggled like two unmarried girls and went on waving, and shouted out greetings to the villages that went unanswered.

Nefertiti kept her own counsel, lurking alone in bow or stern as her moods dictated, bright in her white gown that glowed with sunlight, but dark and thoughtful of face. She barely looked up when one of the lookouts on the boat's mast called out a warning. A large herd of *deby* sunbathed in the water ahead; the fat-bodied river-horses blew through their great, round snouts and shook their tiny ears irritably as the boat glided through their midst. Nefertiti did not even jump in startlement when one of the *deby* raised its head above the surface and roared, opening its huge, pink mouth and thrashing its jaws against the side of the boat, very near to the place where Nefertiti stood. She only gazed over the rail in bemused curiosity, and did not bother to look back as the creature as the boat slid past.

That night they anchored in a place of great silence. Just

before the musicians started up their joyful commotion, Kiya felt the thick, expectant quietude of the land pressing all around her, like the heavy wool blankets she had snuggled under on Mitanni's winter nights. She stared out at the nearest shore—the eastern one—trying to discern what about the place felt so strange to her, so deep and watchful in its silence. But she could make out nothing but the faint silhouette of black cliffs against a purple-dark sky, seeded with its array of stars. Long after the musicians had played the night's final tune and Kiya had crept into her bed, the sense of silence—of something ancient and watchful crouched in a posture of long waiting—remained.

The silence was broken at dawn, by a long, high cry. It shivered through Kiya's restless sleep and jerked her rudely to wakefulness; she stumbled from bed, pulling on the simple tunic-dress she had left on the floor the night before, and wondering at the cry. It sounded again—a piercing call, a human voice strained to an uncomfortable limit, caught somewhere between the two passions of triumph and fear.

She realized that it was Amunhotep's voice.

Kiya threw the door of her cabin open, rushing onto the barque's deck as Sitamun and Nefertiti also emerged, staring about in panic.

Amunhotep swayed in the bow of the boat, facing the east. His hands were raised to his temples, and he clutched at the braids of his short wig with trembling fists. As Kiya and the other wives stood gaping, unsure whether they ought to hasten to his side or stay well away, Amunhotep's legs gave way beneath him. He collapsed onto his knees, his stare fixed on the horizon. He threw back his head, mouth open in a silent ecstasy, and shuddered as if an arrow pierced his heart.

Kiya pushed past Sitamun and Nefertiti. She staggered to

Amunhotep's side, calling out his name, asking what ailed him. But he did not answer. He did not seem cognizant of Kiya's voice at all, nor of her touch when she took him by the shoulders and roughly shook him. Finally, despairing and frightened by his inexplicable fit, she knelt beside him, and looked toward the eastern horizon where his glassy eyes stared.

Here, the lush greenery of the Black Land had receded, or perhaps it had given way to some great, god-rent breach in the invisible wall that held the hostile desert of the Red Land back from the river's edge. A vast swath of yellow sand swept from a fringe of desperate, waterside greenery back toward the eastern cliffs. The cliffs themselves drew closer in this place than they dared come elsewhere in the Iteru's long valley. The great, high barrier of golden cliffs, shadowed with cool violet clefts, curved in the shape of a horse's hoof. At the far end of this sweeping arch, the flat line of the horizon dipped in an abrupt, shallow indentation, then rose again just as sharply some small distance away. It formed a perfect, sheer-sided indentation in the horizon, and in that space, the edges of its great, fiery disc exactly filling the gap, the morning sun was rising.

"Aten," Amunhotep whispered. "Glorious god! I see you--I feel you. Do with me as you will."

A T THE KING'S INSISTENCE, the captain lowered a small landing boat over the barque's gilded, painted side. A team of oarsmen rowed Amunhotep ashore; accompanying him at his command, the King's Wives huddled close together in the small boat, wary and silent as they watched their royal husband.

Amunhotep shivered with his fervid zeal as the boat's hull scraped ashore in the thick, sandy muck. One of the oarsmen helped the women to dry land, but when the King's Wives were gathered together on that barren stretch of sand, Amunhotep commanded all the rowers to remain with the boat. He gestured curtly to the women and strode away up the dry valley, his face turned always toward that strange, shallow break in the horizon.

Kiya shared a long, cautious look with Sitamun and Nefertiti. Sitamun's eyes were thoughtful beneath the fringe of her wig, and Nefertiti's cheeks had paled with the return of that fleeting, regretful pain. None of them spoke, and at last, Kiya turned on her heel and followed Amunhotep across the sand.

She was the first to reach his side. "Husband," she said, reaching for his hand. "Pharaoh. What is it? What do you see? What inspiration—"

He rounded on her suddenly, barking, "Quiet!" with such force—with such stark, impatient anger in his eyes that Kiya nearly tripped over her own feet and staggered to a halt in the sand.

Sitamun took her by the elbow, giving her a silent, tight-lipped nod of sympathy.

Stunned by this shift of mood—Amunhotep had never shouted at her before, and had certainly never looked on her with any feeling other than tenderness—Kiya scuttled toward him again.

"Amunhotep, please! You're frightening me!"

This time when he turned, he seized her by the shoulders, holding her so tightly between his hands that she gasped and writhed.

"Don't you see it?" he panted. "The image—the sacred word—the Aten itself!"

"I don't understand," she said. Her voice was rising very near a shriek, and she struggled to master it. "You aren't making sense!"

Amunhotep jerked her hard, spinning her body in his

grip until she faced the eastern horizon. The sun was still climbing up out of that shallow cleft, but Kiya could not discern its special meaning, nor fathom why it had affected the Pharaoh so strangely.

He leaned close, his breath rasping in her ear, and whispered, "It is a sign—a portent just for me. The god speaks to me—he speaks to me alone, and I hear him, and understand." Spittle from his lips flew past Kiya's face, sparkling in the dawn's golden light. "Yes," he said, "power—potency—the force of the sun! The creative force, the source of all light and life!"

One of his hands left her shoulder, and Kiya tried to twist away. But in the next moment his fingers clamped on her breast, his grip as sharp and painful as the talons of a hawk. Kiya gasped and threw herself against his restraint. He only held her all the closer, all the harder—and when he pulled her back against his body, she felt his arousal building.

What madness is this? Her thoughts spun, frantic and desperate, as she fought back against his strength. *The sun has taken hold of him—this place has taken hold of him—it has turned him into a lion!*

But no—as Kiya kicked and twisted and thrashed, struggling to remain on her feet in the sand that caught at her ankles and slid beneath her heels, she realized with a dull throb of fear that Amunhotep had been a lion all along. Nann had been right, always right: he was violent and unpredictable, and had only hidden those tendencies to keep Kiya complacent. And Tiy had been right, too. Tiy's truth was the most awful, for its bluntness now struck at Kiya's spirit with a hard, heavy blow. The sound of it rang in her head and shuddered down her spine. *He must be controlled. He must be brought to heel, before it is too late.*

"Now," Amunhotep hissed in Kiya's ear. "Undress and get on the ground, on your hands and knees."

Kiya's stomach froze in her belly. She ceased her struggling, and stared wide-eyed up at the break in the cliff. "Now? Here?"

"You heard me. Do as I say."

She could feel the other women's eyes on her, and the eyes of the rowers on the little landing boat. She could feel all the eyes on the barque, the servants and oarsmen and the captain, the musicians and jugglers, staring out at her struggle, her shame. She could feel the sun's eyes most of all, all-seeing, bright, uncaring.

"No!" Kiya gave one last, powerful wrench. She broke from his grasp and tumbled into the sand; the neckline of her tunic dress ripped and parted as his hand tore from her breast. She scuttled backward in the deep sand, trying to stay clear of him long enough to regain her feet. Amunhotep advanced on her, his erect phallus deforming the line of his kilt. He growled deep in his throat.

But before he could reach for her again, Sitamun stepped calmly between them. She laid a hand on his chest, and Amunhotep, blinking down at her in surprise, paused.

Nefertiti slipped around his heaving form to stand beside Sitamun. "Patience," she said in a cool, commanding tone. All the wavering uncertainty and pensive darkness that had followed her down the Iteru was gone, and she moved and spoke with the pure, divine confidence of a priestess. "Now is not the time, nor the place. Remember, you shall have your sons, my king, but only *after* you've ascended."

Nefertiti turned him away from Kiya and the cleft in the horizon, and slowly, arm in arm, she walked with him back toward the landing boat.

Sitamun offered her hand, and steadied Kiya on her feet. Kiya draped herself in Sitamun's arms, weeping against her neck, coughing and heaving as the tight, thrumming energy of panic receded, leaving a sinking stone in its place. The weight of it settled deep into her gut.

"Are you all right?" Sitamun asked gently.

Kiya didn't know how to respond. Her breast ached from where he had gripped it. She was certain it was bruised. Her tunic was torn—ruined—and one of her ankles hurt her. But these injuries were small, compared to the cavern of blackness that yawned where once her heart had been. It had swallowed up all her joy—all her pleasure at the river journey, and far worse, all her joy in Amunhotep's love.

Tiy was right to call me naïve. I am a witless child—a fool.

"What was that?" Kiya asked, swallowing her tears. "What made him react so?"

Sitamun pointed up at the line of the cliffs. The sun had pulled itself free of the shallow cleft, and now climbed, uncaring, into a soft, blue sky. "It looks like a certain glyph," she said.

Kiya shook her head.

"A word in the sacred writing."

"What word?"

"The name of the Aten," Sitamun said, and wrapped her arm around Kiya's waist. "Evidently he took it for a sign. Lean on me, if your ankle pains you. I will help you back to the boat."

Kiya could not look at the rowers. She hunched in the boat beside Sitamun, and Nefertiti kept Amunhotep's hand in her own, whispering in his ear, all the way back to the great pleasure barge. Kiya shivered and quailed as the men helped her from the landing boat to the deck of the ship, and allowed Sitamun to lead her to the privacy of her cabin, calling for strong wine as they went.

But before Sitamun could shut the door, shielding Kiya from the Pharaoh's presence, Kiya chanced to look back at the eastern horizon. Her eyes rested on the break in the cliffs, the image of the glyph that had broken her husband's façade and shattered Kiya's dream-like naïveté.

Is it too late, Tiy? She sent the thought out like a prayer. *Can I still do the work you laid before me? Can anyone?*

Kiya was sure of only one thing now: she was bound in marriage to a madman. And it might be far too late to leash him—to save Egypt from his strange visions, to save herself from his brutal hands.

Sitamun

Year 5 of Amunhotep
Beautiful Are the Manifestations,
Great of Kingship,
Who Upholds the Sun

W HEN KIYA FINALLY SLEPT, her bruised body
curled upon itself like the frond of a tender fern,
Sitamun rose carefully from Kiya's bed and slipped from
her cabin. Sitamun had remained all day at Kiya's side,
listening to her heartbroken cries, massaging her temples,
dabbing salve on the purple-red bruises that marred the
soft, white skin of her breast and shoulders.

She had made Kiya sip broth from a bowl, but had
eaten very little herself, and when she emerged from the
confines of the cabin to find the sun sinking in its red
fire over the western shore, the cooling air of evening
sharpened Sitamun's appetite with a sudden, insistent
force. Her stomach rumbled and pinched.

The captain was weighing anchor near a cove of bright-
green reeds. They rustled in the rise of the evening breeze,
their stems whispering and chattering together. Sitamun
leaned on the rail and watched the reeds dance, swaying
to the soft refrain of their hushed chorus. On the shore, a
thicket of vines leaned heavily toward the water, and their
long, waxy blossoms began to open, one by one, as night
approached. Some small animal moved amid the foliage,
and then was still. A night bird called, *crake-crake-crake*, in
the gathering dusk.

What peace and beauty is here, Sitamun thought wearily, *far from the House of Rejoicing, and all the memories it holds.* She would remain, if she could—if the gods would allow it. She would find her way ashore and make her own West Bank—her own palace out of starlight and vines. She would never return to the past.

The soft, low tones of Amunhotep's voice carried across the barque's deck. Sitamun looked around. He stood in the bow of the boat, the paleness of his white kilt blazing against the onrush of darkness. The sight of him, his dreamlike luminosity, drew her heart as readily as it drew her eye, catching and holding her attention, her *self*, as tightly, as relentlessly as Amunhotep had seized Kiya that morning. She watched as he sank onto one of the overstuffed cushions that served for dining stools. She felt each minute movement of his body in her own muscles and bones. Her mouth was dry. Her stomach ached with longing.

The servants brought a table, and then food from the braziers. Amunhotep sat staring down at the platters and bowls, unmoving, as the reeds rustled and hissed with their faint, green breath.

Sitamun slipped quietly across the deck. He looked up as she neared, his brow furrowed and his mouth open, ready to send the approaching servant away. But when he saw that it was Sitamun, the frown left his face. It was the first time in years that he had not looked upon her with disgust or disappointment. Her heart warmed, a very little, with encouragement.

"May I sit?"

He nodded.

"How is my Kiya?" he asked as Sitamun sank onto the large cushion beside him. "My poor little monkey."

"Her wounds will heal, with time." Not the wound in her heart. Sitamun well knew that some pains cut too deeply; some blood welled forever.

She helped herself to his food, and Amunhotep did not try to stop her. The bread was soaked in honey, but even it was not as sweet as her brother's simple nearness. She closed her eyes as she ate, and felt the warmth of his body reach across the small space between them, sinking into her flesh.

When she had eaten her fill, Sitamun watched the last sliver of the dying sun fall below the indigo hills. Amunhotep watched her face for a long moment—she could feel his eyes upon her, and she was glad, in that moment, that she was young and beautiful, that she could delight his eye—that he gazed at her alone, at least for the space of these few, precious heartbeats.

"You like it here, don't you?" he asked.

Sitamun gave a tiny laugh. He had mistaken her smile for joy at the place—the green banks and the river's open freedom—not for his proximity, and the peaceful intimacy they shared. But she recalled the gentle music of the reed grove, and the creature stirring unseen in the thicket, and she saw that Amunhotep was not wrong, after all.

"I love it here," she said. "I would make it my home, if only the gods would allow it."

He sighed and nodded. His gaze drifted out across the darkening river, and the smile faded from Sitamun's face.

"I wish the gods *would* allow it," she said with sudden force. "Why can't I—why can't we...?"

He chuckled. "Leave it all behind? Abandon the House of Rejoicing, and let it crumble to mud-brick dust? You wouldn't like that—not truly. No one wants to live like the *rekhet*."

"No," she agreed. "I'd build my own palace. Someplace bright and new, made just to my own liking, and far from the West Bank. Far from Father's tomb, and Mother's schemes. Far from Waset and all the trouble at Ipet-Isut, the priests of Amun and Mahu with his guards."

He regarded her with open amusement. It was good to see his smile return. Sitamun pushed the bowl of honeyed bread toward him, and he chewed a piece thoughtfully.

"Perhaps we could build a palace, after all," he said.

Yes, she thought with desperate need, with a terrible, hollow ache beneath her heart. *A palace of our own—just you and I. Let us leave Kiya and Nefertiti behind. Let us forget everything—the priests and the rekhet, the Hawet Ben-ben and Gempaaten. Let us forget new gods and old gods. Let us make a palace for our hearts. It will be as it was, once, long ago, when we were innocent children who loved one another, and love was enough for us both.*

"Perhaps," Sitamun said slowly, testing the idea as if it were a silk thread on the verge of snapping, "perhaps we could build it in that great valley of sand." She dared a glance at his face, and watched his features go still with inspiration. "That place below the cliffs, where you saw the Aten rise."

Amunhotep did not answer. He stared into the darkness, his eyes wide and glassy, as if stricken by a holy vision.

Do it, Sitamun prayed. *Take me away from the House of Rejoicing, and take yourself away, too. Far away, where you can cause no more unrest, and make no more demands on the gods—on any of us.*

"I would follow you," she said, losing all her confidence. Her voice wavered, and she clutched at her own hands in her lap. "I would dedicate my life to a new palace, a new temple—if you build it, I will follow. I am not the best of your wives, I know. I am not the most beloved, nor the most beautiful. But I would do anything for you, Amunhotep. You know I would."

"If you would follow me, would others?" His eyes on her face were intense, and full of need.

"Yes," Sitamun said at once. "Yes, of course! You are the

Pharaoh." Inside her heart, she knew they would not. The nobles of the West Bank would be as pleased to be rid of Amunhotep as the priests on the eastern shore. And Tiy—she would be best pleased of all. She would recall Smenkhkare from his secret seclusion, and with her youngest son as figurehead, the former Great Wife would set about restoring the peace in Ipet-Isut, healing the damage Amunhotep had done. But she said only, "You can command them, you know. They will do as you say. That's the divine right the gods have granted you."

"Divine right," he said, tapping his long, pointed chin. "Perhaps you are right."

"I am," she said. "I know it. Build a palace, Amunhotep—build a new city. Build a new world." *And we will inhabit it together. The two of us, alone, leaving Egypt to return to its old ways. We will return to our old ways, too. You will come to love me again.*

"It would be a great act of creation, to make a city out of nothing."

"An act of creation worthy of the Aten's great priest."

He stared into the distance once more, enveloped in that same pensive silence. Then he regarded Sitamun with sober focus.

"Do you love the Aten, sister?"

"Yes," she said at once. "I do."

"Then let it be as you say. I shall make raise up a city from the dust. I shall call life from dead sand and stone, just as the sun's rays do."

He kissed her then. His lips were sweet with honey, and tasted her own with a tender passion Sitamun had not felt since she was a child.

It will be well, she thought with dizzied awe. *He will leave Egypt in peace. He will make the world anew, a place just for us to dwell. And I will join him at the place of his creation.*

Tiy

Year 5 of Akhenaten
Beautiful Are the Manifestations,
Exalting the Name,
Beloved of the Sun

THE GARDEN WAS FRAGRANT in the mid-day light, the raised flower beds and great pots of delicate blossoms suffused with the lazy, drifting spice of pollen and petal. Tiy walked slowly along the edge of the lake, hands clasped behind her back, her sandals whispering through the grass. The central dimple of each round, flat lotus leaf held a drop of golden sheen, but Tiy was barely aware of that swath of dazzle, the blanket of sun that lay across the lake's surface like a blanket draped over a soft and welcoming bed. All her thoughts were for the king's excursion, for Kiya and Amunhotep, and her hopes—the last of them, she knew; the final, ragged shred—were thin.

But the garden offered its solitude like a friendly hand, cool and green and open. When she walked here, as she had done each day since the king's great pleasure barque had left the quay, she could feel the threads of her hope with startling clarity. Their texture was fine and frail, but they pressed into her palm with an insistence, an itch that would not be denied. Here, she could close her fist and hold them tightly, clinging like a spider in a strong wind, holding tight to its delicate, shivering web.

She kicked a pebble along the lake wall and stalked after it, clenching her right fist around her hope. She found it and kicked it again. It snickered as it tumbled through the grass, as if the gods themselves whispered with quiet laughter. Tiy scowled, and squeezed her fist all the tighter.

Rapid footsteps on a distant garden path brought Tiy out of her reverie. She drew herself up and turned, searching the tangle of the garden for the source of that intrusive urgency. When she recognized Huya's short, swinging wig and purposeful stride, Tiy's mouth fell open, and her stomach lurched with a sickening wave of misgiving. She stood still, the pebble forgotten, and watched him approach.

Her steward bowed when he reached her, but even before he'd bent himself fully, Tiy said impatiently, "What is it?"

"Ipet-Isut," he panted. "I came as quickly as I could."

"The temples? What has happened?"

"It's finally boiled over, my lady. Mahu's soldiers have struck, and the priests are rioting in response—"

"Struck? What do you mean?" Tiy swept past him, gathering her skirt in both hands so she could stride as fast and fierce as a king.

Huya whirled to follow, and spoke rapidly as he jogged at her side. "They've gone into the heart of the Temple of Amun itself—taken all the offerings—and from the other shrines and gods, too."

"Surely even Mahu wouldn't dare to be so bold." To take offerings left for the gods was nothing short of an outrage. It reached far beyond Mahu's prior stirrings, his threats, both oblique and pointed, to those who failed to visit Gempaaten.

"Mahu didn't act on his own," Huya said. "He did it on the Pharaoh's orders."

Tiy stopped her headlong march so suddenly that Huya overshot her by several steps before he stumbled to a halt.

"The Pharaoh is downriver, sailing on his barque," Tiy

said.

Huya bowed again, as if the obeisance might deflect the bewildered anger he could surely sense building in Tiy's *ka*. "No, my lady. The king returned in the early hours of the morning."

"Gods damn him." She hitched up the hem of her skirt again and spun toward the soaring, ornate wing of the House of Rejoicing where the king's chambers lay.

"My lady!" Huya called. "He is not in his chambers."

Tiy's feet staggered numbly on the path, and she froze in place, wide-eyed, breathing hard, like a beast sunk to its neck in a mire of mud. She had no need to ask where Amunhotep was, if he had not returned to his chambers. She knew.

TIY TOOK THE SWIFTEST BOAT she could find to the quay outside the temple complex. She sat tense and silent at Huya's side, staring out over the bow at the eastern shore, as if by need and will alone she might push the boat more quickly to its destination.

Long before they reached the quay, Tiy could see the signs of strife at Ipet-Isut. Danger and confusion hung in the band of agitated dust that spread over the high wall of the complex, and hung like a banner unfurled from the peak of the Temple of Amun. When they were still a dozen boat-lengths away from the mooring, Tiy heard clearly the surge and roar of angry voices. The shouts from Ipet-Isut drowned out the sound of the oars.

Her *ka* burned and rippled with a fury she had never known before. When the boat made landfall, Tiy shoved her way to the ramp and was standing on the quay before she even knew it, with Huya's voice rising insistently over the din, begging her to wait for him and the soldiers he had brought along for guards. Tiy did not wait—she *could* not wait. Impelled by the twin forces of a deep, hollow desperation and seething rage—at the gods, or the king?— she moved swiftly into the roiling, jostling crowd, and Huya and his soldiers had no choice but to run to catch up with her.

Tiy fought her way forward, knocked from side to side, bruised by the hard, surging force of male anger. All around her was the stink of men—their sweat, their hot breath as they shouted, the sharp, metallic odor of honed swords and spilled blood. Mahu's contingent of soldiers had grown to a frightening size. *Where did he get the funds to hire so many?* Tiy wondered vaguely as she was bounced off the shoulder of one guard and rebounded from the back of a shouting priest. Still she fought her way up the landing, to the towering wall of Ipet-Isut, where the tussling was only fiercer, and the voices of men louder and angrier still.

Huya's guards encircled Tiy with their hands on their sword hilts; she paused in that momentary shelter to catch her breath, and to take in the vision of chaos. Now she could see that a line of Mahu's soldiers were pushing their way into the gates of Ipet-Isut, and that priests— and a few *rekhet*, Tiy realized with wonder and horror— were attempting to bar their passage, standing with arms linked, surging in waves of sweating, shouting humanity to try to force the soldiers back. Now and then a priest would fall, to be kicked and trampled by his fellows until the wave subsided and those who stood above him could pull him back to his feet. It was little wonder that so many fell, for the wide mouth of Ipet-Isut's outer gate was slick and wet with blood.

As Tiy stared, one of Mahu's soldiers fought his way back out from the complex's interior, clutching a leather bag close to his chest. The bag was fat and full. One of the priests made a lucky grab, wrenching the sack from the soldier's grip. It flew through the air, scattering glass beads and a silver cup, then landed on the blood-darkened ground. Golden chains and ivory combs spilled from its guts; a fine platter rolled along its edge, crossing the mouth of the gate as if fleeing from the riot. At the sight of the rescued treasure, the priests and their *rekhet* supporters sent up a hoarse cheer.

"Come!" Tiy turned away from the gate, making her way along the great, carved wall, where images of Amun smiled down, benign and unconcerned. As they passed the quay, the crowd thinned abruptly, for both priests and soldiers were intent on the activity at the gate. Tiy pulled her skirts to her knees and ran, her teeth and bones jarred with every leaping, pounding stride, her lungs burning with the effort. She rounded one corner of the wall and headed east, squinting at the edge of Gempaaten as it peered past the old, strong shoulder of Ipet-Isut. Gempaaten's newness, its white, arrogant sheen, was stark and offensive in the sunlight.

Tiy was gasping and disheveled by the time she reached Gempaaten's gate. A steady line of Mahu's soldiers crept through the opening, bearing sacks of plunder from the Temple of Amun. More soldiers formed a checkpoint of sorts, driving back the few priests who still tried to rescue the stolen offerings to their gods.

"Make way for Lady Tiy," Huya shouted over the rumble and rage of the men. "Stand aside for the King's Mother!"

The soldiers made a narrow gap in their ranks, and quickly, Tiy slipped through with Huya close on her heels. They fell into step with the train of heavily-laden thieves, moving steadily down the aisle of deep, hot sand toward Gempaaten's open-topped sanctuary. Tiy trembled and heaved for her breath, praying that her cool composure would return to her before they reached the temple's inner courtyard. Mahu's soldiers paced along, stern-faced and silent, bearing their sacks of treasure like ants marching to the heap of their nest. The huge, flat-topped pillars to either side of the aisle stared down in stony impassivity.

Finally, the ranks of pillars fell away, and the temple opened on the vast interior sanctuary. Tiy halted at its edge, staring in horrified wonder at the vision. Amunhotep's rows of stone altar tables were mounded with gold and electrum, with all the gifts and baubles left for Egypt's old, true gods. A soldier brushed past her, and upended his bag over the nearest table. Chains of gold, offering bowls, and silver cups rattled as they fell, upsetting more treasure from the heap already piled on the table. The goods tumbled to the sand and lay forgotten around the altar's stone feet. There were fifty altars at least, spaced at perfect intervals, and each one was piled high with the goods seized from Ipet-Isut. Even the food offerings had been taken, the scraps of meat and bowls of milk placed at Mut's shrine by hopeful mothers and the great, bloody sides of beef meant to nourish Amun on his daily trek across the sky. The meat was rapidly spoiling in the fierce sun. The sickening odor of corruption filled the still, hot air between the walls of Gempaaten.

High above, the colossal statues of Amunhotep looked down from their slitted eyes, smiling at the gods' ruin with haughty pleasure. Their bright paint flared in the mid-day light, and they seemed ready to step from their vast stone plinths, to swing their thick, womanish limbs in implacable strides, to reach down from their great height and take, and take, and take yet more, until the world was bare and dry.

"Mother!" Amunhotep stood at the far end of his sanctuary, observing the plunder of Ipet-Isut with grim satisfaction. He lifted one hand, beckoning; and because there was no other sensible thing to do, Tiy went to him.

She did not look to the right or the left as she passed rows of laden altars. She did not see the frantic glare of sun on gold, nor smell the rotting flesh, nor hear the monotonous moan of the flies. She stared straight ahead at her son—at the thing she had unleashed upon the world, the monster that had come from her own body.

If he has stripped the Temple of Amun of all its wealth, all its power, then I cannot even raise Smenkhkare to the throne. There would be no power to back him, no men of great influence to rally the nobles to Smenkhkare's cause. And worse— far worse—no treasure to pay soldiers. Amunhotep had seized it all. All the wealth of Egypt was in his hands, with not one flake of gold left to pay a single soldier to fight against Amunhotep for Smenkhkare's ascendancy.

Tiy stopped several paces away from her son, her feet sinking deep into the scorching sand. To his right stood Nefertiti, dressed in her priestess robes, her face pale and her eyes terrible with comprehension. To her left, Sitamun trembled, clutching at the neckline of her gown. Her mouth opened, but she said nothing. It didn't matter; Tiy could read guilt and the shock of an unpleasant surprise in the hunch of her shoulders, the devastation of her face.

When Tiy's stare fell upon Kiya, the Hurrian fell to her knees, weeping and rocking in the sand.

"Tiy," Kiya wailed. "I tried... I cannot... He is beyond me!"

"Get up, girl," Tiy said coldly. "He is beyond all of us now."

Amunhotep beamed at Tiy, his eyes flat and empty, staring through her body to a great, golden vista that only he could see. "Mother," he said. "You've come just in time to see it—the glorious transformation, the rising of the sun."

"Just in time, indeed," Tiy said. "What are you doing with all this wealth—with the treasury of the gods?"

"I am going to build a city. A great, new city on a golden plain. The Aten has marked it with his name, staked out the place where he wishes the Two Lands to begin anew."

"The Two Lands have no need of a new beginning," Tiy

snapped. The heat hammered down on her; her head throbbed beneath her heavy wig, and sweat beaded on her forehead and neck, dampening the linen of her gown beneath her armpits.

"But they do," Amunhotep insisted, still peering, dazed and misty, into the light and shadow of his temple. "Sitamun made me see it: a new city, a new world. Egypt made anew."

Tiy cut a hard stare in her daughter's direction. Sitamun covered her face with her hands, and her body shook with a silent sob of regret.

"My country will have a new capital," Amunhotep declared. "We will leave Waset behind, its stink, its corruption, its masses of priests and *rekhet*. I will rebuild the world, after my own vision—a place of beauty and peace, where no foul air will ever touch us, where we will live like gods."

Tiy took one lurching step toward him, torn between revulsion at his wide-eyed, panting zeal and the need to make him see sense, to restore his wits and save Egypt from this mad, frantic ruin. "You cannot move the capital city," she said. "You cannot make a world without priests and *rekhet*. They are *necessary*, my son. The gods need—"

"There are no *gods*," he hissed, though he did not look at her. He did not cease to stare upon the glory that danced before his *ka*. "There is only one. There has ever been but one, the sculptor of creation, the breather of life. The force of creation itself is Egypt's god, and I will see the Aten properly revered."

Tiy's heart pounded. "Amunhotep—"

"That is not my name!" His eyes sharpened on her face with a sudden, hateful force, those black depths stabbing a threat into her *ka*.

Tiy stumbled away from him, gasping.

"I am Akhenaten now," he said, and Tiy, caught by the

power of his fury, exposed to the mallet-blows of the sun, could only nod in acquiescence.

"But the city," she said, praying that the gods would make her voice gentle, cajoling. "The temples. To move them is folly—"

"There is no folly in a god's whim," he said. "I am the god on earth. I will do as I please."

He truly believes it, Tiy realized. A bead of sweat broke from her nape and slid down her back, tracing a slow course down her spine that made Tiy shiver. *The madness that infected his father has become his madness, too. But it grips Young Amunhotep a hundred times tighter than it did my husband. Oh, Amun, help me!*

He turned his slow, lustful smile on Nefertiti. She did not tremble or retreat from his leer, but Tiy could see her niece's long, smooth throat tighten as she swallowed her anxiety.

"This day," Amunhotep said—*Akhenaten* said, "this day is my glorious dawn. The High Priestess has promised me that I will climb the skies to their greatest heights. I set my foot on that path today, in this very hour. Only a god can *make.* I will raise up a new capital from barren sand. I will make it fertile—I will cause it to swell with life. I am building Egypt anew—I am making the world to my vision. Like a god—like a *god!* I am rising to the sky, breaking free from my horizon. And soon I will soar at my zenith, higher than any god has ever flown."

Kiya let out another long, shuddering cry. The smell of corruption was thick and choking. Tiy's right hand clenched into a tight fist. She lifted it, stared down with dull curiosity at the lines of her knuckles, the tight, desperate grip of her fingers, the dryness of her skin in the sun's merciless light.

Inside her fist, burning against her palm, she felt the last fine, brittle thread break and slide from her useless grasp.

ABOUT THE AUTHOR

Libbie Hawker writes historical and literary fiction featuring complex characters and rich details of time and place. In her free time she enjoys hiking, sailing, road-tripping through the American West, and working on her podcast about Jem and the Holograms.

She lives in the San Juan Islands with her husband Paul. Between her two pen names, she is the author of more than twenty books.

Find more, including contact information and updates about future releases, on her web site: LibbieHawker.com

Made in the USA
Lexington, KY
30 March 2018